Ebon Rebellion

Shadows of Otherside Book 4

Whitney Hill

BENU
MEDIA

EBON REBELLION

Benu Media
6409 Fayetteville Rd
Ste 120 #155
Durham, NC 27713
(984) 244-0250
benumedia.com

To receive special offers, release updates, and bonus content, sign up for our newsletter: go.benumedia.com/newsletter

ISBN (ebook): 978-1-7344227-7-1
ISBN (pbook): 978-1-7344227-8-8

Library of Congress Control Number: 2021906988

Cover Designer: Pintado (99Designs)
Editor: Jeni Chappelle (Jeni Chappelle Editorial)

For anyone who has decided to fight for what's theirs.

Chapter 1

Life comes at you fast, but elven fists come faster.

Three elves circled me, all unarmed, not that it mattered. My gaze darted between them as I tried to read who would do what. Two were Darkwatch. The third was a high-blood, not Darkwatch but trained in both self-defense and auratic attacks.

He swung, I leaned back in a dodge, and the four of us flowed into a dance.

I was doing well at holding them off until the door leading to the bar's main floor creaked. Someone was coming.

My half-second of inattention was exactly what Troy Monteague had been looking for. He swept my feet from under me and had me face-down on the sparring mats, my right wrist twisted up and between my shoulder blades, before I could finish shouting, "Goddess *damn* it!"

I reached for Air, and Troy hunched lower on my back, wrenching my wrist higher. He smelled only of herbs and male sweat, not of the meringue scent that would signal drawing on Aether.

"No cheating, Finch," he murmured. The nearness of his voice and the weight of his body pressed tight to mine sent shivers over me that weren't fear. Allegra and Iago moved to intercept whoever was interrupting our training session as Troy added, "You can't allow situational awareness to become distraction. What would you do if I had bronze on you now?"

Bronze would cut me off from my magic. I froze, the heat of attraction going cold as I flashed back to my escape attempt at

Jordan Lake. My breath came a little too fast as I remembered one of a group of elven terrorists sitting on my back as Troy slipped bronze over my arm, sealing my fate.

As soon as he sensed the change in my mood, he was off me and three paces away. "I'm sorry," he said, keeping his distance as I scrambled into a seated position and scooted to put my back against the wall. The skin around his eyes tightened as he fought to keep his face impassive. "I didn't mean to—"

"It's fine," I said, voice rough. I dropped my head, inhaled deeply, and held it against the burgeoning anxiety attack. *Leith is dead. I killed him. The Redcaps are dead. Troy and I killed them together. Callista is gone. Artemis has her, thanks to me.*

Gone wasn't dead though, so that last enemy still kept me up at night. Callista had escaped the gods' prison once, so in my mind, she could do it again. A concern I'd have to deal with eventually but one that was lower on the list than the humans boiling over about the vampire Reveal eight weeks ago and the elves splitting on the alliance. And when I say "splitting," I mean I had three individuals solidly on my side, versus three whole Houses on the other. I suppose it shouldn't have been surprising that the faction who'd had a bounty on elementals like me for millennia wouldn't just roll over and accept a sylph staging a coup, ousting the Triangle's previous head bitch in charge, and establishing herself as the area's arbitrating power.

Especially now that I wasn't just a sylph anymore. I took another deep breath, reaching for calm as I remembered my own power. Sometimes I wondered what was more offensive to the elves: the fact that I'd gained control of Fire, Earth, and Water in addition to the Air magic I'd been born with, thus becoming the first primordial elemental since the last Great Flood, or the fact that I was the only child of an elven prince by a djinni, both of them slaughtered along with his entire House for the crime of having me.

Elves hated unfinished business. Especially when it walked, talked, and had elemental powers.

"Who's here?" I pulled myself together and re-opened my bond with Troy. He'd already unblocked it from his side, and the sense of wary frustration throbbing through to me was probably as much for reminding me of our contentious past as it was for having been interrupted at a teachable moment. When I looked up, he was crouched off to the side, casually keeping himself between me and...

"Roman?" I frowned, looking him over. He hadn't changed: tall for a werewolf, sturdily built, and handsome, with stormy grey eyes and dark brown hair cut short on the back and sides. He was also my ex, and he was supposed to be on the other side of the state.

"Hey, Arie." He frowned hard at each of the three elves blocking him from coming all the way into the sparring studio I'd converted from what Callista had used as a basement dungeon. The energy in the room ratcheted up toward dangerous as he stood there with fisted hands. "What the hell is going on?"

I'm fine. Thanks for asking. "Training. Is there some kind of emergency? We weren't expecting you back in town," I replied, sharper than I'd intended. I didn't like the little flutter in my chest or the flip-flop in my belly at the sight of him, and it made me mouthy.

Roman relaxed and offered a little smile, like he could smell the reason for my mood and liked it. "The kobold at the bar said you were down here. I heard fighting."

And, of course, came to the rescue when I didn't need it and probably after Zanna told you not to. I sighed and couldn't help a glance at Troy. He'd kissed me at the vampire Reveal two months ago. I'd liked it and shouldn't have. Neither of us had spoken about it again, but the elf could give Roman a run for his money in the looks department and I'd enjoyed the physical nature of our new sparring routine a little too much the last few weeks.

I cleared my throat, pulling my mind away from thoughts of Troy's body close to mine, alongside lingering memories of Roman's in much more intimate situations. "Yeah. No more hapkido, but I still need close-combat training."

"With elves?" Roman's tone was less than courteous, and I frowned.

Allegra pulled back to look at him, chin tucked, arms crossed, and eyebrows raised. "What's wrong with us?"

Roman's eyes darted between them again, his face fixed to stubbornness. "From what Vikki has passed along, y'all are the last folks I'd expected to find near Arden. In a friendly fashion, at least." A hint of a wolfy growl entered his tone as he focused on Troy. "Especially that one."

I closed my eyes and rubbed my temples, counting it a blessing that—for the most part—the hierarchically-inclined elves seemed content to let me do the talking. "Roman, the situation here is a lot more complicated than it was when you left."

When you broke up with me to go back to your estranged fiancée and toxic-ass family.

The words, both said and unsaid, hung between us for a long few heartbeats. He had the grace to look embarrassed.

I just tried to keep my temper.

"Wait for me upstairs, please." I was supposed to be in charge here. Might as well pull rank and end the public awkwardness. If he was going to turn up unannounced, I had to establish my boundaries hard and fast.

Roman bristled at the tone in a way that he wouldn't have before, when he'd always acted like I was the alpha in our relationship. Then he took a last, long look at each of the elves with the silver eyes of his wolf and went back upstairs without a word.

"Ass," Allegra muttered as she checked her locs in one of the mirrors against the far wall, tucking those that had come out of their bun back into place. She'd pass for Black among the humans, with skin only a few shades of golden brown lighter than mine and honey-colored eyes. "As though anyone with ill intent could get to you in the bar."

"Troy and I managed against Callista." I winced at her hard look. That was a sore point for her and a defense of Roman, neither of which I particularly wanted to do. "But yeah. Sign on the door."

"Boundaries," Troy mused. When I looked at him, his black hair had fallen over eyes the color of moss on sandstone. He ran his fingers through it to comb it back off his face, not looking away from me.

I broke eye contact first, hoping they'd take my flush for exertion and praying that he thought the flustered snarl of my thoughts was because of Roman's sudden appearance—not because I'd kind of wanted to resettle his hair for him. "Yeah. Exactly."

"What's the story with the wolf?" Iago was a Luna, average height and vaguely Hispanic in appearance. I wasn't sure why he'd sided with me when the rest of his House was inclined to follow the Monteagues, but Troy and Allegra vouched for him.

"Eldest Volkov son," I said, unwontedly clipped and short. "Formerly exiled. Accepted back into the pack several months ago. I have no idea why he's back in town."

"I know all that," Iago said gently. Sometimes it seemed like he did everything gently, until he was sparring. "I'm asking why it felt like I was watching a lover's quarrel."

"Because we used to be lovers." I spun away and grabbed a towel, my face flaming more than a little now as I headed up the stairs.

Allegra was waiting when I finished freshening up in the bar's bathroom. I couldn't read the expression on her face as she asked, "Do you need me to stay?"

"For...?"

She shrugged. "Moral support. Backup. Not every day your ex randomly comes back to town and busts in on you with another man on your back." Her eyes twinkled for a moment before she sobered again. "I think Troy wanted to offer, but he said something about giving you space and headed out."

Decent of him. We were still navigating my bad memories and his role in them, despite the changes in the last six months and his efforts to make amends. After some initial missteps, he'd become surprisingly good at respecting the boundaries I'd set and, even better, at anticipating when I'd be enforcing them—part of the reason why I wasn't bugging him about when he'd get around to breaking the mutated Aetheric bond between us. "I'll be okay. I just wish I knew why Vikki didn't warn me."

Allegra pulled me into a hug. She was one of the few people I'd allow it from, and I patted her back awkwardly. When she pulled away, she said, "Maybe she didn't know. From the last report I saw, things are a little shaky out west. Likely why ex-horndog is here. If she does know, she's probably as pissed as you, given her ambitions."

"Fair." I pressed my lips together in annoyance. Vikki's plans to start a new werewolf pack probably meant keeping her elder brother out in the mountains near Asheville and her younger brother trapped in wolf form and eating kibble from a dog bowl.

Either way, Roman was here now. "Thanks for the session," I said. "Same time on Thursday?"

"Sure." She studied me. "You want the boys back as well?"

"If they want." I caught myself crossing my arms and turned it into an awkward clothing adjustment.

Her grin said everything. "I'm sure Troy wouldn't miss it. Take care, Arden. Let me know if there's any news about next steps for dealing with the mundane protests."

When I sighed and nodded, she hustled for the front of the bar.

I stood there a few moments longer, gathering myself. Roman had been my first real relationship. He'd also been the first person I told about being a sylph—voluntarily, anyway—and despite my initial resistance to being in a relationship or falling in love, I'd done both. The betrayal I'd felt when he'd decided to take up his family's offer to return to the pack and re-establish ties with a woman he'd been betrothed to as a teenager had cut me deep. I hadn't had time to process it before being thrown into the next crisis and managing the Reveal, but the eight weeks since then had given me plenty of time to rehash everything. Usually in contrast to my shifting feelings for Troy.

Which was fucked up, given I'd learned that his grandmother had slaughtered my parents and destroyed my father's House.

Shaking my head at my own mess, I steeled myself, found a neutral expression, and made my way to the front. Roman was in a booth by the door, a bottle of beer in front of him. He looked up as though he'd sensed me, and I raised a hand to signal I'd be with him in a minute.

Zanna, my kobold landlord and new full-time barkeep, looked up from restocking the beer fridge. "Your wolf is rude. Didn't offer greetings. Ignored the sign."

"I know. He's not my wolf anymore but sorry anyway," I said. He was apparently here for me, so it made zero difference to Zanna. This might not be my home, but the four-foot fae could curse a bar as easily as a house and nobody wanted to drink beer that was actual piss, now that they'd learned the hard way that legend was real. "I'll talk to him."

"See that you do."

"How's everything otherwise?"

She glanced at one of the TVs I'd asked Terrence's leopards to install as part of the bar's retrofits. "Fine in here. Getting worse out there."

I turned and scowled at the ticker rolling across the bottom of the screen: PROTESTS ESCALATE IN FRONT OF DURHAM CITY HALL. I scanned the signs being pumped in the air by agitated protesters. There seemed to be as many pro-vampire as anti-fang. The humans had thought the Reveal was a hoax for a good couple weeks, but then the New York coterie had followed suit with an event of their own, then Miami. New Orleans, Austin, and Los Angeles had followed, and then the vampiric Reveal had gone global. Even then the humans had thought it was some kind of publicity stunt...until a body had hit the street.

Then the "fake news" became all too real, and the humans didn't like it one bit. They also didn't seem to know what to do about it. Sales of garlic and crosses had spiked before they realized neither had any effect on vampires. Shit had briefly gotten violent and had stayed at a simmer of unrest for weeks as politicians and law enforcement pleaded for calm.

Because Raleigh had gone first, the Triangle was one of the epicenters of the protests. Everyone was looking to North Carolina to see what tone would be set. In a state that was purple at best during the mundane presidential elections, none of us knew whether we were looking at a new apartheid state or an evolution in human nature. Things were manageable in the bigger cities, but drive an hour out and you were in iffy territory.

Sighing, I turned away from the TV, filled a glass with soda water, and dropped in a slice of lemon. "I'll deal with it." A tension headache tightened in a band around my head, and I muted the bond enough that it wouldn't afflict Troy. "Somehow. Roman first."

Zanna nodded and eyed me from behind her wild mane of curls, her brow creased in worry.

Grey eyes watched me intently as I made my way across the bar, stopping to speak with people on the way. It hadn't been Callista's way—she'd ruled with the iron fist—but I wanted to do things differently. After growing up alone, isolated, and endangered, I sought to build alliances. Even Othersiders couldn't help wanting to respect, if not like, the people who put themselves in charge, so I tried a less aloof route.

So far it seemed to be working. At least, I thought it was working. People brought me information voluntarily because they thought I could help, rather than because I'd bullied, blackmailed, or abused them. Whether it was everything Callista used to get, I didn't know, but I couldn't lead the Triangle worrying about what she'd had. Besides, we had newcomers in town, drawn by rumors of me or, in the case of the valkyrie sipping an ale in the corner, by the possibility that the protests would turn violent.

Roman leaned back in the booth and smiled as I sat down on the other side of the table. "Quite the thing you've got here, Arie."

I shrugged, proud of what I'd done in the last few months but irritated by his using my nickname. All the same, I tried for the same neutral friendliness I gave everyone else. "Yeah. A lot of work, but the community seems happy."

"So what's the story with training with elves? With Monteague?"

Ah. So it's more Troy than elves in general that bother him. Interesting. "We have an understanding," I said carefully, wondering why he was making this an issue.

"Arie—"

I didn't like the condescendingly patient note in his tone. "I appreciate that you may still see me as an extension of your pack, but..." I shrugged again. "You left. I made the deals I had to make in order to survive. That included agreements for security, training, and information with whoever was willing and able to offer them. Is that going to be a problem?"

The grey in his eyes shifted to storm clouds then to silver as his jaw clenched. "Not so long as Blood Moon continues to receive equal consideration," he said grudgingly.

"Of course. Just like House Monteague and the Raleigh coterie did when I was with you." I leaned back and sipped my water. The bubbles had already started going flat from my circuit around the bar, but the lemon had infused nicely. "Thanks for your understanding. Now, what brings you to town personally? Is Vikki going back to Asheville?"

Roman's jaw clenched, and he looked away.

Submission or uncertainty?

He spun his beer then took a long sip.

Uncertainty, I decided, recognizing the motion.

"I need your help," he said in a tight voice when he set the bottle down. "I want to overthrow my father."

Chapter 2

I stared at Roman, not quite sure I'd heard correctly. Or rather, I knew I'd heard correctly and really didn't fucking like what I'd heard. Where Vikki had come with patience and cunning, Roman wanted to use a battering ram. Always.

"Excuse me?" I hissed. "Overthrow. Your father. The alpha of the biggest werewolf clan in the Southeast? And you want *my* help?"

He fiddled with the now-empty bottle and signaled the bar for another one, clearly stalling for time.

"Before we get to that, you're gonna need to apologize to Zanna," I snapped, annoyed all over again. This was *not* what it meant for me to be the arbiter of the alliance. "In fact, I'd go do it personally rather than summoning her over here like some kind of maid."

He frowned, looking completely confused. "What'd I do?"

"It's what you *didn't* do—greet her properly when you arrived. Then barged past the sign telling you to stay out of the back." Something ugly tightened in me as it occurred to me that he wouldn't have dared do that when Callista was in charge. I set it aside for later, our old pattern with a new twist. "Zanna is a *kobold*. You know that, and you know better. Courtesy. Rules. Order. Hospitality. Come on, now!" I didn't have the patience to remind a werewolf to honor the fae, and he was a grown-ass man. Whatever his feelings were about me or being back in town or this batshit request about his father, he had to do better.

Funny how quickly I was re-evaluating my earlier wisdom in dating him, now that I was no longer in such a vulnerable position.

With a put-upon sigh, Roman slid out of the booth and approached the bar. From the curl of his shoulders and the pep in Zanna's form as she hopped onto a stepladder and got in his face, he wouldn't make the mistake of crossing the kobold again.

Good. It rankled that he hadn't offered either of us basic respect. I didn't know if it was because he'd reclaimed some footing out west or because we'd been intimate once upon a time or something else entirely, but it was bad enough that the elves were on the verge of open rebellion. I didn't need more of it from someone I'd once given my heart to. Come to think of it, this was exactly our old pattern—I'd thought being together meant people having my back and keeping me in the loop, and he seemed to think it meant having that person available for whatever was more convenient than doing things the hard but correct way.

My phone buzzed, and I fished it out as I watched the scene at the bar. It was a text from Troy.

Everything okay?

Just peachy, I swiped back. I started to apologize for the mental load, but the only reason we were bonded was because he'd committed magical trespass and hadn't been able to break the magic when my inborn Chaos had warped an Aetheric tracking tag. I had nothing to apologize for, even if it was nice that he was decent enough to check. That was why I'd agreed to having the bond open—so that he could play bodyguard without constantly having to be here.

The phone buzzed again in my hand, but I put it away as I sensed Roman returning and looked up. "Well?"

"Arie, I hate to drag you into this, but shit is really not going my way back home." He slid back into the booth with another beer and a second glass of sparkling water for me. Probably his idea of a peace offering. "Pops is still Pops, just older and crankier."

"Older, crankier, and still prejudiced against those who can't shift fully?" I guessed.

Roman's jaw clenched. "Yeah."

"Your mom?"

"Happy to have me home but pressuring me on Ana."

I sipped my water to give myself a minute to wrestle with despondency. "What's she think of all this?"

A half-smile tugged the corner of Roman's lips. "She's progressive enough to make it work. Doesn't have a problem with my shift."

I read the conflicts in his body language even as I did my best to bury the stab that went through my heart at his wistful expression. "But there's a problem there as well, or you'd have gone to her pack for help rather than coming here."

"Yeah. She fell for someone while I was gone, a guy who can shift fully, and her family thinks more like Pops. So she's got to decide if she chooses me, becomes next in line for alpha female of Blood Moon, and possibly loses her pack—which would go against the whole point of the arrangement. Or she chooses Cyril, reneges on the agreement to marry one of the Volkovs, and keeps her family but offers an insult that could mean war between the packs." The tension in his face finally matched that in his body. "Sergei pulled some shit with her, so she wants nothing to do with him. Her family doesn't care; they want a full-magic Volkov son, and Sergei's it. She's been stalling for years with the excuse of completing a PhD program, but she's graduated. Time's up."

I was beginning to see why Vikki wanted to start her own pack. All of this was so ugly—the prejudice, the forced choices, the willingness to overlook what had probably been assault of some kind on Sergei's part in pursuit of power.

My stomach tightened. "How does removing your dad play into this?" Vikki had said their mother effectively ran the pack, but it sounded like that only went so far.

"Both pack alphas refuse to renegotiate. If I'm alpha, I can break the treaty and let Ana do what she wants without a war hanging over her head." He offered me a tentative smile. "You know me, Arie. I'm a romantic. If it was just an arrangement, I could at least hope that we'd come to love each other. But an arrangement with war as the alternative? I'd always wonder if I'd forced her."

I sighed. I felt for him—I really did—even if his talk of wanting to fall in love in an arranged marriage hurt all over again, given that it was what he'd left me for. Especially given that, since he'd left, he'd been calling me off and on with hints and wishes that I'd barely been able to steel my heart against.

Hell, I even felt for Ana. Nobody should be treated as Roman and other magical "runts" were by the werewolves, and I didn't like the pieces I was putting together about how they treated their women either. I'd asked Terrence about it, and the wereleopard obong had sneered and said something about backwards wolves. At the same time, I really did not want to get caught up in the family nastiness that was the Volkov pack. I was too busy trying to manage the fallout from the Reveal and keep myself safe from the elven queens.

There's never just one battle. They all intersect. Maybe there was something I could do from here. "What do you need?" I asked neutrally.

Roman's shoulders rose and fell in a jerk. "Get rid of Niko."

"I'm gonna need you to be more specific."

"Vikki told me about how you made the sorcerer's corpse disappear." He lowered his voice. "You have more than just Air now, right? So…"

Horror and outrage gripped me, and I dug deep to say it, since he apparently refused to. "You want me to use my elemental powers to kill your father and make it look like an accident."

Roman stiffened at the flat anger in my voice. "Well. Yeah."

"You want me to be an executioner. An assassin." The anger was no longer flat.

"You got rid of Torsten, didn't you?"

My jaw dropped. "Is that what people are saying? That I… What? Eliminated Torsten and installed Maria as Mistress of Raleigh?"

"That's what one might infer if they read between the lines." He narrowed his eyes in the way he always had when he thought I was being needlessly stubborn.

I couldn't speak for a moment. I'd known that dealing with Torsten and Dominique—the succubus who had actually killed Torsten—with only Troy as a witness would come back to bite me. I just hadn't expected it to be Roman doing the biting.

"How dare you," I said, low and so outraged my voice was cold. I wrestled down an instinctive reach for Air. "Yes, I have had to kill to get here. To *protect* myself. I do *not* go out of my way to commit murder for power, and I didn't kill Torsten."

A flush reddened Roman's cheeks. "I thought you'd help me."

"Roman…" I slumped and closed my eyes as I did a breathing exercise, counting to five. I'd imagined seeing him again. Not quite daydreaming, just running through scenarios. What would it be like? What would I say?

It had been a waste of time. In none of my scenarios had I envisioned him coming back to town to ask me to kill his father and then being hurt when I turned him down.

I decided to change tactics. "Have you spoken to Vikki about this?"

"She doesn't know I'm in town yet," he said sullenly. "I came straight here from Asheville."

Great. Just great. He was lucky none of Terrence or Ximena's people were in the bar today, just witches and a clutch of Modernist vampires. Vikki had been working hard to address some of the damage the wolves had done with their arrogant, even imperialistic dealings with the other were groups, and Roman had come trotting back like nothing had changed—or even needed to.

If there was one thing I was learning the hard way, it was that people didn't like change, especially if it meant they had to be more accommodating when they were accustomed to thinking only about themselves. Roman would have to be handled carefully. He hadn't said he'd come back for me, but there'd been more than one hint in our check-in conversations over the last couple of months, and I'd seen the jealousy in the narrowing of his eyes at Troy.

I reached across the table and squeezed his hand, consciously loosening my face to match the conciliatory gesture. "Talk to your sister, okay? She's been doing good work. There might be another solution."

He covered my hand with his bigger one and squeezed back. "Okay, Arie." Flushing again, he met my eyes with a sheepish expression. "I guess I got ahead of myself again, huh?"

I shrugged and reclaimed my hand before he could get ideas. "A little."

"You doing okay?"

There it was, the thought that I was someone more than a useful piece in a plan. Nice of him to remember that. "Doing my best. The protests make things dicey, but Maria thinks she's making progress with the politicians. A few donations, plus some research sponsorships for the universities. They'll be the first in the country to get verified vampire interviews. The historians are chomping at the bit, and the geneticists are jealous as hell."

"I bet. You did good with all that." Sighing, Roman downed his beer then stood. "Guess I better be getting on. I'll let you know what Vikki says."

I forced a smile and gestured at the bar. "Great. You know how to reach me." Translation: don't stop by my house.

He hesitated, as though waiting for me to stand for a hug or something, but I stayed where I was and sipped my drink. I'd be polite, but I was not reopening that can of worms. He'd made his choice and his bed, and I was not about to come lie in it again. Even without fleeting thoughts of Troy, I had more self-respect than that.

"Well, bye now." Roman rocked awkwardly on his toes.

I saluted him with my glass. "See ya around."

When the door shut behind him, I forced myself to stand tall and make my way back to the bar rather than slouch dejectedly in the booth. That had sucked, big time.

"I'm going home," I said to Zanna. "Anything need doing?"

"No. Good night, tenant," she said, eyes on the TV in the corner.

"Call me if anything comes up or if Iago makes any progress on the deed and assets."

Zanna scowled at the reminder that the bar wasn't *legally* hers yet, even if she'd happily accepted it as rent payment in perpetuity. Iago Luna was a bar-certified lawyer and was quietly tracking down all of Callista's assets and having them transferred to me. The weres had found a stash of cash, gold, gems, and artifacts while they were renovating the basement, from which I'd paid them for work they'd offered to do voluntarily.

The rest went to Iago to pay off fees under the table. One day, all of Otherside would be out to humanity. I intended the bar to be a legal source of income when that happened, because Goddess knew I was struggling to keep Hawkeye Investigations running with all my new duties for Otherside. Not demanding protection money was probably a mistake, but for now, I was trying to show how I was a break from the past—how we could do things differently.

Never thought I'd see the day where I'd become an optimist, but here we were. I needed something to hold on to, given the way things were going.

On my way home, marching humans with signs, bullhorns, and flags crowded the streets. They seemed equally split between pro- and anti-vampire. Their dress ran the gamut from the stereotypical vampire Halloween costumes to bright yellow T-shirts with the timber rattler from the Gadsden flag atop Comic Sans text that read, "Don't drink from me."

They seemed more interested in shouting at each other than going after the vampires for now, but all of Otherside was waiting for them to erupt again. A few humans had started calling themselves vampire hunters, but mundane law enforcement cracked down on that when a goth kid had been mistaken for a vampire and staked through the heart. Things had calmed back down to just the protesting and some anonymous threats to known vampires, but we were approaching another boiling point. I wondered how many elves were scattered in the crowd, either keeping an eye on things or stirring them up, and whether the protests were why the Houses hadn't moved against me in force yet.

I tapped my fingers on the steering wheel as I waited for an intersection to clear. We'd predicted this, to some extent, but in some ways we very much had not. Otherside had existed in parallel to human society for as long as there had been humans. As the human population exploded, edging us out, we'd grown ever more adept at anticipating and manipulating them. But we were at a pinch point, having waited perhaps a little too long to recognize that the elves could only do so much to misdirect— and only when they wanted to. The vampires and weres could only turn so many. The fae could only cast so many illusions. The witches might be okay with the resurgence of interest in metaphysics lately, but that assumed having confirmation the occult was real didn't send the humans back to the Salem Witch Trials.

The djinn and others who could change planes might be in decent shape, but mundanes were inventive. They'd had to be. Given enough time, they'd come for the interplanar Othersiders as well. Especially with the mundane media networks taking every opportunity to spin this bigger and no shortage of demagogues willing to speak ever more outrageous bullshit.

I gunned the engine of my Honda Civic hatchback as the intersection cleared, eager to get the hell out of town. Maybe take a bubble bath to ease the ache I knew I'd have in my shoulder later, the one Troy had wrenched.

Troy. There had been an awkward two weeks after the Reveal where I'd avoided him and Allegra, not sure how to feel about them, given their grandmother had destroyed my family. Then I nearly hurt a mundane at hapkido and realized I'd grown too strong and fast, and was too new to it, to risk sparring with humans anymore. After chewing all my nails down to the quick and my roiling emotions bugging Troy enough that he'd sent three texts, I'd called him and asked if he'd help me with training.

My life had fallen into a strange sort of limbo since then. One that had gone on for too long and shouldn't have needed Roman returning to shake me out of. It was time to stop making excuses and take some action.

Chapter 3

I bypassed my front door when I got home, heading straight for my clearing on the banks of the Eno River. I needed to be out in the fresh air, alongside a body of water and land I'd apparently formed a connection with, anchored by a bonfire pit I'd dug out after Fire had manifested. A place where the elements were in balance for me and therefore easiest to practice with. Taking action would likely mean using my powers, and given how new everything except Air was to me, practicing was not optional.

The waning moon overhead gave just enough light for me to see by even filtered through trees, and I easily followed the now well-beaten path down to the riverbank. The heat of the early July day had given way to a warm night humid enough that Water felt closer than usual. Fireflies flashed in the undergrowth, signaling for mates with an eerie yellow glow. The purling of the river over its stone bed and the scent of damp soil and water plants beckoned. As an elemental, I needed this piece of wildness—especially since gaining three more elements. It might have been better with someone to share it with, but for now, solitude suited me. I had too much to think on.

I started with Water, the element I struggled with the most, while I was still fresh. Even after eight weeks of daily practice, my heart pounded at the surrender required to fall into it. I could grab Air, embrace Fire, and to some extent, coax Earth.

Water? A shitshow.

I had to relive and get over being drowned, to start, and then fix myself to the unnatural act of surrendering. Everything in me was about fighting or luring. Surrender was not something I did.

It was why I was taking a break from practicing with my fellow elementals. Val's undine sister, Sofia, lost patience with me during a session and snapped that I needed therapy. She wasn't wrong, but who the hell was I gonna talk to? At the same time, I couldn't keep claiming their time when it was obviously a me problem, so here I was.

Sitting at the river's edge and trying to fall into it without physically falling in was the longest, hardest part of the night, worse even than gradually adding in the other elements until I was working with the same weird primordial ball I'd made in desperation to destroy the unreality Callista had created when she'd tried to escape to the Crossroads. Troy had helped the first time, and it had been fresh enough to go quickly the second. But it took forever when I was practicing on my own. Faster each time but still too long given what I'd be up against.

That's why you practice.

I focused again on surrender, on falling…and with a mental splash, I had it. Gritting my teeth against the sensation of being underwater and reminding myself to breathe, I nudged Earth. It obliged me tonight, coming to me with a rumbling sigh. I worked with Water and Earth for a bit, tracing the root systems of the trees, containing river water in vessels of Earth and making mud pies to launch into the river even as I focused on keeping myself separate from its sedate flow.

Only when those powers came smoothly did I reach for Fire, carefully splitting my attention to light the fuel in the pit. I'd only gotten the balance right last week. Holding elements without using them was exhausting and took all the finesse I'd gained over the last six months.

Air, I called last. It came to me as joyfully as ever, and I relaxed as the familiarity of my natal element filled me. Lightning crackled across the fingertips of my right hand as I let it blend with Fire, the two elements as sympathetic as Water and Earth.

Now came the hard part.

With the utmost care, I pulled the chords of each element closer. It was like adding instruments to a musical piece, getting them all to start on the right beat so that the song could continue without sounding like a train wreck. I breathed slowly, sweat beading on my forehead as I tried to ignore the bites of mosquitoes.

I jumped when the little ball consisting of all four elements snapped together, as it had in the bar the night I'd ended Callista's rule. I didn't quite understand how it worked, other than that it was a concentration of reality. One that could cancel the unreality required to make interplanar jumps.

As though drawing all the elements together had been a beacon, a ripple signaled the imminent warping of reality. Someone was coming from another plane, and from the power behind it, it was a god.

I stumbled away from the opening portal, putting my back against a tree as I steadied my grasp on the elements. When Neith stepped through, twirling her *was* staff as the red linen strip holding her hair back fluttered in the wind, I wasn't sure whether or not to be relieved. Neith was the goddess I encountered most often, almost a patroness, but she was still one of the Old Ones who wanted me to help end the world.

"My lady," I said, trying to find respect under all my fear. If I was going to have to keep dealing with the gods, I'd have to stop fearing them.

"Little primordial." White teeth flashed in a grin. "We are so pleased to see how much you've grown this last season."

The edge to her voice made my stomach clench even more than the weight of her power. "I try."

"Shall we see how much you have tried?" Neith circled me, not giving a shit that I had my back to a tree. "The Mistress of our Wild Hunt should be able to stand against anything on this plane. And since we are here now…"

Fuck. I didn't have the slightest idea how to fight a goddess. My best guess was that it involved my primordial powers, so I hurled my ball at her when she made her way back in front of me and lunged with her staff.

She laughed as she deflected, sounding delighted. "Excellent! Already so fearless as to cast at one of the High Ones!"

A deep, existential fear sank into me at the joyful tone. Of all the faces of the Goddess, Neith was one of her oldest and wildest. Defiance wouldn't enrage her, as it had Artemis. It would challenge her at best, amuse her at worst.

She struck, her staff slashing toward me in the moonlight. The curved end held an edge I hadn't noticed before, one that could probably steal my soul as well as my life if she wanted it to.

I deflected with Air as I dodged aside, barely escaping the strike without losing flesh or blood.

"Good!" The goddess lashed out again.

Dancing to the side, I tried Earth this time, pulling the ground from beneath her feet. It did nothing. She simply floated above it rather than falling into it. Snarling, I drew on Fire. A tree exploded as a bolt of lightning missed her and sank into it.

Her staff lashed out again, and I wasn't fast enough to evade it. A deep slice in my right flank sent a sheet of blood cascading down my hip, and Neith frowned. "That was far too easy, Huntress. Don't tell me you're still relying on your bonded Hunter as a crutch."

Hunching around my wound, I pushed hard with Fire. If she'd been anything less than godly, it would have worked. As it was, the fringe of her kilt smoldered before she phased out of this plane and then back again, completely untouched.

"Better," she said.

Storm clouds roiled overhead where we'd had a clear summer's night before. I swore. We couldn't have this happen twice in a summer, or the mundanes would start asking questions, especially now that the vampires were out. It was as though using my powers guaranteed some sort of weather disturbance, and the stronger I got, the worse the effects were.

"What do you want?" I didn't dare to lift my eyes from her lithe, circling form.

"Domination." A lazy slash of her staff drew blood from my right bicep when I was too slow to divert it with Air, followed by one to the outside of my left thigh. She was playing with me, like a cat with a bird.

"So why do you need me?" I panted, trying another half-formed ball of primordial power.

It staggered her half a step when it sped past the guard of her staff, and she grinned. "Because you can do that." She circled again. "And because we lost our original primordial powers after the world was formed. Imagine our delight when we realized that elves and djinn could create copies, however pale. Our fury when their petty politics sundered their custom of breeding more...until now."

We exchanged another flurry of attacks. Mine broke my heart as they warped my clearing—only one in a handful made it to their target. Hers pulled blood and strength from me as those I failed to block bit into my flesh.

"Enough," Neith said, finally. "You are not quite ready to lead the charge. But you are close. Much closer and much faster than we'd dared to hope when Callista first brought you to us. Until next time."

Reality stretched and thinned as she made another portal and disappeared.

I fell to my knees, gasping for breath as I looked at my precious clearing. Using primordial powers had warped reality, giving me a glimpse of what might happen during the Wild Hunt. Trees suddenly grew at right angles. The river splashed upward at its center, arcing to cascade back down in an unsupported waterfall. Random rocks and a square yard of flaming dirt hovered in the air, and leaves swirled as wind spun counterclockwise.

Jaw clenched, I pushed through an overwhelming exhaustion to correct the damage. In a way, it was better practice than learning to fight had been because it forced me to lean into what was *wrong* with the world in order to set it right. I had a feeling I'd need that knowledge someday, probably sooner than I'd like, and my intuition was rarely false.

Unfortunately, it also took what little reserves I had left after holding off Neith. When everything was righted, I collapsed to my back in the dirt, tasting blood. My heart thundered so hard I thought it'd burst from my chest, and I couldn't seem to get enough air into my lungs. My head pounded, and the earth sang where my blood seeped into it, delighting in the unintended sacrifice. My eyelids fluttered. Maybe if I let go, that would stave off the Wild Hunt. I'd accomplished what I'd intended for myself—a place of my own in Otherside. Maybe me not being here anymore was for the best. A wave of exhaustion tugged at me.

No. I've fought too hard for it to end like this.

I wrestled the blackness eating away at the edges of my vision as my blood fed the soil beneath me, deepening my connection with it. Desperate, I reached for Earth, trying to make it stop pulling at me, crying out in pain when all that did was make my blood pound faster and seep into the ground with greater speed. The earth rumbled.

My breath was coming fast. Too fast. My healing powers were better than ever, but Neith's staff wasn't from this plane. I was bleeding out faster than my body could regenerate. Darkness clawed at my mind, threatening to pull me under.

It can't end like this!

Then I sensed something I hadn't expected, a tense ball of masculine concern and Aether approaching. One that should have been in Chapel Hill, definitely not getting closer, full of agitated worry. I set aside my pride and dropped all the walls in the bond.

Here. I'm here.

Troy burst into the clearing. Dirt and dead leaves flew as he skidded to a stop, and the moon made the gold flecks in his eyes glow as they fell on me.

"Finch," he breathed, darting to my side.

I reached for him, barely managing not to pass out.

"What happened?" he snapped as he sank to his knees beside me. "You were practicing like usual and then all of a sudden…"

"Goddess," I breathed, squeezing my eyes tight and choking on a groan as pain caught up with me. Was Troy's imminent arrival why Neith had left? The gods had hinted that I'd need a Hunter to be at my most powerful. Would I be powerful enough to stop their Wild Hunt? Didn't matter just now. "Neith."

"You need a doctor."

"No. I'll heal."

Something that looked like fear hovered behind Troy's eyes as they darted around the clearing and then back to me. His nostrils flared, and he shuddered. "Finch, you've lost enough blood that, if you were human, I'd be waiting for your last breath. More than Maria took."

"Oh." That was bad. Worse that I hadn't realized. That was probably why I felt cold all over, despite the summer heat and humidity that'd been so oppressive earlier. "Shit."

"Yeah. Be still."

The command should have sparked fear in me. He'd used it to steal my will before dropping me in Jordan Lake, but they were just words now. I let my eyes close as he settled a hand over my forehead, thumb and forefinger pressed into my temples.

"Just physical damage," he muttered. "Damn. I'm not a Sequoyah. I don't know if—"

Darkness washed over me, and the world spun.

"No! Stay with me."

That was interesting enough that I roused. "Why do you care?"

"Because I do." He scooped me up in his arms. The scent of crushed herbs and fear was almost overwhelming. "Stop talking."

My blood throbbed in my veins. Part of me was freaking out. I was bleeding badly, and elves were a predator species. The other part was just kind of surprised that I'd survived long enough against a goddess that I might be of interest to an elf.

"Are you going to eat me?" I rasped.

Troy glanced down, frowning, then back up as he stumbled on the uneven path. "I'm not a wyvern."

"Those are still around?"

"Not anymore," he said grimly. "Elementals weren't the only beings my people hunted."

Silence hovered between us as we approached the house. He hefted me long enough to get the sliding door on the deck open then looked around, obviously at a loss as to where to put a bleeding elemental.

I giggled. Everything was light and floaty. "Anywhere. You know your way around."

"Stay with me, Finch," he muttered, before deciding on the kitchen table. That couldn't be good. If I was okay, he would have just put me on the bed or the sofa.

My vision swam, and I might have blacked out for a moment because Troy was gone and then he was back with my completely inadequate first aid kit.

I giggled again. "Seriously?"

"What the hell else should I do?" he snapped. "Do you want to go to the hospital?"

It was a fair point. "Leave me alone and see what happens, I guess."

The stricken look on his face should have sobered me up. "I can't do that."

"Another mission," I slurred. There couldn't be another reason for him to save me. "Yay."

Muscles bunched in his jaw, and I reached up, trying to touch his cheek. He looked so worried. That wasn't right. He never worried. My hand flopped to the side before I managed to get more than halfway there. "I don't feel so good." I swallowed hard as nausea roiled.

"I told you. You've lost a lot of blood." Troy's eyes darted over me impersonally. The fear I thought I'd glimpsed was gone, and the Darkwatch agent was here. That was good. If I was a mission, I'd live. Troy never broke his word, and his word was always involved if he was on a mission.

Still, I couldn't let him worry. He was so uptight that he might have a heart attack, and I was getting to like having him around. It had gone from being infuriating, to frustrating, to convenient, to…maybe something else. If I hadn't been loopy on blood loss, I might have been more concerned about that evolution, but all I said was, "Don't worry. I'll heal."

"Finch, you—"

"The gods wouldn't throw away their toy." My eyelids fluttered, and I fought for consciousness.

"Not on purpose," he growled, apparently deciding that the deep slice on my flank merited the most attention because he ripped my shirt the rest of the way open and leaned closer to it. "Who knows how long it's been since they played with mortals."

He had a point.

I started to tell him so when his brow pinched and he said, "You are mortal, right?"

"Duh."

"I don't know if I'm relieved or more distressed," Troy said flatly, not sounding like he was either.

I winced as he started cleaning the wound before pinching it together and taping it shut. After two attempts at speaking with a dry mouth, I managed to ask, "Why do you always turn up?"

His pretty eyes met mine before refocusing on his work. "Who else is going to hold the Triangle together? Especially now that we're Revealed?"

I didn't have an answer for that, other than that he'd better pray they wouldn't have to find out in the morning.

Chapter 4

An ice-cold sweat and a stomach clench woke me. I swallowed hard, taking slow, deep breaths, because if I was going to hurl I'd probably choke on it before I could move. My head throbbed with my pulse, each beat sending a dagger so sharp it burned through my brain. Fine tremors shook me as I focused on breathing. My tongue felt too big. My eyes were gummed shut, and I squeezed my eyelids closed tighter to try to work enough tears out to open them. This power hangover dwarfed the one I'd had after fighting the vampiric sorcerer and then feeding Maria. Made sense. Bigger fight, more blood lost.

I felt like I'd died and gone to hell, but I was alive.

I was on the couch with a blanket pulled over me and a glass of water in reach at the edge of the coffee table. When I reached for it, bandages tugged on my torso, arms, and legs. My hand shook so hard water spilled onto the floor. I drank some in tiny sips, spilling more on my chest and wincing at the weight in my throat as it went down. The salt-sweet electrolyte taste suggested that Troy had mixed up a batch of oral rehydration solution while I was knocked out. My stomach roiled, and I paused until it settled some then slowly finished it.

Setting the empty glass aside, I looked for the elf, sensing him nearby. The faint light of near-dawn showed him slumped in my armchair. I bristled, the fury at the sight of someone in *my* chair clearing some of my brain fog, until I remembered that he'd saved my life. Again.

I supposed I could forgive him, especially since he could have just let me die and follow through on what he'd said at Umstead State Park when the alliance was formed—that he'd thought I'd die before he'd have to worry about the unintended bond between us. That he'd fixed me up inclined me more toward gratitude now that I was lucid. I tried to sit up then spasmed as every wound I'd taken the night before hollered like a hit dog.

My gasp of pain drew Troy awake and upright with the guilty look of a soldier caught napping on the job. "Finch," he said in a gravelly voice, rubbing his eyes and inhaling sharply before stretching.

"Still alive," I croaked, managing to get myself a little more upright.

Troy rose with enviable grace for someone who'd just woken up after having fallen asleep in a chair. He crouched next to the sofa, glancing at the empty glass. "What do you need?"

Booze was too little, too late at this point. I couldn't imagine an elf prince cooking me breakfast, but fuck it. "Some food to settle my stomach. Peppermint, ginger, or chamomile tea. More of that devil juice." I flopped a hand at the empty glass.

"Okay." His fingers were cool and his eyes distant as he slowly reached to check the pulse in my wrist then laid a hand on my forehead. "You're still not quite normal. For you, anyway."

"Probably because I feel like three different kinds of shit." I held myself very still, not quite sure what to make of his gentle touch or the way it made my heart skip.

"Fair," he murmured, resting light fingers alongside each of my wounds before rising. "I can't tell if there's infection or if you heal so fast that it only feels like there is."

"Likely the latter. I've never had an infection. Just near death," I quipped.

The look he gave me suggested he didn't find that funny, and that made me grin perversely. My lips were so dry they cracked.

After grinding his teeth at me, he went to the kitchen. The clattering of cookware made a bizarre contrast to the silence of elven movement. Pans clanged, water burbled as it boiled, something plastic opened and reclosed, but of Troy, I heard nothing at all.

I couldn't help comparing the fact that he'd asked what I needed, rather than just assuming or going to cook something for himself, with Roman's behavior the first time he'd slept over. Roman had done the dishes after helping himself to breakfast, but he still hadn't asked about cooking anything in the first place. I wondered whether it was a cultural thing, given the relative position of women in each faction, or an individual thing. Probably a little of both. Troy might be a prince, but he'd always be subordinate to a queen, whereas Roman had been born to be an alpha.

A steaming cup landed on the table, smelling of chamomile and ginger. Troy left it and went back to the kitchen so quickly it seemed to have been pulled from another plane.

"Thanks," I croaked.

"Finch, we need to work out a better system," he said over the sound of something frying. Bacon, from the smell of it, and I frowned as he added, "I'm trying with the boundaries, but you've got the gods and the Houses gunning for you now. I might not make it in time to help next time." I almost didn't hear the next thing he said under his breath. "And I don't want to bury you."

Swallowing past the sudden lump in my throat, I focused on the part that I could do something about. Talking kept my mind off the hangover. "What do you mean, the Houses are gunning for me? As if they weren't already."

"Alli sent a text while you were asleep. The Conclave made a decision at midnight. Monteague, Luna, and the remnants of Sequoyah have decided to reject the alliance so long as you're at its head. My being here like this is treason," he said, voice tight. "All elves owing loyalty to one of the high Houses are required to re-swear their fealty."

My face went cold. "When's the deadline?"

I startled as he approached so silently that he seemed to appear as magically as the cup of tea had, the air molecules catching up almost belatedly. He put a plate laden with food on the table and crouched easily next to it, looking completely blank even as the bond roiled with half-suppressed emotion. "Three hours ago."

"What?" I swallowed bile. "Did you go?"

"No."

My throat closed. "Monteague—"

"I'm not sure you can call me that anymore." His smile was bitter as wormwood. "I couldn't do it. It's wrong. Besides, I swore a blood oath to the alliance and you as Arbiter."

I stared at him, dumbfounded. Never in a million years would I have expected Troy to break his word to his House, at all let alone over me. "So what happens now?"

"If anyone finds out about the bond or the fact that I'm helping you, I'll be arrested and executed. Painfully." He pointed at the plate, as though he hadn't said anything earth-shattering. "You need more protein."

My mind whirled at what he'd been saying as I looked at the plate, heaped with more bacon and eggs than I'd ever eaten in a sitting, and the package of jerky he'd dropped beside it. "I think there's plenty."

"No, I mean generally. I need double the protein intake of a human. I don't know how much the djinn need, but a half-human, low-blood elf would still need more than the balance I saw in your fridge. That might be why your power hangovers hit so bad. You'd probably heal even faster too."

I frowned, never having considered that there might be something I could do about the hangovers other than stave them off with alcohol. I ate like a human because that's how I'd been raised. Now I wondered if Callista might have known better and done it on purpose—along with steering me toward alcohol as the key, which would keep me isolated and weak as I sought not to drink so much or use enough of my power to unlock Chaos.

"I'll keep that in mind," I said slowly. "Thanks. Are you eating anything?"

"I didn't want to assume you'd be okay with that."

My eyebrows raised so fast I thought they'd fly off. "When you commit to a thing, you really commit, don't you?"

Troy shrugged, looking like he wasn't sure whether to take that as a compliment or not.

"Be my guest." I reached for the plate with a wince as healing cuts pulled against medical tape and bandages. "Least I can do is make sure you get breakfast."

He came back with a second plate heaped as high as the first. "I was going to leave this for you for later, but…"

I flipped a hand. What he'd already put in front of me was more than enough, regardless of his thoughts on protein needs, given that I never ate breakfast. The amount of food and the smell was making my stomach rebel again, but I knew I'd feel better if I settled it.

Troy eased down next to me on the couch, and we ate in silence as I grappled with the elves' hatred of me going so deep they'd spurn the whole alliance and the benefits we could all gain from working together, simply because an elemental was at its head. It was one thing to know that people hated me enough that they'd kill me if they had the chance. It was another to recognize with cold certainty that they hated me enough to spite themselves and everyone else, rather than get over it and grow into the future. The food went down like every bite would choke me, tasteless and heavy, as the full impact of what Troy had said—what he'd done—hit me.

To my surprise, I cleaned my plate while deep in thought. Troy gave me a knowing look when I lifted my eyes from the empty plate, blinking in confusion at having done so. I did feel dramatically better with the protein-heavy breakfast than I had with my usual grain-based attempts at settling my stomach.

"Thought so," he said, setting his own empty plate aside. "Callista fed you like a human, didn't she?"

"Yeah. I guess she did."

Silence stretched as I put the plate down and leaned back into the couch, closing my eyes to feel vitality growing in me a little more quickly than usual. The headache was already easing, and my stomach wasn't in a state of imminent revolt. The cuts from Neith's staff itched like hell, but the goddess had been toying with me, not aiming to kill. I'd be fine. "I might be able to keep my meeting with Maria later at this rate."

"Finch—"

"I'm going."

When I opened my eyes, his scowl matched the frustration burning in the bond.

"Thanks for looking out for me though." I swallowed hard, still blown away by what he'd done. "And for choosing me."

He shrugged, slouching on the couch and resting his hands over his belly in such an uncharacteristic display of casualness that I couldn't help staring. Was this what he was like when he relaxed at home? Normal? Accessible?

His eyes flicked to me, and he blushed slightly but stayed as he was. "What are friends for?"

I warmed. "Are we? Friends?"

"Well, I wouldn't disown myself for just anyone," he said drily. "And we did just have a sleepover."

Holy shit. Was that a joke? I coughed a laugh and mimicked his posture, wincing as the cuts tugged again. "Okay then."

Troy relaxed. His eyes wandered around my living room, though whether he was cataloguing it or evaluating it for defensive positions, I couldn't tell. He asked, "You're really going to go to Raleigh rather than take a day off?"

I shrugged. "The humans aren't going to stop protesting just because the gods are coming. I mean, hell, if we told them, they might actually riot. The sooner we can get them squared away, the sooner I can refocus on dealing with the Wild Hunt."

"The Hunt and the Houses."

"Them too." I pushed down the spike of fear in my gut. "Which brings us back to what to do about you committing treason."

Everything about Troy went very still—the bond, his body, his expression. "It's my choice."

"Which you're making on account of me." Nope, still could not wrap my head around it. "I don't know whether to thank you or ask if you need to get your head examined. Are you serious about this?"

"It's the right thing to do. Yes, for you. But Val and Laurel and the other elementals haven't done anything to deserve being targets either. They helped us with the lich when everyone else sat on their thumbs and spun."

I frowned at the mild vulgarity of that statement, not accustomed to hearing that kind of thing from Troy, but he continued as though he hadn't noticed.

"I was sworn too many different ways, Finch. The easier choice would have been to take you along with me to re-swear to the queens and just be done with all of it. But that wouldn't have been the *right* choice or the one that served the greater good for all of us."

"Okay, but *why*? How do I know this isn't another deep cover, like the Redcaps? You were with them for so long they trusted you to kill me. Twice." I crossed my arms and gave him a hard look. Savior or not, Troy *always* did things by the book. If I wasn't part of a mission, there had to be something else.

"Javier." The name of Iago's half-brother fell from Troy's lips in a whisper.

The bond twisted with such sick rage and shame that I had to hold my breath against the nausea it drew up.

"I'd told myself that his death was a sacrifice for the greater good. Leith's terrorists had to be stopped before they toppled the matriarchy." The rage boiled into a fury, shading his expression and hardening his tone. "The Conclave had an opportunity to do better. They could have addressed the problems that drove the formation of the Redcaps. They could have *listened* to me when I told them you and your alliance were the way forward for Otherside. Instead, they let Javier's death be for nothing, and they ordered me to keep you under surveillance when you clearly only acted because you were being pushed. By Leith. By all of us."

"Because I wanted to be acknowledged as a person and have space for myself." Tears choked me up, and I didn't know what was drawing them out. Only that I couldn't breathe with the weight of the emotions in my chest.

"Yes. As you were right to do all along. I can't forgive them. I won't. So I picked an oath. Yours."

There was something else underneath his words, something I couldn't read in his tone or the sudden flatness of his emotions.

I couldn't tell if he wanted me to push or was afraid that I would. I agreed it was the right thing to do, but as I sat there studying him, I couldn't figure out why it bothered me that he'd risk his life to help me and the other elementals or that he'd advocated for me to the Conclave or that, finally, someone had chosen me. Did I even deserve it?

As though he'd read my mind, Troy tilted his head just enough to look at me sideways. "You're allowed to receive help from others, Finch. Especially when it's to redress a wrong. This is the bare minimum you're owed."

That hit me in the gut hard enough my breath caught. Was that it? Had I internalized a belief that because I was always giving, and always stepped on, that I deserved it?

The elf prince—former prince?—who was now apparently my friend and protector watched me until he saw that it had sunk in. "So, when are we going to Raleigh?"

"We? I told you—"

"There are going to be attempts on you," he said bluntly. "The Captain isn't a bad man or an evil one. But he's served the Conclave his entire life. He'd die for the matriarchy. Even if he knows this is wrong, he will follow orders. The Conclave formally withdrawing support from the alliance is step one. Step two will be to remove you. Probably capture, if they can, to draw it out and make an example. Kill, if not. Where's your pendant?"

"My..." I reached for where it usually hung around my neck with cold fingers, panicking when I found it gone until I remembered what I'd been doing yesterday. "I take it off for sparring days. I didn't know if it would be safe for Iago to see." Shit. Iago and Allegra. *What happens with them?*

"Wear it. Openly. Any high-blood elf will recognize a prince's amulet, even if they don't know the House. It'll mean they try to take you alive to find out where you got it. They'll assume you're under someone's protection, unless they recognize it as the House of Onyx. That will give me time to get to you."

I couldn't breathe as my heart pounded, making my wounds throb painfully. Cold chilled me to the bone. My head spun. Troy was talking about kidnapping, assassination. *My* kidnapping and assassination. I almost screamed when his gentle fingers turned my face and my heart made that weird flutter again.

"Hey." The gold flecks in his eyes seemed brighter than usual. "You will get through this. You're tough, and you're not alone. Okay? But if my people are coming for you, then I am *asking* that you let me help, in whatever way I can. You are owed."

"Okay," I whispered past stiff lips and a tongue dry with fear. I'd really thought myself safe. I had allies. I'd gotten rid of Callista. I'd led the Reveal. I'd helped keep everyone stable through the first spike in anti-Otherside violence from the mundanes. Throughout all of it, I'd dealt with everyone as fairly as I could, striving to do what was right for all of us. But it wasn't enough.

Something dangerous and ugly flickered to life in me.

It would never be enough.

Because the elves didn't want compromise, progress, equity, fairness, or justice. They wanted a status quo where they remained comfortably superior, leaning on the victimhood of a story of Atlantis from thousands of years ago. Nearly wiping out elementals wasn't enough either. The elves wanted all of us—all of their bastard children—gone.

Not all of them. Troy had withdrawn, giving me space to process without going anywhere. He was steady in the back of my head, not judging, just waiting.

"Maybe it's a good thing the tracker warped," I said weakly.

A smile flickered on his lips. "I was hoping you'd see it that way because every angle Alli and I have investigated looks like it would backfire pretty badly. It's only gotten worse as you've grown into your power."

Cold fear fled, replaced by something warmer I didn't recognize. "Are you saying—"

"For now, yes. You're stuck with me." He sighed, heavy with regret. "I'm sorry. I'll keep trying, but..."

Pitching a fit wouldn't fix this. I couldn't ask the djinn, and they were the only ones other than the gods who would know anything about using Chaos. I closed my eyes and found the neutrality that infuriated me when Troy was the one exhibiting it. *Let me accept what I can't change.* "Okay."

"You're taking that better than I thought you would."

"It is what it is, and for now, it means you turn up when I might be bleeding to death. Silver linings." A thought occurred to me, and I carefully kept myself blank. "You have another safehouse, don't you? In Durham. There's no way you'd have gotten here so fast if you were in Chapel Hill."

After a silence long enough that I cracked an eye and looked at him, Troy crossed his arms. "Yes."

The weres would be furious if they knew.

I sighed. "You're right. We are going to need to work out a better system. One that doesn't have you drawing the attention of Terrence and Ximena and get you caught up in a turf war trying to save my life. Durham is neutral ground but not *that* neutral."

"You're not going to tell them?"

"I should. Are you engaged in any missions against them?"

"No. You became enough of a threat to the queens that the Captain pulled me off everything else."

I turned to face him full-on, trying to get a sense of his feelings about that before I realized it didn't matter. What did matter was that I trusted he was telling me the truth. "Fine. Not my business then. If there's a dispute raised, I'll step in, but I'm not y'all's momma. I just arbitrate. And carry out coups, apparently. Might run with the Wild Hunt if I feel cute."

Troy snorted, and the tension in his shoulders eased. He stiffened again when I pushed myself up with a groan. "What are you—"

"I need to get the bandages off before the cuts close up over top of them. Hurts like a bitch to get the threads and shit out." I braced myself on the couch until my head stopped spinning then started shuffling to the bathroom as Troy rose, looking frustrated.

Never would have guessed that the guy who dropped me in a lake to drown would willfully commit treason to patch me back up now...or be worried about me healing up. Beyond that, though, a plan was unfurling in my mind. And I didn't think Troy was going to like it.

Chapter 5

As I tossed bloodied bandages into the bathroom's trash can, it occurred to me that the elven surveillance network would probably be working overtime on a missing prince.

"Not to sound ungrateful, but won't they be tracking you or something?" I pitched my voice so he'd hear me from the living room.

Troy's response came from the door behind me, making me jump. "I saw where this was going yesterday afternoon. Switched the lojack on my car to a different vehicle in Chapel Hill, swapped the plates, cut the biotracker out—and the backup one they thought I didn't know about." He showed the inside of his left forearm then lifted his shirt to show me a nearly healed slice on his hip.

I pulled my eyes away from his bare skin with an effort. "And what, nobody knows about your Durham place?"

"Paid for it in cash two months ago via a shell company."

"Allegra?"

He winced. "Doesn't know. Or didn't. I mirrored my SIM card on a dual-SIM phone and left the phone they'd be able to trace in the same car that has the lojack. Haven't answered her messages yet."

I stared at him, boggled by the resources, planning, and him really going all-in. "Isn't she like your bodyguard or something?

Your knight? She's going to lose her mind, and she'll know exactly where to look for you."

"I wanted her to have plausible deniability and room to make a choice for herself. She can choose me—choose *us*—or them. They'll find me eventually, but I needed to buy us all some time." He crossed his arms and looked at the floor. A shaky feeling had started to tinge the bond, like none of what he'd just explained had been real until he told me.

A sinking in my gut felt like my limited version of the Sight trying to come through. I hugged myself. "It won't be enough."

"I know." A haunted look darkened his eyes as he looked up. "I just need to evade them long enough to plant the seeds that will discredit Keithia."

My stomach clenched into a knot. "You've got to be shitting me. You're planning on dying."

Troy shrugged, the lift of his shoulders heavier than usual. "If I have to. It was going to happen sooner or later. At least it'll be doing the right thing now." He looked away then back at me with renewed intensity. "The gods are coming. I felt Artemis's power when she carried us through the Veil and the dregs of Neith's in the clearing last night. We don't have anything or anyone that can stand against them except you. You have to make it to the Hunt. That's what matters for the greater good, not just for Otherside but the world."

I clenched my hands into fists to stop them from shaking. How had this escalated so quickly? "What seeds?"

"That the Solari heir lives." A twisted smile tugged at the corners of his lips. "The Lunas are only a high House because they took the Monteagues' place when we ascended to the gap left by Solari. Keithia assured them it was legal. If you live, it's not. The Lunas will splinter. The cowards will cleave to Monteague. The clever will ask what else Keithia has been hiding. The brave will start digging."

My jaw dropped, and I shivered at the implications. "You're not just committing treason. You're burning everything to the ground."

"And salting the earth," he said grimly. "I tried, Finch. I tried to do things the legal way and hold to my oaths. But they kept doing the *wrong thing*." He finally met my eyes. The gold in his seemed to spark with something deeper than frustration. "They kept hurting people. Using *me* to hurt people. Javier and you are just the ones who finally made me see it."

I scrubbed my hands over my face. This was exactly what we'd tried to avoid with Torsten's old guard and the Modernists: the splintering of a key faction that would leave us vulnerable to the mundanes. Troy had to know that, which meant I had to trust this was truly the only way to resolve it.

For now. I hadn't busted my ass this hard to risk everything falling apart now. Something else would come to me, but for now, I had shit to do.

Troy frowned when I looked up. "What?"

"We need to do two things. First, buy you more time. Second, get the pressure off the vamps. They've handled the Reveal on their own long enough."

"You look like a woman with a plan."

"Something like that." I studied him, wondering if he'd go along with it. He'd had a lot of pretty words about doing the right thing. Turning traitor on his House and people was a start, but he hadn't really done anything except not turn up when summoned.

He waited. Tension grew the longer I considered, but he didn't push me.

"An eye for an eye," I murmured, still not even sure myself I wanted to go through with this.

"And blood for blood," Troy finished cautiously. Otherside justice was very clear. That shaky feeling came through the bond again, before he squashed it and straightened, falling into a parade rest as his eyes deadened. "Who's the target?"

A chill rippled over me. He'd already paid the debt we'd agreed for magical trespass in the creation of the bond, yet he offered his skills again without question.

But being willing to kill was one thing. What I had in mind was something else.

"You," I said softly, not taking my eyes from him.

Troy paled and what felt like a fight-or-flight response rippled through the bond before he got it under control. He didn't say a word, although wariness tightened the skin around his eyes and the muscle in his cheek twitched as he waited for me to explain.

"You said five things. First, you weren't sure I could still call you a Monteague. Second, the pressure is created by the risk of discovery. Third, you chose the oath to me over the others. Fourth, you need to plant seeds to discredit Keithia. Fifth, those seeds lie in the fact that House Solari was not entirely destroyed."

To his credit, Troy pieced it together. "My life for your father's. A prince for a prince."

"Yes. Your *life*, not your death."

He frowned, his eyes searching mine as he wrestled down an impulsive reach through the bond. "You mean—"

My heart pounded, and my mouth was dry. "What would happen if I claimed you as mine? For real this time, not just sending a misleading photo."

With a sharp inhale, he shut down his side of the bond. "How so?"

I leaned on the bathroom counter, trying to figure out what was going on behind those pretty eyes for him to react that way. "However makes it legal as far as elves are concerned. I dunno. Help me out here. If I'm the last and only living daughter of the prince of a high-blood House, that makes me...what?"

"A queen." His voice roughened with an emotion I couldn't read.

My heart skipped. "Even with a djinni mother?"

He frowned, his eyes searching the ceiling as though elven law was written there in blood. "It could be challenged. There isn't a case like yours recorded, to my knowledge. But your paternal grandmother was a queen. Given her resistance to the Conclave's orders, she had to have accepted you as her legitimate granddaughter, which would have made you heir-apparent. The argument could be made."

"Fine. How would you beat a challenge to that?" I tried to say it like my head wasn't spinning at the implications. Me? Queen of my own House?

"I'd re-establish your legitimacy." His gaze snapped back down to mine. "By finding the royals of another House to speak for you publicly and align with your platform. Better still, to change Houses to yours."

I lifted my eyebrows, glad that my wild brain sparkles had actually come to something.

Troy swallowed, hard, and the first sheen of sweat broke out on his brow. "I'll do whatever it takes. My grandmother went too far with your House. With your family. If she won't right the wrong done by House Monteague—by her—then I will."

"Even if it means calling Keithia and declaring?"

His pupils dilated, and he swayed on his feet as more blood drained from his face to leave him a sickly yellow. "Yes. Whatever it takes."

I narrowed my eyes at him. "Are you saying that because you feel guilty or because you truly believe that's what's right?"

He swallowed, looking ill. "If I said both, would you hold it against me?"

"No. But I would want you to go away and think about it." I crossed my arms as I tried to find the right words and the

47

courage to speak them. "I've been alone my whole life. Hiding who and what I am. Fighting for scraps. Fuck, for the right to simply exist. No community. No partners. No advisors or family or friends. No nothing until I was forced out in the open in January. I don't want you at my side unless you choose to buy into that wholeheartedly. You've seen what it meant for me, every ugly part of it. I mean, hell, you were part of it."

Troy breathed deep, his gaze going distant with memory before it sharpened on me again. He nodded, jaw clenched. The wall in the bond came down a little, giving me a peek of guilt and deep remorse.

"So. We can do things your way. I'll keep managing on my lonesome as arbiter while you work on the Houses in parallel, and I'll be grateful for the help from an ally who's come through before. Goddess knows I need a buffer while I work on the mundane reaction to the Reveal and find someone to go next." I fixed him with a look I hoped was serious and not just uncertain. "Or you publicly renounce Monteague. Keep the name or don't. I don't care. But you choose me. Not your House, not the Conclave, not the Darkwatch, not your laws. Me and the alliance. In whatever capacity makes this legitimate, whether that's bodyguard or fake prince consort or whatever the hell else you can think of."

"I don't do fake," Troy said hoarsely.

"Fine. Then come up with something that works or tell me no."

"Finch—"

"Just go think," I said, suddenly too tired and frazzled to go through this anymore. "Please. Go back to your safehouse. Get drunk. Have a real good think. Because after Roman—" My voice cracked, and I looked away, swallowing past the lump in my throat as my shoulders curled under the weight of my past. I wondered why I was talking to Troy about this. "I put everyone else first. I will no longer surround myself with people who think they can call me friend or ally and not do the same. I can't."

Troy pressed his lips together, looking anywhere but at me. "Okay. But first, what was the second part of the plan? To take pressure off the vamps."

I winced and spun away, limping in a two-step circle. "Another group needs to come out. More than one would be better."

"Do you already have thoughts on who?" he asked warily.

"No, and I need to see Maria first."

"That's why you're good at this."

His tone made me look up sharply, and I frowned to see the approval on his face. "What do you mean?"

"Callista would have just decided. She did, in fact. The Sequoyahs were the weakest and the easiest to spin, so they were her tool. Until you figured out something else."

I looked down at the floor, not sure how to feel about that. "For all the good it's done."

"Stop, Finch. The humans aren't in your control. You let Maria volunteer her people. Now you're going to see what she needs as a next step. That's all you can do."

His words made me uncomfortable. I should have managed it better than this. I couldn't help but feel as though there wouldn't have been protests and deaths if someone more capable, more experienced, had led the Reveal.

"Stop overthinking," Troy said again.

"Stop reading my mind," I mumbled, equal parts annoyed and looking for a reason to listen to him. Maybe this was why I kept finding myself working with him, despite our past conflicts. He had the political experience, training, and self-confidence to lead but no outlet. I had the power and the opportunity but neither the experience nor, deep down, the confidence I needed. Something about that irked me, but now was not the time to throw away the help. Troy's hard-on for duty and the greater good made it a little easier to trust him, now that he was determined to use it in my favor to whatever extent.

"If you can, get some rest before you see Maria." Troy backed out of the bathroom doorway. "Before the collapse hovering under the bond puts you flat on your back."

"Yeah," I said grimly. Adrenaline and focus had kept the shakes at bay, but I still hadn't recovered from the previous night's physical exertions or this morning's mental shocks. "Thanks for patching me up. And breakfast. Don't let Keithia kill you."

"I'll try."

We had an awkward moment of staring at each other before he offered a nod that was almost a salute and left.

I stayed where I was, leaning with my hands on the counter and looking at myself in the mirror as the front door opened and shut, trying to figure out what the hell had just happened and who I was becoming.

Chapter 6

Getting into Claret through the front door was going to be downright impossible. I studied the protest going on outside the wine bar above the main entrance to the vampire coterie's nest, scowling as much from the lingering hangover as the scene in front of me. Metal barricades and police in riot gear stood out front in untidy rows. One of the windows had a spiderweb of cracks in it from where someone had thrown a brick. There'd be another way in—or several—but vampires were cagey. Maria might trust me, but other than the Modernists who'd been at the Reveal, the rest of her coterie barely knew me. They wouldn't be too happy with an outsider knowing one of the secondary entrances to their nest. What a fucking mess.

This had to be resolved. Fast. With Troy's revelation about the Conclave, I had to assume that the elves might be agitating the humans, using their extensive political and financial networks in mundane institutions to hedge against rather than support the vampires. I didn't think they'd risk themselves by instigating outright action against another Otherside faction, but they'd settled the humans when the lich was involved and prevented riots. They could have done the same here.

Then again, maybe they were just scared of being outed themselves. My lip curled at the idea that they were letting the spotlight stay on the vampires out of cowardice. Of course, they probably called it being smart.

Frustrated by everything about the situation, I pulled out my phone and called Noah. Maria's second had been more readily available in the last few weeks and therefore had a quicker line to her ear than the phone she ignored.

"What?" the vampire said sharply.

"I'm outside Claret." I kept my voice soft, hoping to avoid the attention of protesting humans.

"I hope you're here to offer blood because my mistress has her back against the wall. Not that she'd admit it."

I weighed that against my still-healing wounds. Boundaries. "If I hadn't faced off with a goddess last night, I'd say yes. But I can't. Not today."

"A goddess? The Wild Hunt is that close?"

"Look, I just need to know how to get inside without riling the mob." I kicked a bottle fragment into the patch of dirt surrounding a struggling tree. I'd never understood why humans planted trees in the sidewalk and told themselves it made a difference when they kept cutting down whole forests. "Let Maria tell me off directly, how's that?"

"Fine. Meet me at Wilmington and Hargett."

I tucked my phone away when the call ended and started walking, keeping an ear cocked toward the conflicting chants.

"My body, my choice! Vamps should have a voice!" shouted one side.

"All lives matter!" shouted the other, bland and repetitive in comparison to the pro-vamp side willing to offer their blood voluntarily to the undead population. That second chant flat-out baffled me, although it seemed to be what humans said when they refused to acknowledge that some lives mattered less than others in the systems they'd built. I supposed they felt acknowledging vampires would make their own lives matter less, but why it had to be a zero-sum game was beyond me.

Noah was waiting for me on the corner, dressed in jeans and a black hoodie despite the hot, sunny afternoon. His neutral expression didn't hide the pain in his eyes. I'd barely reached him when he rocked into motion.

"Come on," he said. "Quickly."

We both kept our heads down as we headed north on Hargett. At the parking garage, he paused abruptly. I almost kept walking, nudged by a subliminal message. *Nothing to see here. Nothing to see.*

Noah's mouth firmed as he rapped on the battered metal door I'd missed the first time. It swung open to reveal the skinny vamp who usually acted as the back-room bouncer when the bar was open. He eyed me then stepped back, pulling the door open wider and making space for us to pass.

"Fae magic?" I asked when the door swung shut behind us. I hadn't realized it would affect me that strongly.

Noah grunted an affirmative as he flicked on a light to reveal stairs going down. At the bottom was another metal door, which he unlocked with a key from a ring of them and gestured me through. He sniffed as I passed. "You weren't joking about the gods."

"Nope."

"How badly were you injured?"

"Nearly died." I grimaced.

"Yet here you are." He inhaled as he passed me again to take the lead, deeper this time. "You found a Sequoyah to heal you?"

"Ah, no. Troy made it in time to stitch me together long enough that my healing abilities kicked in."

I couldn't read Noah's expression when he turned around to look at me. "You're spending a lot of time with our Prince of Monteague lately," he said in a tone that wasn't quite neutral. "Anything the rest of us should know?"

"I'm his assignment, apparently." I couldn't say anything about the bond. Not only was it magical trespass, but the more people who knew a secret, the more likely it was to be shared. "The Darkwatch and the Conclave don't want an elemental with my strength running around unsupervised."

He chuckled, breaking the beginnings of tension. "I see. Poor you. That one has always had more honor than sense, and he's like a damn python. Once he gets his teeth into you and pulls you in, there's no escaping his coils until he's done whatever his duty calls for."

My shoulders eased. I'd found Maria's second to be both utterly loyal to her and prone to running hot and cold. Noah was a good man, just a mercurial one. He would've liked to see me with his mistress, but it seemed that Troy wasn't a threat. Interesting, given the dynamics I'd observed between Troy and Maria. The alliance between House Monteague and the Raleigh coterie had been in place at least as long as I'd been alive, and those two had history that seemed to lean toward the personal.

"Luckily for me, it seems like his sense of duty is saying to keep me alive," I muttered, thinking about this morning. How much could I let myself accept from Troy?

"Luckily for all of us." Noah turned a corner and took a second flight of stairs down then stopped in front of another door. He glanced at me as he shuffled through his key ring for yet another key. "What aren't you saying?"

I flushed and hoped he'd take it for anger and not residual...whatever I was feeling after a morning with Troy. "I learned this morning that the Conclave has decided to break treaty. They're going to withdraw from the alliance. I'll likely be targeted after."

Noah went dead still, not even breathing until he said, "You could have led with that. Hekate curse them."

He unlocked the door, pushing it open to reveal a long, dark hallway. A sheet of gauzy fabric hung over the far end. Flickering light and warmth suggested a fireplace.

I eased my shields down and let my passive powers extend, reading the air currents. Nothing stirred on the other side, but then again, vampires could remain perfectly still.

"Mistress," Noah called as he started forward. "I've got Ms. Finch."

"It's about damn time," Maria called back.

She was waiting for us when we pushed through and entered what had been Torsten's throne room. Her princess-cut dress was a rich plum today, deepening the brown of her eyes and making her emerald hair pop. The pulsing power I'd come to associate with Torsten's presence wasn't in evidence yet, but it was close. Torsten had been over a thousand years old. Maria was pushing half that but had drained an elven prince and drunk from me just months apart. She'd also had several elves before that. Torsten had punished her for it back in January. How strong would she be in time?

"Why did Noah's agitation spike just now?" Maria laid a protective hand on his shoulder.

"Hello to you too." I looked around the cavernous space. When Torsten had been Master of Raleigh, it had been stark, weighed down by dark colors and functional, angular furniture. Maria had brought her trademark brights to the space, added more soft furnishings, and installed new lights. I didn't know why she needed a fire in early July, but the room was much more comfortable than it had been. I wondered if that made it more dangerous—a seductive lure versus the openness of an obvious threat.

"Poppet," she said with a blend of patience and irritation.

I crossed my arms and cocked a hip. "The elves are quitting the alliance."

Her pupils dilated, filling her eyes with black. "Excuse you?"

"Exactly. The Conclave has elected to reject any alliance that includes me," I said flatly.

Maria and Noah exchanged a heavy glance, and his jaw clenched. Her head shifted slightly, barely suggesting a negation. I got the feeling that they were communicating telepathically.

"Where does our dear prince land?" she asked in a dangerously soft voice after a few heartbeats.

"With me." My voice was rough, and I couldn't quite meet her eyes. I was beginning to suspect the reasons for Troy's allegiance went beyond simple right and wrong. Given the vampire's interest in me, I didn't know how that would be taken.

"What a relief." Maria's hand slipped from Noah's shoulder, and she squeezed his arm before flouncing back to the oversized throne that dominated the back of the room.

I followed. "Is it? He's committed treason, Maria."

"Yes." She settled amongst the new cushions. "Troy has always been progressive for an elf, especially when Allegra or Darius—her twin—are around to guide him."

Allegra has a twin? I frowned, vaguely remembering a Darius being mentioned at the Reveal but not who he was. *What's the story there?*

Before I could ask, Maria continued. "It takes our princeling a while to get there, but he'll do the hard work in the end. The real wonder is that Keithia allowed it to get this far without executing him. She must be getting soft. Or she thinks the example she made of his father fifteen years ago stuck."

She propped her chin on her hand, an emerald-haired Thinker with distant eyes, as I wondered what example Keithia had made. Troy had said his father had left or was gone, nothing about an example.

"We had Troy pegged as the preferred successor to Monteague years ago," Maria said. "Difficult, given the necessity that he become a king in his own right but not impossible even with a full-blood sister ahead of him in line. I daresay that's part of why Keithia despises him so much, despite the loyalty he's shown up to now. He has the potential." Her eyes cut to me. "He just needs the right partner."

Noah stiffened, his gaze locking on me as well.

This was *not* what I'd come here to discuss today, but a puzzle piece fell into place. It was suddenly difficult to breathe. I flashed back to the night the alliance had been formed, and a little comment she'd made after drinking from me earlier this year. She knew something. "Telling me to hate fuck him wasn't an idle suggestion or a tease."

Maria's gaze weighed heavy on me, speculative and, for once, utterly lacking in flirtation. "An elemental of your strength could only have one origin, baby doll. Tell me I'm wrong. Tell me that pendant you used to keep so carefully hidden didn't belong to your *elven* father."

I went cold as I clutched my pendant and everything inside me tightened. "You knew?"

"No." She flashed fangs in her smile. "Not for sure. Not until I tasted you and even then, not for certain until just now. But once I had your blood on my tongue…well, there is only one possible way for a trueborn elemental like you to exist, and we just happen to have a tragic story that fits right here in the Triangle. The elves refused to see it. Not me."

I wavered on my feet before sinking onto the cushions of her red jacquard couch and burying my face in my hands. "Who have you told?"

"Nobody except Noah." Soft footsteps and shifting air currents told me she was descending from her throne. "And I will tell nobody. Nor will Noah. But Arden, you have to understand how important this is. You're the solution to so very many problems in Otherside."

"If I break everything that caused those problems." My throat tried to close around the words, and my head swam.

"Precisely." Maria knelt in front of me, ignoring Noah's disapproving growl as she took my hand with one of hers and tilted my chin with the other. "Face it, Roman was never going to suit you, nor would Terrence or Ximena allow you to take up with a wolf. I understand why you weren't going to be able to choose me, no matter how much desire I can smell on you." Her rueful look held me captive. "But Troy? Arden, poppet, he can bind the Houses to you. To all of us."

I recoiled even as I rose and pulled free of her clasp. "No. Fuck no. Nobody *allows* me anything."

A sad smile curled the corner of Maria's full lips. "How many times have you told yourself that, only to wake the next morning and find another way to work within the existing system?"

Her coffee-dark eyes bored into me, and I stood there, face cold, horrified and unable to answer.

The buzzing of my phone saved me from having to. I fished it out. "Finch."

Doc Mike's voice came down the line, tense and afraid. "Arden, I think we have a problem."

Maria's pupils dilated as she listened in.

"We, as in Otherside, or as in—"

"Otherside." He was almost drowned out by the sound of traffic, which meant he was out walking to ensure our secrets weren't overheard somehow by mundanes. Not that Wade Avenue was the safest place to walk, by any means, but I supposed he found it safer than anywhere else. "All unusual cases are now under special review. That healthtech startup, Verve? They got state backing somehow. Anything that gets flagged by their systems needs a secondary review."

"Goddess damn all of it." I scrubbed my free hand over my face. The alliance had seen this coming, but we'd hoped it would take the mundanes longer to connect the dots. "The lich case?"

"Under review." Doc Mike sounded strained, as well he might. He'd been kidnapped as part of that event, and while he hadn't been gone long enough for anyone to report him missing, it meant all of that evidence, and anything else he'd touched, would probably be considered unreliable. That meant open to reinterpretation—and that added danger to all of Otherside.

My blood froze. The case involving the mundane influencer Torsten had been pushed into draining had been handled by Doc Mike as well and was directly linked to me. I'd called it in, thinking to outmaneuver Callista's hail Mary play from beyond the Veil by doing exactly what no Othersider in their right mind would do—turn it over to the human system.

Of course, it wouldn't just be the elves mucking things up now. The humans would have to jump in as well. The elves probably pushed them, the bastards.

"Arden?" Doc Mike sounded lost and shaken. "What now?"

I rubbed my temples with my free hand and dared a look at Maria, knowing that she could hear every word. "Leave it with me."

"I can only stall so long."

"I know," I said more sharply than I'd intended. "Trust me, Doc, I know. Hang tight. I'll take care of it. Keep me posted, okay?" When he confirmed, I ended the call and turned back to Maria. "I know that we were going to discuss what to do about the protests, but we need to get everyone together. Now."

Chapter 7

Raven Rock State Park looked much the same as it had when the alliance's key players had met here weeks ago. Tall loblolly pines and mixed oaks offered some shade. Though the Cape Fear River was a bit of a hike away, I sensed it meandering below the cliffs, wide and deep and slow. Something about it bothered me, but I couldn't say what.

The sandy soil under foot was littered with dried pine needles and granite pebbles, along with a few carelessly discarded granola bar wrappers I picked up and threw away. The heat and humidity were worse now that it was summer, as were the flies hovering over the picnic site's trash cans. I plucked at my shirt as the hundred-degree heat index sent sweat rolling down my back, even in the shade. My head thudded with a dull headache as the sun exacerbated my blood loss, adding to the sullen mood precipitated by what Maria had said about Troy and Roman. About my relationships in general and what I might be *allowed* by the rest of the alliance.

The setting might be the same, but the players had changed somewhat. Troy came alone this time, and Vikki was at Roman's side rather than Sergei. Terrence had brought Ximena, the wereleopard and werejaguar leaders looking as solid as ever. Laurel, my oread friend, stood awkwardly off to the side, looking fiercely at the elf as though she was waiting for him to show another face. Janae, still acting as the witch representative, had brought Hope. Noah was here instead of Maria, continuing the vampire tradition of sending a second to deal with matters outside the coterie. I hadn't called Duke, given how we'd left things the last time we spoke. Big group, but with all the new Othersiders coming to the Triangle, we'd eventually need to look at expanding the parliament even further. All of them had rebuffed my outreach though, still preferring to watch from the shadows for now.

The other change from the last time we'd been here was that it now felt unified, maybe. Like we were all here for a common purpose, rather than our own individual missions and goals. That wasn't to say none of us had our own objectives. It helped that we'd fought together since then, some of us more than once. Maybe we could get through this.

If today's news doesn't push anyone to the breaking point.

"Doc Mike called," I said as soon as everyone had settled, perching on a picnic table or leaning against a convenient tree. "The healthtech startup I bugged back in January has come to an agreement with local government. With the vampires out, they figured out that some of their stranger results might be because of Otherside. Not that they know us by name, but…" I shrugged.

"We need to move faster." Vikki spotted the problem immediately.

Nodding, I met each of their eyes. I knew what Maria wanted to happen: all of the rest of Otherside out right fucking now. But that wasn't a decision I could make for everyone. All I could do was push them there and support the vampires as they'd always supported me. "Right now, the pressure is fully on the vampires. Sooner or later, the mundanes will realize their tests aren't picking up vamp or just vamp. They'll wonder who else—what else—is out there. That'll mean hunts, like in the bad old days when they actually believed in our existence."

Everyone dealt with that in their own way, but they all looked scared. Everyone except Troy. He only settled into calm, even when I peeked through the bond. His hazel gaze met mine when I frowned at him, and the corner of his lip twitched as though he'd aborted a smile. I looked away when I felt Roman watching me.

"Noah," I said, pretending I hadn't noticed my ex's attention, "your coterie is the worst affected, not only because you're out but also because of the open case associated with Torsten's error. Why don't you share what Maria's asking?"

The werecats watched with sharp eyes. Vikki placed a restraining hand on Roman's arm as he took a breath, ignoring him when he glared at her.

"It's as Ms. Volkov says," the vampire second said in a voice like an owl winging through the night, soft and deadly. "We need to move faster. We need another faction Revealed. Preferably all of them, but we'll be happy with one or two more to start. We can't have this startup pinning every inconclusive violent death on the vampires, or there will be hell to pay. For all of us."

Roman glowered. "And just who—"

"I'll take care of it," Troy said in a tone equally as grey as Noah's had been.

I stared at him, as did everyone else.

"If I can spoil the test results, they won't have anything conclusive. It'll give us a little more time."

"You. By yourself." Doubt was heavy in Roman's tone. "Are going to spoil all of the test results in a healthtech startup that knows they have holes because they hired Arie to find them."

I bit my tongue and tried to keep my face even, annoyed that Roman was using his nickname for me in a professional setting. Vikki frowned and eyed him sideways, as though she didn't like it either. Or maybe it was his attitude she didn't like.

"At the very least, I can get rid of the ones associated with Torsten's case." Troy's calm was fraying on the edges in the back of my head, but he still looked outwardly chill.

Roman had a point though. Even for one of the Darkwatch, it was a tall order—and this Darkwatch agent was compromised.

I sighed heavily enough a breeze stirred before I could yank it back, and everyone eyed me askance. Fair enough. I usually had better control over my powers. But usually I wasn't exhausted from surviving a visit from a goddess and aching from fast-healing but still-present wounds.

"I'll help him," I said. "I know my way around. If he can manage the networked systems, I can heat the samples enough to spoil them without it looking like outright sabotage or theft."

"Finch—"

I gave Troy a steady look until he raised his hands. He wasn't going to talk me out of this on the basis of me needing rest or to hide from elven assassins or anything else. The alliance needed time. I'd help him buy it.

"If that's settled, there's a second item," Troy said instead of continuing to argue with me, looking as though the words were being dragged from him. He glanced at me, waiting for my nod before continuing. "The elven Houses are withdrawing from the alliance."

Roman muttered under his breath, and I caught a couple of swears. Terrence and Ximena exchanged looks like they'd expected this, while Vikki's expression turned calculating. Laurel shivered and edged closer to me, looking as though she was seeing the resurgence of elven bounty hunts against our kind. Noah just sneered. Only the witches accepted the statement with any equilibrium, waiting to hear what else Troy would say before judging.

"The queens consider my and Evangeline's oaths null and void." Troy flushed with such a deep shame that I burned with what washed through the bond. He glanced at me then away. "They won't consider an agreement made with an elemental lawful."

Vikki narrowed her eyes at him as she pinched Roman to shut him up. He blushed a deep red, still ignored by his sister as she glanced between Troy and me, gears turning. "Then what are you doing here, Prince of Monteague?"

"Upholding my oath to this alliance and to Finch as its leader." Even without a weapon, Troy was dangerous—and he looked it just then as he glowered at Vikki, hands on his hips and not a drop of sweat on him despite his wearing all black in this heat.

The beta werewolf took in my lack of surprise. "You knew?"

"I did," I said, a little unsteady at Troy calling me the alliance's leader and not the nominally less explosive title of arbiter. "I found out this morning. Rather than sit on the news, I called everyone together to have a voice in a parliament. Like y'all wanted."

"So we did," Vikki agreed, a tight smile tugging at her lips.

Her brother scowled at all of us with an extra helping of vinegar for Troy, who ignored him as thoroughly as Vikki had. As cunning as Roman was, the she-wolf was clearly the brains of the family. No wonder she wanted to start her own clan, where she'd be able to exercise it on her own rather than through an alpha male.

"It's just nice to see an elf playing for all of us, for once," Vikki added.

From the look on Roman's face, he didn't buy for a second that Troy was playing for all of us, but Vikki had set the tone and he had to follow it if he didn't want the wolves looking as divided as the elves had a couple of months ago.

"What does that mean for you, Arie?" Roman's eyes were the stormy grey they got when he was pissed.

"She'll be hunted," Troy answered bluntly before I could come up with a reply.

Behind me, Laurel gasped.

I turned enough to put an arm over her shoulder, trying to be reassuring. "Me, not the rest of you," I murmured to her. "I'll make sure of it."

"But he'll tell them!" Laurel protested.

"He won't." I leveled my hardest look at Troy. "I'll make sure of that too."

Roman scoffed. "You're really going to pin your life on *his* promise? It's not even that his sister broke faith. He drowned you once already."

"He what now?" Ximena's eyebrows lifted. Terrence pursed his lips and crossed his arms as he leaned back, giving me a look suggesting I was being an extra special kind of foolish.

"I did it." Troy crossed his arms, jaw clenched as he defiantly met everyone's accusing, disgusted eyes. Shame and guilt rippled through the bond, with a chaser of stubborn pride and determination. "She was captured by Leith Sequoyah's elven terrorist group. I was in deep cover with them and following elven law, but that is no excuse for what I did. I was wrong, and I regret my actions. I'm making amends. Or trying, at least."

A knowing look eased over Janae's features as she connected the dots between the current situation and the sympathetic elven magic she'd sensed lodged in my aura a few weeks ago. When I nodded, she leaned close to Hope to murmur something quietly enough that I couldn't hear it.

I scowled but let it go. "What Troy did is being dealt with." I hoped I sounded like a hard-ass and not like a little girl out of her depth among alphas, princes, and favored seconds. I stared everyone down, commanding the respect I'd fought so hard for. "He's here today, facing all of y'all, when he could have been back home with his family and House feeding them information.

Or delivering me battered and helpless to Keithia, given that he spent last night putting me back together after Neith decided it was time for another of her tests."

The fact that I was now defending the man who'd just been following orders two seasons ago didn't escape me. It felt gross and uncomfortable, but maybe progress was like that. Even for the wronged party, as much as I might dislike it.

My statement raised eyebrows on the weres. The witches' gazes darted between Troy and me, and I wondered if they were trying to sense the bond when goosebumps prickled with life magic. Noah looked bored.

"I don't know what to say about a face of the Goddess turning your way, but if he's not in another deep cover, then he was disowned." Vikki looked slyly at Troy.

"I disowned myself," the elf snapped, the calm façade shattering as his fists clenched. The scent of burnt marshmallow flared, only to disperse as he took hold of himself and let go of Aether.

Unimpressed, Vikki cocked a hip, her long brown ponytail swishing as she shook her head. "You expect us to believe that the most powerful elven prince in the Western Hemisphere just gave it all up?"

Troy's face darkened. "Yes."

I blinked. Western Hemisphere? Not just this area? Or even this country?

"For what?" She looked me up and down, a smirk curling her lip. "Don't tell me you think an elemental is a hot piece of ass? Or that you'd have a chance at tapping it, if what my brother says is true? What do you really want, *prince*?"

As much as I liked Vikki most days, she had a nasty streak sometimes. It seemed like this was one of them, but I held my tongue, despite the implied insult to me. Troy needed to fight this battle, not me, as much as it bothered me that the group's earlier unity seemed to be shattering and we hadn't reached a consensus on what to do about a second Reveal.

The bond roiled with so many shitty emotions that I shut down my side of it. Troy must have had some hellacious training to stand there, keeping his expression relatively neutral, and take the accusations—even if they were well-deserved.

"I owe a debt." He clenched his fists. "My House owes a debt. It will be paid."

"Enough," Noah said as Vikki opened her mouth again, surprising me. "This isn't the elf we need to worry about. He's here, speaking on something that could have been left to Ms. Finch to deal with rather than facing you lot. Take the ally you have. Worry about the foes who've declared themselves."

The vampire second glanced at me, and I smiled tightly to signal I had no objections to his taking the floor.

"If our Prince of Monteague and Arbiter Finch say they can take care of our mundane problem for the time being, my coterie will accept the help. But if you think for a heartbeat that we'll let it stop there"—he smiled to show fangs in a naked threat—"you're sadly mistaken. Another species is coming out, if the coterie has to expose them ourselves. Decide amongst yourselves, or we'll decide for you."

"Hey!" Roman snarled. "That's not—"

"If the word 'fair' is the next one on your lips, wolfling, I'll break all of your teeth and feed them to you," Noah said.

I couldn't help but notice Terrence and Ximena nodding approvingly. Or Vikki grimacing. For every two steps forward Blood Moon's beta female took, one of her brothers dragged them a step back. Roman's time at home seemed to have turned him into someone much more like Sergei, and I didn't like it. And maybe the alliance wasn't as unified or as solid as I'd thought. The realization exhausted me. It felt like I'd never stop being disappointed.

"You'd try," Roman muttered, grunting at Vikki's elbow in his ribs.

"Stop," I broke in. "Monteague and I are going in. Another group is coming out. That's all there is to it. We made an alliance because we knew times were going to get tough. Well, tough times are here. It's time for action."

My big girl voice must have worked because as I looked at each group in turn—the weres, the witches, Noah, Troy, and Laurel—they all stiffened, whether in anger or fear or resolution, and they all stayed silent.

"Okay then," I said. Gentling my tone, I added, "You've all had two months to think about coming out and supporting the coterie. Now we need a few volunteers. Please don't make me voluntell someone. If I don't hear from a willing party in the next three days, I'll be calling all y'all back here, and we won't be leaving until we decide. Even if it means drawing straws."

With grim nods and heavy sighs, everyone signaled their agreement.

"Y'all know where to find me," I said by way of dismissal.

As everyone filtered back toward the parking lot, Janae approached. "Do you need healing, child? You seem a mite peaky."

I started to decline out of habit then decided that if I was going to break into a building tonight I could use the help. "I'd be grateful, Ms. Janae. Anything you have for blood loss or general vitality should do it."

"I have just the thing." She dug in her purse for a small packet of what looked like home-pressed tablets and tapped one out into her palm. "Take this when you get some water. In the meantime…"

She took my hand and one of Hope's. Hope took my other hand, and I shivered as the two witches drew on some of the life in the plants surrounding us. They chanted briefly, and I hissed an inhale, stiffening in surprise as my headache cleared and the slightly woozy feeling I'd been ignoring dissipated. A few aches I hadn't been aware of eased.

With a last murmur, the witches eased down on the magic then released my hands.

"Thank you," I said. "That's much better."

Hope smiled brightly as Janae said, "Thank you for trusting us. I know that doesn't come easily to you."

I flushed, a little ashamed that they were right, given that they were allies.

With a kind smile, Janae squeezed my shoulder then hesitated when I didn't move to join them in the walk back to the parking lot. "You're not coming?"

"I—there's something I need to do." With my head clear, I'd just figured out what was bugging me about being near the Cape Fear River: it was the one my parents had died in.

Before I could ask Troy or anyone else, including myself, to make a choice about House Solari, I had to face my own past.

Chapter 8

It hadn't occurred to me to visit before now. The past had been closed to me, and my parents' deaths were so distant that I had no memory of them.

But now that I had the truth about myself, I had to go, even if this wasn't the point where they'd died. I had to acknowledge them. Acknowledge myself. Because if I didn't know who I was, I'd never figure out where I was going. I'd always be a tool for the rest of the alliance, rather than a true leader.

And I was sick to death of being all things to all people except for myself.

It was a weekday, so the park was emptier than usual. I downed Janae's little tablet with water from the steel bottle I'd shoved in my bag then clattered down the narrow, rickety wooden staircase quickly, with no other hikers waiting in the platforms for me to pass. When I got to the bottom, scattered hardwoods hid most of the river, but the late afternoon sun shone on the tannic brown ribbon in flashes between leaves and stone.

I trudged down to the river's edge, hesitating briefly at a sign that said the trail ended. Two thick trees leaned out over the river, and I climbed the easy one, hitching myself up some more when it slanted. When I was out over the river, my thighs clenched the tree trunk with more than a little fear. It wasn't Jordan Lake, but my unknown parents had died here.

"The Solaris weren't cursed away from water, if that's what you're thinking. At least, not as far as I know."

I nearly fell off my perch as Troy's voice echoed flatly over the wide river.

When I had my balance enough to turn and glare at him where he leaned against the high rock face behind me, he added, "You didn't really think I was going to leave you alone in the middle of nowhere, did you? Especially not somewhere my kin could claim a particularly symbolic victory if one of them was here."

"I kind of did," I said. "I told you to go think. Goddess! If you're going to sneak up on me, at least do me the courtesy of having the bond open so I can see you coming." I should have been paying attention. Even if he didn't make a sound, I'd have sensed the air molecules shifting with the disturbance of something the size of a body. I'd just been too caught up in my thoughts.

Unbothered, he shrugged, opened the bond, and pushed off the rock to stand at the river's edge. "I'm thinking the elves need to be next," he said. "And that it needs to be me who Reveals us."

I frowned then figured out where he was going. "As in, without telling the rest."

"Yes. We take care of the healthtech startup tonight, while the queens are still debating what to do about me not re-swearing. Then I have two more days to spread my rumors. While they're off-balance with that, I make a little public appearance and show the mundanes what else goes bump in the night."

I shivered, recalling when he'd used the phrase to try intimidating me back in January, then shimmied back until I could slide off my tree and stop twisting my neck to look at him.

"The Houses will be too busy doing damage control to worry about me for a few days. I like it."

We stood side by side at the river. Irony tripped through me, as did more than a little guilt. Was it wrong to stand next to the descendent of the woman who'd killed my parents? And here, of all places?

It'd be worse to hold it against him. That would make me as bad as they were over Atlantis. I didn't owe him the high road or forgiveness or anything at all, really. Nor did the elementals owe any of that to elves in general. But for me, for where I was and the path I was walking…it felt like I had to try. Some might call it a bad compromise, but I had to take my allies where I could find them.

Troy must have been having similar thoughts because the bond echoed with both our guilt, uncertainty, and grief.

We stood like that for a while, just breathing, until some of the spiky edge left his thoughts. It eased from mine too, the big river lazily slipping it away as being in nature calmed me. Both of us slowly relaxed.

I glanced at him, reading the unusual serenity in his mood and easier posture. "You need this almost as much as I do, don't you? Being out in nature."

"Yes."

"But they never gave you enough time for it."

"No." Bitterness slid through.

An idea occurred to me, one that felt right even if it scared the bejeezus outta me. Maybe I could give him a little more ammo to use against the other elves. Or better, show him why elves hunting elementals made no sense, if they needed nature as much as we did.

After some more thought, I said, "Do you trust me?"

"Yes. Why?"

No hesitation. That was nice. "Sit. Give me your hand and open up as much as you can."

We sat on the riverbank. His hand slipped into mine, big, warm, and dry. A spark jumped between our palms, but I was used to it by now. I made the conscious effort to unfocus and fall into my magic, hoping this would work.

The sense of the air moving came easiest. It was as simple as stopping my active control over my power. I could taste the difference in the moister water coming off the river, compared to the drier, more mineral flavor of the wind skirling along the rock face at our back. The leaves made a million vibrations, each of them telling me where the tree was occupied by a bird or a squirrel. It divided as it flowed around us, meeting again on the other side to create a distortion where we sat, even as it flowed into and out of our lungs.

Fire, I sensed mostly in the warmth of the sun and the memories of the igneous cliffs behind us. The rock drank in the sunlight that filtered past the trees, reminiscing on what it had been like to be lava. A little more fire lived in the dryness of some of the sticks under an overhang to our left, sheltered from the river's flood and the rain. They'd catch easily with a spark or a careless cigarette, and I pulled my attention away from them, lest I encourage that spark with a thought.

The ground beneath us tasted saturated by water. Potential hummed through it, the anticipation of every seed or buried cicada nymph waiting for its time. Some of the sand remembered being rocks that fell off the cliff face, so long ago that I almost forgot to breathe as I fell into it and my body aligned itself with rock time.

I eased back and carefully, so carefully, eased into a surrender to the river water.

It wasn't as easy as it was with the Eno. I knew that river, having lived next to it for years. The Cape Fear River was wider and slower, deeper in the middle. I pulled my thoughts away from thinking about how difficult it would be to cross in flood with a baby and focused on the humidity in the air around us, the salamanders on the bank, the fish arrowing through the depths, and the turtles sunning themselves on rocks before letting myself fall under completely. Decayed vegetation gave it an acidic taste to my magic's senses, and I eased away, still not comfortable with the reminder of Jordan Lake.

Troy's grip tightened painfully as he experienced nature like I did when I wasn't closing it out. When I pulled my attention away from the living world, I realized that he'd started drifting, lost in depths I floated in naturally. I carefully gathered him back in and let him go, sighing regretfully as I tamped my power back down to a level where I could function the way I had up until this past spring.

Opening my eyes with a slow languor, I inhaled deeply, resettling myself. Troy and I were leaning heavily against each other, and I shifted away.

He stiffened, gasping as though he hadn't breathed the whole time, and stared at me with tears in his eyes. "That's how you live? All of that? All the time?"

I shrugged and shook myself. "It is if I don't focus, now that I have all the elements. The other elementals tell me I have a power signature now, so I have to lock it down and shut all of that out if I don't want to set off the mundanes. Besides, it's hard to think if I don't quiet it."

"You do have a signature. Like a humming or the fan in a wind tunnel starting up. Finch…" He visibly gathered himself, staring at me in a combination of shock and horror. "This makes what my people have done even more of a crime. We call ourselves the stewards of nature, but you *are* nature. The embodiment of it."

I glanced at him sideways, wondering if he was having a religious moment, and slid my hand out of his grip. "Okay."

A grim expression flashed across his face, and an ominous feeling rippled through the bond. "That's it. That's why the elves had to wipe the elementals out. It has to be. Elementals are closer to the Source than we are, and my ancestors couldn't bear it. Otherwise why not go after the djinn? We had a much longer history of enmity with them, even if it was broken by periods of peace and marriage alliances."

"I always wondered that myself." I kept my eyes on the river in an effort to settle the roil his side of the bond was making in my mind and stomach. "It always seemed odd that the djinn would have pushed their children into something so futile, or that elementals would just snap and drown Atlantis without any provocation. I have no bloodlust. Never have, except when Leith had my back against the wall or I was under attack. I don't want to hunt or kill or anything really, other than be left alone and just…thrive. Like, fuck, I don't even have the teeth that you or the djinn do." I sighed. "It's not just me, either. All Laurel wants is to tend her farm and grow things. Val wants to use her magic to help keep people safe. Some of our powers can hurt others, but that's like a knife—it's the intent of the wielder, not the tool itself. I dunno, maybe other elementals are different, but I think it's pretty telling that we let ourselves be pushed to the edge of extinction and went into hiding rather than pulling another Atlantis, don't you?"

"We must have done something first." A low growl slipped from Troy, and I glanced at him to see fury tightening his features. A sense of betrayal echoed through the bond. "The elves must have pushed the elementals into an act of self-defense. Someone is lying. They have to be. And that would mean I did all those things to hurt you to uphold a law based on a *lie*."

I frowned, wondering what was most offensive to him—the lie, the impact it had on his honor, or what it had driven him to do. In my pocket, a buzz announced a phone call. I rose and wandered off a little way to take it, leaving Troy to wrestle with the revelation that maybe all the history he thought he knew had been wrong, told through a lens skewed to paint the elves in the best, or most victimized, light.

"Hawkeye Investigations, this is Finch," I said, not recognizing the number.

"This is Detective Rice, Raleigh PD. I'm calling to see if you can come down to the station, Ms. Finch." His tone gave nothing away.

I spun back to Troy, finding him on his feet, head cocked as he tried to read the bond. After a brief hesitation, I stepped close enough that he could hear the call.

"Hey there, Detective. You got a job for me?" I asked in a light tone.

"I'm afraid not, ma'am. We're re-interviewing everyone associated with the Umstead hotel death from a couple months ago. Wondering if you might be able to take a look at some evidence." The detective's voice had hardened, as though daring me to decline.

Troy grimaced as I said, "Sure thing. I can be there in forty-five minutes, if that works?"

"That works. Thank you for your cooperation."

I hissed as the call ended then let my frustration out verbally when that wasn't enough. "Dammit."

"Indeed," Troy muttered as he pulled out his own phone and answered. Detective Rice, again. When he'd given the detective the same neutral agreement I had, he asked, "What's our story?"

"You're asking me?"

He lifted his eyebrows. "I didn't call you the leader earlier just for show."

I crossed my arms and looked out over the river. The timing of this pinched, and that made me suspicious. It had been weeks since we'd last been interviewed, and before his latest call, Doc Mike had said the case was marked as being on hold because they couldn't find anyone matching Torsten's description to bring in for questioning. Not a surprise, given that I'd struck a bargain with the succubus who'd set up the whole mess to take Torsten's desiccated corpse to the Crossroads. So why now?

Think, Arden. What's the worst-case scenario?

"An elf talked," I said, sure of it. "One of the EMTs or a CSI. Shit, I should have seen this coming."

Whether it was arrogance or naiveté, I'd been optimistic about the odds of getting the elves to play nice over the Reveal. I should have known it would come to this.

Troy scowled and opened his mouth then winced and looked aside. "It's what I would have done," he agreed grudgingly.

"Especially given the way they looked at me when you came up playing boyfriend. Double that for you not turning up to re-swear and that no longer looking like an act." I peered up at him. Blood drained from his face then flushed back up as his expression firmed. I'd expected regret, but it was determination that came through the bond.

"I'm going to need to move faster than I thought." A frown pinched his brow. "We'll go together."

"Are you kidding me? You know that if they called it in, they'll be watching for me to turn up. They'll see you with me."

Troy pressed his lips into a grim line. I could practically feel the gears turning through the bond. "So be it," he said after a long pause.

I stared at him, unable to reconcile this Troy with the one who'd named me an elemental to the Redcaps and carried out Leith's order to drown me. "What the hell is going on with you?"

"You still don't quite believe everything I've been saying. I can feel it. The doubt in the back of your mind."

When I grimaced and looked away, heart pounding at the truth of it, he gently turned my face back to him with two fingers on my jaw.

"This morning, you told me to go and think." The sun picked out sparks of gold in his gaze, and I did my best to focus rather than falling in. "There's nothing to think about. There's only what's right and what isn't. Standing with you is right."

"Monteague…"

"Don't call me—" His voice hitched, and he swallowed as a wave of melancholy swept through the bond, so thick and choking I shuddered. "I won't claim that House anymore."

I looked at the sky, wondering why the hell I felt bad for him. *Because I'm not a cold-hearted, hateful bitch. Because he has everything I ever dreamed of having, and I'm still not convinced I'm worth giving all that up for.*

I shoved that ugly thought in a box to examine later and refocused on the dejected elf in front of me. "Fine. But you cannot be seen with me yet. We have to do the Verve job, and if they know we're together, they'll know to look for you near me. We'll do the job, and then you can satisfy your honor. Okay?"

He studied me, looking like he wanted to disagree. "Okay. But let me do something first."

"What?"

"A formal oath. It'll protect you against a few things. But I have to put it on you since you can't put it on me." When I nodded, heart pounding, he knelt and bowed his head. The scent of Aether burned strong as he took my hand. "I, Troy, former Prince of Monteague, renounce all previous claims, titles, and obligations to that House. I accept the claim of Arden Finch

Solari as my queen and swear my life and death to her service. And so it is."

I shivered as Aether prickled over me, arrowing into my aura and then shooting back to Troy through the bond.

He grunted and rose, expression tight as though it'd hurt then bowed his head. "My queen."

"Thank you." I didn't know what else to say. My head spun. I hadn't realized claiming him meant an oath, but I'd asked it, and he'd agreed. Just like that, he was mine and I was, technically, a queen.

We left the park without another word. Silence hung heavy on both of us, even as he handed me a small radio receiver and another one of the dime-sized earpieces we'd used when we'd fought the lich.

Chapter 9

The chairs at Raleigh Police Department were as hard and sticky as I remembered from my last visit here. Troy had pulled off into a coffeehouse, presumably so we wouldn't turn up together and raise suspicions among the elves or the mundanes. I had to assume he had some way of staying under the radar, given that there was no way in the nine hells that his people weren't looking for him, swapped lojack and plates or not. My stomach clenched, and my breath grew short every time my mind drifted to his little speech. I figured out why it scared me so damn bad: I hadn't actually thought he'd do it.

I'd been trying to drive him away.

Quick, heavy steps pulled me out of my thoughts before I could examine them further, and I slapped a smile on my face as Detective Rice approached.

"Detective! Good to see you again." I rose and met his extended hand with a firm clasp.

"Ms. Finch. Thanks for coming down on such short notice." He eyed my rumpled clothes, creased where sweat had dried. "I hope it wasn't too much trouble."

"None at all." I fluffed my hair as I followed him, hoping it covered the earpiece. The humidity had made it wild enough that it should be fine, but I still worried.

Worry turned to ice in my gut when I picked up the scent of burnt marshmallow as we passed the main floor and headed down a small hallway. "I thought this was a friendly visit," I said coolly. "Any reason why we're going to the interrogation rooms?"

"Like I said, we'd like to review some evidence."

Rice didn't say more, and I didn't push, trying to balance the need to keep Troy in the loop with not looking guilty as fuck.

The source of the Aether became apparent as soon as we entered a small room with a double-sided mirror.

"This is my colleague, Estrella Luna with the Crime Scene unit." Rice gestured to a dark-haired, dark-eyed elfess seated on the side of the table with two chairs and no handcuff loop.

"Ms. Luna," I said, heart pounding as I took a seat. My silver knife, the one I'd used to tear up the wound in the vic's neck to hide Torsten's bite marks, was in a plastic baggie in front of them. I'd done it to keep attention away from the vampires, and the elves knew it.

"Ms. Finch." The woman's hard gaze flicked over me. I didn't know if it was to do with me or if she just had resting bitch face, but I assumed it was the whole elemental thing and returned it steadily.

The look eased as she smiled at Rice. "Clayton, would you mind grabbing some water? While you're up."

The detective nodded. "Sure."

When his footsteps had receded, Estrella shut the door then flicked her thumb along her palm and looked at the camera in the corner. The red light started blinking, and I caught the barest glimpse of something black in her hand.

"Where has the Prince of Monteague been?" she asked in a terse whisper, staring intently at me.

A pit grew in my stomach. They had to be desperate to find him if they'd dare asking me directly. "How the hell would I know?"

"He seems awfully attached to you."

"Keithia mighta set him to watch me. That doesn't mean I see him. He's a sneaky fucker." Everything inside me quivered, as it had the day Leith Sequoyah had walked into my office. The difference now was the elves knew who I was—and I knew my own power.

"You captured him once. How do we know you didn't again?"

Was she asking because they suspected him or because they didn't and thought the only reason he hadn't showed was because of me? Which kept me safer?

"Why do you care?"

Before Estrella could answer, Rice's footsteps approached. The elfess flicked her thumb again and pocketed whatever she'd been holding. The light on the surveillance camera returned to its threatening, steady red.

"So you're sure you've never seen this knife before, Ms. Finch?" she said as Rice opened the door, juggling three mini-bottles of water dewy with condensation.

I lifted my brows, asking permission as I reached for the plastic baggie. Estrella pushed it toward me. She had to turn a gasp into a cough when the Aether dart she tried sending when our fingers brushed rebounded sharply off my shields and went straight back into her.

Bitch.

"You all right?" Rice looked between us.

I ignored him, faking a concerned look for Estrella before turning my attention to the knife in front of me.

"Fine," she said. "Thanks for the water. Damn allergy meds dried my throat up."

With a grunt, the detective settled into the chair next to hers.

"Nope. Never seen this." I slid the knife back over. "What's it got to do with the crime scene?"

"It was recovered there," Detective Rice said. "My CSI colleagues think it was used to make it look like our deceased had been stabbed."

I frowned as though that wasn't exactly what I'd done and offered my smoothest lie. "Sorry, Detective—are you suggesting the vic hadn't been stabbed? I mean, I'm the one who tried to stop the bleeding and performed CPR. I saw the wound. All that blood."

"A wound that had two unusually deep punctures on either end," Estrella said.

Playing ignorant, I said, "So, are you trying to say he was stabbed more than once or—"

"Stop, Ms. Finch," Detective Rice said. "You were there assisting the hostess with a matter. That hostess claimed she was a vampire not minutes before you discovered the body. There was a room full of them. Now we have riots in the streets and the public demanding we give these creatures human rights. *Human* rights." He scoffed.

A chill settled over me as I saw what he was angling for. "It sounds to me like you're asking me to help you pin this on someone. A vampire someone. But that would be unconstitutional and unethical if there's no hard evidence to support it."

"It's not unconstitutional if they're already dead. Or hell, if they're not even human."

The angry fear in Rice's tone hit me like a slap. I dared a glance at Estrella. She looked grim, like she'd been tasked with a mission she didn't want, but her lips pressed tightly together. She wouldn't speak against this. That they were being open with it while this interview was being recorded told me either someone would disappear the tape later or the whole station was in agreement with the sentiments. Either way, not good. I needed to shake them off this, fast.

"Of all people to want to plant evidence or make false accusations against a member of a group struggling for their rights," I said softly, "I didn't expect it from a Black man."

The detective recoiled. "How dare you."

"No, how dare *you*." I snapped. "I came here as a professional courtesy. What you're asking is not only morally wrong, it could get my private investigator's license revoked. Am I under arrest?"

Ire snapped in the depths of Rice's brown eyes. "No," he said after grinding his teeth and looking like he was trying to find a reason. "But don't you leave town."

I rose, debating whether to press my luck. The hell with it. "Times are changing, Detective. Whatever anyone thinks of the vampires, they were always there, from what I hear," I said. Then I shifted my glance to Estrella. "Those who can't get with the program might well find themselves on the wrong side of things—and the oppressed never stay quiet for long."

Estrella stiffened, hearing my threat for what it was. Rice just sneered at me, but it looked weaker than before. Thoughtful, as though my invoking his race had put him on the back foot. I supposed he'd thought he was one of the good cops until right this moment.

The elfess cleared her throat. "I think that's all we needed. I'll walk Ms. Finch out."

I kept a careful distance between us as we retraced our steps to the front, but she leaned closer. "Monteague is next on our interview list."

"Looks like you've found him then. Why ask me where he is?"

She reached for my arm, and I danced aside quickly enough that a passing officer stopped in his tracks. Dammit. My reflexes were improving as my powers grew, and that had been a little too fast for human. Blinking and shaking his head as though he hadn't had enough sleep, the officer passed between the wide space now between Estrella and me.

"I'm trying to help," she hissed when he'd moved out of earshot. "You need to keep him with you."

I stared at her, shocked enough to forget myself, and jolted myself into a walk when she reached for me again. "Funny way of helping, with whatever you tried to pull earlier," I snarled under my breath. We were almost to the door. "Why should I trust you?"

"Because we all need Troy."

"Who the hell is 'we all'?"

"The Ebon Guard. And you."

"Never heard of them." My gut burned. First the Redcaps, now some Ebon Guard. The elves seemed to like their super-secret, color-coded groups. That hadn't worked out so well for me before.

"Few have. We want to keep it that way. We also want Troy."

I paused at the door, eyeing her suspiciously. "For what, and why should I care?"

"We want him to lead us."

This cryptic shit was getting tiring. "What the hell for?"

"To protect you. They're coming for you, Finch. Soon. You're not alone, and neither is he. We just didn't know you existed until a few months ago. We've been trying to figure out which side of the fence Troy was going to fall on for about that long. If he wasn't missing last night because you captured him..." She shrugged. "Maybe he's seen the light. Maybe he'll help us."

Studying her, I tried to decide how to turn this about. Maybe help sow Troy's little seeds. "You didn't know I existed, as in what I am? Or the Solari thing?"

Her eyes flew wide before dropping to the chain disappearing into my shirt, where I'd tucked my pendant out of habit, and I hoped I wasn't about to make a huge mistake in following Troy's advice to be more obvious about it. Heart thundering, I casually ran my finger around the chain as though I was adjusting it and let the gold-wrapped onyx pendant thump onto my chest.

If I'd thought her eyes were wide before, they bugged out now.

"Have fun interviewing Troy," I said when all she did was sweat and stare, leaving her with her shock and heading back out into the hot summer evening. I scanned the parking lot for anyone waiting and spoke just loud enough for the earpiece. "All clear. Meet me at the bar when you're done."

I texted Maria a warning about what had gone down then spent the drive back to Durham listening to them try the same shit with Troy with even less success. I had zero reason at all to trust a random elf playing mind games, but she'd said the same thing Troy had: someone was coming for me.

Fine. That was credible enough, especially when she told Troy the same thing while walking him out. But some secret guardian society all ready to help me? Pfft. They'd had months to make themselves known as allies. To stand up to Keithia and do something to actively help me. Why now?

I didn't trust any of it, at all. Not their motives, not their mission, not their altruism or whatever so-called good intentions might have been behind Estrella's declaration that I wasn't alone. None of it. I'd lived under a death threat my entire life simply for existing, and all of a sudden these chuckleheads wanted to pop up because they finally perceived a crisis. For all I knew it was performative, and they'd make a good racket so that the rest of the alliance didn't kick them to the curb when the gods came for the Wild Hunt—but sit on the sidelines when I needed them most.

Troy, I might see my way to trusting. Eventually. If he didn't fuck this up.

I'd watched his evolution over the last six months. He'd approached me at every turn. Apologized. Owned responsibility. Taken action that was ultimately costing him his House, title, and family. I might not want to admit it, but he was, as Maria had said, doing the work.

But some random elf I didn't know from Lilith? Nah. I'd need to see some serious proof first.

When I pulled into the bar's parking lot, Roman's battered F-150 was there. I sighed, slumping, wondering which of the Volkovs was waiting for me. It would be a while before Troy could get up here and meet me to plan the Verve job, and I'd wrapped up my last mundane case last week without selecting another. With the protests for and against vampires ramping up alongside Independence Day last week, it didn't seem wise either to be distracted or too closely involved with humans. I dunno what being an American had to do with supporting or opposing vampirism, but patriotism seemed to have lit a fire under both sides. In any case, it meant I didn't have many excuses to avoid Roman, if it was him. After the way he'd acted at Raven Rock, I wanted some space.

I tapped my fingers on the steering wheel, debating whether to go in and sift through whatever information had come in or wait for Troy at home.

A low wolf's howl made the decision for me.

"Shit." I slid out of my car and glared at Sergei.

The werewolf trapped in wolf form was in the bed of the truck, and he grinned at me, tongue lolling.

"Asshole," I snapped as I passed.

Sergei yipped again as Roman appeared in the bar's doorway. The overhead light made shadows where my ex's hair fell over his face.

"Roman," I said in greeting as I slipped past him. The cedar-and-musk scent of werewolf lifted from him as I passed, and goosebumps rippled down my arms at the memories the scent invoked. Warm nights, cool sheets, salt sweat, and…I shoved the distracting thoughts aside.

"Arie," he returned, sounding smug as he followed me in. He stayed just far enough that I couldn't call it clingy as I popped behind the bar, but his little smirk told me he'd caught the scent of my remembrance.

"Hey, Zanna." I pushed through my irritation to offer a genuine smile to my kobold landlord-turned-friend. "How's things?"

"Quiet." She shook her curly mane out of her eyes before hopping up on a stepladder to serve the witch who'd ambled over for a refill. Once the transaction was complete, Zanna eyed Roman, clearly debating what to say in front of him. Roman didn't budge.

I sighed. "I'll check the reports in a bit, okay? I have some business to take care of tonight, so I won't be in long."

The kobold's brows rose. "Business."

"We need to buy time to decide who's being Revealed next."

Zanna took that at face value, not reacting beyond filling a highball with soda water and dropping in a thin slice of lemon for me.

"I'll catch you up when I get home, okay?"

"You do that, tenant. The Chamber of Lords has been rumbling."

I grimaced, and Roman's cocky smile slipped. The fae lords and ladies had been content to stay in their realm for long centuries as the humans expanded, leaving their subjects to choose whether to come or go from this plane. "Rumbling" couldn't be good.

"We'll talk," I promised, waiting for her solemn nod before turning back to Roman. "I assume there's something I can help you with?"

"Can we talk? Alone? Please." He nodded to Zanna, who stared at him with undisguised hostility.

I debated whether I wanted to be alone with him and whether my reluctance to grant the request was because I was trying to punish him. I wouldn't know until and unless I went with it. Maybe I was being too hard on him. He'd asked, rather than cornering me in the parking lot.

Zanna's eyes weighed on my back as I led him to the office that had once been Callista's. I'd replaced all the furniture that had been shattered in our fight and upgraded the computer to a sleek laptop but left the big-ass silver sword hanging on the wall behind me. I didn't have the slightest idea how to wield a sword—knives, guns, and magic were more my speed—but it made an impression and reminded the few people I had back here who I'd claimed this place from.

I didn't sit down, hoping to signal that I wanted to make this quick.

Roman shut the door then took in my crossed arms and neutral expression. "Arie, I've missed you."

A headache blossomed, as did an ache deep in my heart. I could not afford this, not now. "Roman—"

He cut me off. "You can't trust Monteague. Don't go with him tonight."

Chapter 10

I stiffened, jaw clenched. "What have you heard?"

Roman reached out to rub along my arms. I closed my eyes, swaying a little, allowing it but not leaning in the way my body wanted to. I didn't want to admit it, but I'd missed him too. I missed being desired. I missed his touch, his attention, his…everything.

"Babe—"

That broke the spell, and I stepped back, though it made me ache even deeper. "Don't call me that. Not when you're with someone else."

Sighing, he rubbed the back of his neck. "Maybe not for much longer. Things are getting worse back home."

"I mean, one of the first things you said is that you wanted me to kill your father for you, so…" I shrugged, pulling a wry face.

"Come on, Arie. We used to be good together."

"Did we?" When he just looked confused, I added, "I really wish you'd stop with the nicknames, especially in front of the alliance. Can you not see how that undermines me?"

He just frowned at me, looking bemused, studying me as though he just had to find the right thing to say to make me fall back into bed with him. The worst part was I wanted to, he could probably smell it, and all of that annoyed the living hell outta me. He was trampling what little pride I had.

"You *left*, Roman. That was *your* choice, not mine. I'm moving on. You need to as well. Be with Ana or don't, but I need someone who will be there for me. Who will choose *me* first." The words I wished I'd said sometime before now poured out of me so fast and so hot I had to force myself to stop, turning my back to him and leaning a hip against the desk.

"So that's it? No second chances?" The puzzled hurt in his voice arrowed to my core, making me feel guilty then resentful that he kept stepping over my lines. *He'd* left *me*. Couldn't he see why *I* was hurting?

I can't do this. "Why can't I trust Troy?"

"Oh, it's 'Troy' now?"

Disbelieving, I turned back around, my temper flaring at the naked jealousy in his tone. "It is when he's lost his House and probably everything else supporting me, which is a hell of a lot more than I'd ever dreamed anyone, let alone an *elf*, would do. It's sure as shit more than *you* did."

We glared at each other. I had the uncomfortable thought that if there was anyone I was going to hate fuck, it'd probably be Roman.

I took a breath and tried to calm down. I was better than this. I had to be because I was nominally in charge of this damn alliance. "Is there a reason you're making accusations?"

"I'm trying to help you." His voice held the exaggerated patience of an adult speaking to a child. "Lupa's teats, I found him pinning you to the floor!"

"So what? You nostalgic for our runs in the woods or something? Pissed off about an elf on top of me when you can't be?"

Okay. Maybe I wasn't better than this. Maybe I'd been trying to be for a little too long now.

Thunderclouds had nothing on Roman's face. "I can see you wouldn't listen to reason even if I presented it to you."

"What reason?" I pulled my hair off my face in exasperation then froze as my thumb skipped over the plastic of the earpiece I'd forgotten to remove from behind my ear.

Shit. Troy could hear all of this if he still had his receiver on. I flushed, deeply embarrassed, then used it to fuel my anger. "Roman, this is not what the alliance should be about. Running around behind the others' backs and making unfounded accusations. If you have evidence, tell me. If not, I need you to back the fuck off. We can have a professional relationship, but I cannot do *this* anymore."

"I just can't believe you're so desperate for support you'd ignore that he's just waiting for another chance to hurt you!" Roman snapped, hands on his hips to make him look even bigger. "Arden, he's an elf. He's already hurt you. If you want to be naive enough to trust a damned elf who's already proven he's willing and able to *kill you*, that's your business, but don't punish me to the point that you can't see I'm trying to keep you safe!"

Feeling as though he'd slapped me, I bowed my head. My insides churned, and my skin felt too tight. Part of me screamed that Roman was right, that I couldn't trust an elf, any elf, including Troy. Callista had taunted me with the same words when I'd fought her. But my thoughts were there too, as were Maria's words, and Noah's, and Troy's back against mine in battle. His calloused fingers pinching my wounds closed as I lay bleeding on my kitchen table. At the end of the day, Maria had never asked for anything other than what I was willing to give, and Troy had given up everything to do right by me.

Roman had given me up.

As petty and selfish and small as it made me feel, I couldn't let that go. When I met Roman's eyes, he huffed a sigh at whatever he saw in my expression or smelled on me and shook his head.

"Fine," he said sourly. "Learn the hard way. I'll be in town a few more days to hash out a few things with Vikki."

The implication that he'd be there to pick up the pieces laid heavy between us.

"Thank you," I said hoarsely, scrabbling for the last bit of dignity I could summon. I hated this, and I hated that I had to swallow my own anger and hurt feelings to get him to leave. "If there's nothing else, I have a mission to plan."

Roman rocked on his feet, as though he was going to embrace or kiss me, then left, pulling the door closed again behind him.

As I collapsed into my chair, my phone buzzed with a text message. Blood rushed to my face as I read the note from Troy.

Not going to pretend I didn't hear all of that. Won't hold it against him. He means well. Be there in 10.

"He even takes the high road. Fuck," I muttered then went hot all over again when I realized Troy could hear that too.

It could have been a ploy, but I didn't think it was. Troy had been too genuinely angry about whatever lie he thought he'd been told earlier for him to be telling me one now, and the bond shared his acceptance and regret as he drew closer.

I dropped the phone on my desk and pillowed my head on my arms. I really, really wanted the situation with Roman to be anything other than what it was. But every interaction we'd had since he'd left threw up red flag after red flag, and looking back on our relationship, a few had always been there. He might finally be choosing me now, in his way, but it wasn't the way *I* needed. It made me feel icky or ungrateful or like I was being too demanding. Shouldn't I just be happy Roman cared, even when he was still working things out with someone else? But every time I relented on what I wanted—what I needed—I ended up regretting it.

Why did dodging a bullet have to feel so shitty?

I was unenthusiastically reviewing my notes on Verve Health Solutions when I felt Troy close enough that he had to have entered the bar. After a long pause, probably to greet Zanna and pay his respects, he started drawing closer again.

"It's open," I called before he could knock.

He slipped in as soundlessly as he'd approached, and we stared at each other.

"I appreciate what you said," Troy finally said. Everything about him was carefully neutral, from his face to his body language to the hum of the bond between us.

That was it. No promises, no guilt trips, no barbs. It was a relief, but I just shrugged listlessly, too tired of all of it to want to talk about any of it. "I have the plans for Verve here. Notes on entry, exit, security, and my recommendations based on what I was able to access during my penetration test."

"May I?"

I slid the rolling chair to the side to make space for him to come around the desk.

He leaned forward, weight on one hand with the other tucked behind his back as he studied everything. I kept waiting for the reflexive panic to come at being so close to an elf in a closed space, but he was tamping down on Aether and all I smelled was fresh herbs, male sweat, and the lingering traces of city night. He was being careful, very careful, not to be a threat. Hell, even more careful than when we sparred and there was actually a possibility of his hurting me.

I wavered between getting closer to see the plans and keeping my distance. Had I finally lost my fear of him?

Troy glanced at me as though the thought had caught his attention, but all he said was, "This matches what Callista provided the Darkwatch. A team was sent in to make sure we had a backdoor into their systems, so assuming nothing's changed, I should be able to get us in. I'm more concerned that the Conclave will make an attempt on you tonight."

I frowned. "Did Estrella say something I missed?"

"No, Detective Rice was present the whole time, so all I know is what I heard from your conversation and what you heard of mine. Thanks, by the way, for dropping the Solari name into it. Makes my job easier." He offered a lopsided smile before returning to his study of the building plans. "It's just that Estrella will have to report back that she's seen us both. The Conclave will probably order the Darkwatch to take one or both of us. That means we're likely both under surveillance or will be soon."

I blinked. "But you still came here?"

He gave me a tired look then turned back to the plans again before skipping to the section about the electronic keypad manufacturer. "I have a decryption key for this one. Easy in. Cameras are standard, easily hacked even if the network backdoor has been discovered and patched. Are your bugs still active?"

"No. The batteries will have died a few months ago. As far as I know, they were never replaced."

"Okay." Troy straightened. "Then let's get going. You head out first. I'll follow and see if anyone trails you."

And who watches your back? I wondered.

***

I parked at the back of the lot in the next office park over from where Verve was, having noted on my last visit that it lacked cameras beyond those on the door. Troy should have been right behind me, but he'd fallen back somewhere. A shiver ran over me as I wondered if he'd picked up a tail.

He'd shake it. I had to trust him. For now, I'd scout.

Tugging at the black cap I kept in my car and keeping my head down, I walked through the thin row of trees between the two complexes. Mosquitoes buzzed in my ear, and I swatted at them as I made a short hop over the ditch at the bottom when I smelled swamp. My foot still squished in mud, and I grimaced, pausing to scrape it off on the grass when I got to the other side. It wouldn't do to track some in and leave evidence.

I took the opportunity to pause and evaluate the building. It was mostly dark. A few lights had been left on inside, but those looked like desk lamps that had been forgotten. No cars were in the lot, and no silhouettes moved in the windows. Still, I stuck to the pines ringing the parking lot as I made my way around the perimeter. It couldn't hurt to make sure there was as little as possible of me to erase from the tapes, just in case something was missed.

As I approached a picnic area in a small patio clearing in the trees, the wind shifted, bringing me the scent of burnt marshmallow.

Elves.

I scrambled to put my back to a tree and crouched, heart pounding, as I eased my shields down just enough to get a sense of the air molecules shifting. Someone was mirroring my crouch to my left, away from the building.

"It's me, Finch," Troy hissed at the same time I realized how close he was in the bond.

With a heavy exhale, I rose. "Where'd you go?"

Grim satisfaction slithered through the bond as he slipped past me, heading for the door. "Needed to cause an accident."

"You what?" I caught his sleeve and pulled him up short.

"The first attempt was supposed to be on the road. There will be two more teams of three out tonight."

My fingers cramped on his sleeve as the reality of what he'd been saying hit me. Kidnappers and assassins. It was already starting. The elven tendency to do things in threes meant this would be a long night. I checked the lead-and-silver blade I kept to defend against elves, reassured to find it on my hip.

Troy squeezed my shoulder quickly. "Come on. They won't try again until we leave the building."

"How do you know they won't just call the cops to report a B and E?" I stumbled after him, mind whirling.

"Because they're still Othersiders. They can only torture us if we're alive and in their custody, not in a mundane jail cell."

Fuck. I watched Troy's back as he messed with the door panel then the alarm system, paying attention with both physical and magical senses. Roman's exhortation not to trust the elf echoed in a corner of my mind, and I tried to wall it out of the bond. If Troy noticed it, he didn't comment. Maybe it was enough that I'd shut Roman down.

Once inside, Troy paused to listen as I read the air currents.

"Nobody on this floor," I whispered, keeping my head angled to hide my face from the camera with my cap.

"I'll deal with the building security. Can you find the samples?" he asked. I nodded, and he pressed a key card into my hand. "That should get you in."

Tucking it into my pocket, I headed for the stairs to the basement, my mood sour at having to be underground. The breaking and entry passed in a rush of adrenaline as I speed-walked to the secure lab, praying Roman had been wrong and this wasn't some elaborate deep-cover trap on Troy's part.

Worry about it later. Keep Otherside safe first.

The keypad took forever to give me its welcoming beep, and I sweated for every millisecond. Cold, dry air smelling of electronics and chemicals seeped out. The only shift in the air molecules came from the same place as a mechanical whirring— some machine in action, preparing samples for the next day.

A scuffing footstep behind me was Troy's polite warning. I slid away from the door to make space for him, and he headed for a computer on the opposite side of the room.

Sliding into the chair in front of it, he said, "If I turn off the climate control and temperature alarms, can you heat the space enough to ruin the samples?"

"Sure. But we should probably be outside the room when that happens."

He flicked a glance at me to gauge my seriousness then bent to his work.

I stalked through the room, trying to determine where the most logical heat source would be. This had to look natural, an unhappy accident, or we'd intensify the hunt for more Othersiders rather than sidelining it.

"Make sure sample number two-zero-two-one-four-one-seven is in here," Troy said. "That's the one from Torsten's case."

By the time he grunted that he was done, I'd confirmed the presence of the evidence from Torsten's case and identified two options to ruin it all: a ventilation fan and a heat exchange system. I could stop the fan with Air and soften the piping enough for it to burst with Fire. Val had mentioned the dea of old acidifying and corroding metal as well as melting it, but I didn't want to risk activating that and, say, turn my own blood to acid. Or Troy's, for that matter.

"Wait by the door." I focused on embracing Fire without letting it run wild in the flammable chemicals in a case along one wall.

It came more easily than usual, drawn by the heat in the pipe. Gritting my teeth against the anticipated burn I'd have on my hands, I hovered my palm up and down until I found a thinner spot. The steam within the pipe grew hotter still as I fed Fire into the metal as slowly as I could. Sweat rolled down my face, more from nerves and strain than the heat shimmering under my skin. It wouldn't just be my hands burnt this time. I'd probably have something like a sunburn all over from trying to hold enough to work with but keep it controlled. From the door came Troy's uncomfortable shifting. I blocked him out.

If the second elf team was hunting, we didn't have time for me to be distracted.

Chapter 11

With a ping, the pipe reached its melting point. I jerked my hand and the rest of me away a bare second before steam burst out in a tight whistle but kept pouring Fire into it until it was wide enough to stop whistling. Backing to the door, I wove a chord of Fire into the metal of the pipe to keep building on its own and switched to Air, making it heavy enough to stop the fan. A loose tie-off of the chord would fade and let the fan free later, when it was too late.

The heat and humidity in the room rose dramatically.

"Out," I said tersely when I bumped into Troy.

He guided me out backwards with a hand on my shoulder as I kept working, weaving Fire and Air together to heat the room well past anything comfortable for most living things. With Troy's touch, Water was easier to surrender to. He'd pulled me out once. He could do it again. I boosted the humidity in the room, setting the complex chord of magic in a loop as Troy closed the door to a crack to keep as much air as possible trapped inside.

A pop announced the first spoiled sample as the little plastic lid burst open. More followed. I kept pouring heat into the chord, wanting to be certain that there was no recovering anything in this room. I felt bad for the people Verve might have been helping with their analyses and studies, but I'd feel worse if one of my Othersiders was harmed by their work. Given the human reaction so far, I didn't trust the biases of mundane scientists.

I wavered on my feet as dizziness hit me. I'd never woven Fire with that much control, and the strain was dragging at me. No nosebleed, for once—the effort was control, not strength.

"Easy, Finch." Troy supported me from behind with a hand at the small of my back. "A little more."

Nodding, I took a deep breath and shook my head to clear the sweat threatening to drip into my eyes. With a sound like cheap fireworks, the rest of the samples burst in a cascade. We could no longer see through the foggy glass. I gave up trying to stand and knelt so that I could focus on sending my awareness of Water through the room, finding each of the little tubes as points of heat and all of the chemicals splattered within their containers and cases.

"I think that's all of it," I said hoarsely, shutting the door and wiping my fingerprints off with my shirt. "Whatever didn't boil will be contaminated by the bacteria that'll grow come morning."

Letting go of the chords of magic to fizzle out on their own, I let Troy support me with a hand under my elbow when I staggered. "Clearly I need to practice more," I said, embarrassed both for how weak such a short working had made me and for how stupidly grateful I was that he was here.

"Don't worry about it. We all need a little help sometime."

Help or not, I was glad he let me struggle up the stairs on my own rather than trying to carry me. Once outside, the breaths of air I pulled deep into my lungs were sweet...until I realized it wasn't the freshness of the outdoors. It was the cloying confectionary sweetness of meringue, and it wasn't coming from the door behind me where Troy was resetting whatever he'd done to break in. It was coming from the trees surrounding the parking lot.

I shoved exhaustion aside and whipped the breeze into a stiff gale, pushing it outward. A masculine curse came from both behind me and in front.

"Second team," I rasped as Troy darted out and to the side, finding cover behind a trash can.

"We have ten seconds to move out of the cameras' arc of visibility before the loop I put them in ends," Troy said tightly.

"Split up and run?"

The bond suggested he didn't like that idea at all, but we couldn't be caught on video. "Go."

I didn't need to be told twice. Aether prickled along my skin. I tightened my shields as much as I could and took off, angling for the other side of the road and the trees there. I didn't hear feet behind me, but I could sense the disturbance of two bodies moving through space, catching up fast. A third chased Troy. Apparently, I was the more valuable target. Not clever of them, given Troy was the deadlier one.

I hit the sidewalk then the tree line and immediately went ass over tits as the ground suddenly dropped away. Tucking into a ball, I bounced over broken sticks and pine needles, grunting as a branch found my ribs and praying I wasn't going to wake a copperhead. A tree broke my fall at the bottom, half knocking the wind outta me, but adrenaline pushed me to my feet.

Not fast enough.

"Got ya, bitch," a rough voice snarled as someone tackled me into the undergrowth.

All the training I'd been doing with Troy, Allegra, and Iago snapped to the fore. Fear disappeared, replaced by clarity. There was no time to grab my knife. I swept aside the descending hand. Bronze flashed in the distant light from a parking lot. I pressed my open palm to the elf's chest and called lightning.

With a choking gurgle, my assailant fell to the side and flopped like a landed fish as the electric burst overloaded his heart.

The other one was smarter.

While his partner clutched at dead leaves and seized, the elf still on his feet pointed a gun at me. "I'm loaded with bronze," he said softly. "Let go of your magic and come with me."

My heart thudded as though it was trying to beat for the guy on the ground as well as me. "No."

He shifted his aim to my thigh. "I won't ask again."

As I tensed to roll away, a shadow fell on him from behind. A crack rang out in the night. Not a gunshot. A neck breaking. The elf with the gun dropped, and the shadow moved to the one I'd electrocuted, finishing him with a sharp blow to the throat. Cartilage crunched. Breath gurgled.

"Arden," Troy breathed, dropping the shadows and grabbing me by the arms as I stood with my jaw dropped. "Are you okay?"

"You didn't hesitate." I stared at him. The shakes from my earlier exhaustion were joined by an adrenaline crash. "You killed them."

His expression tightened. "I won't let them have you. Are you hurt?"

"No." I couldn't quite find my breath.

Troy killing Redcaps had been a mission. This? This was killing fellow elves purely to keep me alive. And I hadn't missed that he'd called me by my first name again.

With a last squeeze and a worried twinge of the bond, he let me go and started searching the dead. He pocketed the wallets. "The third team is still out there. They've lost two in as many hours, so the last one will regroup before making their attempt."

"Why do you feel anxious?" I located my cap where it'd fallen off in my roll down the hill, brushed the leaves off, and put it back on.

Troy finished with the bodies and nodded toward the slope to the road. We were halfway up, with him steadying me every time my tired feet caught a branch, before he said, "I need to leave you alone for a day or two."

"Planting your seeds."

"That, and I need to call in these fools to keep the Darkwatch busy with a coverup while I break into the archives to find out what the hell this Ebon Guard is. See if we have allies or more trouble."

See if we *have allies.* Troy committed when he decided to do a thing, but there was commitment and then there was this. He'd sworn an oath, but it still surprised me.

We made it back up to the road and crossed. I pushed myself into a trot, not liking to be out in the open, and Troy's worried approval in the bond kept me moving despite my tiredness until we reached our cars. We stood awkwardly—or at least, I felt awkward, looking up at him and wondering again at how much he'd changed.

"Are you going to be okay to drive home?" His gaze flicked over me, the skin around his eyes tight with worry.

Fatigue pulled at me, and the beginnings of a minor power hangover pounded behind my eyes. "Guess I'll have to be."

"Okay." He rocked on his feet, clearly not believing me but not foolish enough to press me. "I'll see you at the next meeting at Raven Rock in three days. Do what you have to do to stay safe until then. Even if it's staying with the Volkovs."

"Troy—"

"I mean it." He brushed a curl off my face. "Stay alive, or this was for nothing."

All I could do was blink, my mind scrambled, as he rocked again and headed for his car. Shaking off the forbidden thrill of his touch, I got in my own car and led him out of the parking lot. We went the same way for a few miles then split off.

Not wanting to risk an attack at my home, I headed for the bar. I had a cot in the storeroom in case of emergency, the building was heavily warded, and it was the community watering hole for the tri-city area. The last kidnapping team might dare Roman's house, but they wouldn't risk pissing off all of the local Othersiders by attacking the bar.

At least, I hoped so. After all, it's what I had done.

I pulled right up to the back door when I got there, darting from my car to the door with keys ready in my shaky hands. I was getting strong enough that the power hangovers were lessening, but I still needed something to eat and at least a little booze.

The night smelled of old beer, fried food, and metal and oil from the nearby train tracks. No Aether. Looked like Troy was right about the third team pulling back. Maybe I'd get some sleep.

Not if I'm worried about someone messing with my car.

A wall of Air would be invisible to anyone except another elemental, and it'd thwart any would-be saboteurs. Just like the block of Air at my house but around the whole car. I pushed through a headache to set the chord then turned back to the door of the bar. Slipping inside, I locked the door behind me and flipped the switch for the security shutters.

He called me Arden.

The thought kept echoing as I shakily poured myself a double rum and downed it neat then followed it with a second before heading for the storeroom with a third and a couple bottles of water. We had some jerky back there plus some bar food I could prepare in the small kitchen. I sent a text to the various alliance factions while the food spun in the microwave, telling them that Verve was handled for now. I didn't mention the elves, nor did I send anything to Allegra. Troy knew, and if he wanted her to know, he'd find a way to tell her. At least, that's what I told myself. Really it just hurt somewhere that after her protestations that magical Black girls had to stick together, I hadn't heard from her.

Give her time. For all you know, she's playing the game from the inside.

Once I'd gotten some protein into me and steadied myself, I peeled off the earpiece and locked it in my desk drawer before washing up in the bar's tiny box shower. Zanna hadn't appeared, which meant she was spending the night at home.

The bar seemed bigger and emptier when I was alone there. The new wood from the fixes Terrence's guys had done didn't feel as threatening as the old building had, soaked through with Callista's presence, but this still didn't feel like *my* place. Hawkeye was mine. Except that my PI firm was slipping away from me as I poured more time into Otherside.

Detective Rice's request made me wonder if it was time to give it up entirely. The shape of the world was changing, and while it'd be useful to have me working mundane cases, I had to draw a line somewhere. If I didn't take cases that required me to plant evidence or rat out Othersiders, would the local police departments still hire me?

Did I want them to, if that was their attitude?

I could take the cases and then scuttle them. Too much of that would get me dubbed unreliable though and eventually go against the point of taking them to begin with.

There were other ways to protect and support the community. They'd require me to make more hard choices about who I could trust, but they'd use my gifts to the fullest. The Verve job would look suspicious no matter what we'd done, but nobody else would have been able to make it look like an environmental failure. Mundanes never considered elementals in their films and TV shows. They might be paranoid now, but they'd still look for a logical explanation even in the face of vampires being real. They always did—except for the conspiracy kooks, who'd probably land on some overly complex government plot rather than elementals.

I switched on the overhead fan for the illusion of air flow then turned off the lights and used my phone's flashlight to find the cot. As I settled in and finished off the rest of my rum and a bottle of water, I tucked my lead-and-steel elf-killer under my pillow and studied the knot in the back of my mind that was the bond with Troy. It was open but muted, heading in the direction of Chapel Hill and giving me an echo of tiredness, determination, and deep down…righteous concern?

Maybe I could trust him, after all.

What did that mean for Allegra? She and I might have been friends, but she was fiercely protective of Troy. More worryingly, what did it mean for me that a powerful elven prince had killed people sent to bring me in?

I didn't have answers. Lulled by rum and exhaustion, my brain switched off.

***

"What a curious creature you are."

My eyes snapped open, and I groaned, finding myself in the empty white expanse of the Crossroads. I didn't recognize the masculine voice that had spoken. When I turned, there was no one there.

"Most curious indeed."

The voice came from the side this time, and in the corner of my eye, I spotted a figure. Tilting my head just enough to keep him in my peripheral vision, I said, "Who do I have the honor of addressing?"

Couldn't hurt to be polite, even if whoever it was probably intended to drag my life into a new circle of hell.

I got the impression of white teeth flashing a smile in a dark face.

"I am the orisha known as Eshu-Elegba." With light steps, he came into view. A palm full of popcorn never depleted as he tossed a few pieces in the air and caught them in his mouth, one by one. "I am Master of the Crossroads. Among other things."

"Oh." I swallowed, hard, and knelt. I had no idea who I was dealing with, but Neith was the only goddess who'd been content to take her respect in blood or wine rather than a show of submission.

"The gods of the hunt love to meet in my Crossroads, pulling mortals in and passing through, yet they always seem to forget I can see them. Ogun came to me after your first visit, little elemental, but the others...mmm. Their impatience for their Wild Hunt makes them forget courtesies." He smiled again, looking equal parts amused and wicked. "It inclines me to offer you a favor."

"A...favor?" I swallowed hard.

Elegba raised a black eyebrow.

I bowed my head. "You honor me."

"I do. And what a trick it shall be."

My blood ran cold. I'd gathered this wasn't a god of the hunt, but I hadn't clocked that I was dealing with one of the tricksters. He might be offering a gift, but that coin could as easily land on its edge or in someone else's pocket as in my favor.

"I shall grant you travel through my Crossroads, one time and one time only. Such is not usually afforded to beings of the golden hour, only those of light or those not anchored to the earthly plane."

I risked a glance upward to see Elegba smiling to himself, as though this was a fine trick. As I thought about it—it might well be. Grimm had once said that my elven father, a being of shadow, had robbed me of the ability to travel freely to and from the Crossroads. Nobody would expect me to be able to get here on my own. That could bring strategic advantage.

The god's smile grew as he glanced down at my comprehension. "Good. You understand my magnanimity."

"I believe I do, my lord. Thank you."

"All gifts have a price. It will hurt. But should you wish to use your boon, simply call out to me." He gave me a last amused smile, his eyes distant as though he was imagining the responses of the other gods, and then the Crossroads melted away to leave me in the dream of a storm-swept coastline that had come to me off and on for the last eight weeks.

Troy wasn't in the dream this time, but the clouds on the horizon were stormier than ever.

Chapter 12

With no natural light coming into the storeroom, I overslept. Zanna crashing in around ten with a harangue about people with nothing better to do yet too busy to come home at night got me up, rumpled and sore. I didn't bother to correct her, just smiled at her caring enough to be grouchy about my not being home last night.

My usual power hangover was practically gone, and I made a mental note that maybe Troy had been right about the protein intake. The thought turned his way told me he was still alive, an unusual focus tingeing his thoughts. Talking to someone, maybe. Convincing them. I pulled back before he could notice my attention and helped Zanna move boxes while I planned my day.

Top of the list was addressing the risks to the vampires. None of the other parties would be willing to risk a Reveal of their own until and unless I could prove we could keep the vamps safe. They might make noises of agreement when we were all together, but I'd seen that play out before with the lich. They'd balk if there wasn't enough in it for them, especially if it was dangerous. Maria had only led the vampires out because she'd had no other choice, given the Modernist schism. The djinn would stay hidden on the ethereal plane, and the elves were already set against us. Even if Troy forced them out, they weren't in a position to work willingly with the vampires.

That meant getting the witches or the werewolves to play ball, since the leopards and jaguars had negotiated lying low as part of their participation in the alliance and nobody had heard from the fae beyond Zanna's comment about rumblings between themselves.

Dragging this out would only make the other groups more reluctant as each one faced human resistance. The sooner a rep from each major group in Otherside was out, the safer we all would be—if only because the danger would be evenly shared. No shirking, no takebacks.

Which meant I'd be spending the next two days politicking. I rested my elbow on the bar and leaned into my hand, munching on some peanuts. It was protein, right? I pursed my lips, considering the options. *Start with the wolves.*

They'd be the biggest pain in the ass, even if Revealing a second predator species would probably freak out the mundanes. With Troy dragging the elves out, that'd put the onus on the three biggest factions to equally share in dealing with the response. I hadn't missed how everyone had been skimping out on their share of support duty. If they were out, they'd have no choice but to help for their own safety.

Maybe the wolves and the witches. The local coven probably wouldn't be keen on it, but we had to balance the vampires.

"Busy day ahead?" Zanna said amidst a clatter of bottles.

I winced at the noise as she restocked the fridge. "Seems so." Rapping my fingers in an uneven pattern on the bar, I debated my next move. "How much time has Roman been spending here?"

The kobold's snort seemed a little too big for her size. "All day. Every day. Staring at the door. Should put 'lost dog' on a poster in the window." She started whistling "That Doggie in the Window."

I almost choked on a peanut as a surprised laugh made my wind go the wrong way. "I'll sort it."

"Good. Bad for business."

I doubted that but didn't argue with her. "Hey, Zanna, do you have any way to get a message to the Chamber of Lords?"

She gave me a level look from under her mane of curls. "Trouble, tenant?"

"I, ah, fucked with some elves yesterday. Between that and the vampire protests, I need to figure out Otherside's options before I get backed in a corner."

Zanna's eyes didn't leave me as she pointed the TV remote and stabbed the button with an aggressive jab. The morning news poured out.

Top story: environmental hazard at a local healthtech startup.

"You?" she asked as the newscaster described the tragic accident that had resulted in the loss of all samples and records.

I bared my teeth in a savage smile.

Zanna nodded, the ferocity in her gaze matching the sharpness of her teeth in her sudden grin. "Good. Be the wind."

"I'll do that." I slid off my stool. "Let me know about the lords and ladies, okay?"

I took her grunt as agreement as I headed out to my car. Satisfied the wall of Air I'd set around it hadn't been disturbed in the night, I stretched out my senses and read the air. Nothing moved except birds and the old trickster hare, although a faint whiff of sulfur suggested the ragged-looking black dog I suspected was really a fiend or a gytrash was back. The scent was old though, and I didn't think he'd shifted to his humanoid form. Still just snooping then. As far as I could tell, nothing waited for me. Taking a deep breath, I forced my feet to move and got in my car.

The whole drive over to Roman's, I debated whether I was going about this the right way. I'd said I'd give all the factions three days to decide for themselves, but here I was making the choice and trying to talk them into it.

Nothing for it. I'd seen what they would do without a push when the lich had been an issue: absolutely fuck all. Months of me waiting around for each faction to talk amongst themselves and come to the conclusions that would serve all of us came to nothing until my friends were kidnapped and I was pushed into making the tough decision.

Looked like I was still making the hard choices. I just wasn't going to wait for my friends to be in danger this time. And I knew the wolves would be cagey. We all knew they were in one of the better positions, but that hadn't stopped them from trying to wheedle and negotiate every single point before. My stomach felt like it was full of snakes as resentment burned my chest. Why was I always having to push people into doing the right thing? Why was I always having to push *Roman* into it?

Sergei was chained to a tree in the yard when I pulled up. His deep bark trailed into the beginnings of a howl, more like the alarm call of a real wolf than the warning of a dog. At this rate, he was going to get animal control called on himself and save me some trouble.

I shook my head at him as I got out of the car, leaning against it until Vikki stuck her head out to see what the ruckus was about. I waved, glancing at Sergei and staying put.

"Hey, girl!" She crossed the yard barefoot, shushing Sergei and pointing at him until he dropped to his belly as she passed. "Roman didn't say you were coming by today."

"That's because I didn't tell him," I said in a low voice. "Something's come up. You got time?"

"Sure," she drawled. "Roman's in the shower. It'll give us gals a minute to talk."

I followed her in, turning one of the chairs at the dining table to face the rest of the room—and put my back against the wall.

Last night had been a little too nasty with Roman, and I wasn't a hundred percent comfortable being here.

Vikki noticed but contented herself with an amused flash of her eyebrows as she poured me a glass of water and piled some shaved deli meat on a plate. "Eat, drink, and be welcome. No harm will come to guests under this roof," she said, setting them in front of me.

I relaxed a little at the generic formality and toasted her with the water. "I come with peaceful intent and will honor my host."

She sat in the chair opposite, and I pushed away a twinge of regret as the scene mirrored the night Roman and I had broken up. The slice of pastrami I swallowed went down in a lump as I pushed the memory away.

"I'm surprised at you, Arden," Vikki said.

Mouth full again, I raised my eyebrows for her to continue. The meat in my stomach was easing the last vestiges of the hangover, and I was keen to clear it away before Roman joined us and gave me a fresh headache.

"If someone had done to me what Monteague did to you, their throat would be in my teeth."

"That's 'cause you have teeth," I muttered between bites.

Vikki laughed. "Fair. Point stands though."

I ate a little more to give myself space to think. "How is it any different to you coming here and offering your throat to Terrence and Ximena? Or Roman asking me to kill your father?"

All of the bemusement washed out of Vikki, and her blue eyes sharpened. "Roman what?"

Shit. The shower switched off, and I waited for the expected hum of Roman's razor before answering her in a low voice. "He didn't tell you?"

"Tell me fucking what?"

I fought the urge to scrub my hands over my face, not wanting to take my eyes off the increasingly tense beta werewolf in front of me. "That's why he came back without telling either of us. He wanted me to kill Niko and make it look like a freak act of god so that he could take over the pack and free Ana from any forced choice between him and this Cyril."

"Bastard. That bastard son of a flea-bitten…" Vikki stood and paced the room. Angry energy practically crackled from her. "He told me Pops had sent him to verify that the deal was being properly managed. I believed him because it's exactly the kind of toxic, sexist horseshit that Pops would pull and figured he was going along with it to see you."

"I mean, I'm not saying he didn't come for that." I chewed and swallowed a slice of honeyed ham. My stomach twisted around it as I wrestled with whether I was doing the right thing. "I'm just saying you're not the only one with ambitions involving the removal of your father."

The sound of the razor cut off from the bathroom. "Vikki! Are you burning something?" Roman called.

"Arden's here," Vikki replied in a voice just shy of a snarl.

I plucked at my shirt, embarrassed that it was the same one I'd worn last night, and sniffed it. "I smell like burning now?"

Vikki shrugged. "If you've been working with Fire. Personally, I noticed the power signature first."

I grimaced and tried shielding harder.

"Arden?" Roman stuck his head out of the bathroom. A brown towel wrapped his hips and his hair was slicked back. The woodsy cedar-and-musk scent that rolled out of the bathroom was all him, not aftershave, and heat washed over me as a more erotic memory swam up, shoving aside my earlier bad feeling.

"Hey," I said, flushing deeper at Vikki's knowing, if slightly bitter, expression.

His lopsided smile made it seem like we hadn't said some real ugly words to each other last night and drew more memories. "Hey, yourself."

I needed to wrap this up and get outta here. "I gotta talk to you two about something. When you're dressed."

"Sure," he drawled, much as Vikki had earlier.

When the bedroom door shut behind him, Vikki turned to me. "A hint?"

"Another Reveal."

She leaned back in her chair, chewing on her lip as she thought furiously.

I finished the plate of deli meat and the water by the time Roman came back out, dressed in jeans raggedly cut off at the knee and a baby-blue T-shirt that looked new. It hugged his biceps and brought out the hints of blue in his grey eyes, and I had to grit my teeth to stop myself from reacting favorably. I might be mad at him, but he was still a damn fine-looking man.

He grinned as though he could smell it on me anyway, and he probably could. "You're still in one piece. Guess I'm glad I was wrong about Monteague. This time, anyway."

I took a breath, praying for patience. "That's actually part of why I'm here."

"Oh?" both Volkovs said together.

"The elves aren't wasting any time."

Vikki pursed her lips. "They're after you already?"

"Yeah. Troy stopped one attack on the road last night, and we stopped a second after destroying the samples at Verve. All things in three with them, so I'm waiting for the third team even now."

Roman scowled, though whether it was for the danger or my mention of Troy, I couldn't say. "They won't stop till you're dead, Arie."

I gave him an annoyed look at the use of the nickname but didn't speak on it. I needed him agreeable, not ornery. "I'm sure you're right, but—"

116

"You should stay here," he interrupted. "It'll be safer than you by yourself."

All I could do was stare at him for a minute. Did he really think getting back together was just going to be a matter of wearing me down and creating an opportunity? And where the hell did he think I'd sleep when he and his sister and their doggy-ass brother were already staying here? *Aw hell no.*

"That's…gracious of you. But I don't think it's a good idea."

"You got a better one, I'm all ears."

Vikki rolled her eyes at her brother, lips pressing together like even she was tired of him.

I bit back a nasty response and tried to keep my voice even. "Actually, I was thinking this means we can't afford to waste time on moving forward like we did with the lich."

Vikki's face blanked as she figured it out, but Roman asked, "What are you saying?"

"Seems to me that if you want to put your pops in a hard spot, all you have to do is reveal the wolves."

Roman blanched as Vikki nodded, but each of them stiffened as they avoided looking at the other. I stopped myself from filling the silence with more words and ignored the buzz of my phone in my pocket.

"That's quite an idea, Arden," Vikki said at last, eyes hard on me.

I shrugged, striving for ignorant nonchalance. "It is what it is. All three Volkov pups are here, while both alphas are out west. Y'all are both telling me that's not by accident? Or that you don't see any kind of opportunity there?"

Roman shook his head stubbornly. "I don't like it. Humans like hunting wolves too much."

"They like hunting Othersiders in general too much, and the wolves have more numbers than anyone except the vampires. I'ma tell you the same thing I told Maria: this is your one chance to take control of the narrative. You really want to be found out by accident?" I raised my brows and tilted my head as I rose and edged toward the door. There wasn't much else to say, and I didn't want to give Roman an opportunity to piss me off again.

"You're not staying?" His voice held more than a hint of a growl to it, though whether that was for the opportunity I'd just dropped in his lap or for me coming and going before he could really do anything about it was hard to say.

"The longer I stay put somewhere, the more likely it is the Darkwatch finds me." I avoided his stricken look by pulling my hair up into a bun. "Thanks for the hospitality, Vikki. See y'all in a couple of days at Raven Rock."

"Sure thing." She gripped Roman's arm when he started to speak, and he settled.

"We'll be in touch," he said after scowling at his sister.

I said my goodbyes and saw myself out, giving Sergei as much of a snarl as I got when I passed. I had backup plans to make because, as much as I wanted to, I just couldn't trust that Roman would act in everyone's best interest.

Chapter 13

I was almost home when my phone rang. I didn't use my phone while driving, but there was enough going on that I didn't dare leave it for later. I pulled off into a gas station and checked. The buzz earlier was a text from Allegra, but the incoming call was Noah.

Frowning, I answered. Noah never called. It was always Maria calling me, or me trying to reach Maria via Noah.

"Noah?" I said when the call connected to dead air.

Instead of the vampire second's even tones, a rougher male voice came through, muffled as though through fabric. "Come now, Maria. You don't truly expect me to believe that you defeated Torsten, do you? You're much stronger than you were, to be sure. But not Viking strong."

"The question asked was who is master in Raleigh. The answer is me, Giuliano. *Me.* So make your challenge or back the fuck off." Under the tight, balanced tone of her voice, Maria sounded furious. "I extended you all the rights and privileges owed to one of your station, which is far more than required given your abrupt, unannounced, and frankly rude arrival. Don't push me."

"As you say…Mistress." The voice I took to be Giuliano's was heavy with delayed threat and mocking respect. "I'll bide, until Luz arrives this evening. Then we shall see who is master in the Middle Seaboard."

"You do that," Maria said. Poison dripped from every syllable. "Until then, get out and relearn guest courtesy. You embarrass your coterie, your master, and yourself." After a pause, Maria's voice came through closer than before. "Get Arden here. Now."

"Already working on it, Mistress," Noah said. A rustling noise came through right before Noah's soft voice. "You caught all that?"

"Yes. On my way." I didn't need to know what was happening. I could guess. As Maria had feared, the rot eating away at Torsten's coterie had made them too tempting a target to ignore. With the former master's library and Maria as potential prizes, the other East Coast coteries had to have been waiting for Torsten's fall. The added chaos of local mundane unrest made the opportunity impossible to pass up.

Noah hung up, and I spun out of the gas station in a squeal of rubber.

I'd never made it to Raleigh so fast. Remembering yesterday's process, I parked in the same deck as the secondary access. Noah was waiting for me when I stomped up, fury boiling in my blood at the audacity.

He scented the air as I passed. "You're angry. Good."

"Damn right I'm angry. Who the fuck do they think they are, coming to *my* fucking region without my say-so?"

When Noah didn't respond after shutting the door behind us, I spun to face him. He raised his hands, looking afraid of me for the first time in our acquaintance. "I am at your service, Arbiter. Let me show you to my mistress."

With an effort, I took myself in hand and nodded for him to lead the way. Where the hell had this sudden rage come from?

Troy. The bond roiled with it. Whatever he was doing had him furious, and it was leaking through to me. With an effort, I shut it away. That didn't clear it away fully though. Some of it was all mine, enough that my usual reticence about being underground was absent. Whether I'd wanted to or not, I'd adopted all of the Triangle as mine. Had Callista been in charge, Giuliano or anyone else would have checked in with her first, as was proper. This challenge to Maria was a threat to me as well, and as much as I didn't want to be a second Callista, I couldn't allow it to stand if I expected to keep my position against more aggressive Othersiders.

Having the power to stand alone didn't just mean for myself. It also meant standing for those who stood with me. This was just the first time I'd had to reckon with it against an outside force, rather than an internal one.

Seething, I followed Noah into the throne room. Maria paced in front of the roaring fire in the clockwork-jerky motions of an undead not bothering to hide what she was.

"What?" she snapped as Noah entered the room. Her expression sharpened when I emerged from behind him. "You got here quickly."

"I won't have this," I said grimly. "Not against my allies. Not against me as Arbiter."

"Good. Then you'll be my guest at the welcoming ceremony later."

I had no idea what that would entail, but I nodded.

Her gaze shifted to Noah. "Get her something to wear. Don't tell anyone she's here."

"Yes, Mistress."

With a tilt of her head, Maria gestured for me to follow her. Her new living quarters were larger than before, but that just allowed more space for the same stained-glass-writ-large effect that she'd taken with the rooms that had been hers as second.

"Nice upgrade," I said.

"I could wish you were seeing it under more amusing circumstances, but what's most important is that you're here," she replied.

"About that—what the hell is going on? I only caught the tail end of you dressing down Giuliano."

Ire snapped in her dark eyes, a depth of rage I'd never seen in her before. "The cowards are scared. They think things have gotten out of hand, and since Raleigh led the Reveal, the New York coterie wants me to abdicate in favor of Giuliano so that he can be the voice of vampirism. If Luz is coming up from Miami as well, they intend to hit me with a double challenge."

"Can you beat them?"

Maria grimaced and settled into an overstuffed armchair the same emerald shade as her hair. "Not one after the other, no. Giuliano became a *moroi* at the beginning of the Renaissance. Luz toward the end of the Reconquista. Assuming their masters granted them access to more powerful blood ahead of their journeys here, it'd be a draw with Giuli and a defeat to Luz."

I paced the room. "So Luz is the bigger threat?"

"By far. She was always a zealot and never afraid to fight for whatever inflamed her passions. She's the warrior of the two. Probably still carries that damn mace around. Giuli can use a sword, but he's a better politician."

I had an idea, but I didn't like it and didn't know if Maria would. "What if I made them fight me first?"

"Excuse me?" The perfect blankness of her expression made it difficult to guess how she was feeling.

With an effort, I kept myself still and pushed on. "Would they have contacted Callista before entering the territory?"

She nodded, a single down-and-up jerk of her head.

"Okay. Zanna knows to call me if anything like that comes through to the bar. I presume you would have done the same had they followed the correct forms. Which means I'm equally within my rights to claim offense. Correct?"

Another sharp nod.

"Okay then. I'm not in any shape to make you another blood donation to fight them off yourself, not after Neith's trial and with more attacks from the elves coming. But I could thrash them to within an inch of their lives with elemental magic, no problem."

Maria leaned back in her chair and steepled her fingers. "I'm surprised at you, Arden. I wouldn't have thought you willing to expose yourself like this."

I shrugged, trying to pretend my stomach wasn't roiling with discomfort at being seen. "I'll be honest, I hate this plan. But if I'm going to say I mean no harm but take no shit, I have to be willing to back up the 'take no shit' part. I wanted a place in Otherside. I have one. The fact that it's not what I imagined doesn't matter. You helped me see that."

The stiff mask finally broke, and Maria's smile sent warmth curling through me. "I'm proud of you, baby doll. I'd expected to have to knock some sense into you before you owned that."

Wrinkling my nose, I offered a lopsided smile of my own. "Yeah, well...everybody seems to wanna step to me this week. Maybe nipping it in the bud now will let me take a vacation. Or at least a damn day off. Hell, I'd be happy with a solid nap."

"Don't count on it." She rose and came to me, rising on tiptoes to brush a quick kiss on my cheek before going to an armoire of rich ebony carved with flowers. As she shifted through it, muttering about what to wear that would be both elegant and aggressive, I opened my phone to check the message from Allegra.

Where's Troy? she'd written.

I grimaced. If he hadn't told her, I wasn't about to get in the middle of it. That didn't bode well for him. Probably not for me either. I could only deal with one problem at a time though, and the one in front of me would serve two ends: shoring up my more consistent allies and keeping the elves off me for a few more hours.

Whatever you're doing, Troy, make it fast.

The next hour passed in a blur as Noah swooped in and out with various options for me to try. Apparently my denim shorts and black T-shirt weren't quite fancy enough. The bustle kept my mind off being underground—for the most part. Maria had the fans going full-tilt after she caught me looking at the ceiling for the umpteenth time.

For me, we finally settled on supple, black leather pants and flat-heeled boots with a sleeveless silk top that would match the gold flare of my eyes when I was using my power. For her, a royal blue suit-and-pants number that looked like something the Three Musketeers would wear with buckle shoes. The tomboyish look was a departure from her usual ultra-feminine dresses or skintight commando garb, and I couldn't help lifting my brows in question.

Maria shrugged. "We'll all be in period costume. Maybe not the one we were born to but something that recalls the old days. At least I can move in this if shit hits the fan."

The door opened, and Noah stuck his head in. "Mistress, Oscar just sent word that Luz has arrived at RDU."

"Arriving this evening, my left tit," Maria muttered. "I thought they might play it like that. Thank you, Noah. Assemble everyone in the throne room. Fancy dress and bad attitudes, my lovely."

"Yes, Mistress." He darted a worried look between Maria and me, one that hardened in warning when it landed on me. When I tilted my chin up in challenge, he ducked his head in a tight nod and left.

"You're getting better at owning your power, darling. I'm glad. Play the bitch today, hmm?"

"I won't be playing."

She offered a toothy grin sparking with mischief. "Good. Let me introduce everybody. Then feel free to kick ass in whatever way you choose."

"Sure." My heart pounded at the coming confrontation.

"Oh, and let your shields down. This is the last place you want to appear less than you are."

With that comforting comment, she headed back out to the throne room. After a deep, steadying breath I dropped the shields keeping a lid on my power signature, dug deep for my best approximation of the violent confidence Troy always exuded, and followed. Hopefully, the humming crackle of power seeping from me would override the thudding of my heart. As Maria settled on the throne, I leaned against it, arms crossed and attitude bad, as she'd directed Noah.

The massive throne room was lined three rows deep with utterly motionless vampires in clothes from bygone centuries. I hadn't realized the Raleigh coterie was that large, even after the housecleaning they'd done earlier this year. Not a single breath stirred the air. No movement sent disturbed ripples to me. The roaring fire was the only motion in the room other than mine. We could have been standing in a mannequin warehouse.

It was starting to grate on the animal part of my brain that registered a threat when a quick knock preceded the door opening. A pair of vampires swept in, followed by an entourage.

"Maria! Look at you, all grown up." Luz matched her childishly high-pitched voice, in that she was a beautiful woman with slim hips and a flat chest. Bright green eyes shone with a savage desire to hurt someone in a heart-shaped face, her lightly golden skin making her look like she'd just come from the tanning salon. Brown hair fell in rich waves to her waist over a floral-pattered dress that looked like something straight out of a Jane Austen flick.

Her hand rested atop that of a singularly ugly man I took to be Giuliano. A heavy brow jutted over a nose that had been broken a few times too many to heal properly before he'd died. Clever brown eyes narrowed at me, as lips so thin they were barely there pressed so tightly together they practically disappeared. He was dressed to suit his original time, in white tights, ballooning crimson pants patterned with fleur-de-lys, and a matching poofy-shouldered jacket over a white shirt, the laces undone halfway to his bellybutton.

Behind them, their small retinue of vampires from backgrounds the world over were dressed in period wear that would have fit anywhere from the Song Dynasty to Elizabethan England to Great Zimbabwe.

"Luz. Look at you, still thinking you can take things that don't belong to you," Maria replied snidely.

A little girl's giggle crawled down my spine. "Oh, Giuli, you didn't say that she'd found a sense of humor."

I gritted my teeth, already annoyed.

"I don't think she's joking, my dear," Giuliano said. I recognized his voice from the phone. He frowned, eyes darting between Maria and me before they settled on me and widened.

"Shame. It'd make all of this easier." Luz looked me up and down and sneered. "New pet?"

Maria's tone was cold. "Before you get around to offering a challenge, Luzy love, you owe someone an apology."

"Oh?"

"I'm sure you must have heard we have a new Arbiter here in the Triangle. Arden?"

I straightened and offered a half wave. "I'd like to say it's good to see you. But I try not to lie to people."

Luz pursed her lips and looked me up and down. I didn't miss the pinch in the corners of her eyes as she opened her mouth to reply. She hadn't expected me to be here.

I didn't let her speak. Pulling on Air was tough this far underground, but I'd had enough practice that I didn't break a sweat as I looped a chord around both Giuliano's and Luz's ankles, hoisting them up to dangle upside down before tying it off. Before their startled entourage could react, I wound a third chord around them, walling them in.

None of the vampires in the room moved as I took my time approaching the two who thought they could roll up into my territory without so much as a hello.

Giuliano, apparently the more intelligent of the two, hung silent even as he flushed red with obvious fury.

Luz needed a lesson.

When she opened her mouth again, I slapped her with Air, not breaking my measured pace.

"I don't recall inviting either of you to my region," I said when I was standing in front of them, letting anger tinge my voice even as I kept it low and even. "Maria and I have an excellent working relationship, so I'm certain your arrival didn't slip her mind. Which means you're either rude or foolish. Which is it?"

"Bitch!" Luz shrieked.

This time, I indulged in slapping her with my hand. "Bit of both then. Probably for the best that you didn't see me first. My kobold despises rudeness. Either way, I guess we're gonna do this the hard way."

Chapter 14

Giuliano swallowed. If he hadn't been hanging upside down, he probably would have paled. As it was, there was too much blood rushing to his head. "Luz, shut up. The power signature is coming from Ms. Finch."

A smile curled over my face. Not a nice one. "So you do know who I am. You just thought you could walk all over me and my friends here in Raleigh."

This time, our visitors kept their mouths shut.

Remembering how unsettling I found it, I circled them, giving their retinue a hard look as I passed behind their leaders. They watched, many with eyes bled to full black, all with their attention on me. A quiver ran through Giuliano as I passed behind him. Luz tensed, fisting her hands uselessly.

"Y'all really thought you were gonna... What? Turn up, depose Maria? And then?" I snarled at them as a thought occurred to me with the feel of the Sight. "Ah. I wasn't supposed to be here, was I?"

Maria descended from her throne, holding one of her katanas loosely at her side. "What are you saying, Arden?"

"Did Keithia call you? Or Evangeline?" I asked our guests, harsh as a death rattle.

Neither Luz nor Giuliano reacted, but someone behind them gasped at Evangeline's name. Luz's expression soured.

"Tell me, before I shake you both so hard your fangs fall out." I circled again for psychological effect, giving the chord of Air a jolt that twanged with a discordant note only I could hear. When I was in front of them again, I steeled myself and embraced Fire, letting a ball hover over my palm like I'd practiced with Val. "Or we could try something a little more fun."

Giuliano quivered, the wild look in his eyes growing more frantic as I drew closer, but he didn't answer. Luz sneered, baring her teeth, but I stayed focused on Giuliano. My bet was that he'd faced fire before and hadn't come out of it well.

I brought the ball of flame closer and crouched as I let it dance in Giuliano's face. I mentally prayed they wouldn't actually make me burn them. "Come on now, y'all. I'm sure you've heard barbecue is our state's specialty. You ever heard humans are supposed to taste like pork? I dunno if vampire still tastes like human, but we could find out. Only real question is whether we go Lexington-style or Eastern-style on the sauce."

I pulled a little more Fire into my ball until it was the size of a large grapefruit and sent a burst of Air to make the fireplace flare as well.

Giuliano struggled harder.

"It was Evangeline," he said hoarsely.

"Shut up, Giuli," Luz said.

He snarled at her. "The deal is broken. The terms were that the elemental is removed. She's clearly more powerful than we were led to believe."

"We can still—"

"No."

I let go of Fire before my hand could do more than redden with a mild contact burn and glanced at Maria as they bickered back and forth, their united front and power both broken. Behind them, their entourage oozed uncertainty as they glanced at Maria's people lining the wall. The gathered coterie stared back hungrily. Maria wore an expression of barely contained savagery.

Hell, I'd be pissed too if I'd been set up for a fall like that by another faction. Oh wait, I had been, and I was furious.

"Enough," I said coldly. "Maria, elven involvement makes this a factional coup, not an ascendancy challenge. I will deal with the elves. These fools are yours."

"Put them down." Maria's grip tightened on her katana. "And free their people."

I glanced at her, confused, but did as she asked. The tension in the room notched up as Luz and Giuliano caught themselves with the speed of the undead, not managing it with any grace but avoiding broken necks.

Maria smiled beatifically. "Per the Articles of War and Ascension…children, dinner is served."

She suited actions to words, cutting off Luz's cry of "No, you can't—" with a flick of her sword. Blood spurted from a deep, vertical gash alongside the pretty vampire's throat. A mirror image of it opened in Giuliano's throat, and then Maria and Noah fell on them as the rest of the coterie bore the visiting retinue to the ground with silent glee.

I backed away, my gorge rising as the scent of hot copper and wet ash grew alongside the screams of the would-be conquerors. I wanted to run and get as far away from here as I could, but I'd allowed this to happen.

I'd stand and watch, so that later, I'd remember what happened when I allowed reluctance and wishful thinking to stop me from taking the hard road. If I'd confronted the elves before now or at least done something about Evangeline, Maria might not have been endangered by the princess's ambitions and hatred of me.

It took a long time for the feeding frenzy to die down. The visiting vampires' screams turned into moans then silence.

"Are they dead?" I whispered when Maria rose and stretched as though reinvigorated.

She shook her head. "Just drained. They'll sleep for a time while they recover. Long enough for us to sort out this mess."

"Okay." Relief eased the tightness in my muscles. I'd killed people but in self-defense. This would have felt like crossing a line. I kept inching closer to that line, and I was desperate not to cross it, even as I kept finding myself in situations that nudged me to stumble over it.

Noah rose from Giuliano and wiped his lower lip with the back of his wrist then licked the blood off like a cat. "Orders, Mistress?"

"See Arden out. She's spent enough time underground today. Then see to cleaning this up."

I brought my gaze down from the ceiling. Maria offered me a small smile but didn't move to hug me, as though she understood my mind wasn't right for it just then. Noah waited expectantly for me to follow him back to Maria's bedroom to grab my things.

"Keep the clothes," he said when I moved to change back into what I'd arrived in. "I'm sure my mistress would agree your assistance was more than worth it."

"Thanks." It'd be too damn hot outside for leather, but fuck it, I'd been wanting a pair of leather pants for ages. I stuffed my other clothes in my backpack and followed him back up to the secondary door.

"You keep surprising me, Ms. Finch," Noah said as we reached it. "Stop underestimating yourself and lean into your instincts. That, and keep Troy close—regardless of what the wolf says."

"I'll remember that." With a last nod, I cracked the door enough to find the street empty and slipped out.

Dread pooled in my guts as I jogged up the flight of stairs to where I'd parked my car. If the elves had been coordinating with the other East Coast vampire coteries, they had to know I'd be here. There was still the last team in the first set of three. They might attack in broad daylight but not this close to the coterie.

Or maybe they would.

I froze as I spotted three mismatched elves leaning against my car, all dressed in the loose, black cotton that seemed to be Troy's Darkwatch uniform. It looked like this team had a high-blood from each House—one to attack my mind, one to subdue my body, the third to break my spirit. I drew hard on Air as my mouth dried and my heart tried to slam its way free of my chest. The public be damned—I wasn't about to be taken.

The blue-eyed Sequoyah dangled a bronze cuff from a finger. "Don't make this difficult. None of us wants a scene, right? Kneel and put this on."

They must have overridden the parking garage's cameras if they were doing this so brazenly. There'd be no witnesses. No way for Troy to track me.

But why rely on a savior?

I snarled, wrestling with panic to find clarity and settling on boldness. "No."

"Kneel, Finch. My cousin won't save you this time," the Monteague said. "Don't add to the clusterfuck your Reveal has already become."

Lifting my chin to the imperious angle I'd seen on Keithia at her bitchiest, I prayed Troy had been right. "A daughter of the House of Onyx does not kneel."

The Sequoyah and the Monteague frowned.

But the Luna jerked as though I'd slapped him. "What did you say?"

I lifted the chain around my neck and made sure they could see my pendant. "Gift from my father. Like it?"

"It's a fake." The Sequoyah rolled his eyes. "Enough stalling."

I dropped my shields almost all the way, leaving just the bare slip I'd need to yank them back up if the Monteague tried a mindmaze. "Is my power signature a fake too?"

That gave them pause.

I pushed harder, summoning lightning to dance over my fingers and willing the elves to break. "You killed the cameras, right?"

The Sequoyah paled.

"'Cause if you didn't, I will. The gods are always looking for offerings. Your kin will never know what happened to your bodies."

Sweating, the Monteague pulled hard on Aether.

"Stop." The Luna squeezed his boy's arm when the Monteague started muttering. "I said, stop. If she is who she claims to be—"

"It doesn't matter," the Sequoyah snapped.

The Luna scowled at me. "It *does* matter. There's a point of law in question."

I held myself ready for attack, adrenaline pounding through my blood as three of the Darkwatch tried to decide which law took precedence in the case of my life. A ridiculous giggle bubbled in my chest, and I choked as I swallowed it.

The Monteague shook the Luna's hand free and bared his teeth at me in a sneer. "The only law that matters is that she's an elemental. Capture and death, Troy be damned."

"Then do it without me. Queen Keithia has some things to answer for first." With a last grim look, the Luna backed away from us, hands out to his sides.

"Traitor," muttered the Sequoyah.

"Ass," the Luna shot back. "Did you not hear the bit about the gods? If you don't see what's happening here, then you'd best pray you don't survive to see the Wild Hunt."

That got through where the legal debate hadn't. The remaining two elves flicked glances between each other then after their fellow. I pushed a little more crackle into the lightning still wreathing my fingers, hoping to push their broken consensus into a departure.

It worked.

"You haven't seen the last of us." The Sequoyah's glower would have been more threatening if I didn't see the doubt in his eyes.

A thrill ran through me, cutting through the fear. "I have for now. You best think on what your friend said on your way back to Chapel Hill. Unless you think you can ride the Hunt yourselves." I cocked an eyebrow and sneered in derision. I didn't know if *I* could manage it myself, but they sure as shit couldn't.

With a last ugly look, both elves turned tail.

I waited until they'd gotten into a black SUV a few rows down and driven away to let go of the lightning and hustle to my car. Not for the first time, I was grateful that it was a touch-lock rather than a key. I wouldn't have been able to manage a key just then. As soon as the door was shut, I stabbed the lock button then hit it again just to be sure. I needed a damn minute to come down from the adrenaline high of backing three high-blood elves down by myself. Not even a year ago, I'd practically shat myself when one elf hired me completely unawares.

I'd grown. Under the lingering terror, it felt damn good.

Part of me still wanted to run back down to Maria's lair and seek shelter there, but I didn't. The coterie had its own battles to fight, which were partly my fault. Giuliano and Luz had been eyeing the Triangle for years, from the sound of it, but I had led us into the situation that had precipitated their shift from eyeing to snatching.

I took a deep, shuddering breath.

"You've got this. You are the baddest bitch in town," I whispered as I started the car. I used the voice feature to dial Troy as I crawled out of the garage, on the lookout for the Darkwatch elves to try something desperate, like ramming my car.

Troy picked up halfway through the second ring. "What happened? I didn't want to risk distracting you by calling."

The naked worry in his voice went a long way to easing something tight in my gut. "Evangeline talked the New York and Miami coteries into an attempted coup. Maria and I put that down. The third Darkwatch team was waiting at my car in the parking garage when I left."

"Goddess damn—I wondered where they'd disappeared to. You're not hurt?"

"No. I bluffed them down. You were right about the pendant."

"Mixed team?"

"One from each House. The Luna broke off first, after I mentioned the House of Onyx. Something about Keithia needing to answer for something." I exited the parking garage, navigating the tight streets on my way to the onramp for 40 West.

"You did good. Kept your head. Showed your strength. Exactly what you needed to do."

"Well shit. Thanks." I flushed and cleared my throat, embarrassed at his approval.

"Remember it, because the next attempt will change the pattern."

Uncertainty prickled over me again. "Oh."

"You've proven too difficult to take by direct force, so they'll try something else. Probably a distance attack. Maybe guile. Maybe a frame job. Can you hang tight another day?"

"Gonna have to, aren't I?" Normally I would have said that in a biting tone, but all I could manage was breathlessness. I gritted my teeth and tried again. "Yeah. I got this."

"Good. I'm making headway. Just need a little more time."

"Okay. Thanks. Oh—one of your cousins was on the squad today. They know you're helping me. Allegra texted me looking for you as well. I didn't answer her."

Troy's dark chuckle sent chills down my spine. "Took them long enough. Thanks for the warning. Let Alli stew a little longer. I want her to be sure she wants to join us. I'll be waiting for the rest. Take care of yourself, Arden."

Before I could say the same, he ended the call, leaving me to drive home with a nauseating blend of anger, fear, and anticipation churning in my belly. If I'd thought Troy was scary before, I wasn't sure what would happen if he decided he believed in the cause he was fighting for.

Or what it might mean if that cause was me.

Chapter 15

I didn't like the idea of spending another night at the bar, but I liked the idea of my house being attacked again even less. Yeah, I had protective and defensive wards set up by the djinn, the witches, and a kobold, but the elves were pulling out all the stops. Troy's talk about a distance attack had me thinking of flaming arrows bursting through the windows and burning me out, medieval shit like that. He'd once said that if he was serious about coming for me, he'd wait in the woods or lure me out. If the Darkwatch handbook had inspired that, why tempt the elves into trying something and depriving myself of my home for a second time this year? They'd have to be willing to risk pissing off the weres and other unaffiliated Othersiders by coming to Durham, but that hadn't stopped Troy.

My thoughts whirled like the spiced rum in the glass in front of me as I agitated it in circles. I was making progress on multiple fronts. I just couldn't see past the paths that had led me here. I kept trying to see, in hindsight, what I could have done differently. Because that was what good leaders did, right? They were introspective. They learned from the past. They identified turning points where things could have gone differently. Where people wouldn't have been negatively impacted.

"The wind just keeps blowing." Zanna hopped onto the bench opposite me with a bottle of beer.

I looked up from my rum, blinking away my thoughts and trying to focus on her. "What?"

"Learn from the past but don't dwell on it. Keep blowing."

Frowning, I drank half of my rum. "I'm not dwelling. I'm reviewing past events to find points of improvement."

The kobold's eyes rolled like they were fit to bounce right outta her head. "You're scared to go home."

"I—" My frown turned into an outright scowl. "Why invite trouble? I thought you'd appreciate me not drawing the elves there."

She sighed, clearly finding patience. "Trouble will find you here, there, anywhere. Leaves on the wind, blocking a gutter. Happens every season. Do you leave home for it?"

"No, but that's just—" I shut my mouth and finished my rum. Answering her literally was not going to do anything for my point.

She stared at me unblinkingly, her brown eyes not leaving me as she pulled on her bottle of beer and replaced it, unerringly, on the exact ring of condensation it had left when she lifted it.

"I don't want them to fuck up my house. Our house," I muttered, breaking eye contact. The other patrons were giving my booth a wide berth, eyeing us with tight faces and hunched shoulders. There was something satisfying about having their respect, or at least their fear, even if it was counterproductive to my efforts to win everyone over.

Zanna gave me a look like I was unforgivably short-sighted. "You want them to fuck up the bar instead?"

"No, but—"

"Get out. Go home. Claim your land. Keep it."

The intensity in her voice forced my attention back to her. For the first time, I realized that while she called me "tenant" and expected her dues, she might also consider me an equal partner in the care and keeping of the house. Maybe even relied on me in a way.

Troy had called me out for playing the victim before. I needed to consider how deeply that had dug into me under Callista's guardianship. Dug in, or maybe more accurately, had been instilled. Dominique, the succubus who'd killed Torsten and been banished by me in turn, had said that Callista had always feared me. I'd reflexively called bullshit, but puzzle pieces kept dropping into place, unveiling the many little ways the nymph had undercut me or turned me against myself to keep me limited and pliable.

I shivered. She'd turned me into my own worst enemy, undermining me with hefty servings of self-doubt, fear, and defensiveness. Sure, the elves were assholes of epic proportions, the gods were trying to use me to destroy the world, the djinn had turned their backs on me, and my ex wanted to use me to kill his dad.

But the common theme was that I kept accommodating it. I kept reacting. I kept curving around all of this shit like a light breeze encountering a brick wall, when I had it in me to be a damn hurricane and blow it all down.

Did everything need that heavy a touch? No. But even the threat of a major hurricane had folks on the coast boarding up homes and businesses and fleeing inland for safety.

"Be the wind," I murmured.

"Now you see." Zanna rose and headed back for the bar, taking her time, despite a growing queue of customers. Not that any of them were making a stink.

Part of me was still trying to find the balance between who I wanted to be and who I was afraid I'd need to be in order to get everyone in line before the Wild Hunt. Not asking for the responsibility I now had didn't mean I could simply abdicate it just because I'd prefer to mind my own business being a wild thing in the woods.

It was time to step up. Not just because I had to but because there was something in it for me.

Like I'd told Troy once, there had to be a goal pulling you forward, not just a fear pushing you. So what did I want, now that I was able to practice my magic openly and had power and allies?

The thought occupied me on the drive home and then while I cooked and ate dinner. It hummed in the background as I did a few chores and got caught up on the bare minimum needed to keep Hawkeye Investigations running while I dithered over what to do about it. What did I want, now that I had space to think beyond not being in hiding?

Did I want my birthright? Rebuilding the elven House that had been my father's and claiming Troy to serve me had a certain justice to it beyond simply using them as a tool to destroy Keithia. An elemental? Queen of her own House? I snorted a laugh and shook my head at even floating the idea. A year ago, I wouldn't have dared. But I was still acting like it was just a thing I'd be pretending at rather than a real possibility.

Sighing, I decided I was wound too tight to think clearly about it. The wards had been quiet, and Troy was out there, keeping them all busy. As paranoid as I'd been at the bar, he'd said the next team would take time to regroup. If I was going to take some time for myself, tonight would have to be it.

A bath. I hadn't willingly submerged myself in water in months, not since Jordan Lake, but the more I struggled to work with Water, the clearer it was that I had to get over it. I was crippling myself by not being able to work with all the powers at my disposal.

Not only that, but the confrontation with the Luna earlier reminded me that I needed to work on all aspects of my magical defenses, not just the combative ones. Going up against a lich lord, a vampiric sorcerer, and a rabisu in the space of a few weeks hadn't done my aura any favors, and Iago had frightened me with how easily he'd been able to blanket my aura in Aether. That had been for a good purpose, but what might the Lunas try in a fight?

Stop making excuses for needing to recharge.

I went out to the garden to gather some herbs to protect my spiritual field—hyssop, rue, lavender, basil, and rosemary— extending my senses as I did. Nothing was out there except for the deer and small animals. Someone might be blanketing their magic like Troy could, but the animals wouldn't be going about their business with elven hunters in the woods. There was nobody out there, not today.

Back inside, I grabbed the sea salt from the kitchen counter and ran the bath, stirring a generous amount of salt in and scattering the herbs over the water as I said a small prayer. As a precaution, I closed off the bond with Troy. What I was doing this evening was my business.

With a last blessing over the water, I stripped and gingerly got in. I stood there for a minute convincing myself that it was okay. With a deep, decisive breath, I sat down so quickly that water sloshed over the side of the tub.

I was too shaky to be annoyed at the mess, gripping the edge and trembling. The water was warm as blood, not cold as ice. It was clear, not darker than death. There was nothing in the bath but me and my herbs. No corpses. No clinging ropes or water plants.

My lungs burned from the breath I hadn't realized I was holding, and I gasped so hard that I started hiccupping. But I could breathe. It was air filling my lungs, not water. There were no elves waiting in a warehouse on shore. There were none in my woods.

It was just me, and I was fine.

Shuddering, I eased lower into the water, willing the herbs to soothe me and the water to bless me. I was fine. I was healing. It was a process, and I'd finally found the courage to take the first real step after months of reliving my near-death in my nightmares. I had everything under control.

Slowly, the tremors stopped. I focused on my body in a wave, consciously relaxing muscles and easing deeper into the water. Everything was fine. I was fine. I could let go.

And just like that, Water greeted me, a gentle enfolding that held and supported me, accepting my surrender and offering a balm in return.

I jerked upright, losing the element in my surprise. "The hell?"

Swallowing past the thud of my heart in my throat, I got a hold of myself. Went through the process of relaxing again. Let go...and managed not to panic when Water returned.

"Okay then." I'd need to find a way to speed up the process, but here was a method that wasn't connected to making myself relive being drowned. Something tied to relaxation, rather than the memory of fighting my body's desire to take one more breath.

Tentatively, I made a sphere of bathwater, trapping a basil leaf inside and hovering it in front of my face. The water was as happy to be contained in my sphere as it was in the confines of the bathtub. It didn't rage to be free and consume, like Fire did. It didn't resist, like Earth did. It clicked then that that was why I'd struggled. I was used to fighting everything—including the water in Jordan Lake. But there was no fighting Water. There was only flow. It could be diverted, dammed, channeled, or transformed, but there was no real way of fighting it.

In that, it was like Air. Zanna had been guiding me toward this all along, whether she realized it or not. *Be the wind.*

Something in me eased, a knot around my heart and in my guts that had probably been there since January. One bath wasn't going to heal all the damage, but it was a start. Maybe the nightmares would ease off. And maybe I could see my way to taking Troy's efforts to be a better person at face value, rather than holding on to pain and suspicion.

Insight flashed in me like a lightning bolt. That's what I wanted. To heal.

I wanted to be not just functional or okay but good. To let go of the crushing anxiety and fear that Callista had used to control my life and the elves had fueled. To put down the weight of my trauma. I didn't just want enough power to stand alone. I wanted the space to find out who I was and build relationships with people who embraced that self. Not the scary powerful self who had the magic to remake the world or the tired and beaten self who was constantly on defense. The self who was me, at my core, buried so deep and for so long I didn't even know who she was.

Tears burned, and I let them fall as I gingerly slipped back down into the water. I hadn't seen any of this. I'd been clutching so hard at gaining strength and power I hadn't looked past it to see what it would mean beyond claiming space. Now I wanted it so bad I ached.

A vision of what life *could* be unfurled behind the veil of my tears. I could find real freedom. Explore the new depths of the world that my growing magic revealed in greater detail each day. I could finally take a vacation and just exist, happily and peacefully, without the constant thrumming crush of paranoia and anxiety creating a background track to my life and mind. Curtailing the elves would free my fellow elementals to associate with me. I could take the time to find a partner and not worry that they'd be killed for associating with me. I wasn't naive enough to think my problems would just disappear—as long as

I held power, someone in Otherside would test it—but I could claw out some Goddess-burned breathing room.

I could find space to heal and to blossom.

All I had to do was end the elven threat, get the rest of Otherside revealed, and do something about the end of the world. But now that I knew what I wanted, nothing was going to stand in my way.

Chapter 16

I was almost surprised to wake alone and in one piece the next morning. Sunlight pierced through the blinds and slanted over my head. I stretched both my limbs and my magic, letting down my shields completely to taste the world. The open windows brought the damp promise of the day's humidity and the rich scent of the woods in summer, pine and honeysuckle blending with the faint smell of river water. Birds sang their good mornings, and the dauber wasps under the eaves buzzed.

I felt good. Lighter than I had in a long time. Almost hopeful, in a way that seemed rebellious and transgressive. I *would* be okay, and fuck everyone who thought they could keep me down. Smiling, I rolled over and hugged my pillow, savoring the feeling. And it seemed that I wasn't the only one who'd had a good night. A whisper of satisfaction came through the bond from Troy's end. A slice of pain echoed alongside it, swiftly muted on his side, as though he didn't want me to know. What had he been up to while I was having my little breakthrough?

New energy and purpose sparked in me as I got myself dressed in cutoff shorts and a black tank top cut high enough that my pendant would stay on top. After a long hesitation, I went to the box where I kept the callstone Duke had left me and put it on, tucking it under my shirt, close to my skin. I might not like the idea of a djinni being able to listen in on me, but it was the only thing I had that represented my mother and it seemed wrong to focus exclusively on the damn elven pendant. I'd never know Ninlil, but it sounded like she'd done the hard part: taking the first step to change the world. Whatever had first driven her to seek my father had required her to embrace a vision of what Otherside *could* be. I'd honor that, and I'd embody her dream.

Once I'd had my morning cup of tea on the deck out back, I gave in to my curiosity and desire to get shit moving and called Troy.

"Morning," he said with the sleepy pleasure of a sated lion. "I'm glad you called. I have news."

I cleared my throat and tried to push aside the unwonted warmth curling through me at the rumble of his voice. "Yeah? Anything to do with whatever's hurting you this morning?"

He made a noise like he was stretching and regretting it, half groan, half hiss. "Yes, actually. Sorry, I thought I'd muted that."

"It's fine. I, ah…I'm glad you're okay."

"Mmm. I think I believe you."

I shivered as heat that had nothing to do with the rising sun warmed me further and, flushing, remembered myself enough to mute the bond a little.

The amusement in his voice suggested I hadn't done a great job of it or not soon enough. "I took care of the third team last night. The one that came after you in Raleigh."

"Dead?"

"No. I needed them to carry a message I no longer have the access necessary to deliver. But they won't be walking again anytime soon."

I didn't quite know what to say to that. He'd killed at least three elves and now decommissioned another three to protect me or carry out whatever crusade he was on. I settled on, "Thanks."

"Trust me, it was my pleasure. I should have turned traitor years ago."

The satisfied darkness in his voice worried me a little. He'd always done what he'd needed to do to complete a mission, but I'd never particularly gotten the sense he'd enjoyed it before. Did that mean I had a moral obligation to reel him in?

No. Keithia made this bed. She can lay in it—or die in it. I hardened myself. It was time to get over the idea that I wasn't a killer. Troy might have been the hand wielding the weapon, but it was on my behalf. I was a survivor, and I'd been the one to pitch the plan claiming him. I'd own this.

"I guess I'll look out for that second wave then." I tried to keep my tone light.

"Yes. But that wasn't all."

"Busy night for you."

"I used the team's access codes to break into the archives looking for information about this Ebon Guard that Estrella mentioned. All I could find were heavily redacted records. The Guard existed but were apparently such a threat that knowledge of them is beyond even my old clearance level. Probably reserved only for the Conclave. Maybe the Captain. Nobody should even know the words 'Ebon Guard' for something this secret."

"Sounds promising."

"Definitely. Enough that having a more private chat with Estrella is next on my to-do list." He sounded a little too pleased at the prospect of another hunt.

"You gonna be okay, Troy?"

"You care?"

I paused. The question hadn't been laced with sarcasm, as it might have been once. It was a little too carefully flat, as was the caution in the bond.

"Yes," I finally admitted in a shaky whisper. "I started coming to terms with Jordan Lake last night. I want to move past it. Not just because it makes it easier to work with Water. I need to find a way to heal."

The heavy sigh from Troy was accompanied by a weird fluctuation in the bond, kind of like the mental equivalent of a heart palpitation. "Good. That's…really good. Thank you."

"You're welcome?"

"You don't owe me the effort," he said quickly, as though he'd said something wrong. "You owe me nothing at all, and I'd still help you either way. Shit. Now it sounds like I think you're doing it for me. I don't. I just…"

I waited, shifting on my chair as the sun gained strength and he gathered his thoughts or looked for words.

"Most people don't get second chances." The words were delivered in such a quiet tone, with such a deep wave of melancholy through the bond, that I had to wonder if he was thinking of his father and whatever correction Maria had hinted at. "I don't deserve one. I don't deserve to be near you, and I shouldn't have kissed you. But…"

My breath caught, and my fingers rose to my lips as I remembered all the past conflict blending so harshly with all the future possibility. Possibility that I still didn't know was right, even if I could forget my lingering attraction to both Roman and Maria.

Troy sighed. "But nothing, I guess. Never mind. I'm sorry, Arden." He cleared his throat, and a shifting sound made me wonder what color his sheets were. "There was one more thing. I think Evie is going to make a play for Niko Volkov."

I shook off my confused feelings and the abrupt change in subject. "What kind of play?"

"The deadly kind. With all three pups here in the Triangle, Niko is vulnerable. He has only Irina to stand as successor, when either of his sons would be more palatable to the wolves.

Particularly Sergei, given Roman's situation. They're much more conservative than our cats."

"Shit. We're looking at another attempted coup?"

"Yes. It looks like they're adopting Callista's plan."

"Divide and conquer."

"Exactly. And accelerating it."

If Evangeline and Keithia pulled off that kind of coup, Roman would get exactly what he wanted. He'd head home, which might not be such a bad thing for me personally, but I didn't think it'd help Vikki much. Niko dead might even be enough to get Sergei a pardon. That'd leave the Volkov's beta female holding uncertain territory here in the Triangle, with her personal ambitions coming to the fore right when I needed as much stability as possible to deal with the elves.

"I can't afford that just now," I said in a hard tone. "Do you know when?"

"I'm working on it, but after what I had to do to get into the archives, I've been blacklisted. You might be target number one, but I'm a close second on their hit list."

I tilted my head back to look at the sky peeping between the tall pines. "I'll do what I can about the Volkovs. You stay alive, okay? I need allies. Breathing ones, not martyrs."

"As you command, my queen." Both his words and his soft tone sent a shiver over me. In a more normal tone, he added, "I'll be in touch every six hours from now on. If you don't hear from me, assume I'm captured or dead and act accordingly. I'll do the same if I don't hear from you."

Shivering, I set down my phone as the call ended.

My queen.

My thoughts from the night before stirred again. Claiming what was mine and rebuilding it as a path to healing. What did it even mean to be a queen? What did *I* want it to mean?

Inclusion. Safety. Those were good starts. I tilted my head back again, staring at the sky and trying to figure out what my next move needed to be. The day warmed as I thought through what else Evangeline might try—I had no doubt that all of this was instigated by her, even if it was enabled by Keithia. The heir-apparent to House Monteague had apparently reached the active part of her political training. If divide and conquer was her plan, killing Niko Volkov was an excellent countermove to my neutralizing Giuliano and Luz, assuming it wasn't a planned escalation.

I tapped my fingers on the arm of my chair. All Troy had been able to tell me was that the old wolf was a target. Odds were good that the elven team was already out west, either on standby or actively preparing. I needed to get ahead of it.

Roman would be the harder one to bring around, but he technically had the power if he and Vikki were both here. I sighed and scrubbed my hands over my face. I could social engineer this, but it was going to be a fine line. Roman needed to think going along with me was his idea. It would be easier to call Vikki and work through her, but Roman had always had certain notions about what he deserved. Undercutting him by going to Vikki would set him firmly against me.

Or...you could divide and conquer. Following the lead of the elves felt shitty, but Roman's lingering feelings for me combined with his drive to be the alpha of Blood Moon made him dangerous. Unlike Troy, Roman wasn't burying his own objectives for the greater good. He'd find a way to use me—again—and tell himself that it was in everyone's best interest, but his guiding stars were his ambitions and his ghosts.

Not that Vikki didn't have her own ambitions, of course. She was just more objective in pursuing them, having included Terrence and Ximena in what was developing into a sort of reparations project. I wasn't naive enough to think that Vikki's plans weren't for herself above all, but the incidental effects would do more to support all my allies rather than only herself. If she was smart—and she was—she'd pull her allies east to the Triangle under the guise of holding the land ceded here then dig in while the Volkov and other packs fell into infighting over leadership of the clan. A smaller ally was better than one that was completely distracted.

Decided, I called Roman.

"Are all of you at home? Just the three of you?" I asked when he picked up.

"Yes, and good morning to you too," he said, sounding put-off.

I ignored his mood. "I have news. Put me on speaker."

After a long pause that felt like he was trying to decide whether to argue with me, I heard the phone clatter to the table as he called for Vikki.

"It's Arden," Roman said as footsteps came closer. "Okay, we're here, and you're on speaker. What's so urgent you can't say good morning?"

"The elves are going to attack your father," I said bluntly. "I don't know when or how."

"Your princeling told you this?" Vikki said after a moment of silence.

"Yes. He's carrying out counter-ops to keep his kin busy while we get a plan together to support the vampires."

"Credible?" She raised her voice to be heard over a deep growl I assumed came from Sergei.

"I'd say so. Evangeline manipulated reps from the New York and Miami coteries into coming here and making a play for Maria. I dealt with that yesterday after seeing you. That means the vamps will be wary of more elven outreach and she needs to shift her focus to another of my allies. The wolves are the strongest faction remaining."

"I have to get back to Asheville," Roman said over Sergei's ongoing rumbling growl in the background. The wolf yipped in agreement.

Exactly what I thought he'd say. Time to engineer things. I only felt a little guilty as I injected a hint of uncertainty into my tone. "Roman, are you sure? It could be a trap. I…wouldn't want anything to happen to you."

"Don't worry, babe. Trap or not, we can handle it."

I smiled bitterly. We were back to "babe" at the smallest suggestion of weakness on my part. Again I was struck by the contrast between Roman's idea of care and Troy's. The elf built me up and stood at my back. The wolf pulled me down and stood over me. I was certain Roman thought he was doing what was best for me, but I'd never felt more vindicated in my decision to let him go and not wait for him. I'd still be in the box I'd been in when he'd left.

Vikki cleared her throat. "I should stay here. We finally have a foothold on prime territory that Pops had his eye on for years."

More silence met her declaration.

"What?" She sounded annoyed. "We can't risk the Farkas pack coming down from Virginia. If all three of us run back home, what's to stop those curs from edging in?"

"Sergei could stay," Roman said.

The wolf bark-howled his agreement.

"Absolutely not." My stomach clenched.

Roman shushed his brother. "Reckon that's for us to decide."

I hardened my tone. "Reckon that since I'm the one he tried to screw over and the one who could turn all three of you over a log and thrash your asses like I did the outta-state vampires, it's for me to decide. Don't make me pull rank, Roman. You won't like it if I do."

"It's like that?" he said in a low voice I didn't like at all.

I consciously softened mine, feeling like I was walking a knife's edge. "Only if you force it. I support the need for y'all to do something, but that thing cannot include Sergei remaining unsupervised or in man-form in the Triangle. We can revisit it when the elves are dealt with. Not before."

Easing my tone and throwing him a bone for possible renegotiation seemed to mollify Roman somewhat. "Fine. I'll head home with Sergei today. Vikki…"

"Don't worry, big bro. I got this," she said, a bit twangier and lighter than usual. She was playing him as much as I was.

"You'd better. We can't lose this land. Arie, anything else?"

I mulled over whether to remind him someone needed to be revealed to support the vampires then decided to coordinate it with Vikki. "No. Thanks for being so understanding. I hope the intel is wrong."

"Hmm." The hint of savage satisfaction in Roman's tone made me wince. He'd be getting exactly what he'd asked me to do, without losing face by going to another faction. "Thanks for the tip, Arie. Hang in there with the elves. I'll be back as soon as we have everything sorted out."

"Sure," I said, irked by everything he'd just said and trying not to let it show. "Bye then. Drive safe."

Not long after, my phone buzzed with a text from Vikki. *Well played. If you're free later, I'd like to swing by and discuss next steps with you and the cats.*

Be my guest. I'll see if they're available, I texted back, finding a bitter smile. I would rather things hadn't turned out so ugly with Roman, but I'd play the cards I'd been dealt.

Chapter 17

For someone who hadn't ever had people round before this year, I certainly found myself entertaining quite a bit this summer.

We stayed in my house this time, within the wards. Lola and Joachin took posts at the front and back doors while Vikki, Terrence, Ximena, and I sat stiffly around my dining table. Ximena fingered the deep gouge Neith's gift had left in the surface. I don't think she was aware of doing it.

"It's time for the wolves to come out," Vikki said tersely, not bothering with a lead-in.

Terrence's eyes flickered to the peridot green of a leopard's for the barest second as he clasped his hands in front of him. "What brought this about? Your brother didn't seem keen on the idea the other day."

Vikki's smile was more of a snarl. "Both my brothers are headed back home to deal with a threat to our father."

Both werecats stiffened. If they'd had tails, they'd be lashing them. I leaned back in my chair, trying to remove myself from this as much as possible. It had to be Vikki's show, or it would look like I'd pushed her into it.

Ximena caught herself rubbing the gouge and grimaced, rubbing her hand on her shorts. "That'll be the opportunity you were hoping for then?"

"I'd like to prepare for it to be, but only with both of y'all's blessings." Vikki leaned forward, glancing between them.

"What does that preparation look like?" Ximena's tone was guarded. From what I'd gathered, she'd been against the plan to cede what little land the cats held to the more powerful Blood Moon clan in exchange for a voice they should have had by rights.

The tightness in Vikki's body suggested she was trying desperately not to fidget. "I get a message to my people in the clan. Tell them to stand ready. If the threat succeeds, they'll flee here and beg sanctuary. Either way, as the clan's sole representative in the Triangle, I overturn Roman's objection to us being the next ones out."

Ximena narrowed her eyes, tensing as though to pounce. "Beg sanctuary? To stay on land you already hold?"

"To stay on land I'd cede back to you in exchange for recognition of my new pack. As I promised. Y'all are owed justice." Vikki finally gave in and squirmed before catching herself.

Terrence caught the movement and offered his cat's smile. "There's more to this than justice for a pair of cat prides you didn't give two shits about before this summer. Speak, Viktoria."

I frowned, eyeing Vikki sideways as I tried to work out why the hell she was so nervous about this. She hadn't been anywhere near as anxious when she'd offered the plan to begin with.

The werewolf slumped with a heavy exhale. "Sergei's bullshit isn't the only reason why Ana stalled on the marriage pact with the Volkovs."

Her deep flush and the sweat on her brow spelled it out for me. "Oh, shit."

Vikki grimaced at me then turned back to the werecats and whispered, "Ana's my lover."

As Terrence and Ximena exchanged confused glances, I said, "Does the third guy know?"

"Cyril is our front. We've been best friends since we were whelped. Ran every full moon together until this summer. When Sergei…did what he did, Cyril stepped in to protect Ana."

Terrence started chuckling.

"What the hell are you laughing at?" Vikki snarled, flushing a deep red with fury as the scent of musk flooded my kitchen.

The wereleopard shook his head and blew his breath out. "Love conquers all, including injustice. For love of another woman, you would shatter old Niko's empire. Not only that but hand part of it to cats."

Ximena's aggressive posture had softened. She reached across the table and squeezed Vikki's hand. "Thank you for your honesty. That paints a much clearer picture and offers motives we can understand. Next time, start there. It's more believable than one of Niko's get suddenly gaining a thirst for justice and reparations."

The look she exchanged with Terrence had me wondering again just what their relationship was. Not that it was my business, but weres were almost rabid in their insistence to keep breeding within the species. They'd have to start biting people to turn them, otherwise, and that was a big no-no.

Unless the weres are out. I cleared my throat for attention. "Are Acacia Thorn and Jade Tooth not worried about the wolves increasing their numbers by turning humans if they're out and the cats are not?"

Vikki recoiled, grimacing. "I wouldn't."

"But some of your people might," I said gently. I didn't need another factional war on top of the elves. This needed to be sorted right now, not later.

Terrence nodded thoughtfully. "It would be a condition of sanctuary. Births only. No bites."

"Accepted," Vikki said without hesitation.

Ximena looked out the window and tapped her fingers on the table in a pattern. "How many wolves are we talking about?"

"How many would you be comfortable with?"

The cats exchanged a look.

"No more than a third the total number of combined cats in the Triangle," Terrence said. "And you'd be expected to help us with holding—maybe even expanding—our territory to the surrounding counties. Mundanes keep developing the land around here, and game is thinning. We can't have pressure on our hunts from both humans and wolves."

Ximena nodded her agreement.

"I won't take the wolves to war for you," Vikki said.

Terrence wrinkled his nose. "I had enough war in the Marines. Not fixing to fight it here. But if Blood Moon brings battle east, that's on you and yours to handle."

Vikki chewed on her lower lip. "Okay, I can see why that's fair. I don't like it, but it's fair."

"Anything else?" I said when they all fell silent.

"Forfeits," Ximena said. "I'm sorry, Vikki, but the wolves have a history. Roman paid a forfeit when he petitioned to live and hunt in the area. We'll expect the same from every wolf who settles within fifty miles of Durham."

I hadn't known that and wondered what Roman had paid. He'd been a teenager without much to offer when he'd arrived, or so I'd thought.

Blanching, Vikki said, "That would take your sphere of influence out to Greensboro, Rocky Mount, the Virginia border, and most of the way to Fayetteville. You don't hold that much land right now."

"But we should." Ximena's soft voice held threat in it. However sympathetic she was about Vikki's story, she was not and never had been anyone's fool. "We need assurances none of your people will share Niko's ambitions, and we need room for our own to spread out, deeper into the less-populated areas of the state. The wolves can keep the lands they already hold west of 77 and north of 81, but we're tired of being confined to the Triangle when there's more territory—more safety—available. If you're bringing the wolves out, people will start wondering about other shifters. We can't be an easy target."

I held my tongue, although I really, really wanted to make sure we weren't going to set up a future turf war. If Vikki was balking, Roman would be livid. He'd have his hands full dealing with pack and clan succession if all of this came to pass, but I knew my ex. He'd have something to say on it. On top of that, I had no idea what he'd do about his betrothed being his sister's forbidden lover.

Let Vikki and Roman manage each other. I was the Arbiter in this situation, not a warlord or a queen.

Vikki scrubbed her hands over her face. "I request a night to think on it."

"Granted," Ximena said. "But think quickly. This threat to Niko must be urgent if the boys have run back to the mountains already and you're here with us alone. We'll expect an answer at the next alliance meeting."

Terrence nodded, and Vikki pressed her lips together, nodding with a quick jerk of her head. She was stuck and she knew it, but she was too wily not to try finding a way to eke out a little something more.

"Okay then," I said. "That covers the territory discussion. What about the wolves coming out?"

"We'll do that regardless of what happens in Asheville." Vikki looked out the window as though seeking mental space from the negotiations. "Roman will be pissed, but Ana will go for it if I tell her it paves the way for us to be together. She'll bring the Farkas pack around."

I frowned, remembering the way she'd spoken of that family on the phone earlier. "Ana is from the Farkas pack? But I thought—"

Vikki flipped her hand. "I was playing on the boys' thinking that the Volkov pack is superior by default. I don't give a cat's tail—um, sorry y'all—but yeah, I don't care if the Volkovs go to hell in a handbasket. I've been working for years for reform. Not just for me but to bring Roman home too."

"Backwards," Terrence muttered.

Vikki tensed. "Excuse me?"

The wereleopard's face twitched as though barely holding back a sneer. "We don't care who you love or how well you can shift. We look after our own."

Ximena's hard expression suggested she agreed, and I stepped in before we could backslide.

"Okay. Vikki agrees the wolves will be the next faction to come out. Troy was talking about dragging the elves out as well, so y'all can do a double-header. And maybe we can get a witch in so it's not just a bunch of predators. The mundanes have been losing their shit all summer. We need to show them someone a bit more benign."

For a few heartbeats, Vikki said nothing as a flush rose into her cheeks. "Part of me wants to ask why I should do it if Monteague already volunteered." She looked at Terrence and Ximena, who were watching her with the intentness of their other forms. "But I guess the more of Otherside that's confirmed as out, the more the rest can hide."

Terrence offered a lopsided smile. "For a little while, anyway. We're not so naive as to think we can stay hidden forever. We just need a little more time to shore ourselves up is all."

"And werewolves are the beastie everyone knows. Yeah," Vikki said. "Arden, can you get Monteague and the witches on the phone? Or better yet, get them here? If y'all are okay having elven royalty in Durham outside the bar."

Years of long practice kept my face straight at the implication that Troy might not already be in Durham, and more recent experience kept me from giving myself away in a jump of heart rate.

"If it's alliance business, fine by me," Ximena said.

Terrence nodded.

I slipped my phone from my pocket, resting my wrist on the table as I tapped through for his number. "Troy was planning a hunt today, so I don't know that he'll be around just now. I'll try him first."

The weres all perked up.

"A hunt?" Vikki asked.

I rapped my fingers in a line along the table, trying to decide how much of this was alliance business and how much was elven. "There've been some further developments with the elves. Troy is following them up."

"You always called him 'Monteague' before," Ximena said, her eyes narrowing as they shifted to red-gold. "Something change?"

"He's—there's been a change in his House situation," I blurted, flushing as I remembered he claimed my House now. *I don't have feelings for him. He's just useful.*

Terrence whistled low and long, eyebrows up, and leaned back in his chair as he exchanged a glance with Ximena. "We wondered if it'd come to that after the last alliance meeting, but that boy's always been so…dedicated."

Ximena snorted. "Try hardheaded."

I grimaced. "Trust me, when he said he was dropping Monteague, it was a hell of a surprise to me too."

"I can imagine," Terrence said. "Maria said once that his duty would be either his death or his elevation. Reckon it might well be both at this rate."

"It might well be," I said softly. That was Troy's choice. I couldn't own as mine what Keithia and Evangeline might or might not do to him for it. All I could do was keep dragging all of Otherside forward, one painful step at a time.

I pushed the thought aside and dialed Troy.

He picked up after three rings. "Arden? It hasn't been six hours. Are you okay?"

"Fine." I looked toward the sliding glass door leading to the deck and the backyard. "I'm sitting in on a negotiation with the weres. Can you come up to my place for a meeting?"

"Vikki ready to bring the wolves out?"

"Yes. Ximena and Terrence are here as well."

"All three clan leaders at your house? Right now?"

"Yes." I glanced at Ximena. "They're okay with you being in Durham if it's on alliance business."

"I see." He sounded as though he was reading into that exactly what I'd intended—that I hadn't told them about his having a safehouse in Durham but that he'd have an excuse if he needed one. He sighed. "I think Estrella knows I want a private chat. She's been very careful all morning."

"So…"

"Give me an hour."

"Hang on." I glanced at each of the weres in turn. "Is an hour okay?"

"Faster than I'd expected," Ximena said, head tilted, the little curl of her lips not quite Terrence's cat-like mocking look but one that suggested she was reading into the situation.

"An hour's fine," I said to Troy, leveling a warning look at the werejaguar.

He hung up without saying anything more, probably counting on the weres' superior hearing to let them eavesdrop and not wanting to give them more than he already had. I called Janae and repeated the request, gaining a nervous agreement from her that someone would be here if two other factions were also coming out but only after I promised to come to the rescue if the Salem Witch Trials kicked off again.

"Who wants to spar?" I asked to break the awkward silence.

Chapter 18

The weres indulged me in some hand-to-hand combat training while we waited for Troy. I think they were honored to be asked, if the looks of shock followed by enthusiastic grins were any indication. Up until that point, I'd only trained with elves—they were the greatest threat to me. But they weren't the only ones with something to offer.

Nobody likes feeling like they owe someone else, whether justified or not, so I figured asking for their help in keeping myself alive might go some way toward lessening any feeling of obligation they might feel for my efforts on their behalf. Resentment toward Callista was what had opened the door to all of them working with me, and I was always conscious of that.

Sarah, the red-headed witch who'd helped with the fight against the vampiric sorcerer, turned up forty-five minutes later. Vikki brought her around to the back yard, and they carried on discussing with Ximena about how exactly they wanted to do our second Reveal. The plants seemed to quiver with Sarah's nerves, and I hoped she was up for this.

After a little more than an hour of getting my ass kicked and learning some new tricks, I felt Troy's nearness in the bond and ignored it, remembering my mistake when Roman had appeared in the basement last time I'd practiced and determined to finally catch Terrence. The wiry little man was my size, but his Marine training and wereleopard reflexes meant he'd beaten me in every bout.

Including this one.

"Damn!" I slammed my fist against the ground, pinned by Terrence right as Troy came around the side of my house.

Troy didn't make any outward reaction, but the bond practically stabbed me with a sharp protective urge, forcibly curtailed.

"Nice one." I accepted Terrence's hand up and nodded respectfully. "I'll remember that trick."

"You nearly had me." The wereleopard slanted a mischievous glance at Troy. "Maybe I should thank the elf for arriving when he did and ending the session."

I almost brushed off the comment, except that Terrence was breathing hard and massaging his shoulder. I wondered why he'd gone into the Marines when he was so keen to hide what he was and how the hell he'd managed it. Witch magic, maybe, or silver. Or maybe just iron self-control. I hadn't caught a whiff of his cat while we were sparring.

"Next time," I said, rather than indulging my curiosity.

"Glad to see you're taking our discussion seriously, Finch," Troy said drily, shaking hands first with Ximena, then with Terrence, Vikki, and Sarah. All of us raised our eyebrows at the clear evidence Troy had been in a fight: a healing black eye and split cheekbone, bruised knuckles, a bandaged left forearm. He was in dark wash jeans and a close-fitting forest green T-shirt that showed the curves of his muscles, making me think he'd been making more of an effort to blend in as he looked for an opportunity to talk to Estrella.

"She'll be dangerous soon," Vikki said from where she'd been watching on the bottom step of the deck. She eyed Troy. "You been training her?"

A curl of satisfaction slipped through the bond, jerked back as quickly as the protectiveness had been as Troy nodded. "Me and a couple of others."

Terrence shook his head. "The Wild Hunt must surely be upon us if elves are teaching elementals how to fight."

"Indeed," Troy said coldly. It didn't take sharing a bond with the man to tell that he didn't like that idea. He shifted his attention to Vikki and Sarah. "The wolves will come out? And the witches?"

With a nervous nod, Sarah said, "Yes. I volunteered. I want to show that we have something to offer."

Vikki shrugged, her nerves only showing in the thicker scent of musk on the air. "The wolves will if I reveal myself while my brother is dealing with y'all's machinations."

Troy grimaced. "I'd apologize for that but—"

"But it's not you playing Machiavelli. No worries, Monteague. I know the shape of things."

Troy stiffened. "I don't claim that House any longer."

Nobody answered him for a moment. Then Vikki grinned. "That what happened to your face?"

The grin slipped when Troy echoed it with far more savagery than I'd seen on him before. "Something like that."

"Sheeit," Terrence said, drawing the swear out. "Does that mean you're gonna share with the class for once?"

A muscle twitched in Troy's cheek. The bond gave me the impression he was wrestling with himself. His eyes flicked to me, and he sighed deeply. "I suppose I have to now, don't I?"

"Might clear up a few things," Ximena said.

Sarah just looked uncertain, like this was all above her paygrade.

With a movement too stiff to be casual, Troy leaned against the deck railing. "I'm forsworn and, for the moment, on the run from the Conclave and the Darkwatch."

I crossed my arms and pressed my lips together when he glanced at me again. I supposed that since I hadn't formally declared myself queen of House Solari to the alliance, he couldn't formally declare himself as mine. We hadn't worked out exactly what that entailed beyond the oath in any case. Another item on the to-do list.

The scent of cedar and musk crested as the weres grew agitated, and the honeysuckle vine twining around the deck railing grew a few inches.

Troy continued before they could ask any questions. "Finch is public enemy number one on their list. I'm a close number two. Rejecting House, queen, and the Darkwatch all in the same day would be bad enough if I hadn't also chosen to keep an oath to an elemental."

"And then kill the teams sent after me," I muttered.

The others reacted with varying degrees of surprise, stiffening and eyes flashing.

"That too," Troy said. "Sets a bad precedent. Then the Captain found out about Evangeline's move against the Raleigh coterie and refused to approve Darkwatch resources for what is essentially an act of war against another faction, even if we all know it plays into Roman's plans nicely. So Evangeline sent a team of Monteague House Guards to Asheville."

Vikki scowled. "With Keithia's blessing?"

"Yes, as far as I can tell."

"Bold play." Ximena's gaze darted between Troy and me. "So what's going on between the two of you?"

"He's my bodyguard," I said when Troy just looked at me. Amusement-tinged satisfaction danced though the bond, so it seemed he was okay with that.

Ximena looked equal parts skeptical and amused. "Mmhmm. Lots of boldness to go round, I see, given what we heard about his past actions at Raven Rock. But okay. I guess that means he'll want free passage into and out of Durham."

"Or he already has it," Terrence said slyly.

Troy kept his face neutral. "And if I did?"

Vikki's expression sharpened, but she held her tongue.

The cats exchanged a look. "If you did," Ximena said, "You'd owe the usual forfeit plus an asshole tax for not following the proper procedures."

"We'll write off the death part of the deal though, seeing as you're needed to protect Miss Arden here," Terrence added, glowering. "But don't make a habit of crossing us."

I barely held back a grimace. I'd known but said nothing. Then again, it wasn't mine to tell.

"Understood and appreciated," Troy said. "Double the usual?"

"That'll do," Ximena said. Terrence nodded, and they all shook on it, leaving me wondering what the hell the usual was. I'd ask later.

Troy straightened, wincing and rubbing the ribs he'd broken a few weeks ago. "About the next round of Reveals then. Have you all agreed on anything yet?"

Ximena glanced at Sarah and Vikki. "Only that we need to do it fast, record it on a phone, and that Sarah will go last to show we're not all predators."

"Okay. Viktoria, if you're amenable and Finch consents to the use of her land, I propose we do it here and now. I can strip the geodata from the file to keep our location anonymous."

I fisted my hands on my hips and looked at the ground, not liking how rushed this was after all the careful planning of the vampire Reveal but not seeing another option. If Troy was being hunted and was the only elf willing to commit to a Reveal, we had to get it done before the next round of Darkwatch teams had a chance to take him out. Roman and I had gone for runs in the woods but mostly along the river. If they stayed away from it, it should be unrecognizable as my land. It'd get back to him eventually, but I wouldn't mind the breathing space to deal with the elves before I had a furious werewolf ex coming down on me.

One question came to mind. "Troy, is this going to make it harder for you to track down the Guard?"

"Not if I use shadows to obscure my face."

"Okay," I said, carefully controlling my body language in the hopes of looking confident. "And Sarah? You gonna be okay?"

Her face pinched. "I might lose my nannying job. But it's the right thing to do."

"I'll talk to Zanna about hiring you on at the bar, okay? We can help keep you safe and make sure you have work."

Sarah brightened. "Oh! Thank you, Miss Arden. I'd appreciate that. I used to tend bar while I was at college."

I offered an encouraging smile and turned to Vikki. "You need anything?"

Vikki shivered, looking paler than usual as she took a deep breath and looked at the sky. "Lupa suckle and protect me." Pulling her eyes down to me, she added, "If this goes wrong and I get hunted down...tell Ana I love her and I did it so that we could have a chance to live openly. In all ways."

Suddenly choked up, I nodded solemnly. Something shivered through the bond from Troy, and I felt his gaze on me.

"If the worst should happen, our pact will stand, Viktoria Volkov," Terrence said in a low, grave voice. "Those of your people who need it may find sanctuary here. Ana will be an honored guest. I do so swear."

"I do so swear," echoed Ximena.

Vikki nodded, lips pressed together, and straightened. "Worth the risk then. Arden?"

"Follow me." I led the little band to the gate Zanna had installed in the back of the fence in lieu of repairing the gap where the tree had fallen on it. It made it so I didn't have to climb over or walk out the front and around to get to my riverside practice.

Troy, Vikki, and Sarah followed closest behind me as I turned in the opposite direction of that I used to go with Roman. They murmured back and forth over what to do and how, settling on Troy recording Vikki's shift from a naked crouch so that she wouldn't shred her clothes or get done for indecent exposure. Then he'd draw shadows and turn the camera on himself. Then they'd show Sarah working with plants.

It all sounded small, the kind of everyday magic any of us had, but my heart thundered. There would be no coming back from this, for the mundanes or Otherside. Not that there was any other choice. But still.

I sent a group text to the rest of the alliance as we went deeper into the woods, away from the road and the river both. By the time I'd reached a small clearing, I'd gotten replies from Janae, Noah, Val, and Laurel with confirmations, good luck wishes, and more than a few swears. After another thought, I sent the same message to Zanna and Doc Mike. Neither the fae nor the human sensitives were formally part of the alliance, but I couldn't let this just drop on them.

"We're good to go with the rest of the group," I said when I had their confirmation. "How's this?"

"I'm happy if Viktoria and Sarah are." Troy had walled off the bond on the way over, probably to hide whatever he was feeling about deepening the betrayal of his people. He might enjoy the fighting part, but everyone in the alliance had dragged their feet over the Revealing part. That it had fallen to him had to have him feeling a certain kind of way.

Vikki looked around the clearing and sniffed a few times, taking in the smells. "Sure. Good a place as any."

Sarah just nodded and sweated.

"We'll stand watch," Terrence said.

With the casualness all weres seemed to have about nudity, Vikki nodded then stripped and handed me her clothes. "Don't drop 'em. I don't like getting burrs up my ass."

I couldn't help a snort of laughter, and her weak smile said that had been her goal. She crouched, looking strong and fierce rather than vulnerable, and waited for Troy to ready the phone. At her nod, he started recording.

"Y'all had to know that the vampires aren't the only ones out there." Her expression was flirty, and her voice was lower and far more sultry than any she'd used before, despite the obvious growl to it.

Then she shifted. Bones cracked as white fur sprouted. Her ears slid to the top of her head as they grew pointed. Her jaw shot forward along with her nose to become a long snout full of sharp teeth. A tail burst from the base of her spine almost as an afterthought. It looked painful as hell, and although Vikki panted, she made no noise until she'd finished.

A massive white wolf with silver-blue eyes shook herself and grinned at the camera, tongue lolling.

As a cloud blew over the sun, Troy cloaked himself in shadows and, to my eyes, was lost in a haze. He tapped the camera button to switch it to selfie mode. "We are Otherside, and we have lived alongside you for as long as your ancestors can remember."

With a snarl, his second set of teeth dropped down.

The elves' dagger-sharp secondary teeth were, for reasons I didn't understand, one of their most closely guarded secrets. From the goggle-eyed looks on Sarah, Terrence, and Ximena's faces and the sudden stiffness of Vikki's posture, I wasn't the only Othersider who hadn't known about them.

The elves will kill him for sure now.

After a heartbeat, Troy hid the teeth, winked roguishly at the camera, and added, "Let us continue to do so peacefully, and there's no need to be afraid of the dark." He turned the camera to Sarah.

"We have so much we could share," she said quickly. With a prickle of life magic, she reached overhead to a trumpet vine and sent every budded flower on it into bloom. "Growth. Healing. Knowledge. All we ask is peace."

Troy ended the recording.

Vikki changed back even more slowly than she'd originally shifted then held out a hand for her clothes. "Fuck but I hate a back-to-back shift."

I handed them over. "Thank you. All of you. I know it's a huge risk. You can call on me for support if you need it, okay?"

Vikki nodded, looking shaken as she hurriedly redressed.

Pain lanced through the bond from Troy—the emotional kind, more than the faint background hum of the injuries from his fight. He'd irrevocably broken any reconciliation with his people. Maybe they would have overlooked siding with me if he'd done something to betray or undermine me, but there was no fixing a Reveal.

Squeezing his arm, I sent a burst of gratitude to him before asking, "What's the plan for getting the video out?"

"Triple check that any identifying data is stripped to make sure we don't lead anyone here to you. Send to local news stations via disposable email address. If I don't see it airing by nine tonight, I send it to a few contacts I have nationally and abroad."

I inhaled and blew a breath out. "Okay. Then let's get back to my place. Drinks on me."

The three weres and the witch led the way back to my house, a new camaraderie between them as Terrence wrapped his arm over Vikki's shoulder and Ximena slipped an arm around Sarah's for a quick hug. Troy brought up the rear, watching my back.

My phone rang with the "Bad Boys" ringtone, and I frowned. *What the hell does Chapel Hill PD want?* "Or maybe not. I'm sorry, I have to take this." I accepted the call. "Finch speaking."

"Hey, Arden, it's Tom Chan."

My stomach clenched. Two police calls in as many days? "Detective, how's things? Got a job for me?"

"Not so much, sorry. Could you swing by the station today though? We've got a few questions about some cases you helped us with."

"It has to be now?"

"We can send a car if that makes it easier."

Shit. First Raleigh, now Chapel Hill. And we hadn't even shown off the rest of Otherside yet.

Tom sighed. "I hate to do this, Arden, but my captain is breathing down my neck with all the protests. Could you do it as a favor? For me?"

I scrubbed a hand over my face, weighing my need to play mundane with my need not to be killed by elves. I was the alliance's best connection with the human police departments though—which meant I was our best shot at gaining intel that could keep us safe if law enforcement turned against us before Maria could finish her work to get laws protecting Othersiders through the state legislature.

"Yeah. Sure. I'll be there in about half an hour. You're bringing the coffee though." I hoped my wary tension didn't carry over the phone.

"It's a date. See you soon," Tom said before hanging up.

Chapter 19

It'd been a while since I'd visited Chapel Hill PD. I was not at all keen on being in elven territory and my declaration that I had to go gave Troy a quiet, carefully hidden conniption, but there was no easy way for me to put off the visit. He insisted not only on me wearing an earpiece but also on accompanying me down, driving separately. He'd gotten a new car somewhere, and it matched mine. I raised my eyebrows when I saw it but didn't ask. I could guess. If there were two of us in similar vehicles with similar license plate numbers, it might buy him the seconds he needed to take action.

The police department was the usual fluorescent-lit space reeking of coffee and copy paper that it always had been. My favorite officer, Rachel, wasn't on the desk, which was a shame. Tom was waiting for me though, dressed in street clothes—jeans that would be stifling hot in the summer humidity and a polo that reminded me of the way Troy tended to dress when he wasn't on missions. His black hair was cut shorter than it had been the last time I'd seen him.

"Right on time," the detective said with his usual disarming smile. "Thanks for coming. I mean it."

"Sure." I followed him back through the maze of desks to his and tried to stay casual as I sat. The godblade seemed to burn in its concealed sheathe at the small of my back. I couldn't get away with carrying the eight-inch elf-killer, but meteoric iron gifted by the gods should handle any Darkwatch attempts. "What's going on?"

"Like I said, a few cases got flagged from your early days working with us."

"Lemme guess," I drawled. "The ones with connections to Raleigh?"

Tom had the grace to blush. "I might have heard from Clayton, yeah."

"Detective Rice has some concerning opinions." I tilted my head and left it at that, trying to suss out whether Tom had similar feelings about vampires.

"Something about you seems…different." Tom studied me, shifting in his chair in a way that seemed unconscious. "You been working out?"

Deflecting. Not good. Despite the easy nature of our conversation, I had a feeling I wasn't going to like where it went. This was how he was with suspects.

"Yeah. Found a new personal trainer." I flexed my bicep to show the muscle I'd developed over the spring and summer, shielded as hard as I could, and prayed that my power signature wasn't leaking. Othersiders would be keenly attuned to it, recognizing me not only as one of the community but also my faction, if they'd experienced it before. Kind of like the scents of magic humans generally couldn't pick up unless the working was especially strong. Completely mundane humans would just experience my power signature as vaguely unsettling—an instinctual reaction, like spotting a lion in the tall grass. Or maybe a sense of the uncanny valley was more accurate. Something would scream at them that I looked human but wasn't.

My stomach sank as any last illusions that I could maintain Hawkeye Investigations any longer were dispelled. I pushed aside the pang that echoed through me at that. Now was not the time.

Tom looked at me sideways from the doodle of a cat he was retracing. "You've always had a rep for being good with weird cases."

Something cold curled through my guts. I forced myself to shrug nonchalantly. "Guess it's a talent."

"Is it?"

I lifted my brows in question.

"A talent? Or is it something else?"

Frowning, I leaned back in my chair. "What are you trying to say, Tom?"

The detective mirrored my shift and tapped the point of his pen against the pad of paper. "I think you know."

"Spell it out for me. For clarity's sake."

Tom studied me, his dark eyes suddenly gaining in intensity as they flicked over me. "Are you human, Arden?"

Blood fled from my face, and it was pure force of will that kept me from swaying. "Excuse me?"

"I have to ask." Tom shrugged, not taking his gaze off me. "Vampires? Who can daywalk?"

That was an easy one to dispel—all I'd have to do was smile to show my decidedly un-sharp teeth—but this had the invasive feel of a witch hunt. First Detective Rice down in Raleigh, now Tom.

Sure, I could give a little. Show my teeth. Make protestations. But me giving a little sent the signal that this was okay and appropriate when it felt like cops looking for an excuse to trump up charges so they could bring you in for "resisting arrest." Nothing about the question was innocent.

I crossed my arms and narrowed my eyes. "Do you? Have to ask?"

"I don't follow."

"It sounds to me like you're trying to step onto a slippery slope. Detective Rice tried a similar step."

"So you're of the opinion that vampires are people?"

"I really don't see what this has to do with the cases I helped you with, *Detective*."

"Come on, Arden. Help me out. I'm just trying to understand."

"I'm still not clear on what though, and if this isn't a paying gig, then I'm sorry but I don't have time to entertain offensive questions and speculation."

He nodded and started sketching a poodle or something. "Okay, that's fair. Who's Troy Monteague?"

My heart thundered. Detective Rice had been suspicious of Troy at the Umstead, and I could only imagine he'd be even more so after their interview. He must have called Tom and asked him to dig. Something was off though. Raleigh PD had called both of us down. If they suspected Troy of something, they would have called him in or sent a squad car for him. I'd had Troy's background checked as part of the Sequoyah case and he'd come up clean, so there was no reason for Tom to be interested in him unless he'd been pointed there.

Now it was the earpiece stuck behind my left ear that seemed to burn. *Go, get out of here*, I willed at Troy. Something wasn't right.

Aloud, I said, "Rice had a lot to say, huh?"

"So you know this Monteague guy?"

I shrugged, wishing I had some water for my dry mouth. "Security contractor from the Umstead job."

"Where the vampires came out."

"Is this about my cases? Or is it about vampires?"

"You tell me." Tom set the pen down. "We've known each other for a while so I gotta be honest, Arden. It feels like Clayton was right. About you hiding something."

My stomach sloshed bile up my throat. I tried not to be obvious about swallowing it back down as I stood. "Nice catching up, Tom. Let me know if you've got a paying job, okay?"

"Whoa, whoa, come on. I'm sorry." The detective stood and held his hands up placatingly. "Can we forget all this? Sit down out back for that coffee we never seem to get? Shit's been wild lately."

I didn't like the edge in his smile and something about all of this had my gut churning, but I was already being suspicious enough by not answering his questions and insisting on leaving. It was coming from righteous indignation rather than guilt, but it seemed my cop acquaintances didn't have the nuance for that. "Fine. Okay. And then I'm hitting the road."

We got three steps outside the back door when I caught the cloying meringue smell of Aether. I rocked to a halt, hoping against hope it was Troy but knowing from the bond he wasn't near enough for me to scent him.

Fuck. Did Tom set me up, or was I followed?

I got my answer when Tom stepped to the side as two suits approached, one male, one female, both looking like Feds. They reeked of enough Aether that the detective frowned and wrinkled his nose as he turned to me, not quite managing to look me in the eye.

"I'm sorry about this, Arden. They claimed jurisdiction."

Numb with shock, I glared at Tom. He rubbed his arms as though he was cold, but I knew it wasn't that. It was seepage from my power signature, drawn out by my agitation. I'd grown too powerful too quickly and had been acting like I could still get away with shielding and keeping my head down. Like I could keep living the same way I always had, with minor adjustments.

I was a fool. There was a reason most of the old and powerful Othersiders stayed in their lairs or spelled the fuck outta humans if they went out. There was a reason Callista had used Watchers instead of doing all the footwork herself.

The elfess, a Sequoyah from the toffee-blond hair and grey eyes, paused with her hand on her unsnapped service pistol. "We're going to need you to come with us, Finch."

"On what grounds?"

"Patriot Act." The elf sneered. A Monteague, maybe, with hair closer to Roman's dark chocolate shade than Troy's raven black. His forest-green eyes were hard as he casually drew his own gun.

"You've got to be shitting me." Maybe I could bluff my way out of this, if Tom was a witness. "I mind my own damn business. Always have. What could I possibly—"

The Monteague's sneer twisted into a snarling grin. "We have reason to believe that you're behind the recent unrest locally. Come with us, Finch. Don't make this difficult."

The Darkwatch. Just as the elves had CSIs, EMTs, lawyers, and hackers, they had people in federal agencies. Anger heated me as I thought of all my good-faith efforts in dealing with the elves. The road to my personal hell was littered with good intentions and wishful thinking.

In the next two heartbeats, I decided the werewolves, elves, and witches weren't the only Othersiders coming out today. I refused to walk into the cuffs of people who wanted me dead.

Tom had shifted out of their way, behind me and to the side, so he didn't see the flaring gold of my eyes when I dropped my shields and drew on Air.

The elves in front of me did though. Faster than human, they fell back and raised their guns. I darted to the side as they fired, away from Tom, fast enough to dodge one bullet. The second slammed through my left bicep, spinning me around and sending me into a car before I slid to the ground.

178

Worse, it cut me off from my magic—and from Troy. The bullet jacket had been coated in bronze.

"What the hell?" Tom shouted as blood rushed in my ears. "You said you just wanted to talk to her! She didn't do—"

"Shut it, Chan, unless you want to go down with her for conspiracy. I'm sure we can make something stick."

I was too busy swimming in pain to do much of anything beyond trying to stand and reaching for the godblade in its back sheathe under my shirt.

"Don't even think about it," the Monteague said, too close. "Alive is preferable, but dead is tolerable."

The gun he had leveled at my head was steady, and his eyes said he'd happily pull the trigger. I froze.

He extended a bronze band and open handcuffs. "Put these on. Slowly."

Grimacing at the pain radiating from my arm, I complied, glaring hatred at him. I'd escaped bronze once before. As long as I was alive, I could do it again—with or without Troy.

To the side, the scent of Aether rose again as his partner mindmazed Tom. "Arden Finch was here," the Sequoyah said. "You took her for coffee, and she left. We were never here. You're going to tell Clayton Rice you don't know what he's talking about, there's no need to surveil Finch's property or her person. She's just weird and private."

"Yeah. Of course." Tom's words slurred.

And just like that, they made sure no humans would dig into what happened to me or draw awkward attention.

Unless they find my blood.

As though he'd heard my thought, the elf holding a gun on me smirked and murmured a few words of elvish. I smelled Aether, though with the bronze I couldn't feel the usual prickle even standing this close to the bastard. With a shimmer, the blood disappeared. It wasn't gone—I could still smell it—but it would be hidden well enough until an elven cleanup crew could get here.

"Let's go," my captor said, wrenching me around by my good arm and hustling me toward a black Suburban.

I slid into a third elf as the Monteague practically threw me into the car. Another Sequoyah?

"Aww, the Lunas don't want to play anymore?" I sassed through teeth gritted in pain.

"Can it, bitch." The elf's eyes rested on the pendant still hanging out of my shirt though, and he pressed his lips together in a thin grimace rather than say anything else.

The Monteague started the car as the Sequoyah woman got in.

"Call it in," she said. "The fallen prince is around here somewhere. I didn't see that truck of his, but I caught his scent. If team two doesn't take him, he'll come for her."

I sneered at her when she twisted in her seat to grin triumphantly at me. "You fucking idiots shot me in broad daylight. At a *mundane police station* in yuppie-ass Chapel Hill. Do you seriously fucking think—"

"Blah, blah, blah," the elfess said. "Do *you* seriously fucking think we didn't have a sound dampening net over the whole area? That our techs can't wipe the video? This never happened."

And as far as Tom will remember, I left.

I wasn't ready to give up. "You will never—"

"Shut her up." The elfess settled back in her seat. Apparently she was the boss of this operation. Good to know.

Before I could say anything else to antagonize her, the Sequoyah beside me socked me in the jaw. I hit the window, tasted blood, and passed out under a wave of Aether.

Chapter 20

I woke in the dark with a throbbing face, a split lip, and an arm that ached something terrible. The chemicals in the new-smelling carpet stank almost as much as the cloying scent of burnt marshmallow.

Groaning, I swore under my breath and rolled to my back. The elves had me. Again.

My left bicep throbbed where I'd been shot. That it hadn't started healing was a bad sign. I reached for Air in a fury then remembered that they'd put a bronze cuff on me when nothing happened.

Still, I reached again.

Nothing. No comforting breeze, no sense of dancing molecules. The room temp hadn't adjusted either, leaving me uncomfortably warm.

Shit.

When I shifted to check my bicep, my hands came up together, bound tight with rope wrapped in duct tape. My feet were tingling where my captors had done the same around my ankles. They weren't taking any chances I could pick cuffs. Smart of them. I checked behind my ear. They'd thought to look for an earpiece and taken that too.

I was in a hot mess of trouble, and if I was cut off from my magic with no earpiece, Troy would have trouble figuring out where I was.

I was on my own.

Pushing aside the burgeoning panic, I forced myself to breathe and use my physical senses. A TV was on in the other room. Anime, from the sound of it. Dubbed. Two male voices were speaking over it with the sound of a fandom debate. Without Air to carry scents and sound, I couldn't tell much more. Elementals weren't the predators that elves, weres, or vampires were.

With an uncomfortable jerk, I shifted to poke around in the bullet wound, grimacing at the flare of pain. It had been a lucky shot—if getting shot could be called lucky—and the bullet hadn't gone deep. The bronze coating was probably doing me more harm than the slug itself. With a pinch against the muscle that made me gag with pain and disgust, I managed to squeeze the bullet out.

That left the fact that I was tied up and in the dark except for the light coming from under the door, with no magic and no allies who knew where I was.

Stay calm. Stay calm.

Options. I needed to evaluate what I had working for me and consider my options. My brain scrabbled and fluttered like a bird in a box. I forced aside the memory of my previous time as a captive.

I still had my pendant and my callstone. They clacked as they swung around my neck. That was lucky. The elves must not have recognized the callstone for what it was or had Leith's daring to steal my pendant.

Option one: use the callstone to ask Duke for help. Problem there was he'd want a hefty forfeit for helping me out of this. If I was going to call him, I needed something solid to offer. Would spoils be enough? Maybe I could lean on gratitude for freeing him from one of Callista's geasa?

Option two: use the Crossroads pass Elegba had granted me. My legs jerked, and I wondered if I'd be able to use the gift if I couldn't walk out. Something told me a trickster would put some kind of condition on it.

Option three: try calling on one of the other gods. But I'd left Artemis's ring at home, locked behind the wall of Air in my closet next to Mixcoatl's arrow and Leith's pendant. I didn't like that option anyway—I would be indebted to them, and that assumed they weren't already watching, treating this like yet another test.

Option four: be patient. Troy's contacts would be receiving the second Reveal video any time now. Someone in Otherside would wonder where the fuck I was. I didn't like that option either though. I wasn't some princess in need of rescue.

That left option five: sow dissension amongst my captors and push one of them into making a mistake. I broke out in a cold sweat at the idea what might happen if I pushed too far, but that was the best option I could think of. Someone wanted me alive, just as Troy had predicted. Having done the hard part, the elves would be reluctant to throw away their work and kill me for being mouthy.

I hoped.

Hope was all I had at this point though. I refused to give in to despair or wait around for a hero. I was my own damn hero. I mean, fuck, everyone thought I was going to ride the Wild Hunt with the gods and end the world. It was time to start acting like it.

"Hey!" I hollered. "Hey, assholes!"

Someone turned the TV up.

That just pissed me off. Grimacing against the pain of the wound in my arm, I sat up, scooted over to the door on my ass, and then dropped onto my back to hammer the door with my heels. "Don't you fucking ignore me!"

I kept pounding until the door was yanked open. My ankles were caught in a two-handed grip and twisted, forcing me to roll onto my shot arm.

Over my pained curse, the male Sequoyah from the car said, "Shut. The fuck. Up."

I wriggled as he spun me around to drag me back into the room. "You need to let me go. Or do you want the gods turning up?"

The Sequoyah scoffed and dropped me, frowning at the bullet I'd left on the carpet.

"I'm serious," I said in my most menacing voice. "The gods of the hunt turn up in my office. In my damn house. You want them here? They're always looking for an offering of blood and bone."

"Then I'm sure you'll do, trussed up and bleeding all over like that. Especially if you're unconscious." The scent of Aether rose.

"They want me to lead the Wild Hunt," I said quickly. "First place I'm gonna lead them is straight to you. I'm gonna go Atlantis on what's left of your fucking House."

The elf froze, glancing at the door which had swung half shut. "Not if I kill you first."

"You're gonna kill an elemental wearing the pendant of a prince whose House was supposed to be destroyed? The one fucking person who might have a chance at turning the Wild Hunt elsewhere?"

My captor hesitated. The burnt marshmallow smell flickered. I was getting to him.

"Come on. You know this is a bad idea," I said in softer tones. "Leith was worried about the queens and their overreach, right? He went about addressing it the wrong way, but…maybe you could do better."

Bile rose in my throat at what I was saying. Leith Sequoyah had been a terrorist, a misogynist, a murderer, and an elven supremacist—the worst kind of asshole. I'd never killed anyone before him, but I'd happily bury my elf-killer in his heart a hundred more times. His whole House had known what he was and ignored it, thinking he'd limit himself to killing low-bloods until he'd gathered the Redcaps around him and it was too late.

That kind of foolishness could be useful.

I held the eye of the Sequoyah in front of me, willing my face to stay neutral at the thoughts of the one I'd killed. "What's your name?"

"Doesn't matter. I'm not freeing you." But doubt had crept into his tone.

"Fine. But maybe you don't want to kill me just yet either. Maybe you wanna go have a think about whether the queens are still overreaching and what a resourceful fellow might do about it. How many of the Darkwatch will die when the gods return for the Hunt and there's no Huntress? I mean, unless you like being a pawn."

Snarling, the elf aimed a kick at my head. I toppled over trying to dodge it and took the blow on my right shoulder instead. A follow-up landed in my gut, knocking the wind outta me as dizziness descended.

"Shut up. Quit with the door."

The smell of Aether crested again, and without being able to sense magic, I was barely able to twist the Sequoyah's efforts.

"Sleep," he said.

I forced my body to slump as though it had worked, but all he'd managed was to make me sleepy. He didn't have Leith's strength, and I'd had a lot more practice in the last several months. I kept my eyes closed as his footsteps receded and the door shut behind him, not bothering to get up. Shit.

It wasn't a complete failure. Getting free on the first attempt was always a long shot. The goal here had been to get him thinking. Doubting. Questioning. To plant the seeds that would grow into noxious vines reaching deep into the cracks of lost faith in the queens and their actions—and failures—of this year.

My focus now had to be on getting untied and free of the damned bronze cuff. It was a solid piece, so I needed my full hand free to get it off. I'd seen nothing in the room that I could use as a sharp edge when Jerkface had opened the door, and the ropes were thick under the duct tape.

I thought in circles for a few minutes then sighed. I was doing it again: trying to do everything myself. *Just call Duke.*

He'd been pissed with me for defending Troy over Grimm's death back in the spring, but seemed to have forgiven me somewhat after I fulfilled a deal to hand over some magical items tuned to his auratic signature. It'd mean swallowing my pride to ask for help, but I'd be a fool not to use the tools the elves had left me.

Grimacing against the pain of bending my arms up, I clasped the stone and focused on a mental image of Duke. "Hey. You there?" I whispered.

Nothing. I massaged some blood into the stone and pushed harder.

"Come on, Duke. I know I'm not your favorite person these days, but I've got a deal for you."

That got a twinge suggesting he heard but was ignoring me.

"Look, I've been trying to give you some space but I could use a favor. It'll be worth your while."

This time he turned his full attention my way and the stone flared red in my hands as his voice whispered in my head. "I'm listening."

"I'm in a bind. Literally. But the jackasses who kidnapped me didn't take the callstone. If you can pop over here and cut me loose, you can have whatever loot they have in the house and plausible deniability for any collateral damage."

"My little bird is willing to kill elves after surrounding herself with them all summer? How intriguing. And morally convenient."

I swallowed. I'd been thinking more of incapacitation but I had to face reality. Someone would probably die.

Duke's mental signature was tinged with amusement. "Still reluctant, even after all they've done?"

"I'm not a killer."

"You keep saying that. People keep dying."

That hit me hard. I didn't answer for a minute, feeling sick and resentful. Lost in my hesitation, I barely bit back a *meep* of surprise as the room brightened and the air shimmered, resolving into the form of Duke holding a dim lantern. He'd used our blood tie to pull himself to my location like he and Grimm had to access Torsten's library.

I stared at him, wondering if this was going to be worth the price. I was still fucked by the bronze in my bloodstream though, preventing me from healing as quickly as I should. I might not want help, but I needed it.

The djinn tilted his head, flicking his carnelian eyes over me with studied indifference. "It certainly seems like you're in a spot of trouble, cousin. I can see why you'd be driven to get over yourself and ask for assistance. Where's our dear Prince of Monteague?"

I sat up and glared, wanting help but also annoyed as fuck about the entire situation and worried about Troy. "You'll take the deal?"

"Now that I'm here, it seems your little godknife isn't the only item of power these elves have. So yes. I'll free you from your bonds in exchange for spoils and a little fun." He grinned, the shadows from his lantern twisting over his face. The laughter in his dravite-colored eyes made me ache as it reminded me of better days.

"I want my knife back." I didn't know why, but the longer it was away from me, the more it itched at my mind. I wanted it back. Now. I needed it.

"Fine. The rest goes to me, and I'm not responsible for any elven deaths that might occur during your escape attempt. I wasn't even here."

I almost got hung up on the deaths part, but I was done being that foolishly naive when I was tied up and awaiting a grisly execution. I extended my hands. "Done."

"And done." Duke pulled a knife from the ether and sliced through the bonds at my wrists like they were butter.

I hissed as blood started flowing freely to my hands again then bit back a groan when he freed my ankles and the pins-and-needles sensation nearly blew my feet off. I yanked the bronze cuff from my wrist and, in a fury, twisted it nearly in half before throwing it across the room and reaching for Air again. It came weaker than usual but still stronger than it had when I first started practicing. I let go, not sure if there were more elves with Troy's annoying talent for sensing when I was powered up and not wanting them to realize I was awake before I was ready. I got nothing from the bond. Was Troy dead?

A crash like furniture overturning and glass breaking combined with raised voices from the other room. When I looked at Duke, he shrugged.

"Did you hurt her?" That was Troy's voice, though I'd never heard him that loud or that angry before.

My breath caught in my throat. How the hell had he found me? Or had he been captured as well? Captured and cuffed would explain the quiet bond.

"Fuck you, traitor." That sounded like the Monteague from the police station earlier.

"Did. You. Hurt her?" Troy repeated. His tone was so sharp it could etch glass.

"Of course we hurt her. Orders. And hell, just for the fun of it," the elfess from before said. "She killed my cousin. My House is in disgrace because of her."

"And it got us what we wanted. You. Stupid enough to walk into a trap," the Sequoyah man added.

"I told you he would." The elfess sounded pleased with herself.

"Never thought I'd see the day," the Monteague who wasn't Troy said, sounding disgusted. "He turned down every offer for years. Is she worth it? I mean, you've bred her at least, to be risking your life for a Goddess-burned elemental. Right?"

With an effort, I tuned them out and refocused on the djinn beside me, praying I wouldn't regret what I was about to say. "Don't hurt Troy. Please."

Duke gave me a sharp look. "Whyever not?"

I opened my mouth then shut it when the answer that came to me was not one Duke would be willing to hear.

He studied me as my face warmed. Then his eyes went carnelian. He cupped my chin firmly with one hand, looking strangely fond even as something in his gaze made me think he was thinking of taking my head off. "So you are your mother's daughter then. Seducing our enemies to win them to a cause. Perhaps Ninlil wasn't as mad as we all thought her after all."

"I wasn't even trying to—"

"Yet the result is almost the same as it was for her. Curious. Well then. I agree. Shall we?"

Aether rippled over him with a burst of lemon peel scent. The light from his lantern blinked out as he sent it Veilside. He grew, shifting into a winged lion with a man's head, until a shedu towered over me in the faint light coming under the door.

I took heart. He couldn't be that angry if he'd chosen the form of a protective spirit. With a wicked grin, I shoved aside my lingering fear and pulled on Air again. A nasty smile curled my lips as I pulled harder, deeper. My night vision sharpened, and I followed the arguing voices to the outline of the door. I was kicking some ass and getting my knife back.

And then the queens were next.

Chapter 21

Wrath made me push my gust of Air even harder than I'd intended. The door blew off its hinges, taking them and splintered chunks of the door frame with it. I strode out, and Duke pounced to stand just in front and to the side of me, tail swishing. He paced to the edge of the room, and I saw what had aborted his leap.

Troy knelt in a circle of six of his kindred, with three more scattered in the room, fury painting his expression despite his hands being bound behind his back and a gun pointed at his head. Hope, relief, and something I was afraid to categorize lit his face when he saw me.

My heart turned over. He hadn't run away. He hadn't tried to do anything political or clever, like he should have done. He'd either come for me or gotten caught planning to, knowing that it would mean his death.

"You assholes fucked with the wrong elemental," I said to the elves holding him. They wouldn't have me, and they wouldn't have Troy either. I pushed past the lingering bronze poisoning to pull in as much Air as I was capable of and started it whirling.

A ceiling fan wobbled in its lazy spin overhead, churning the air currents in the room into a gentle breeze. The mechanical assistance let me reach for them, and I slammed them into a mini-tornado then expanded the molecules to create a concussion of outward force with me at its center.

Duke roared his joy and plowed into the nearest elf.

A gun went off, and I barely bit back a cry as blood spurted. I pushed with Air, a pressurized bomb. Every piece of glass and every window in the room shattered. The acrid scent of an electrical fire curled through the room as the TV exploded. An armchair rocketed into the wall, smashing through the plaster, and the matching sofa blew over backward, trapping an elf behind it.

An elf who held Neith's gift.

Something in my mind wrenched. "That's mine!"

I kept the tornado whipping around me as I lunged for it, snatching it out of his limp hand. As soon as the grip settled against my palm, the itching tension ebbed away. I stood, eyes closed, in the center of a whirlwind, hearing a voice coming from the knife, one I'd never heard before. It sang to me.

"I hear you," I whispered to it. "I will do this."

I opened my eyes as the scuff of a foot warned me of an attacker. A film of red washed over my vision. I caught his fist one-handed and forced him back, drawing on the strength of the blade to overpower the much larger elf, one I recognized. The Sequoyah from the back of the truck, the one who'd kicked me not too long ago.

"You shouldn't have hit me." I tripped him and forced him to the floor. "Y'all definitely shouldn't have stolen my knife."

The elf was a slippery fucker. He half-rolled to dodge my downward stab, bucking upward after a feinted punch to throw me off of him. My foot caught on a toppled end table, and I crashed to the side, barely slithering away as the Sequoyah made a return stab. I cried out in pain as it caught me across the lower back, nearly a kidney shot.

That pissed me off even more.

With a soundless snarl, I rolled to my feet and launched myself at him, completely lost to reason. This time, I made sure to punch him in the face first, like he had me. Then I used Air to trap his wrists to the floor and pounded on his fingers until he let go of the knife.

Blood. Prey. Hunt. Mine.

I raised the godblade for a killing blow.

The elf shouted.

So did someone else from behind me as they caught my wrist. "Finch, stop! He's the last one. We need to question him."

I glared over my shoulder. Troy's face was pinched with the effort of holding me back. Blood dripped from a gash in his forehead, and the knife serenaded the crimson trail.

Hadn't he been bound? A gun had fired. It must not have hit him. That was good, right?

My mind was too fogged to put the pieces together. All I knew was that he was stopping me from doing what the gods demanded: hunting my enemies, the fools who would try to thwart the Wild Hunt.

"Let go, or you're next." My teeth weren't sharp, but my temper was. I let all the elements flood into me. Let him see the raging storms in my eyes.

Pressure built in my mind.

I let go of the elf beneath me and tried to wrench free as I figured out what Troy was doing. "No! Stay out of my fucking head!"

"Be still!"

The knife let me overpower the Aether-driven command but only just. I pushed to my feet. In the fog of my mind, a shedu roared. Blood and Aether scented the air, sweet and tangy and deadly.

"You asked for it," I said, going with the momentum of rising and stabbing at Troy's eye.

His breath hissed out, and shadows danced as he dodged. The knife crooned in my mind as it kissed his ear and tasted blood.

Troy shouted as red painted the side of his face. Then he used my own momentum to plunge the knife into the wall, his body trapping mine. Broken handcuffs swung from his wrists and a burn in the pattern of the standard-issue silver and lead cuffs the elves carried glistened above the left one.

"No!" I struggled physically and mentally, trying to push back. "You can't do this. I'm the knife of the gods, who cuts throats and clears the way for their return!"

Troy was strong though, both physically where he held me pinned and mentally, through the link in my mind. Too strong to challenge directly.

A smile twisted my lips. I had another way.

I let Chaos slither forth. It had broken through vampire glamour. It could find a path to Troy now.

There. A crack.

But going for it left an opening for him as well. "Damn it, Arden, be still!"

Something snapped into place between me and the blade's song. Sudden clarity tightened every muscle in my body as I stopped moving. My breath came ragged into my lungs, and my blood pounded in my ears as I took in what I could see of the room.

There wasn't anything left solid or undamaged, and that included the people.

The blades of the ceiling fan had snapped off, and glass glittered in the lights that remained. Smoke hazed the room. Eight elves lay where they'd fallen, most of them bleeding from ragged wounds made by lion's claws and unconscious or dead, one trapped under the heavy sofa, another with the shedu that was Duke standing over her, claws digging into her abdomen.

One was finding his feet, rubbing his throat where it was already bruising and glaring bloody murder at me, but I had more immediate concerns.

"Let go of the knife, Arden." Troy's voice was soft, but insistent. "You have to let go."

My hand cramped tighter around it. "No, I can't! The gods want this!"

I didn't know how I knew it. I just did.

"Yes, you can." Troy held me unmoving against the wall and fought my efforts to dislodge the knife, but his tone was gentle, if threaded with strain. "Arden, please—don't you move!"

I gasped as his attention slipped from me. The knife's song rose, and the red film started to fall over me again. That couldn't be good. I couldn't lose myself again. "Troy!"

"I'm here. Hang on. Sequoyah, don't take another fucking step unless you want her to kill me and finish what you started with kidnapping her."

The blond elf with the bruised throat stopped coming toward us, his expression now promising a double homicide. The shedu left his downed foe and gave him a casual swat on the shoulder, sending him flying before standing over the elf with a menacing grin.

"I'm here," Troy said again as his attention refocused on me. "Please let me in. We have to get the knife away from you."

Neith's gift raged, a violent cacophony in my head. I was suddenly afraid of the thing even as I wanted to keep it more than ever. I'd never imagined it would twist my mind like this. "Okay."

With my agreement, the pressure dribbled back, like the first slips of water finding their way into the cracks in dry earth.

"One finger at a time," Troy said, his whisper barely there against my ear.

I let my breathing match his. Focused. Peeled my thumb away from the grip. The song intensified, and Troy pushed more of himself through our strange bond, helping me hold it back. The scent of burnt marshmallow and spoiled herbs filled my nose as his body heat rose at my back.

"That's good. Another finger now."

Pain burned through me as I ripped my index finger away. Then my middle finger. Fire raged along every nerve, but I kept going. I forced my ring finger free and, as the pain roared, my pinky. I screamed as my hand cramped, trying to answer the call to take it back again.

Troy hauled my arm behind my back and pulled me away. "Leave it!"

Every muscle in my body spasmed. Troy lost his grip on my sweat-slicked limbs and swore at the Goddess. I went down, panting from pain and relief. As he stepped between me and the wall, I curled into a ball, still struggling not to obey the knife's song, to keep control of the elements and not demolish the entire house in an undirected burst of vengeance.

The elf spoke from under Duke's shedu paw, pain tingeing every word. "Are you seriously defending a fucking elemental?"

"That's exactly what I'm doing," Troy snarled. "She's under my protection. I'm oathsworn."

I wanted to open my eyes, but if I did, the whirlwind raging in my mind would break free and probably kill everyone in the room.

"For the love of the Goddess, why? You—of all people— know the law! Why the fuck would you turn traitor when you had everything to lose?"

"Think about that. Think about what I know, what I had to learn, what I had to do, to make that decision. Really think about it. With Torsten dead, she's the single most powerful being in the Triangle. She has the attention of the Old Ones, and if we kill her now, there is nothing and no one standing between us and the Wild Hunt."

That was exactly what I'd told this fucking fool. Maybe he'd listen if it was coming from another elf.

"The Hunt is really coming?" Sequoyah sounded shook. "I thought it was just some shit she was saying so I wouldn't kill her."

Duke leaned on the elf under his paw, eliciting a pained grunt.

"How do you explain this?" Troy asked. Wood creaked, and I tightened in my ball as I felt the knife in his hand. It didn't like him as much as it liked me. It didn't like the purple taste of Aether as much as it had the wildness of my primordial powers.

"I need it." The words jerked out of me, along with a gust of wind that rattled the blinds half-torn from the windows.

Troy didn't take his eyes off the Sequoyah as he answered me. "I'll hold onto it for you."

"It's mine. Neith gifted it to me!"

"I know. But just for a little while. Just until we sort out what's happening."

I shuddered. That might be okay. I could get it back. Neith wouldn't be angry with me. Maybe. "You promise?"

"I promise."

"This mewling wildling is supposed to be our salvation?" Sequoyah's outraged disbelief lashed at me, pushing me out of my ball.

Duke swatted the fool in the head again. If he wasn't careful, he'd break the elf's neck. Troy wouldn't be happy then, though I couldn't say how I knew or why that would bother me.

I needed that knife.

The Sequoyah might come at me. Like his cousin had, saying he was going to ravage me, ordering Troy's and Maria's bodies to shut down while Roman lay with broken ribs against a far wall. The Sequoyahs had healing magic, but all healers know how best to kill.

"Wildling?" Troy sounded icily calm, which probably meant he was furious. "She's a trueborn elemental and the first primordial in Goddess knows how many generations. But all you see is weakness, don't you?"

Another wave of longing hit me. I bent over my thighs and hugged my knees. Let a wash of power go in a gust of wind. Lighting crackled over my entire body, and the earth rumbled faintly. I grimaced, trying to get control of my magic.

Troy sounded scornful next. "If that's what you think, you're as stupid as Leith was."

"You've got some balls, saying his name to me." The Sequoyah spat.

"The fact that this house is still standing says she has some too," Troy said. "She's fighting the gods right now, Sequoyah. You think you could resist them pulling on your control of Aether through an enchanted object, let go of that object, and then let someone else take it, against everything compelling you to obey?"

In the long silence after Troy's question, I was finally able to wrench myself free of the connection with the knife and let go of the elements. I collapsed onto my side, teeth chattering as the red filming my vision fled completely and shock kicked in. Footsteps made me force my eyes open a crack.

"Breathe, Arden." Troy thumbed my eyelids wider then checked my pulse and frowned.

Lemon-flavored Aether rippled, and Duke was himself again, the tall, lithe Black man, his laughing eyes far too serious. He picked his way over broken furniture. "I have to say, this is all *far* more interesting than I'd expected."

Troy shot him an irritated look. "I thought that might be you. Are you trying to tell me you don't know what's going on?"

The djinni scoffed. "More that I hadn't realized it had gotten this far."

I shivered at his expression and his piercing gaze. Then he shifted the look to Troy, narrowed his eyes, and sniffed as though he was taking in a scent.

Troy froze and paled.

Duke studied us with a face like thunder. "With the gods, or with you, *elf*. Ishtar preserve us. The Council thought the issue was contained with Ninlil's death, but she had to pass her proclivities on to her daughter. And you had to—bollocks. Bloody flaming bollocks."

I couldn't say anything. Didn't know what to say. Didn't quite know what was happening, other than I was both too hot and too cold and I could still feel the godblade tucked behind Troy's belt like a trophy.

I didn't like that, but I fisted my hands rather than trying to take it back. Whatever the gods had intended by making me a gift of that knife, I was my own woman.

I decided what I would do.

In any case, Troy didn't seem inclined to explain himself or anything else, and I decided enough was enough.

"I want to go home," I announced to the carpet. "Now."

Chapter 22

Tremors shook me and a raging headache pounded behind my eyes as we argued over what to do. My demand put Troy in something of a tight spot. He wanted to take the Sequoyah with us for interrogation but didn't want our enemy seeing his hidey-hole in Durham. Troy was a wanted man in Chapel Hill, so the house he shared with Allegra was out, but he was visibly riled by the idea of having said enemy in my home.

We both refused Duke's suggestion of the Crossroads. I didn't need to be any closer to the gods than I already was, and Troy's mind had nearly shattered on just passing through before. It was the only thing other than zombies I'd seen him shudder over.

"How about this?" I leaned deeper over my crossed legs as Troy bandaged the slice in my back with a cheap first aid kit he'd found in the bathroom. He'd already done my arm, stoic in the face of my flinches of pain. "We take him to the bar. You do whatever you like in the basement while I figure out where the hell my car and purse are."

Duke gave the lone surviving elf a chilling stare as he considered it. The Sequoyah tried to return it, but mostly just looked shit-scared.

"I got your car," Troy said quietly. "I swapped the plates with the one I picked up while you were inside the police department, so the car the Darkwatch towed and dumped is the wrong one.

You'll be in trouble with the registration not matching the plates if you get pulled over, so don't speed. Our friend here will know what they did with your purse and phone."

"You have my car?" It was a reversal from the winter, when he'd hidden it from me in an attempt to keep me dependent on him for transportation while we worked on our plan to kill Leith.

"Parking lot at Lowe's. Where they picked me up buying defensive materials. Just like I wanted them to."

The Sequoyah's face reddened, making me feel bold.

"Hey, asshole," I said to our prisoner.

He didn't quite look at me and didn't respond.

I didn't care. This fucker was mine. I fixed him with a look that funneled all my rage at having been hunted and captured into a fine point spearing him. "What's your name?"

No answer. I tensed, ready to jump him.

Troy said, "That's Caelan Sequoyah. Lesser cousin to Leith on his father's side, so not in line for the throne. Much as with Leith, Caelan here has been running side missions that he thinks the Captain doesn't know about."

Caelan paled, and Duke chuckled nastily.

"*This* mission was definitely Darkwatch sanctioned." Troy smoothed a last bit of surgical tape over my wound with a surprisingly gentle touch. It should have started healing by now, but the bronze bullet had been lodged in my arm long enough to poison me. Part of the reason I couldn't quite use my magic at full strength and a raging power hangover twisted my guts. Maybe that was a good thing, given the state of the room. I might have leveled the house.

"Go to hell, traitor," Caelan snarled.

Troy snorted and rose, moving to our prisoner with a liquid grace that was the opposite of Maria when she was hungry but had the same vibe. "Imagine what I'll do to you if you don't tell me what I want to know."

His low, silky tone rippled through me. The bare whisper I got through the bond gave me the impression of a nocturnal predator with prey in sight, readying an ambush under a new moon.

I shivered, scowling at Duke when the djinni lifted one knowing eyebrow. I was beginning to think Troy wasn't anywhere near as simple in his personality or motivations as I'd once thought. Sure, the underlying thread was still duty and honor. But I hadn't seen him when he was actually *enjoying* all that…like I thought he was now.

Why me?

I'd overheard or been told enough to figure out that Troy had thrown away more than he'd told me about when he chose to side with me. So why me? The greater good and wanting to do the right thing made for a pretty speech, but the way his fingers had tingled on my back just now matched the shiver through the bond.

It wasn't just the greater good.

Duke crouched next to me as Troy mirrored the movement in front of Caelan. The djinni watched the elves as he spoke to me. "You see it now, don't you?"

"That he wants something from me?" I muttered, thinking of Roman's warning in spite of myself. I had to be missing something.

"That he wants *you*. Be careful, Arden. He's well and truly chosen you, and I'm not sure you're aware of what that means. For either of you. Ninlil certainly didn't when she allowed it from Quinlan, and look what happened."

"Educate me then, since y'all were completely and utterly remiss in explaining large chunks of my family history growing up," I snapped, jumping when Troy backhanded Caelan with casual, unexpected violence.

Duke chuckled under his breath. "No. I think I'll simply enjoy the show. It's not every day prophecies come to life so literally or so entertainingly. What are you going to do about the state of this house?"

I sighed, irritated at yet more secrets, then shrugged it off. I'd found my own way to this point. I didn't need the charity of his explanations. The house needed to be my priority anyway, before someone called the police.

The place was trashed. I didn't even know where in the Triangle we were. From the fixtures and furnishings and the size of the room, we were in one of the nicer parts of town. That nobody had noticed the sound of fighting was either a miracle or magic—or by design. Maybe all three. The richer neighborhoods spaced the houses out more, put trees between them as barriers. I was tempted to burn the place down, but I couldn't risk the fire jumping to a neighboring yard.

Looking at his nails rather than at me, Duke said, "You could leave it all with me."

I narrowed my eyes at him, managing not to jump this time when Troy smacked Caelan a good one and sent him toppling over. "Eight Darkwatch-trained elves, legally maimed or killed. In addition to our agreement about whatever items of power they have on their persons and on the premises."

"I did save your life."

Scoffing, I rolled my eyes. He might have, but I wasn't foolish enough to let him get away with this much of an overreach. "Rescind your threat to hang me by my intestines. Formally forgive both Troy and me for Grimm's death, to the Council. If you're taking the bodies, you take them as weregild, not as a favor to me or Troy."

"Done." He'd answered a little too quickly, especially given his previous outrage over Grimm's death. Whatever game he was playing had higher stakes than I could see.

"You'll also fix everything up here, report to me on whatever so interests you about these elves and their artifacts, and serve as my eyes and ears in the Crossroads. I want to know what the hell is going on with that knife. *Regular* check-ins, Duke, on my timescale, not a djinni's."

I hadn't been able to take my eyes off the bump the godblade made under Troy's shirt the whole time I was talking with Duke. I needed to know its story.

"Arden…"

"Take it or leave it. I can manage a clean-up on my own. Or you can graciously step in as a member of the alliance and, for once, fucking do something."

"We saw how well your clean-up went at the Umstead. All those cases under additional review."

I glared at him. "The mundanes would have done that anyway. I—"

A strangled shriek cut me off. Troy was leaning hard on Caelan's wounded leg.

"Troy," I said in a low, warning tone. It wouldn't do to have our captive incapacitated here, when we needed everyone to walk out to a car like we were all friends.

Immediately, he eased off. Good to know he'd take orders. I felt like I should have been more bothered about what was happening right now, but this Caelan asshole had been involved in kidnapping me. He'd bound and abused me. Fuck him. I had no sympathy left.

I forced my attention back to Duke. "That's the deal. Help me and the alliance or fuck off."

The djinni's eyes shifted to carnelian. Smoke hovered over him, a hint of his true form. When I didn't back down, he said, "Fine. The deal is made."

"The deal is made," I said quickly. Rising, I added, "Let's go, Troy."

He shifted so that he could keep Caelan in view while glancing at me. Apparently I looked serious, because Troy hauled the other elf to his feet then whispered something to him that made Caelan look sick.

Turning back to me, Troy asked, "Clean up?"

I tilted my head toward a very satisfied-looking Duke. "He'll handle it as a member of the alliance."

Troy narrowed his eyes at Duke as though he knew there was more to it than that but said nothing as he shoved Caelan toward the front door.

"Don't be a stranger, Duke," I said as I followed. "I mean it."

"I'm a djinni of my word."

When I turned around at the note of pleasure in Duke's voice, he'd shifted fully to his natural form, hovering avariciously in front of a painting that probably hid a safe or something. How unimaginative.

"Go on," Duke said, seeing me watching him. "I'll give you the first summary by the end of the day tomorrow."

"You'd better," I muttered, knowing he could hear me.

The front of the house was as nice as the part I'd destroyed in my elemental attack. Nicer, since it wasn't in pieces. Whatever Troy had said to Caelan had the captive elf silent and not fighting us as we reached the front door.

Troy pulled up short. "Finch's things."

Lips pressed tight together, Calean pointed to a door.

I pulled on Air and Fire to make lightning crackle. It was weak, but it came. I listened for a moment then pushed open the door and pressed myself flat against it.

Nobody there. The room looked like a home office, with an imposing wooden desk. My backpack had been emptied across it, and a snarl twisted my lips at the invasion of privacy. From the look of the device sprouting cables, they'd been trying to crack my phone. I hadn't set up the fingerprint lock—which presumably they'd tried while I was unconscious—and I patted myself on the back for that bit of foresight.

Yanking the cables free of my phone, I started to throw the device on the floor then thought better of it and scooped it into my bag with everything else. Might come in handy someday, now that Roman wasn't around to play tech support. I checked my wallet, pleased to find my bank cards, driver's license, and the monthly parking pass for the deck downtown still there. The assholes had taken the cash and eaten my snacks and my gum, which just seemed petty. My stomach grumbled unhappily.

"Keys," Troy prompted when I emerged and nodded.

Caelan grabbed a set from a dish on a console table next to the door. Silver flashed on his wrist, one of the cuffs blended with lead that was apparently standard issue.

"I told you, don't try to mislead me. This doesn't have to be unpleasant. Unless you want it to be." With an eye on the other elf, Troy reached in and grabbed a different key at random, nodding when Caelan slumped.

I let them lead the way out the door, following the elves to the car that chirped when Troy pushed a button.

We didn't speak as I got into the driver's seat, and Troy slid into the back with Caelan. We didn't need to. Sometime in the last few weeks, Troy and I had spent enough time together to know how the other thought.

I didn't know what to make of that.

***

We went in the back door at the bar. Troy shoved Caelan ahead of him down the stairs—literally, from the thuds—and I went to clean up in the bathroom.

My reflection in the mirror was haggard. My tight curls were tangled, and there was nothing I could do about it until I got home and used some conditioner on them. Bruises had blossomed everywhere, painting the rich sienna tones of my skin a blotchy green-black. Nothing was healing at the usual pace, and unaccustomed aches and pains wracked me, forcing me to move more slowly and stiffly than I wanted to.

Despite all that, I felt reborn. Afire with possibility.

The elves were trying everything they could, short of a magical war in the streets. I'd held a team off on my own. My work to grow connections and make allies had paid off, ensuring I had help when I needed it. Not only that—for the first time, I was okay with needing help. I was proud of myself for keeping my head and working through options. I'd been trapped and hella scared, but I'd come a long way from who I'd been in January, when the Redcaps captured me.

Maybe most importantly, I was learning that being the most powerful Othersider in the Triangle didn't mean doing everything alone or doing it myself. It meant acknowledging my power and capability, wielding it responsibly, and accepting help when I needed it.

I had no need to fear the elves any longer. I knew what they could do, what they wanted to do. I knew they would seek to undermine me. Capture me. Kill me.

But I was enough to stand against them. And where I wasn't, I had allies.

Tears brimmed, not in sadness but in relief. I was enough. Me, Arden Finch...Solari. More than that, I had been enough before the heads of each faction had pushed me into leading the alliance. Before my primordial powers had manifested. Before Duke had told me my lineage. Before Troy had told me I was a queen. I had always been enough. I'd just let Callista convince me otherwise, even after she was gone.

No more. I was done with being small when I'd literally been born to change the world.

Chapter 23

When I pushed through the door to the main room of the bar, the only sound was the TVs, all of them on a different channel but showing the same footage: the video of Troy, Vikki, and Sarah.

Overlapping newscasters spoke.

"Breaking news, folks. Disturbing new footage that appears to have been shot on a cell phone—"

"Vampires aren't the only fairytale creatures out there. We have—"

"After extensive checks, this is either a really good deepfake or completely authentic. Incredibly, witches, werewolves and other creatures may also live among us—"

"America is going to hell in a handbasket. That's right, I said it. Heathen creatures of Satan himself—"

I scoffed at that last one, drawing the attention of the mixed crowd of weres, witches, and vampires in the bar just as my phone buzzed with a call.

Zanna pointed the master remote at each TV in turn until they were all off. Tension ratcheted up as everyone focused on me and magic built. The iron-and-ash scent of vampires blended with the muskiness of weres and the not-quite-human scent of witch sweat.

"As you can see," I said into the silence, heart pounding, "the werewolves, elves, and witches are now Revealed in accordance with an alliance agreement to support the vampires. The mundanes will now have multiple factions to consider in whatever they're planning. I will be working closely with the parliament to plan our next steps."

Two dozen pairs of eyes stared back at me, some worried, some looking more beast-like than human.

"Was that Troy Monteague in the video?"

I picked out Joachin at a booth with Lola and two others. "It was."

The werejaguar tilted his head. "We hear he's on the run."

I sent a forceful nudge through the bond. Troy was gonna need to speak for himself on this. "He is."

"So I imagine the queens didn't sign off on that stunt."

"They did not." I couldn't stop the hint of a wicked smile from curling my lips even as I gestured at the mess of my face and the bandage on my arm. "I'm dealing with it. As is Troy."

The door behind me opened. Troy's footsteps were silent as ever as he came up behind me. "What's—oh."

"The video hit the news. Big story." I stepped to the side so we were shoulder to shoulder, rather than him at my back like a bodyguard—or a shadow advisor. He might well be both, but that's not the image people needed to see just now.

Consternation flooded the weakened connection of the bond, chased with a little fear that was hastily smothered with grim determination. Troy said nothing as he pulled himself to his full height and crossed his arms.

I barely managed not to jump when Joachin stood and started slow clapping with big booming echoes. The others in the bar joined him one by one until everyone except Zanna and me had joined in. Confusion and shame echoed in the bond as much as in Troy's uneasy shifting.

The clapping died down quickly, but the tension in the room had eased somewhat.

Joachin took the center of the room. "I cannot speak for our jefa, but speaking for myself, it's nice to see an elf with a sense of community. Y'all'a been strutting around acting like calling your leaders queens makes you regents of the whole Triangle for far too long."

Nodding heads bobbed in the room. Troy flushed and looked at the floor. I just lifted my eyebrows.

"What did it cost?" Lola asked in a soft purr from the booth, eyes narrowed.

Troy brought his head up, face hard. "Everything."

"Title? Properties?"

"Plus my incomes, my positions, and inheritances. My House and my family." A soul-deep emotional pain stabbed at me before he walled up the bond.

"Good," Lola said with a savage smile. "We might applaud you for doing the right thing, but I won't pretend the rest of it wasn't justice."

With a long blink and a heavy, if quiet sigh, Troy nodded.

I met every eye in the room, reading the mood. They'd accept Troy's deep and public humiliation alongside his Reveal as compensation for whatever they thought he might have done. Blood and money weren't the only currencies in Otherside. As long as the consequences with the elves stuck, they'd be satisfied.

The buzz of my phone again reminded me that if this room was in an uproar, others might be as well.

"If y'all will excuse me, I have business to attend to. Zanna, I'd like a word when you have a moment. A round on the house first though please. We're making smalls steps and the road ahead will be long and hard, but we should definitely fucking celebrate."

A cheer rose, and an orderly queue formed as I retreated to the back office. I felt Troy on my heels and didn't object when he slipped in behind me and closed the door.

"Good speech," he said. The new wood creaked as he leaned against it. The cuts and bruises he'd taken over the last few days were healing, except for the most recent. Probably due to poisoning from the lead-and-silver they'd had on him at the house.

I cleared my throat. "I'd apologize for making you explain yourself but..."

"Nothing to apologize for. I factored that in when I made my choice."

When he chose me.

We stared at each other. The old tension of wondering what he'd do had shifted. Still dangerous, just not to my life. More to my heart, now, which fluttered with that thought.

I cleared my throat and sat behind the desk, claiming the place of power in the room.

A smile flickered over Troy's face as he pulled himself up into a parade rest, accepting his part.

"Report," I said, testing him.

"Caelan will take a while to break. He's scared of me but not as much as he is of the queens. I was able to maze him enough that I confirmed a triad of Monteague House Guards were sent to Asheville, but he's resisting anything else."

An idea flashed to mind, and I couldn't help a small smile. "When Maria bit me, she said I reacted like an elf."

"Fell into glamour too far, too fast, which surprised the hell out of us both given that I've seen you look them in the eye. I remember." The words were delivered in tones just barely avoiding a protective growl.

"If we were to give him to the coterie..."

Troy's chin lifted as his eyes narrowed. "A gift of powerful, high-born blood to Maria, who has a particular taste for elves. In exchange for whatever Caelan said while under. That's devious, Arden."

I squirmed a little. This was not who I'd been six months ago. But I hadn't needed to be this person six months ago. I'd accept responsibility for the act. Because I'd have to accept responsibility for what would happen if I didn't.

"Don't get me wrong, I think it's a good play," Troy said softly. "One I hadn't considered because I'm accustomed to keeping everything within the Darkwatch or at least the faction. I just…I suppose I underestimated you, to be honest. I'm sorry."

My phone buzzed again, demanding my attention before I could answer. I glanced at the caller ID. "Roman."

All of the missed calls were from him, unsurprisingly. The other factional leaders had advance warning of the second Reveal. I grimaced. Roman would be furious, but there was no running from it.

Troy opened the door. "I'll speak to the vamp in the bar about ferrying Caelan down to Raleigh then prep him for transport."

"Thanks." I was relieved that he wasn't going to insist on staying. This next conversation was going to get real ugly.

Roman picked up on the first ring. "What the actual ninth fucking circle of hell, Arie? You used my sister against me?"

"Hi Roman. I believe we spoke about the use of nicknames."

"Don't you—"

"Enough," I snapped coldly. Deep in my heart, I mourned what we'd had even as I resented that he still leaned on it. "I did not use Viktoria against you. I ensured that all of Otherside would see the sacrifice the local wolves so valiantly made to support the Raleigh coterie when your sister saw the benefit to all of us and graciously volunteered."

"She *what*? I expressly—"

Keep his head spinning. Vikki is the thinker. Roman just reacts. I raised my voice. "I'm sure you noticed the elves and witches have also been forced out. How's your father?"

A seething silence damn near made me hang up the phone. "Still alive," Roman bit off. "Furious that Sergei and I are home and Vikki is unescorted. If I find out that Monteague son of a flea-ridden bitch played us, I will have his throat, Arden."

"You will not." I pulled on Air as I said it in the hopes that, just as you could hear a smile in a voice, he could hear my power. "He passed on information he thought was valuable to a fellow alliance faction and confirmed it this evening."

"Bullshit. He's not trustworthy!"

"Give it up, Roman! You left." At his silence, I took a shuddering breath and softened my voice. "You. Left. I was very clear. I would not wait for you to figure out your life with Ana or your family or Blood Moon. You were still out the door in less than a week. Everything I'd known—everything I was!— had fallen apart. I was in more danger from Callista than I'd ever been. And you *left*. On the faintest hint of a chance you could get more by *marrying* someone else."

Something that had been broken in me for weeks came to the fore, stabbing me like shards of glass in the chest. "You took what you wanted and thought you wouldn't have to pay for it. Or you thought you were owed, and that the payment included both Ana and me. I fell in love with you, and you still left. Just like everyone else in my life."

"So now you're falling in love with him." The wolf's tone was deep and nasty, like an infected abscess.

"I am learning to trust the one person in my life who has given up *everything* for me simply because it's the right fucking thing to do. Even if it means giving up *his* toxic fucking family and any hope of claiming the power he was born to." I couldn't keep the harsh edge out of my voice. Roman hadn't made that choice, even if it was, on many levels, similar.

"I could withdraw Blood Moon from the alliance."

"You could." I drew on my years as a private investigator to keep my voice even and pretend that statement didn't scare the bejeezus outta me. I couldn't lose the werewolves. "But then y'all would be alone. Revealed. And without anyone to call on for support if and when the mundanes decide wolves aren't an endangered species when they can walk on two legs as easily as four."

The line was quiet except for the sound of wind blowing in the background. I imagined Roman out in the woods. He probably had a gorgeous view for this ugly conversation, all forested mountain ridges and blue skies.

"You best hope your elf bastard was right about that threat against Pops," Roman finally said. "Because honey? If I don't have my hands full here with an ascension, I'll be coming back to the Triangle. And you and I are gonna have a reckoning."

"Good hunting, *babe*." I turned it into a snarl so he wouldn't hear the second heartbreak. I hung up then texted Vikki to make sure Ana and their people were safe. If Roman or Sergei were looking for someone to blame, I didn't want it to be Ana. Goddess only knew why, given that she'd been the reason I'd let Roman go when he decided to leave. Decency and a desire for someone to have a happy ending in all this, I guess. None of it was Ana's fault anyway. It sounded like she'd been treated like a damn party favor until she'd found Vikki.

Pain shuddered over me as I set the phone down with exaggerated care to avoid throwing it across the room. As often happened when Roman and I argued like this, Fire pushed at the underside of my skin. I clenched my fists to keep it contained, squeezing my eyes shut and focusing on my breathing as tears threatened. I hadn't been able to afford to lose my focus when I was just a sylph under a death threat. I certainly couldn't afford it now that I was a primordial with a staggering amount of world-bending power available with a thought.

Did I still love Roman, for his words to hurt this much? I didn't have an answer.

A light tap on the door brought my head up. With jaw clenched, I scrubbed away both tears and thoughts that this wasn't how it should have been.

"Come on in," I said, voice rough.

Zanna slipped in and shut the door. She knew with a glance what was wrong, but she didn't give me another lecture about being the wind. "You wanted to speak?"

"First, how have you been? Do you need anything for the bar?" Whatever my needs, it wouldn't do to insult the fae.

She lifted her brows and peered at me from under her mane of curls. "The bar will keep."

"The lords and ladies," I went on when she didn't say anything further. "I need to know whether they're going to Reveal themselves or if they'll stay in the fae realms. I also need to know where they stand on the Wild Hunt, but keep that subtle if you can."

Zanna drew herself up. "You wish me to speak to them on behalf of the alliance?"

"Yes," I said firmly. The only other fae I knew of for sure was Nils, the tomtar who'd made my elf-killer knife. Various Othersiders had been trickling into the Triangle, but I didn't know them. Zanna had been my landlord—even my friend—for as long as anyone at this point.

"An honor." She narrowed her eyes. "First the bar, now this. Your price?"

I scrubbed my hands over my face. "Zanna, I just need someone I can trust. That's you."

She gave me a sharp-toothed grin. "Not wise to trust the fae."

"I know. But if we can't all be in this together as Othersiders, then we're fucked."

That sobered the kobold. "Agreed. I will take your petition to the Chamber of Lords and ask your questions," she said somberly. "Will need someone to tend the bar for a week."

My eyebrows shot up. "That long?"

Zanna shrugged. "Summer is high season at court. Might be longer."

"Got it. Fortunately, one of the witches is available. Call Sarah. I promised her a job."

"Certainly. Will travel the Veil as soon as she gets here."

"I appreciate it, Zanna."

Seeming flustered, she ducked out, nearly crashing into Troy waiting outside.

I realized that Troy had felt everything I had during the conversation with Roman when he shut the door behind him and just looked at me.

"Don't," I whispered. "I don't need…"

I trailed off, not knowing what he was offering with his presence even with the bond wide open.

"What *do* you need?"

I rose and started gathering my things. "I need to go home. Read through the reports that came in while I was—unavailable. I need a shower and something to eat and—"

My voice broke. *A hug.* I'd been so strong and determined less than an hour ago. Maybe I felt even more deeply about Roman than I'd thought, to suddenly feel so alone and unsure again. This sucked.

The thing I was starting to appreciate about the warped bond with Troy was I didn't always have to say something. He took a step closer and, when I didn't react, another, until he was close enough to signal that he was available. Close enough to hit was the feeling that came to me through the bond and his body language, as he steeled himself.

I didn't want to hit him though.

My mind flashed back to the battle with Callista. Before I could mentally argue myself out of it, I went to him and leaned into his chest, like I had after that fight. Inhaled to find his scent under the elven mélange of herby meringue that used to scare the ever-loving daylights outta me but was starting to be...maybe not quite normal but not a source of terror anymore. Neith's gift called to me from where it was still tucked behind his belt, and I fisted my hands against Troy's back to stop myself from reaching for the knife.

As before, he stiffened then embraced me before I could pull away. "It's not that I don't want this," he murmured in response to my flustered confusion. "It's that I never expect you'll offer it. Because despite walking away from my family and the Darkwatch, I still can't grasp how alone you've been that you'll settle for comfort from me."

A sob choked my next breath. I swallowed it down. Squeezed my eyes shut against burning tears. Was that all it was? That I'd been abandoned and boxed in by too many people, so was grasping at the life raft that was the first person who did otherwise—even if it was an elf? Was I settling?

Rather than telling me not to overthink it, Troy pulled away and gave me space before I could panic. "Let's get you home."

I almost missed the whisper of desire he buried under duty and concern.

Chapter 24

The house was intact when we got there. Not so much as a busted window. Troy didn't sense any Aetheric magic hanging over it. Either the wards had kept everyone away, or they had gotten what they wanted with capturing both me and Troy and were confident of keeping us. I smiled to imagine the queens' outrage.

After a flurry of security checks and a shower, I stood in my bra at the sink, gingerly peeling away damp bandages and dropping them to the floor. The spread of the rust-red stains on them conflicted with the nearly healed gashes I could see. My powers were returning. Good.

Troy hadn't moved from the living room, where he'd been stashing the godblade in a lead-lined box from my bookshelf and then presumably looking for somewhere to hide it. The bond vacillated between longing and denial, desire and self-loathing. He'd been silent the whole drive over, turning off the A/C and opening the windows despite the heat when our scents blended to smell like herbs drying over a campfire after a thunderstorm. We'd very carefully kept our distance as we checked the house, and the zing of…something…had my nerves on edge.

"Are you going to help me or just stand there being indecisive?" I shouted, beyond tired of the churning stomach his conflicting emotions were giving me.

Only the bond told me that he was getting closer. His footsteps were silent. Then he filled the doorframe, six-plus feet of lean, delicious danger.

"What do you need?" His eyes trailed over my body, pausing on wounds rather than my tits or ass.

What a gentleman.

I shifted, turning my back to him so that the bandaged gash under my last short rib was closer. That one might cut through my tattoo, and I was pissed.

Gentle fingers traced the outline of the oversized bandage, seeking a loose edge. The warmth of his body made me shiver, and the scent of herbs made my breath catch. Troy peeled the bandage away slowly, carefully, not pausing when my breathing hitched as part of it pulled away from where it had partially healed over. He laid the blood-crusted gauze aside once it was freed, and I caught the dilation of his pupils as his attention returned to my skin.

The bond shuddered with repressed want. I didn't know what called to him—blood, power, or sex—and for some reason, that thrilled me.

Suddenly, I could no longer ignore the building tension between us.

He wanted me, and I knew it. I could no longer deny that I wanted him too. I let the feeling slither through the bond even as I kept my face neutral and turned on the water, soaking a washcloth to dab the edges of my wounds without looking at him.

Troy inhaled, his breath hissing through his teeth as he scrambled for calm and distance. His face was dangerously blank when I twisted excess water from the cloth and passed it to him. He held my gaze in the mirror as he accepted it.

"You need to be more careful." His voice was much rougher than his touch as he made his way around the edges of the adhesive on my back. "If this had gone deeper, it would have been a kidney shot. You'd be dead."

"But I'm not," I said softly.

Muscles bunched as he stopped cleaning and clenched both his fists and his jaw before dabbing again. "No. You're not."

When he finished, he tossed the washcloth onto the counter with more aggression than showed in his careful touch or neutral expression. "If something happened to you—"

"What, Troy? What could anyone do about it? What could *you* do about it?"

My breath caught as he leaned on the counter, his front pressing against my back as his arms bracketed me. His face disappeared against the corner of my jaw, and the warmth of his breath along my neck made every hair on my body stand on end.

"Don't make me consider that again." His voice was almost too low and rough to hear. "It was all I could think about when you were taken. I hated every second of it."

Warmth flushed through me, plunging low from my core. I wanted more than this. More than these almost moments, close and touching and hinting at more but not going all the way. He might be able to live with playing the pining bodyguard, but I couldn't. I refused.

"Take what you want and pay for it, Troy," I said.

The sandstone-and-moss color of his eyes had darkened to shadowed labradorite when he looked at me in the mirror. "That's a tall order. Are you willing to fill it?"

"Try me."

He shifted his jaw, and his secondary set of teeth slid free of his gums. He pressed his body closer as I stiffened. "Sure about that?"

I didn't reply. Didn't move as he ghosted the sharp points down my neck, his eyes never leaving mine in the mirror.

"Yeah," I managed, tensing again as the scent of burnt marshmallow announced he was drawing on Aether.

"Absolutely certain? You know I only ever come with everything I have."

My heart thudded. In the mirror, I could see the pulse in my throat jumping. I was goading an elven prince, a born predator. I'd killed the last one who'd come at me with everything. Totally different situation but with the cloying scents of meringue and the blood from my bandages hovering in the tight confines, who was to say sex wasn't as intimate as death?

I made my decision and took a deep, shuddering breath.

"I'm not afraid of you anymore. Whatever you bring, I'll throw right back," I whispered.

Troy's pupils dilated, flashing so wide that the only thing stopping him from looking like a vampire was that they didn't expand into his sclera. His hands shifted, one gripping my hip while the other tangled in my hair and pulled my head to the side, exposing a long stretch of my neck.

"Don't toy with me," he growled.

"I'm not. Stop stalling."

With a guttural groan, Troy spun me and lifted me to sit on the counter, my knees falling to either side of his hips as he pulled me to him. Sharp teeth closed to either side of my windpipe.

My pulse throbbed under the points, and it took everything in me not to move.

To trust him.

He was trying to scare me. I could read it in the bond, the near-desperate effort to throw everything elven at me so he wouldn't have to admit he wanted this as much as I did. So he could keep thinking the greater good of all of Otherside was what drove his actions.

Slowly, so slowly, I let my hands creep to his chest. His heart pounded like it would burst free into my hand, and his breathing was the fast-short cadence of someone trying to come down after a hard run. When he leaned away, I leaned in and slowly, carefully, trailed my lips up his neck, inhaling to attach the scent of elves with a new feeling, one I didn't have to fear. One that made me feel powerful.

Troy's jaw shifted, and when he mirrored me, lips on my neck, there was no hint of his sharper teeth. His hands settled tentatively on my hips. Then he paused.

I have to take the lead.

Of course—in a society where women had more power, he would have been taught to wait.

I couldn't help my grin and the surge of empowerment, and he shuddered when it came through the bond. When I kissed the corner of his jaw, Troy shivered again, every muscle taut under my hands as his tightened on my hips. I leaned back just enough to read unquestionable want in his eyes, slid my arms up and around his neck, and kissed him before I could lose my nerve.

Desire rolled over me like the stiff wind of a summer storm as Troy responded. He pulled me more tightly against him, his lips moving hungrily against mine. It was like when he'd kissed me at the Umstead but better because of the mutual buildup.

I lost track of who was feeling what in the bond and decided it didn't matter. We hovered on a knife's edge even as we drowned.

A banging on my front door made the both of us jump, and Air burst from me to scatter everything on my counter to the floor in a clatter of glass and plastic. Panting, we pulled back to stare at each other. Need tightened both our faces, and power filled the room with the choking scent of burnt marshmallow, roasting herbs, ozone, and woodsmoke.

After a pause, the banging started again. With a grimace, Troy glanced in the mirror and straightened his clothes.

"Maybe we should revisit those boundaries." I pulled my T-shirt on, moved past him, and headed for the door.

Frustrated desire, hot and piercing, echoed through the bond behind me, and his voice was rough. "Seems like we already have. Wait here."

I glanced out the front window. "That's Allegra's car. And...mine?" That was confusing, but I wasn't going to give up the point just yet. "We're in my house. The wards would have stopped someone with ill intent. I'll open my own damn door."

"Not when there's a chance you could be taken again. It's easy for anyone to get in a car, and not many people would have known where to find yours." Pain tightened his features as he slipped past me, stopped, and sighed, looking down at the floor then flicking his gaze back up to mine. "Arden, please. I know you're strong. I know you can handle whatever comes your way. But let me do my job."

The knock came again, harder this time. I ignored it, crossing my arms and trying to pull my wits together while my lips still tingled from the kiss. "What's your job?"

"Keeping you alive." When I still hesitated, he said, "You asked me to choose you. This is what that means."

"Okay," I whispered, thinking back to what Duke had said about me not having the first idea of what it really meant. When he put it that way, it was hard to argue. A little knot of pain that had been snarled in me so long I'd forgotten it slackened.

Relief eased the lines of his body. "Thank you."

I waited where I was, leaning against the bathroom door where I could see over the half-wall separating the dining area from the entry. The scent of Aether grew as Troy closed off his desire for me and refocused on defense as he approached the door, drawing his punchblade and keeping it hidden behind his back. I went cold as I realized choosing me meant really choosing me, even over the cousin he called a sister. Assuming, of course, it was her and someone friendly.

He opened the door just enough to see who was outside and speak. "Allegra. Iago."

"I thought I'd find you here," Allegra said. At Troy's lack of response, she added, "Don't be like this. We're on your side. Hers too, even if she doesn't answer her damn text messages."

"How do I know that? I've spent the last two days dodging the Darkwatch and getting caught pulling Arden out of Keithia's trap."

"Do you think we look like this because we fell down the fucking stairs? The House is a heartbeat away from civil war, thanks to you. Evangeline is calling the shots, and Keithia is letting her, may the Goddess burn them both. Luna is in open rebellion, and Sequoyah isn't far behind. We need to talk to Arden."

Troy didn't budge.

"Arden?" Iago called in a voice far calmer than the other two. "Estrella talked to us. She says she told you about the Ebon Guard."

I straightened from my slouch against the doorframe. "Let them in, Troy. Please."

With the slow, stiff movements of a tomcat considering a strike, Troy backed away from the door, keeping himself between me and the other two elves. The bond hummed with enough adrenaline to set me on edge. If he was that unsure of the person closest to him, things had to be worse than I'd thought in the elven Houses. I reached for Air, connecting with it but not doing anything more than sending a zephyr among the air plant bulbs hanging from the ceiling to let off a little tension.

"Stop. Shut the door." Troy brought the hand with the blade in it down to his side—not overtly threatening but visible.

I sidestepped so I could see them and gasped at Iago's black eye and the slash over Allegra's brow and cheek. She was lucky to have the eye, from the look of it.

"What the hell happened?" I asked.

Allegra ignored my question, her eyes darting between Troy, the knife in his hand, and me as she scented the room. "Troy, have you—"

Troy stiffened, but his chin went up defiantly. "Yes."

"Does she—"

"No."

I stepped closer, until Troy stuck his arm out to keep me behind him. "I'll say it again—What. The. Hell."

Allegra narrowed her eyes at Troy. "You really bonded to her."

Bonded to *me?* That didn't sound like the bond we already had. "Someone needs to explain themselves before I catch all three of you about the ankles and shake you upside-down until something sensible falls out your Goddess-cursed mouths."

Resolution made a rock-solid wall in the bond as Troy shifted to glance at me while keeping Allegra and Iago in sight. "It's a hormonal thing," he said. "No impact to you."

"It's an evolutionary trait particular to high-blood elven males." Allegra's emotionless tone scared me more than anger would have. "Their body chemistry adjusts to a suitable female and her alone. Basically turns him into a goose. He'll feel driven to stay by your side and defend you at all costs."

I blinked, not sure what to make of that.

"The benefit to him," Allegra continued, still studying Troy, "is that he'll heal faster if he's close to you. Distance will lessen and eventually break it. I hadn't realized a trueborn elemental would have enough elven pheromones to trigger it. But he would have felt it happening."

Troy shrugged, not looking the least bit guilty or uncertain. "I made a choice."

"Dammit, T, you could have been reassigned."

"I didn't want to be. I owe her. I chose to pay the debt in full, not just in what was agreed. Besides, can you imagine what *your father* would say about his second bonding to an elemental? Even one with as royal a bloodline as House Solari?"

Wincing, Allegra swallowed whatever she'd been about to say.

Iago stirred. "Allegra, let it be. It makes this easier."

Troy and I both tensed.

"Don't worry." Iago raised a hand, slowly, and flipped his lower lip down to reveal a tattoo in the style of an elven House mark but not one that I recognized as local. "We're Ebon Guard. We've been waiting for this day for a long time."

Chapter 25

With a sigh, Allegra also flipped her inner lip to show a tattoo matching Iago's.

"Allegra, what—"

The elfess cut Troy off. "I couldn't tell you, T. I couldn't risk it." She turned to me. "And why the hell didn't you answer my text?"

I frowned at her. "Because I didn't know if you wanted to help him or hurt him, and I didn't know which elves would be on my side. All I had was some random Luna cornering me in an interrogation room dropping vague hints. What the hell was that?"

"Girl, I *told* you that we magical Black chicks have to stick together." Allegra shook her head in exasperation. "I swear to the Goddess, if you're *both* going to be impossible to advise—"

Iago squeezed her arm and cut off her tirade. "Can you blame her? Or him? Let it be. We're all here now. That means the revolution can begin."

With a sigh, I pressed the heel of my palm to my forehead and waved them all to the dining table. It seemed we were all on the same side. For now, at least. "Be welcome in my home. My table is yours, my hearth is yours, and my roof is yours, while you are here."

Troy relaxed when Allegra and Iago answered in sync, automatically. "We honor our hostess. While your home is ours, our strength is yours."

"Fan-fucking-tastic," I said. "Thanks for bringing my car home. I can't remember the last time I ate, so I'm making steaks. Who wants one?"

All of them raised cautious hands. I eyed them and their injuries and pulled out one for me and two each for them. Troy had mentioned their high protein needs, they'd all been beaten to shit, and I had food in the fridge for once. They watched me warily as I grabbed a fork and stabbed the meat with more aggression than strictly necessary. I couldn't even tell why I was pissed off. I just was, and if I couldn't stab anyone else, then the steak was gonna get it.

"What revolution?" I asked as I splashed some Worcestershire sauce on the steaks and seasoned them. *Vegetables.* The elves might not want them, but I did. Setting the meat aside to marinate, I took out my biggest knife and started cutting peppers, onions, mushrooms, and tomatoes into large chunks then skewering them aggressively on little bamboo sticks. Probably should have soaked the sticks in water first, but fuck it.

I looked up when the elves didn't answer, looking uncertain as they watched me handling the knife. Annoyed, I drew on Air to make my eyes glow. "Don't worry. If I don't like the answer, I'll use something that doesn't leave a mark."

Troy snorted a laugh, but Allegra and Iago glanced between us and shifted in their seats.

At a nod from Troy, Allegra cleared her throat. "Our research suggests that the first Ebon Rebellion occurred shortly before Atlantis. One might even say it was the cause for the drowning of Atlantis. Some of the queens decided elementals held too much power over nature. They preferred that we be stewards over the woods and seas directly, not via intermediaries born of iffy and inconsistent relations with the djinn."

Iago took up the tale. "From what we can gather, the Ebon Guard were dedicated to protecting the elementals, who tended to pay more attention to shaping and tending the land than much of anything else. When the queens issued the order to turn on them, the Guard refused. The Darkwatch overwhelmed them and attacked the elementals. Grief-stricken elementals pulled Atlantis down in self-defense. We think they were weakened enough by their efforts that swift retaliation from the queens shattered them and sent them into hiding."

"I was right then." Troy looked sick. "We were lied to."

A chill settled on me as my stomach clenched. This didn't match what Val told me at our first meeting. It was worse, a false history written by the victors. We'd *all* been lied to.

Sorrow tightened Iago's features, and he looked out the window rather than at any of us. "It was why Javier was visiting Claret and giving blood to the vampires. He was hoping to gain entry to Torsten's library for information we couldn't gain clearance for in the royal archives. Leith caught him at the bar and saw the bites."

Troy bowed his head, and I had to brace myself on the counter against a wave of remorse and self-recrimination. It was bad enough that Troy had drowned the man to maintain his cover. Now we found out that not only was it a shitty thing to do, it also hurt what we were doing now. Secrets within secrets had meant none of them had the full picture. I felt guilty I'd been saved then resentful that I felt guilty. It wasn't my fault. It just sucked.

"I'm sorry," I said after a respectful silence. I started piling the food on plates. "You said the first Ebon Rebellion. Sounds like there was a second?"

"We think there were several over the years, but the records are all either sealed, redacted, or missing. But now there's this one," Allegra said fiercely. "We're starting it now. It's time to bring things back into balance. What the queens forgot—but the Guard passed down in oral histories—is the elementals weren't just the earth's stewards, managing floods and wildfires and whatnot. They also kept the world in balance. And the Wild Hunt at bay."

My eyes widened in shock as all the puzzle pieces finally fell into place. "Multiple trueborn elementals meant no single individual could be tapped as Mistress of the Wild Hunt. It'd take a critical mass, or the rest would stop the gods' choice. The wildborn aren't strong enough to carry out the gods' wishes, but a single trueborn primordial..."

"Precisely," Iago said softly. "It was once an honor for djinn and elves to be paired. The one thing we could do to maintain the balance and keep the gods away. We think, anyway. As Allegra said, the records that weren't destroyed were sealed, and oral histories have a way of being distorted over generations. We don't know how often a trueborn elemental developed primordial powers. All we know is what we've just told you."

Gathering up the food, I said, "I'm gonna need a minute."

Troy rose before I had to ask and opened the sliding glass door to the deck. He fired up the grill without a word, gauged my mood with a glance, and went back inside.

Smart man.

I could hear an argument happening behind the closed door but not what was being said. The bond carried something near fury from Troy, blended with the same righteous concern I'd felt from him after he'd dispatched the first team of elves, after the Verve incursion.

Whatever they were fighting about, they could sort it out. I was too heartsick and tired.

Assuming a predator species would want their meat as rare as possible, I made half the steaks rare, half medium-rare, and the vegetables charred and crunchy. All of them perked up as I brought the steaks in. The table had been set and water poured. I pursed my lips and frowned at that then reminded myself I'd welcomed them with hospitality. Elves were naturally more social than I was, although given a few things Val had said, I was wondering whether my intense desire for privacy was normal or another trauma response. I set the meat in the middle without a word, heading back out to double-check the grill was off and grab the vegetable kabobs.

As I'd expected, each elf took two steaks, once I'd made it clear I was happy with one and the veg. When everyone was full, Iago and Troy cleared the table and washed up while Allegra and I spoke.

"How long have you been planning this?" I asked her bluntly.

"It was obvious T had a thing for you weeks ago," she replied, quiet but equally direct. "Shocked the hell outta me given his law-and-order schtick, but it made my job easier. I didn't think he'd go so far as to allow a double bond, given its role in his father's punishment, but he never did understand moderation."

I set that comment to the side for the moment. "And what's your job?"

She studied me. "Depends on where Troy falls and what happens with House Monteague. He outranks me—or did, as a member of the House—so assuming you claim him, I'd take Captain of the Ebon Guard. Answering to the two of you."

"Your father's role, for the rebellion."

Grimacing, Allegra nodded. "I'm in the line of succession for the Monteague throne. But I can't stand what they've become. I don't want anything to do with Evie, our grandmother, or the House. Not anymore."

"Don't you have a twin? What's he think of this?"

"Darius is also Ebon Guard, but the Captain sent him away on a mission. He'll be in when he gets back to town."

"So you'll all throw in with a Solari? Just like that?"

"For a chance to make things right after Atlantis and stave off the Wild Hunt? Yes. Especially if it means keeping my brother out of trouble." Her eyes shifted over my shoulder to where Troy must have been at the sink, making it clear which brother she was talking about.

"Which makes me what in all of this?"

"Queen."

I sipped my water to cover the emotion that rippled through me at hearing someone other than Troy confirm it. A dish clattered, and Troy muttered a mild swear when the feeling hit him.

"What if that means going up against the Blood Moon clan?" I had to think ahead.

Allegra's gaze returned to me and sharpened. "Trouble with the ex?"

"Roman and Vikki weren't on the same page with the second Reveal. Speaking of, what was the Conclave's reaction to Troy?"

"Chaos." The elfess chuckled, amber eyes bright and seeming genuinely amused. "That was very well-played. Perfect timing. Amazing how many hidden factions there were, just waiting for the opportunity to make themselves known. Whether intentional or not, you've managed to well and truly disrupt the elven Houses. If you can sort out a court for a new House Solari, you might gain the Lunas as allies. Or vassals. Depends on who wins." She sobered, her narrowed gaze darting between me and Troy again as a tingle of Aether rippled over me. "The bounty on Troy might be higher than the bounty on you now though, so keep him close. That Aether bond is still strengthening. Together, I think you two could take on the world and the gods. Separated…there's a risk."

I turned to look out the front window, considering everything. It sounded like I was balanced evenly with the elves, as long as the alliance didn't break. I needed to get the queens off my back before turning my full attention to the gods and the Wild Hunt, so they had to be my priority now. The gods themselves were definitely on the list, given whatever the fuck was going on with the knife Neith had given me. I couldn't feel it now, locked in the lead box, but something in my soul itched. I still wanted it, and that scared me.

The werewolves needed to be on the list somewhere, just in case Vikki and Roman couldn't sort out their different visions of the future amicably.

Then, of course, there were the mundanes. The pressure on the vampires might have been eased with this second Reveal, but it didn't take the Sight to know things would get worse before they got better.

I tapped my fingers in an uneven pattern on the table, wanting to trust Allegra but still too wary. "Does anyone know you're here?"

"A few of the other Guards." The intensity in Allegra's eyes suggested she knew I was going to keep some things back. She didn't push though.

"I can call myself queen all I like. Doesn't matter if nobody else accepts it." I half-turned in my chair to watch Troy and Iago dry the dishes and put them away. "I need a critical mass, or I need the Houses broken."

She blew out a breath. "Will delivering one or the other finally get you to trust me?"

"Nothing less," I said grimly, feeling ballsy as hell but no longer willing to compromise.

"Fine. My price is that you keep Troy safe. I can't protect him anymore, not if he's outside the House and I need to play both sides. Don't be stupid, Arden."

I grimaced. "Like I have been?"

"Yes." Allegra scowled. "Seriously, girl. Your position, your power signature, the fact that you're the one thing holding the alliance together? Get you some Watchers, wait for the Guard, or lay low at the bar filtering intel. I don't care what. But fucking stop with running around fixing everything yourself."

"Allegra," Troy said in a low warning tone from the sink.

I flushed, having hoped he couldn't hear our conversation over the kitchen cleanup.

"Mind your business, T," she snapped back. "You're not a king yet, and I'll *always* be able to beat your ass."

Troy grumbled something before switching the water off, but affection was all that came through the bond. They might snap and snarl at each other, but unlike what I'd gathered from the interactions between Troy and Evangeline, there was real love between the two cousins.

Pushing aside the aching question of what it'd be like to have a real family, I said, "You're right. I've been foolish. I'll rectify it."

The room went silent.

"What?" I scowled at the too-blank expressions of the elves staring at me.

"Let's just say 'stubbornness' is one of the character traits listed in your Darkwatch profile," Allegra said drily.

I shot Troy a look, certain that he'd been the primary contributor to said profile.

He winced and cleared his throat. "I, ah, should go clean the grill."

"You do that," I said.

When the sliding glass door had shut behind him, Iago blew out a worried breath as Allegra reached across the table to squeeze my arm. "Seriously, Arden. Please don't underestimate the danger both of you are in. Especially if Evie has bought herself an ally in Roman and Sergei with this play against Daddy Volkov."

"I'll be careful." I wondered if the hint of a glow in my heart was what it would feel like to have a sister. I knew she was probably just pinning her hopes of Troy's safety on me but…hell. Despite my outrage at learning of Keithia and House Monteague's role in my parents' deaths a couple months ago, I had to admit my own desperate desire to have something resembling a real family burned hotter. Part of me felt like I was making excuses though.

"We need to get going before our absence is noted," Iago murmured. "Thank you for the meal."

"Least I can do if y'all can rally a rebellion," I said.

"Don't count your chickens just yet," Allegra said drily as she rose. "But we'll do our best. Iago and I have vetted Estrella and Manel Luna, Ophelia Sequoyah, and Zadie Monteague. Estrella, you've met. Manel works at the 15B Superior Court. Fi is a surgeon at NC Memorial. Zadie is a hacker, a good one, with a day job as a web developer."

Police, judiciary, hospital system, tech. They had key roles covered, for Chapel Hill, at least. A good start for a rebellion. Still…

"When you say 'vetted,' you mean what, exactly?"

Allegra's ruthless smile gave me chills. "You remember how I slipped your shields?"

I grimaced and nodded.

"Elves don't have your tricks to break the enchantment," she said darkly. "Plus Iago has his own talents. We're sure of them."

"Oh." A shiver rippled over me. "Okay then."

The question of whether I could trust her hovered in the back of my mind. I couldn't afford to be gullible. But the one constant for Allegra had always been Troy, and the need to save him from himself and everyone else. I'd trust that, for now.

Allegra fished a cell phone out of her pocket, a cheap burner by the look of it. "If you need us, use the number in this phone. We'll contact you the same way."

"Got it."

As we stood in an awkward silence, Troy slipped back in from outside. None of us missed him settling behind my left shoulder like a bodyguard.

"Make sure Keithia knows where I stand," he said grimly. The bond carried a flicker of fear, swiftly quashed. "I sent the notice, but it needs a validator."

Allegra nodded and closed her eyes, like she'd been expecting that. When she opened them again they were hard as amber. "Abdication and a formal claiming by Solari?"

"Yes. Sorry to make you the messenger."

"It's fine. I guess that means it's time for us to swear too." Before I could say anything, she and Iago knelt and swore the same oath Troy had at the Cape Fear River. "Stay safe. Both of you," she said when they rose.

After they were gone I was left staring at Troy, wondering what the hell to do with him after another kiss and now a burgeoning elven rebellion.

Chapter 26

I spent a couple more hours doing research, keeping an eye on the mundane news stations, and going through the reports Zanna had forwarded and the ones each faction leader had sent me. Maria had sent a note with some early findings from Caelan—the elves were plotting something more than just the assassination on Niko Volkov in Asheville. She hadn't been able to uncover what yet but was enthusiastic about trying again.

So far, the general uproar around verifying the Reveal footage was keeping the mundanes busy, but now that there were more Othersiders to contend with, I figured they'd turn to either pitchforking or legislating pretty damn quick. That assumed, of course, that there was any difference between the two. For those on the margins, there often wasn't, even when they were human. I wasn't expecting Othersiders to get a fair shake, which meant part of my work was figuring out what to do if we were pushed to fighting for it.

The problem was, I couldn't focus.

Troy kept himself busy on my tablet. The tension stretched tighter between us the longer we both minded our own concerns, the edge finer than that on our knives on the table between us. Every time I glanced at him, he was focused on his work, but I could feel the light touch of his attention in the bond when I was working on my own shit.

Suddenly, I missed Roman's enthusiastic pursuit something terrible. I dropped my feet into Troy's lap, intentionally being an ass to push him away if he wasn't going to make a move. I didn't expect him to relax, but that's what he did, slouching in the chair and taking my left foot in a massaging grip as easily as Roman would have.

My brain shut down and recalibrated as Troy's thumb pressed into the arch, and I swallowed a groan of pleasure.

From the darkly satisfied look on his face, he caught the echo in the bond anyway.

"Are you staying here?" I asked, the words flying from my mouth before my mind had a chance to consider them.

The intensity in Troy's gaze grew. "If you're okay with it. My safehouse is only ten minutes away, but that could be the difference in life or death. I can take the couch."

I eyed the sofa that was just big enough not to call a loveseat then let my eyes travel over his six-something frame. "You're not going to fit on that."

He shrugged, his expression neutral. "I'll make it work. I managed in the armchair the other night."

Something sparked between us as I wrestled with a response. "You'd be more comfortable if you took the bed."

My face flamed.

"True." His hands didn't change in their motion on my foot, but something tightened further between us. "I wouldn't kick you out of your own bed though."

"Bold of you to assume I'd be sleeping somewhere else." I flushed hotter. I was *not* proposing to fuck him, but if he didn't stop with the goddamn foot massage...

Discomfited, I pulled my feet free and settled them on the floor.

Troy sighed. "Arden, I'm not going to lie. Bonding to you means that intimacy is more appealing than ever. But my people have brutalized you." The gold flecks in his eyes sparked as a deep-seated anger flared in the bond. "Goddess, *I've* done you wrong. Sex is off the table until you can be around me without panicking when you unexpectedly smell Aether or elves."

I stared at him, the heat of desire going cold so quickly it made me dizzy. Was I using physical attraction as a shortcut to healing?

Probably. And he'd not just heard me but *listened* when I'd said he needed to work to redress the fuckery at Jordan Lake— that meant something. I hadn't figured out what I wanted to ask about this double bond yet, but that bit about intimacy was useful info. Sometimes the best way to gather intel was to act on pieces you already had.

Troy's focus sharpened as I rose to stand over him. He kept his posture faux-casual, leaning against the table even as the hand in his lap spasmed with a repressed urge. Maybe he didn't lack the desire to pursue so much as he was controlling it.

That was interesting. What would happen if I pushed?

I indulged myself in running my fingers through his hair, drinking in the flutter of his eyelashes and then the startled desire that flared to life when I gripped the black locks between my fingers and wrenched his head back. All he did was tense and breathe, pupils wide, and only the scent of herbs filled my nose.

"You like this," I said, hoarse with heady power.

"Yes." Still his hands stayed where they were, away from me, even as they clenched into fists. "Bonding to you makes me crave your touch. But I happen to like this in particular."

Oh, I liked this. The honesty. The control. All of it. Not letting up my grip on his hair, I eased closer then down onto his lap. His breath quickened, his cheek twitched, and the bond spasmed as he tried to hide how much he wanted what I was doing. I lowered my head to his neck and pressed my tongue to the pulse point, enjoying the way it beat faster then faster still when I swapped my tongue for teeth.

The hands Troy had kept so carefully away from me squeezed my hips then jumped away.

"Arden," Troy panted. "I—please."

I pulled back and studied him. "Is that begging?"

The red in his cheeks deepened, but his gaze was steady. "Do you really think security and politics were all I was trained in?"

My grip loosened as I leaned away and considered the implications. "What else?"

"I'd rather show you."

"I thought you said no sex."

"Bold of you to assume I need to have sex with you to demonstrate," Troy said, throwing my earlier words back at me.

For all of three long, slow heartbeats, I studied him. Read the bond. Deciphered his facial expression and body language. Asked myself whether I wanted to open this particular door then asked again.

"Show me then, hotshot." I stood and backed away then gasped when he reached for me.

His hands skimmed over me just long enough to find the balance point that would make it easy to lift me. I bit back a shriek as I found myself over his shoulder, watching the dining table recede as he took me to the bedroom.

He halted at the threshold so fast that I had to brace myself against his back.

"Can I go in here?" he asked.

"You'd better."

He lurched forward fast enough that I had to catch myself again, only for him to lever me expertly over his shoulder and pin me on my own bed.

"I will be right back." Troy's breath whispered against my ear. "I hope those clothes are gone by the time I return."

Well shit. Couldn't get any clearer than that.

Heart pounding in thrilled anticipation, I wiggled out of my clothes, listening to him grab things out of my pantry and drawers and not even caring that he was going through everything in my house again. The light flicked off before he came back, but his night vision was better than mine even with the moon almost new. His shuddering inhale spiked the blood in my veins.

"Arden…"

"You just gonna stand there?"

Light burst forth as he sparked a lighter then lit the two candles held in one hand. He didn't even watch the wicks, his eyes on me. I stretched just for the hell of it and was rewarded with a burst of desire in the bond, hastily tamped down. Whatever he had in mind was for me, then, not for him.

I liked that.

After setting a candle on each nightstand, Troy stripped. Whether intentional or not, the motions were just slow enough to call a tease, and I propped myself up on my elbows to get a better view.

"You're keeping the briefs?" I asked when he straddled my hips, the bed sinking under his weight.

"I told you, I don't need to have sex with you to please you." His voice was heavy with anticipation. "May I?"

I scoffed. "Sure, but—"

Nails along my flanks cut off whatever quip I'd been planning on making, and I arched under his hands with a sharp inhale. I was just healed enough for the movement to feel good.

His lips and tongue made patterns under my ear before trailing down my neck then over my chest, thrilling me even as he avoided anything obvious. Where most men would have gone straight for my nipples or the pearl between my thighs, Troy skipped around them. He didn't lean on the bond, but by the time he'd made his way down to the soft skin of my inner thighs I was panting with want.

"Troy—"

"I'll enjoy it if you beg, but I already told you, nothing is happening tonight," he said, his breath hot against the pulse point of my femoral artery. "Other than you getting comfortable."

I used his hair to pull his head up.

Heat flared in the bond, an arousing blend of frustration and desire.

It took me a moment to convince myself to speak the words racing through my mind. "I want you."

"Too bad. We'll see how things go in the morning."

The feeling of the bond was resolute. He had a plan, and he was sticking to it.

"Fine." I shuddered as I released him and gave myself over to whatever he had planned.

Savage satisfaction rippled through the bond to me. I was too aroused to have enough sense to be afraid. I surrendered to Troy's fingers, lips, teeth, and tongue working me over until I shuddered in completion. The candles guttered with the burst of Air I couldn't keep contained.

Troy growled, a pleased little noise, as he worked his way back up.

I didn't begrudge him the self-satisfied tone of his thoughts. He'd only gone for the obvious parts at the very end, when my body was thrumming with need and aching for the one little thing to push me over the edge. Then he'd given it to me, and kept giving until I called out his name.

As he kissed his way along my jaw, I felt the hard length of him behind his briefs. He wanted me, but he'd meant what he said. His kisses and caresses grew lighter, easing off as I came down from my high.

"How do you feel?" he asked softly.

At a loss for words, I gripped his face in both hands, pulling him down for a kiss.

"Mmph," he said when I let him go. "I'll take that as a positive review."

"They seriously teach you that?" I said after a few seconds of just staring at him.

"Royals, yes. Some diplomacy is best carried out in the bedroom. But if we're lucky, we get to use the skills just for the enjoyment of the act. Like tonight."

My initial tension at the idea that I was a diplomatic exercise eased as he finished his sentence, and I turned to my side before scooting back against him. "What do you get out of it?"

"Do I have to benefit for it to be worth it?" Strong arms held me tighter.

I let him pull me in, shifting to get comfortable before I said, "Yes," in a small voice.

"Peace," Troy said, sounding sleepy. "If I've satisfied my bondmate, the odds improve that I'll see another day."

I clutched his arm to me, suddenly cold at the statement.

This wasn't the first time he'd hinted his life had been at stake along with his title, and it added a layer of understanding about this second bond. The Aetheric bond carried nothing but contentment and relief though, like I'd done him a favor.

Hell, maybe I had. Troy had been caught between so many oaths and obligations among the elves and the rest of Otherside that maybe breaking those and serving just one person and one cause was a blessing. It wasn't for me to say. He was a grown-ass man with more training and experience than me. Without the bond, I would have lain awake, suspicious and wary that a trained Darkwatch agent was taking advantage of me, no matter how much I'd enjoyed it.

With it? I allowed myself to ride his mood into a deep, dreamless sleep.

***

The scent of rosemary and sage tickled my nose, too fresh and too close to be anything from my kitchen.

Elves.

I sat up, gasping and patting for the knife that was still on the kitchen table. My searching eyes fell on Troy on the farthest edge of the bed from me, laying on his side with his head propped on one hand and his eyes sad. His jade prince's pendant sparkled in the morning sunlight, much as my onyx one did.

I gripped the sheets as last night flashed through me—the ecstasy Troy had pulled from my body. My disappointment that there hadn't been more even as I'd let satisfied sleep claim me and chase away the bone-deep fear that had lived in me my whole life. His embrace and the slow, steady beat of his heart against my back. I was safe.

"That's why I said no sex," Troy said. The muscle in his cheek twitched, the one that acted up when he was really upset or frustrated and trying not to show it. "No matter how well I did, one night wouldn't change decades of conditioning. I didn't want you questioning your feelings on top of everything else."

"What feelings?" My voice raspy with sleep—and something else, something stirred by the sight of an elven prince trying to be as non-threatening as possible.

Troy's gaze flicked downward then back up to mine. "We can play it that way, if it's easier for you."

My heart thudded in my chest.

Slowly, Troy rolled to his back, hands folded behind his head.

I resisted for a heartbeat. Two.

Let my eyes travel over his bare chest, his exposed throat.

Three. Four. Five.

Troy didn't look at me, but I saw the tension in his body and felt it in the bond. He knew he was making himself prey. Allowed it, waiting in anticipation.

Six. Seven. Eight.

I eased up to my knees.

Nine. Ten.

Straddled him.

Still he kept his hands behind his head and avoided my eyes.

"Look at me," I said.

He obeyed, and gold flickered in the morning light.

"What the hell is this?"

His gaze pierced mine and dove into my core. "I've forsaken every oath except yours. I want you, not for your power or whatever position I might find with you, but as a woman. Because I have spent the last six months learning about you, looking for a reason not to admire you, and failing."

My breath caught. I felt like prey, but I also had never felt more desired in my life.

"I refuse to make what you've been through worse than it already is, but I don't want to be a fling or a rebound."

I shuddered, and under me, his body echoed mine as his pupils dilated. "What if it helped?"

He swallowed hard, and his eyes slipped to my tits before he could pull them back up. "Arden…"

"What if the only way out is through?" I smirked, unable to help myself. "Or in."

"Is that really what you want? After waking up in a panic?"

"What if I say yes?"

I was on my back with Troy's weight pressing me into the mattress before I could take my next breath. He pinned my wrists over my head and leaned close to whisper in my ear as my heart thudded to send blood scalding through my body. "Then that's too many 'what ifs' for me. For once in my damned life, I'm playing for what *I* want, and it's not a one-bang deal." Pulling back, he met my eyes solidly, his body keeping mine pinned with his hips heavy between my thighs. "You have a choice to make, Arden. I'm not going to pretend it'll be simple to say yes or no either way. But you offered a choice. My life. However it makes your reign legitimate."

I couldn't breathe—not because of his body weight, but because of the weight of his words.

"My life, you have. I'll do what I have to do to stay close to you. The manner in which you claim your legitimacy is your choice. Assign me a title in your court if you want to be a queen. I'd be your knight as easily as your prince consort. But if it's consort…that's a path to king for me. A once-in-a-lifetime chance for—"

"Power?" I wriggled and tried to draw back in sudden bitterness even as I wanted the physical promise of him.

"Love." He released me and rolled off to the side, resuming his open position from before. Only this time, rather than being reassuring to me, it felt like need. Aching vulnerability masquerading as confidence.

Goosebumps prickled over me. Had he said…"Love?"

"Consorts aren't supposed to fall in love with their matches," Troy said bitterly. "Or bond to them. We're supposed to stud. Offer pleasure and advice. And then leave when bid, passed on to the next match. Or be punished, so that we never accumulate enough power to usurp a queen. That was the life laid out for me. Before you."

I blinked rapidly, my idea of the elven power structure rapidly rearranging itself once again. His tone was caustic enough to make it sound like the punishment he'd mentioned had been personal somehow.

Then there was what Allegra had said about his father.

He sighed and scrubbed his hands over his face. "I'm not going to offer you a false choice or require dinner and a movie in exchange for my support. You have me either way. I will fight or die for you either way."

Blood heated my face as, whether Troy knew it or not, he reminded me of Roman's deal back in the winter. He'd offered to help if I agreed to go on a date with him. I'd gone along with it, but it should have been a red flag.

"Then what was last night?" I snapped, grouchy and embarrassed and confused.

Troy glanced at me, reading my expression as much as the bond before he answered carefully. "Your exact words were, 'Show me then, hotshot.' I was showing you."

Frustrated as hell, I decided it was time to get up and take a shower. I couldn't tell him what I wanted from him because I didn't fucking know, and his not wanting to deepen our involvement further without knowing my intentions was fair, whether I liked it or not. The shitty thing was that I wanted what he'd shown me. All of it. I wanted everything he could bring to the table politically and physically. But after years of wishing someone would see me—would choose me, truly and deeply choose me—I was too hung up on what it would mean for *me* to also choose *him*.

Fuck. That saying about being careful what you wished for had slapped me squarely across the face.

Chapter 27

I showered then cooked breakfast while Troy took his turn. The sight of him leaning a hip against the kitchen counter, hair slicked back and with a day's worth of stubble, nearly made me choke on desire and surprise. I hadn't heard him come out of the bathroom and had been too wrapped up in my thoughts to notice the shifting air molecules.

When the food was done, I extended a plate of bacon and eggs I barely managed not to drop. He accepted it. We sat in silence at the dining table. Not awkward, just tense. Considering. Me slightly baffled by eating breakfast at all, let alone with him. Troy seeming very cognizant of every thought running through my head and doing his best to pretend he wasn't until I finally had the sense to put my walls up.

I needed to do something. My skin itched with a need to act.

"If Allegra and Iago are working on the elves, I need to refocus on the rest of Otherside," I said. "The humans are losing their shit. My phone has been going off all morning with alerts on all things paranormal and supernatural. Some of it isn't even real. Aliens? It's out of control."

Even as I spoke, the device buzzed again. Annoyed, I reached to swipe the message then froze as I read the headline. "Shit."

Troy looked at his own phone. "That's putting it mildly."

Riots had kicked off in Raleigh. It seemed too early in the day for the protests to have turned violent, but the mundanes had

had all night to ruminate and argue over the werewolf-elf-witch footage—not that any of them seemed to know what Troy was. Fox News was pushing an outrageous apocalypse-slash-Rapture angle, but even the more progressive networks seemed completely at a loss.

Watching sci-fi and fantasy movies was one thing. Suspecting that myths and legends were real was another. Having multiple confirmed non-human species come out in the open, with most of them seeming capable of eating humans, had been a straw too many after a summer of vampire Reveals and protests. The mundanes had reached their breaking point.

"I have to get down to Raleigh," I said.

"Is that...wise?"

Scowling at Troy, I leaned on the table. "You gonna stop me?"

He eased back in his chair and nodded at the sink. "I was standing right over there when you promised Allegra you'd be careful," he said in tones much more level than I would have managed.

"Troy—"

"Arden. Who do you want to be?"

"Me! I'm..." Words failed as my brain ran in a circle. I couldn't say what I was or who I wanted to be. He was right, as much as I hated to admit it. I'd just been kidnapped. I'd just come to the conclusion that I needed to be smarter about how I moved in Otherside. Yet here I was, ready to run off into the heart of a riot with half a thought, because who else was going to fix it?

Troy waited for me to think it through. Didn't push. Didn't cajole or argue or threaten or belittle me. Just waited.

"I hate this," I whispered. "I thought being Arbiter meant helping people."

Warm sympathy curled through the bond. "It does. But maybe not in the way you're used to doing it."

"Maria—"

"Is older than both of us combined several times over and knows how this works." He raised a hand and started ticking off fingers. "You already helped her deal with her challengers. You got three more Otherside factions out to take the direct pressure off of her. You sent her a gift of strong blood and information last night. Just because the riots are in Raleigh doesn't mean she's in direct danger or that there's nothing she can do on her own."

I paced, not even bothering to hide my agitation. Zephyrs stirred the glass bulbs and their air plants hanging overhead and set the parlor palms to rustling. I was an investigator. It was my job to investigate things. Find the truth. Set problems right. Protect people and find justice. That was more than just what I did—it was who I was.

And now I couldn't be that?

I leaned against the kitchen sink and looked at my feet. I'd made so many promises. To Otherside. To Allegra, to keep Troy safe while she sorted out the Ebon Guard. To Vikki, Terrence, and Ximena, that they and their people would be protected. Hell, to myself, that I'd start doing better—whatever it took to heal.

But I couldn't do any of that if the humans burned the Triangle and caused more fear and rage than the lich lord had because they didn't want to get with the fucking program.

Troy sensed the firming of my thoughts. "Arden, *think*. If you really are going to offer me a place in your court, please just think about this."

I snarled when I saw it.

"The elves did this. They've been managing how far the protests got. We escaped, so they let the pot boil over." I flushed at the pride reaching me in the bond, alongside grim resignation and sadness.

"That's my guess," Troy said softly. "The Conclave went from using Darkwatch teams to capture you to elves leaning on human institutions to—"

"To pushing the mundanes into a riot. And probably using their law enforcement connections to put out a BOLO on Vikki. Likely you as well."

Troy frowned at the last statement. "Goddess burn it. I've been focused on the elf angle. I missed that."

I started pacing again, mind racing. This was like being on the edge of cracking a case, and the old invigoration started chasing out the new frustration. I had to face my fears and my biggest remaining enemy. I had to take the fight to Keithia and the other queens before the elves engineered a situation that destroyed the Triangle. Destroyed my *home*. I couldn't wait for the Ebon Guard to come riding to the rescue.

Elves, like most of Otherside, lived on longer time scales than humans. They thought on longer scales as well. Had I been raised among them or the djinn, rather than as a mundane, I might too.

But humans needed things done *now* to fix the immediate symptomatic problem, not the long-term one or the deeper malady. Much like them, Evangeline was young and still capable of moving fast, still driven by immediacy and revenge, which was probably why Keithia was giving her such free rein. That and, if the heir-apparent fucked up, Keithia had someone to take the fall. Allegra could always be elevated to her place.

This was a problem I was uniquely suited to solve, which took the sting out of staying away from Raleigh.

Troy straightened in his chair when I met his eyes, pupils dilating slightly.

"Orders, my queen?" His whisper carried equal parts fear, desire, and anticipation.

I stalked over to him and ran a fingernail along his jaw to make him shudder, tilting his head up as he had mine a time or two. The inversion of roles felt powerful. "I will take your *advice* and stay away from Raleigh. But I'm not sitting idle. You and Vikki need to be protected."

"I don't—"

I raised my eyebrows, and he shut up, swallowing hard as the bond tightened.

When I was sure he'd listen, I said, "You revealed the elves. The humans might not know it, but your people do. Vikki and Sarah showed their faces. None of you have as much protection as Maria does."

"True."

"You're right. As a primordial elemental, my magic is not the best choice for containing a human riot."

Troy started to relax.

"But it is suitable for other tasks. Like, say, pulling down Keithia and eliminating the fuel source of those riots."

Burnt marshmallow scent rose hard and fast, and my skin crawled with the amount of Aether Troy was handling. Every muscle in his body tensed, and the points of his secondary teeth flickered in a snarl.

I drew on Air and dropped my hand from his face to give him space but didn't back off. I was about to find out if Roman had been right about him or if Noah had. Protecting me had broken Troy from his family. Going with me to destroy his House would be more than most people would agree to.

"I'm not asking you to come with me." I kept my voice slow and quiet as the strain grew in his face.

My heart raced, and sweat broke out down my back. I was dealing with a predator species, one who'd been running on too little sleep, too many hard decisions, and too much loss in the last week. Troy was already cracking. Either way, this would shatter him. Whether the breaking would set him free or destroy him was something I had no control over.

Troy arced backward in intense pain then exhaled heavily and slumped. "You don't have to. I told you—I'm yours."

The smell of Aether faded, and the prickles along my skin eased. "You okay?"

He took a shuddering breath and rolled his neck. Sweat had broken out on his forehead, and the air smelled of rotting herbs. "That was my last oath to House Monteague breaking. I should have attacked you then. A direct, credible, and imminent threat to my House and my—to Keithia. They would have been counting on it as a failsafe."

I blinked, kicking myself. All my big talk and I hadn't even thought of this. Of course there'd been a magical safeguard. "That's why you let yourself bond to me?"

Eyes closed, Troy nodded. "Partly. The biological need to protect you—even from myself—overrode the Aetheric oath. The oath unraveled." He snorted, seeming equally relieved and derisive. "Magic can't defeat blood. Another reason we're not permitted to bond."

"You couldn't have warned me?"

"There's a non-disclosure clause written into the oath."

"Okay." I hoped I didn't sound as shaken as I felt. I wanted to push. My natural curiosity practically demanded it. But I set boundaries for myself. I could extend Troy enough trust and respect to let him deal with this shit in his own way, given what I'd just witnessed.

"Thank you," he said after a wary silence. "Arden, it means a lot to be taken on faith. No matter what or how much I did for the Conclave and the Captain, or how many times I proved myself with blood and death, my loyalty was always in question."

I winced. "I'm not going to pretend I don't have questions. But maybe I'm just foolish enough to look at how much you've tried to prove yourself up to now and give you some leeway."

Troy rose, and I backed up just enough that he could stand without bumping into me. Slowly, he leaned in. Pressed his lips to mine. Slipped his hand to the back of my neck when I didn't back away. I stiffened then softened, leaning into the kiss. The longer we spent in each other's company, the more I wanted these moments.

When we were on the verge of more, he broke it and rested his forehead against mine. "We'll find the balance. Somehow."

I tilted my head and stole one last kiss before pulling away and moving to gather everything I'd need to start a day of investigation. "Until then, I need you and Vikki at the bar with me. Sarah should already be there. The Conclave or the Darkwatch might risk the bar, but then all of the local factions will be against them."

"Makes sense. I can fortify the building's defenses while we're there."

I looked up from the text message I'd been composing to Vikki. "The witches and weres—"

"Did what they could with what they knew. The bar is perfectly safe against human mobs and an excellent choice amidst the riots. It's my people I'm worried about." Troy offered a lopsided smile. "Who better to prep defenses than the man who was once tasked with finding an entry?"

I blinked and shook my head then finished my message to Vikki. I followed it up with a general update to all the faction leaders and their seconds. *Anyone who needs protection should be at the bar*, I wrote. *Anyone who can spare defenders is welcome to send them. I will be handling our enemies.*

As we walked out the front door, my phone buzzed with affirmative responses. If the humans or the elves made an attempt, they'd regret it.

***

At the bar, Sarah served drinks with a subdued nervousness, and Vikki's mood was far from its usual exuberance. She and Troy were reviewing the defenses. The shared experience of having Revealed themselves against the orders of their factions seemed to have tightened the working relationship they'd developed while handling security at the vampire event.

I'd retreated to Callista's office—my office—to review reports. Zanna still wasn't back, and there was no news from the witches or the fae. I was still reading when lemony Aether made me sit bolt upright.

"Look at you, all serious." Duke materialized in the room in his favorite form, the lean young Black man with laughing eyes.

My mind spun as I tried to figure out how he'd gotten past the wards. Then I remembered that I was still wearing his callstone. I leaned back in my chair and clasped my hands in what I hoped would look more like the Godfather than a nervous girl. "Duke. Glad you're keeping to our arrangement."

The djinni tilted his head, looking at me sideways with a sparkle in his dravite eyes as he grinned. "Something like that. Those eight elves bought some information."

"Do tell."

"The elves, or at least the Conclave, think a unified triad of queens can replace an elemental as Mistress of the Hunt."

I sat up, not having realized there might be another way for the gods to get what they wanted. "Credible?"

Duke scoffed. "Not in the slightest. If it were, the gods wouldn't have needed to wait tens of millennia from the last

Great Flood to now for a vulnerable primordial elemental. The Conclave has forgotten, or ignored, that *both* halves of Aether are needed to deal with the gods. An unfortunate shortcoming, but they only live a few hundred years."

Djinn, with their greater Aetheric self-healing abilities, lived a few *thousand* years, so it was no wonder he found elven lifespans a deficit.

I tapped my fingers on the desk, thinking. "They must discount the Ebon Guard as well then."

Duke's attention sharpened, and his eyes flickered to carnelian before returning to dravite. "It has been a very long time since I heard that name mentioned, Arden dear. Pray tell, where did you hear of it?"

I smiled, pleased to know something more than he did and more to keep something from him. "Nunyo. What does concern you is that I need to keep my people safe. And that doing so involves removing Keithia and Evangeline Monteague."

He smiled with violent delight. "How intriguing."

Leaning back in my chair, I decided quickly how much of my plan to tell him. "I have reason to believe the local Conclave is the reason the riots here have escalated so much more quickly than in New York or other cities. I need to knock out a leg on the stool. Today, before the elves realize I'm not taking the bait and heading to Raleigh."

"A wise decision."

"To that end, I need to—"

A sharp, burning pain stabbed my chest below the right collarbone, where I'd been hit by Mixcoatl's lightning arrow. I gasped, curling over it, in too much pain to think.

"Arden?"

Before I could respond, I got a wave of fear and rage and hatred in the bond. I looked at my clean fingers and forced myself to breathe.

There was no blood, nothing wrong with my scar. I hadn't been shot.

Troy had.

Humans were automatically turned away from the bar given the magics anchored in it, and it was unlikely they were even aware of the structure on a conscious level, so there was really only one party that would dare.

Elves were attacking the bar—and all of Otherside in the process.

My connection with Troy cut off abruptly.

Chapter 28

I forced myself to stand as I figured out what had happened. "Troy. Someone's shot Troy."

"Stay here." Duke dematerialized in an eyeblink.

"Like hell."

Troy might be dead. I wasn't sure why Duke would volunteer to check on an elf, but I didn't trust him on it. Lacking any control over the djinn half of Aether meant I had to do things the long way. I vaulted over the desk and dashed out to find the bar in an uproar. A blood-spattered Vikki was making her way to me.

"Arden!" she called.

The crowd let her through, the blended scents of too many agitated Othersiders making the bar reek.

"Back here. Now." I pushed back through the door to the back office. She followed, and the moment the door shut, I asked, "Are you hurt?"

"No. They missed me."

"Where is he?"

She pressed something into my hand. I looked down to see Troy's pendant, the silver-wrapped jade identical in style to the onyx-wrapped gold around my neck. Blood stained the chain, and the clasp was broken.

My heart stopped. "Is he—"

"Not dead." Fear tightened her eyes, and she stank of rotted cedar. "He told me to give you this and forced me away with Aether, the bastard. Before they took him."

"Who?"

The sharp scent of lemon peel cut through as Duke reappeared. "From the looks of things, Keithia's reclaimed her errant grandson." He glanced at Vikki. "Who was the target?"

"I think we both were. Troy looked up right before he took the first hit. It gave me enough warning to move. A second bullet hit the wall. I tried to get him, Arden, but he shoved me away and then stung me with Aether, Lupa damn him." She looked pissed. "They strapped him with something silvery, dragged him into a car, and got the hell out."

I snarled. "Hostage. They wanted to make me come for you two. The same plan in reverse but this time desperate enough to attack the bar. Fuck."

"How very elvish," Duke drawled. "Always iterations on the same plan."

"The problem is they work." I paced the small room, mind scrambling.

"You're not going after him," he said. "I've just pulled you out of the last elven trap."

The twang of a country guitar cut off my reply, and Vikki pulled her phone from her pocket. "Oh no." She paled. "Troy was right on the intel. Pops is dead. Assassinated. Mama is in hiding." She looked at me, stricken. "Roman says the Farkas pack is already howling for the alpha position of Blood Moon. The Monteagues are offering to help him secure leadership of the pack and clan if he keeps Blood Moon out of the action in the Triangle."

"That's why they targeted you as well. If they'd gotten you, it would have been extra leverage to use against Roman. Shit!" I slammed my fist on my desk, misjudging my new strength. A dent appeared in the wood. This had all been coordinated in advance, and I'd been too busy putting out individual fires to see it or do any planning of my own. "What'd he tell them?"

"He reckons it's worth considering." Her expression twisted. "Oh, Lupa. Ana. I don't know if—"

"Call her. Have her go to my place. The djinn and witch wards will keep elves or anyone else meaning me harm at bay, and y'all can lose yourselves in the woods easier than you can here in town."

Vikki darted out, leaving me with an unusually serious-looking Duke hovering—literally—in the corner.

"Whatever else you came for, I need you to wait a minute." I pulled the burner phone out of my purse and dialed the only number in it.

Allegra answered. "Arden?"

"They took Troy. He's been shot," I said without preamble. "They tried for Vikki but left without her when she escaped."

"Shit," she said with a depth of feeling that suggested the word was entirely inadequate. "I knew they were planning an op, but I thought it was headed to Raleigh. This is bad, Arden."

"Is it worse if he gave Vikki his pendant to give to me?"

Allegra's breath hissed. "Oh no. Oh, Troy. You stubborn fucking ass."

"What?"

"He should only have been able to remove it if he broke—" She cut off, sounding strangled.

"The House oath," I finished for her, remembering the non-disclosure clause Troy had mentioned. "He did."

She didn't waste time asking me how I knew. "Then he'll be treated as an enemy combatant and not a wayward prince. Goddess damn you, T. I have to go get ahead of this. Don't do anything rash, Arden."

The line went dead before I could come up with anything else to say, and I looked at Duke as I put the phone away. "Let me guess," I said, more than a little bitterness in my tone. "The opportunity of chaos?"

"As ever, little bird. What say we make a deal?"

"Another one, you mean? Seeing as you're already sworn to the alliance."

Duke inclined his head, eyes sparkling.

"This oughta be good."

He smiled to show pointed teeth. "Have you met your Ebon Guard yet?"

"What does that have to do with anything?"

"I did some digging of my own. Torsten's library and the elven archives are good, but they lost a few things." The cheerful note in his tone grated on my nerves and suggested that by "lost" he meant the djinn had stolen them.

"And?"

"And I think they're part of the prophecy of the Second Great Flood."

I fiddled with my father's pendant, forcing my hand down when I remembered Duke would recognize the nervous habit. "That's the second time you've mentioned a prophecy. Why am I just now hearing about it?"

"Because it was the first one I'd ever spoken, and I've never been sure if it was right."

My thoughts swirled like leaves on a breeze. I was anxious to do something about the elves attacking the bar and, underneath, thought that I might be more than a little anxious about Troy. I had a room full of agitated Othersiders to deal with and needed to figure out what to do about Roman. I wanted to snap at Duke to quit playing games—but what if this was part of the bigger picture?

"You want to make a deal to tell me," I guessed.

Duke smiled.

"Fine. Terms?"

"You've surrounded yourself with elves. You need a djinni advisor."

I blinked. "Excuse you? The reason I've been leaning on the elves is because *my cousins* lied to me and kept me isolated my whole life. Oh and one tried to kill me. The other threatened to hang me by my intestines, until it was more convenient to make a deal over a bottle. I don't even know any other djinn."

"I may have been a little precipitous in that matter, and I could see where Grimm may have overstepped."

"Enough games, Duke." My stomach clenched in a tight knot, and a tension headache was starting. I needed to be doing something, not playing silly games with a djinni.

He huffed and rolled his eyes. "You always take all the fun out of bargaining. Fine. If I've interpreted the prophecy correctly, being a primordial is enough to run with the Wild Hunt but not to stop it. I think you'll need both halves of Aether *individually* for that. You have the fallen shadow. You need the risen flame."

"Elves are beings of shadow. Troy fell from his position as prince," I said slowly, intrigued enough to give him a minute if Allegra was already working on the Monteague angle. "Can any djinni be the risen flame?"

"I suspect not. But I also suspect I know who is."

I couldn't help but feel a thrill. "Does that mean I'm finally going to meet more of my kin?"

"Only if you can find her and bring her back from the dead."

That was not what I'd been expecting. "Ummm...please don't tell me it's Grimm."

"No." His expression fell into sadness for possibly the first time I'd ever seen, and I shivered at its depth. "Iaret has been gone longer than you've been alive. We'll need to work together to get to her. Which is why my deal involves me helping you get your shadow back."

I narrowed my eyes at him. "What the hell is in it for you?"

"I can't simply—"

"No, you can't. You *always* have an endgame. Spill so I can get out into the bar and calm everyone down before they start another riot." I wasn't sure, but I thought I could hear raised voices out front.

Duke's shape slipped into his true form, roiling smoke and carnelian eyes. "Iaret was my lover," he whispered. "Callista separated us. Grimm worked for Callista willingly, but I had to be compelled."

My jaw dropped as my world rearranged itself. "And the geasa weren't enough?"

"Those came later. When I sought to leave her service after delivering you."

Leaning on the desk, I looked at the floor, trying to untangle the web. "Are we really cousins?"

"Yes. That's why Callista chose me. And Grimm."

"So you help me get Troy back. We keep the prophecy on track. What, as a fuck you to Callista now that there's an opportunity?"

He nodded.

"You also serve as interim advisor to balance the elves until we find Iaret?"

"Yes. And after. If Troy, Allegra, and Iago can all serve you, I don't see the wisdom in leaving you to their twisty clutches with just one djinni to advise you. We need to sleep too, you know."

I thought fast. I could use the help getting Troy back if—when—I found him. Having a djinni take me through the Crossroads would be a hell of a better plan than trying to sneak up on the Monteague mansion. I suspected there was yet another layer to the deal, even if it was simply having the chance to sack the stronghold of the most powerful elven House in the country, but I wouldn't begrudge him that.

Not when I was damn well looking forward to doing it myself.

"Provisional deal," I offered. "I want a trial period. Which includes going after Keithia."

Duke pretended to consider it, and I went for the door, swiping a quick text to Val, Laurel, Vikki, Maria, Noah, Janae, Doc Mike, Ximena, and Terrence to let them know what had happened and what I was about to tell the whole damn bar.

"Take it or leave it, right now." I opened the door to go deal with the rest of Otherside.

"Done. Provisional. It is agreed."

"It is agreed." I blew through the door to the main part of the bar.

It was in an uproar. Sarah hovered, looking scared as groups of Othersiders worked themselves up, looking strung out as hell—probably from the lingering scent of Troy's powerful blood on the air.

I didn't bother shouting. A thunderclap of Air got their attention, sending several to cringing or taking cover.

"That's better," I said in my best bitch voice. Taking a moment to meet everyone's eye, I eased into the center of the room, claiming the space of importance. "The Monteagues' attack on the bar will not go unanswered."

"How do you know it was House Monteague?" asked a vampire I thought I recognized as a Modernist.

I just stared at him until he looked away, too young to catch me with glamour at my strength. I was not playing twenty fucking questions today. It was past time to take the local community in hand. I was done being nice. Nice had gotten me here: both Troy and I shot and captured in the space of a few days because the elves couldn't bring themselves to be progressive and thought I was easy pickings. Blood Moon at risk of splintering from the alliance—from me—because House Monteague had the leverage and the taste for an assassination.

Nope. No more.

"Let it be known that House Monteague is censured and cast out of the alliance. Houses Sequoyah and Luna are likewise censured. Should any individual elf come to their senses and re-swear, I won't deny them." I curled my lip in a snarl born of all the nastiness that had been spoiling in me since I found out who I really was and what had happened to my parents. "But the three local high elven Houses will be pulled down and disbanded. I will not have attacks on fellow Othersiders or on this place of neutral gathering. A line was crossed, and blood was shed. Blood is owed."

After a long, shocked silence, a few voices echoed back, "Blood is owed."

More repeated it until the words had rippled around the room. A few people stood taller, looking uncertain but almost hopeful. Maybe my effort to be nice hadn't been a good idea. Had they thought I wouldn't—or couldn't—protect them?

I'd just made a big fucking promise.

I held back a grimace at the idea that I now had to carry through, having invoked blood feud to a roomful of Othersiders. That meant I needed to get going.

But before I did, I needed to address one more thing.

"Otherside is not going to war with the mundanes, not here in the Triangle, not if we can help it. Defend yourselves as you're accustomed if necessary." My stomach turned at the idea that I was sanctioning turning or killing humans, but we could not allow ourselves to be dragged into fighting them now. "But if I find out that Otherside started something? I will rain holy hell down on you and anyone I think was involved. The Wild Hunt is coming. The gods walk this plane. And I will not have us squandering time and effort on dogs when lions have their sights set on us. Am I clear?"

The room burst into noise again, quieting when I dropped my shields to let my power signature ebb out and drew on Air to make my eyes glow.

"Am. I. Clear?" I repeated.

"Yes, Arbiter," most of the room said. The rest just stared at me.

I didn't blame them. I'd kept the gods and my power signature under wraps from pretty much everyone. But their leaders all knew, and now I hoped I'd scared enough of the rank-and-file that we wouldn't have anyone tempted to step outta line.

"Good. Enjoy your drinks."

Duke appeared beside me as I stormed back to my office. "Ishtar above, did we not teach you subtlety?"

"I tried being nice. They walked all over me," I replied as I shut the door. "They can get with the program or they can get the hell outta the Triangle. Or I blow them all down like a fucking hurricane."

Chapter 29

For all my big talk, I was a wreck. My body was tight with the effort not to shake, and the temperature in the room slowly cooled, my passive magic kicking in to adjust it as anxiety made me too warm. I'd ordered Duke to go do something useful after the third quip about the Arctic, slapping the blood-encrusted pendant into his hand so he'd have a blood tie to track Troy with. Allegra hadn't gotten back to me yet, so she either hadn't found Troy or was occupied with something.

Either way, Keithia had outmaneuvered me worse than she possibly knew with Duke's revelation about the prophecy. I swore under my breath at once again having received key information too late to do anything about it. Regardless of what was going on with Troy, I needed him back.

More than that, I had to figure out how to topple three high elven Houses simultaneously. Because there was no way in hell they'd let me take them one by one. It was a four-way chess game, one I needed to turn into the chaotic snapping of Hungry Hungry Hippos. Like the djinn, I could snatch opportunity from chaos. What I couldn't do was keep dancing to the beat Evangeline played.

The Ebon Guard. It'll have to be them. Relying on unknown elves with supposedly good intentions made me itch though.

It wasn't just the elves I had to be wary about either. Roman still hadn't called, an hour after Vikki had given us the news.

Given how vicious our last conversation had been and how much he'd wanted this very outcome, I had to assume that he was either busy with the fallout, letting me stew, or both. Probably both.

Daylight was burning, and my Hunter was gone—which, come to think of it, would be even worse if the gods found out. On top of that, my ex was going to be vindictive, and I had run my mouth on punishing the elven Houses. I slumped forward and rested my head on the desk, wondering when I'd lost control so badly. Callista had never seemed to be as cornered as I felt now, even when I'd come for her. Then again, nobody had ever doubted or questioned that she'd destroy whoever stepped out of line…until I had.

That rocked me back upright. She'd been scared of me, so she'd made me terrified of her. But if I could handle her, then I could damn well handle these fucking elves.

I needed a plan.

Focus, Arden. You've got this.

Part one: rather than concentrating on Roman, I needed to set him aside. He was in Asheville dealing with a regime change. His sister was here, relying on me and the relationship with the local weres to provide sanctuary for her and her lover. The wolves would keep—and dealing with this cluster would give me more leverage with them anyway.

Part two: getting the Ebon Guard organized under me, not doing whatever the hell they thought they were going to do. Given the way Allegra reacted to trying to talk about the House oath, I had to assume she was under a similar one—that they all were and therefore couldn't attack the royals of their own Houses. We'd have to swap them around. I didn't know enough about the ties between Houses to know if they'd go for it, but I had to at least try.

My gut soured. I was much more like Callista than I'd ever wanted to be. I propped my elbows on the desk and buried my face in my hands, mind racing almost as fast as my heart as I tried to reconcile what I was thinking of doing with who I was. A little part of my brain needled me with the thought that this was the easy way out, even if it would be difficult to execute. Killing people rather than negotiating with them? Destroying not one but three high Houses—the entirety of the local elven power structure? As I'd told Troy at the vampire Reveal, there was no going back from murder.

I lost my battle with the shakes and gave in, leaning back in my chair and closing my eyes to do breathing exercises as I embraced Air and let a small breeze rotate through the room. The sword on the wall behind me rattled, drawing a hollow sound from the wood it rested on.

I frowned, pulled out of my thoughts by the odd way the air molecules carried the sound back to me. Rising, I went to study it. From the slight color difference between the wood panels on this wall and the others in the room, this one hadn't been damaged enough to replace when I'd attacked Callista. I doubted the weres who'd done the construction would have dared to touch the silver sword.

Was there something behind this wall?

I stared at it, frowning, fists on my hips. Now that I was paying attention, the faintest wisps of air were dancing along the outline of a door.

Goddess save me, of course she'd put the back door in her office. Everything Callista did was so obvious that I overlooked it, accustomed to looking for more devious plots. When the weres hadn't found the back door I knew existed while reconstructing the basement, I'd assumed Callista had had it sealed up as a precaution or something after I split from her.

From what I knew of the building though, it didn't make sense for it to be here. There wasn't enough wall.

The sharp scent of lemon zest gave me just enough warning not to jump when Duke said, "Have you finally cracked, or is there a reason you're staring at the wall?"

"Callista's back door." I continued my study. "It's here somewhere."

With a startled grunt, Duke joined me. He cautiously placed a hand on the wall, fingers splayed, and I felt a pulse of Aether. "I don't sense anything."

I closed my eyes and invited Earth to join me then snorted at what I found. "Ah. It's only about a foot deep behind the wall. I'd assumed it was insulation space when I swept the building before, but the air molecules are off."

Too busy to pay attention properly. That's how you die. I gritted my teeth at my own sloppy work, trying and failing to give myself grace because of how much else I'd had to worry about in the last few months.

"Shall we then?" Duke asked.

"No. I'm not fucking around with whatever magic she's sealed it with when I have more urgent shit to do. I know it's here now. That's what counts." For safe measure, I put up a thin wall of Air in front of it and tied off the chord of magic with a heavy knot. If anyone did try to come through it, they'd hit a barrier only an elemental could see.

I returned to my chair. "Did you find him?"

"I think so. They're not exactly original, these elves. He's somewhere on the grounds of a big house in Chapel Hill, one warded against djinn but reeking of marshmallows. I was able to get a peek from the other side of the Veil though. There's an outbuilding that seems more likely than the house itself."

As soon as I had the laptop awake and online, I pulled up the address for the Monteague mansion on Street View. My guess was that they'd make life easy for themselves and take him somewhere they assumed I wouldn't dare go, somewhere they'd have prepared to use as quickly as possible on Keithia's smallest whim. "That it?"

"Yes," Duke said. "You can't see the outbuilding from here though because of those trees. It's a little smaller than your house. Probably built as a guest apartment."

I studied the heavy tree cover he'd pointed to. The lot was huge, with mature trees growing between it and all of its neighbors. I'd never seen the back of the house on my visits, but I'd be willing to bet the Monteagues had allowed a good amount of ornamental native ground cover to grow for additional privacy—holly, bayberry, trumpet vine, and the like. It was the kind of neighborhood where I and my Honda Civic definitely would not belong, with the kind of people who would call the police in a heartbeat if a strange Black chick went wandering through people's yards. That gave them an extra layer of security for me to consider beyond whatever magic and sentries they'd have on the grounds.

I rapped my fingers on the desk until Duke cleared his throat in annoyance. I hadn't gotten any further on my moral conundrum, and I didn't bother sharing it with Duke. He had no problem killing elves for any reason and, like most Othersiders, would find their actions against me merited blood for blood.

I was *expected* to take action for their abduction of Troy, given that I'd claimed him.

I was *expected* to fight back, physically and magically, to prove I was strong enough not to be pushed around. Otherside abhorred a vacuum, and if I couldn't fill the one I'd created by deposing Callista, I shouldn't have done it.

Fuck. I'd painted myself into a corner.

"I need the Ebon Guard," I said at last. I was going to give myself a headache if I kept my teeth clenched so hard, but I couldn't seem to stop. I didn't want to say the words. But I'd already made the threat. I had to follow through. "We need to find a way to take the queens of all three high Houses."

Duke's eyes flashed to carnelian and his grin showed pointed teeth. "By 'take the queens,' you mean…"

I swallowed and whispered, "Kill."

"Good. My first bit of advice, Arden dear, is to say what you mean. Especially if you don't like it, although Ishtar only knows why you wouldn't want to be permanently rid of the meddling bitches." He studied his talons rather than meet my glare. "They destroyed your whole House. You weren't breathing when I pulled you from the river, you know. Your little baby lips were blue."

I hadn't known, and I froze at the abrupt segue. I knew my discovery had freed him from the geas preventing him from talking about my origins, but our strained relationship had kept me from digging.

Duke flicked his gaze up to see my response. "Quinlan was already dead. Keithia saw to that personally, though he survived long enough to get you and Ninlil to shore. Ninlil had taken a mortal wound to shield you, but the river almost did the work for Keithia anyway. Taking Troy from her, especially now that she has to have learned who you are, would have been intolerable." His face and tone softened slightly. "There was never any other choice. You're not Callista if you tried to put the past to rest peacefully and failed. Appeasement never works on dictators or royalty."

Cold sweat broke out as I processed what Duke had just said. A phone buzzed. I fumbled with numb fingers before realizing it wasn't my phone but the burner.

"Arden? Are you safe?" Iago asked when I answered.

"Yes. I think Troy is being held at the Monteague mansion in Chapel Hill."

"Goddess burn it, that explains why Allegra isn't answering. Are you..." The uncertainty in his tone as he trailed off brought me out of my funk.

"I won't let Keithia win. But I need the Guard to keep the other Houses busy while I go in. I know about the House oaths, so I know you can't go after your own Houses or talk about actions against your own queens. There has to be some way around it though."

"You know?"

"Troy broke his," I said softly, feeling odd all over again about what he'd done and what it might mean.

"Ah. That's why he...hm. Clever. Risky but clever." He went silent for a few moments.

Not knowing what to say, I waited, sweating while Duke leaned against the wall, looking bored.

"Leave it with me," Iago said. "How soon are you moving on Keithia?"

"Soon. Make sure Allegra isn't there." I needed to go home, change my clothes, and gear up with Neith's gift. Troy hadn't told me where he'd hidden the lead-lined box containing the godblade, but there were only so many reasonable places in the house.

I didn't dare call on the alliance for help with this. My plan was to literally tear the house down, and I couldn't risk exposing Terrence and Ximena's people or the witches. The Raleigh coterie would be pinned down by the protests, and the wolves were out. Zanna was, as far as I knew, still in the fae realm treating with the lords and ladies.

That left me. And Duke. Against an entire House. At least I had the djinni in play for once.

"Soon it is." After a pause, Iago added a self-conscious sounding, "Be well, my queen, and may the Goddess grant you victory."

I was too stunned to answer before the phone clicked off.

Chapter 30

It took longer than I'd thought it would to find my knife but only because Troy had hidden it somewhere accessible at his height and I was used to looking at mine. Duke watched, bemused, as I blew through the house, repeating the prep Troy had done for us when we went after Callista and leaving everything ready on the counters. First aid kit, extra bandages, water, and the shotgun I kept on top of the fridge for home protection loaded and ready with lead-and-silver shot. I didn't know what state Troy—or I—would be in when we got back, but I had to assume bad.

"You still haven't mentioned what your plan is for actually getting inside," Duke pointed out.

I checked the elf-killer hanging from one hip, the Ruger LCP on the other, and the godblade tucked in a sheathe at my back. I was getting more comfortable with wearing the weapons, and Neith's gift was pleased, somehow, if a knife could be pleased, to be back with me. I didn't like the sensation or the way it grew hot when it got too close to the bigger tomtar-made knife.

"You're going to take me through the Crossroads," I said. "Grimm carried me through and framed it so that I wouldn't lose my mind. You can do the same, right?"

"I—" He frowned. "Hm. I suppose I could. I keep forgetting you can't get there on your own, but that doesn't mean you can't pass through. I wouldn't make a habit of it though."

I tensed, thinking of all the times the gods had pulled me in. "Why not?"

He tilted his head side to side, as though he were considering his words. "I'm not certain of the long-term effects. You got the knack of all four elements readily enough and I suspect you have a touch of the Sight, so you might well learn to create Chaos spheres and dreamwalk like the elementals of old were said to do. Or you might just get lost somewhere in the In-Between until your mind splintered like an elf's. Chaos is…chaotic."

"Thanks, I hate it," I muttered.

Shrugging, Duke studied me. "Say I get you through. What, by the Bull of Heaven, are you planning to do then?"

"Drop me as close as you can. I can sense and avoid or push through Aether, but Elves can't sense or defend against elemental magic unless they have a lich to work soul magic for them." I paused mid-thought, wondering what had happened to the artifact the lich had taken from Mason Farm, then set it aside to pursue when I had time. "So I huff and I puff and I blow the shit outta that ugly-ass mansion, distract them enough to get onto the grounds. Once I'm through, you can use the callstone and our blood tie to follow."

"You're going to walk through elven Aetheric traps." He sounded utterly unimpressed.

"You can come out of the Veil anywhere, right? Drop me onto the roof. I can cushion the fall with Air." At least I hoped I could. The idea had come to me as it came outta my mouth.

That got a bark of laughter. "So I drop an elemental out of the sky onto a presumably unprotected roof. You make your way down without breaking anything and undetected in broad daylight."

"Maybe waiting till dusk is better." I didn't like the idea, but having the rescue interrupted by Chapel Hill PD coming through to investigate calls about a woman dropping out of the sky wouldn't help anything.

"Dusk. When elven strength waxes. At a new moon, when their magic peaks."

"That's where you come in. You're telling me a djinni several millennia old is no match for a bunch of elves?"

"And if *your* elf is inside when you blow the mansion down or light it on fire or whatever?"

I shrugged off the peculiar feeling of Troy being *my elf*. "He won't be anywhere exposed. It'd be too easy for me to get to him. Besides, you said yourself he's probably in the outbuilding."

Duke studied me, smoke curling from his man-shaped form. "For the record, this is ludicrous."

Frustrated, I threw my hands up. "What the hell else should I do? We can't have an outright war in the middle of the Goddess-damned mundane suburbs, and that's the only alternative if we're going to end Keithia and recover Troy. I can't ask the other factions to help with this when they're all tied down. I'm asking *you*, since you were so hot on being an advisor. If you have a better idea, let's fucking hear it."

While I fumed, Duke's gaze wandered around my kitchen. "When we built you this house, I never imagined this would be a discussion we'd have in it. Callista was so certain she could contain you until she was ready to sell you to whichever god she had her deal with."

I went cold. "This is a conversation we need to have but not now. Right now, I need to get ahead of Keithia and Evangeline. Stop derailing. Can I count on you?"

"Always so impatient. Very well, little bird. We'll do it your way."

His eyes sparked and he looked distinctly pissy, but if he was calling me "little bird" then he'd indulge me.

"Thank you, Duke," I said. A glance out the window told me I had a few hours to kill. "I'm going to see what Iago needs to set up his attack. Make yourself at home."

***

I had no idea what would happen to the bowl of popcorn I left on the ground when we crossed over but given my ballsy play, it seemed like acknowledging Eshu-Elegba couldn't hurt. The journey through the Crossroads passed in a blur, partly because Duke didn't do more than make it a suggestion of a forest and partly because I was too busy freaking out over the folly I was about to undertake.

Duke stopped so fast I would have crashed into him had he been corporeal. As it was, I passed through his true form, a lance of ice shooting down my spine as I choked on smoke.

"Last chance to find another way," he said.

I shook my head. "We're doing this. Now."

"Then I hope you stick your landing."

The world twisted, and my guts went with it. After a half-second of the terrifying freefall I remembered from being thrown into Jordan Lake, I barely got a cushion of Air under me before dropping unceremoniously to the roof.

Immediately, I flattened myself. My heart thudded, my breath rasping, as the setting sun half-blinded me where the last rays stretched over the trees. I had to assume that for all this looked like a normal suburban home, it was probably wired for surveillance and set up for defense. I dropped my shields just enough to send a pulse of Chaos outward. Nothing sparked, and a shaky grin spread across my face.

They hadn't thought anyone might fall out of the sky. Good.

Squeezing Duke's callstone, I gave it a nudge of Chaos and focused on a mental image of him. "Come on through."

With a shimmer of hot air, Duke manifested beside me in his true form. Savage joy radiated from him. "I don't think I've ever been inside the wards of an elven stronghold. Maybe there's something to be said for bold plans."

"Especially if I ask you to a sweep for artifacts before I destroy the house?" It had occurred to me on the trip over that the residence of an elven queen had to have at least a few nice trinkets laying around, and I wasn't above liberating those along with Troy.

Carnelian eyes flashed in the low light. "You spoil me, little bird."

"Go. If you find a blade like Troy's, I want it. You have until I give the signal."

"Which is?"

"A lightning bolt through the house. Maybe stay in that form, hey?"

Duke didn't bother to answer, whirling away to fly down the chimney. Djinn were beings of smoke and flame, and I'd already hit him with lightning once. All it had done was get his attention. He'd survive a strike to the house and any subsequent fire. It might even make him stronger.

The evening sky was filled with towering clouds suggesting thunderstorms, their undersides painted in purple with the fading light and hiding the early stars and jet trails. As I had in the fight against the vampire sorcerer at Falls Lake, I gathered the elements to me, suggesting the oppressive heat and humidity might want to become a summer storm. Then, I'd had to wrench Water into submission. Now, with my newfound understanding, I found that space inside me that wanted to let go, wanted to heal. Pressed myself into the hot shingles and, with gritted teeth, shut out my fear and dared to dream.

Water swirled around me, obligingly mixing with the dust I pulled closer in the atmosphere to boost the clouds, then fall as rain. With half a thought, I got the wind to pick up. In the distance, thunder rumbled threateningly.

I couldn't help my grin of triumph even as my blood pounded in anticipation.

With the stage set, I belly-crawled to the edge of the roof and peered over, spotting the outbuilding with little difficulty. The prickle of Aether was strongest there. I couldn't read what it was, but my guess was something nasty.

Letting my shields down a little more allowed me to sense the disturbances in the air around the property. My range was a hell of a lot farther than it had been, and I picked up a pair of figures on the covered back porch. Impossible to see who they were without being at ground level, and I wasn't keen on the idea of killing any mundane guests they might have.

Crawling to the edge of the roof, I found a corner lacking windows and fronted by some ornamental grasses. Not great cover but better than nothing.

A spark of lightning fried the camera watching this side of the house. They'd know someone was here now, but maybe they'd think it was just the storm. I wasn't going to wait around and see if they'd send someone to check. After a last read of the air currents, I gathered my courage and dropped from the roof, cushioning myself again with Air. I couldn't use it to fly, but damn if this wasn't useful. I'd been sleeping on myself and my power. The thought that Callista had been right to be afraid made me grin, and I felt the snarl in it.

Masculine voices came to me on the wind, and I shielded hard to lock down my power signature before I could be noticed.

"—taking forever to break."

"She's not trying to break him. She's setting an example."

My heart leapt into my throat. They had to be talking about Troy. I crept closer, staying below the line of the windows and darting from one clump of grass to the next.

"You seen him yet? It's worse than what she did to his father."

I didn't know if I could pull down a lightning bolt big enough to destroy a house on my own yet, but I certainly could with a little help. I crept up the stairs to the porch, drawing my elf-killer.

"Good," the first one said. "Fucking traitor, taking up with elemental scum."

Fury flared to life in my chest, redoubling when the second man spat. "Exactly. May they both rot in hell."

"I'll meet you both down there." I downed the first with a kidney shot then launched myself at the second, tackling him to the deck with a thud and pressing lead and steel under his chin. "Where's Troy?"

Aether roared to life, and I didn't wait to see what he'd do with it. Hot, sticky blood spurted as I cut his throat, covering my arms and splashing in a spray across my cheek. Copper and meringue burnt to ash were all I could smell. Green flame ignited on the blade, and I spun back to the first elf, writhing in too much pain to cry out. Power built in me as I stabbed him through the heart.

I had to give it to Keithia—she seemed to breed her people for power as much as looks. The magical backwash from these two was almost as much as I'd gotten from three Redcaps, and I staggered as I rode it.

Shouts rang out in the house. Someone putting a borked camera and an Aether flare together to get trouble.

They were too late.

I was aboveground this time, with a storm already growing overhead. It took next to nothing to channel my magic into the heavens. I reached with blended Air and Fire as I thrust my hand to the sky and clenched my fist.

"I am the wind." I thrust my fist to the ground, pulling magic with it. "And I am vengeance."

Blinding flash. Superheated air. The crack of wood shattering drowned out by the immediate, deafening clap of thunder. I spun away, throwing up a shield of Air a half second too late to avoid catching a few splinters and a contact burn. Swearing, I leapt from the deck.

Three elves boiled out of the outbuilding, and from within the smoking ruins of the house, a shedu roared. As I raced forward, I swept Air ahead of me, fueling it with the remainder of the power I'd stolen from the two sentries on the deck. The elves in front of me staggered, and I followed my gust with a looping chord of magic that anchored them to the ground as surely as ropes would.

Shouting rose from the neighboring houses as humans tried to figure out what was going on. The Aetheric wards must have included a strong suggestion to stay away because nobody came into the yard.

I had to make this fast.

With grim disgust for myself and the path I was on, I killed two of the three elves, praying that the tree cover and wards would shield me from witnesses. Power roared into me, stronger than it had for the other two, and I funneled some of it into the ground. The foundations of the house and the small outbuilding shook, as did the trees ringing the property. There'd be no covering this up, but for now, the mundanes were unlikely to think of elementals and the elves would be too busy mitigating the impacts of the riots to defend whoever survived this.

I crouched beside the last elf. "Is Troy inside?"

"Yes." His voice shook, and even in the low light of dusk, I could see the terror in his eyes.

"Is he alive?"

"Please don't—"

Not liking the sound of that at all, I plunged the knife into his heart.

Chapter 31

The scene when I burst into the outbuilding was horrific.

I found myself in an open-plan room with a small kitchen. A glowing brazier on one of the counters offered the only light. Aether, blood, and burnt flesh made the air reek. Crusted spray that looked black in the dim light painted the walls. More pooled on the floor beneath a crumpled form hanging from the cracked ceiling in chains, one arm badly broken. Strips of skin weeping blood swung loosely from the body, and two more shadows crouched, ready to attack.

It took my brain a moment to catch up. That had to be Troy hanging in chains, and if all the blood in the room was his, he wouldn't be alive much longer.

My stomach heaved. Only recognizing the shadows as Keithia and Evangeline, bloodied knives in hand, was enough to make me choke down everything in my stomach. I let out a wild, unrestrained burst of Chaos instead, tripping every spell in the darkened room and making Evangeline cry out in pain.

"You'll die for this," I snarled at Keithia.

Rage overruled fear, and I rode the currents of the power I'd stolen from the elves outside.

"And for my parents. I swear it. There will be no peace, no compromise. Just this House pulled down to salted earth."

Keithia sneered at me, hatred burning in her eyes. "You'd have to get out of here first to manage that. I don't know how you got in, but you won't get out again." Aether darted at me. "Drop the weapons."

The boost in my power let me fend her magic off. I blocked it, although shielding that hard meant I'd struggle to use my own magic. I'd need a different play this time. I wasn't hiding who or what I was anymore, so I could use my power to the fullest.

I pretended to stagger, buying myself a moment to block off the room with a massive wall of Air. Nobody was getting in or out.

Keithia advanced, lashing out with another burst of Aether. "Drop them, filth!"

"Fuck you." Before her magic could connect, I lashed out instinctively with a slice that snapped the Aetheric attack back into her. The punch of Air I followed it with was the most satisfying thing I'd ever done.

She dropped, gasping for breath around the sucker punch she never saw coming. I sent one at Evangeline as well, not wanting to kill her but not able to leave her. She was still in high school, for fuck's sake. I had to have a line. Killing kids was it.

I didn't have the same compunction about Keithia.

The queen recovered fast. She had the same liquid grace I'd seen in Troy, not at all diminished by her age, and the surety of her movements said she knew how to use her knife.

She edged to circle me. I shifted to prevent it, raising my elf-killer in a guard.

Keithia struck again with Aether, lunging forward with her knife at the same time. Again I sliced at the purple wash of magic with Chaos made stronger by elven heartsblood, splintering it this time, willing it to needle back at her. I had no idea what I'd done, but Keithia screamed and faltered.

I put all the excess power I had into a massive push with Air. It blew Keithia and Evangeline into the nearest wall, bowing it and sending another crack to join the one my earlier mini-quake had already put in the ceiling. Plaster dropped in dry crumbles, and the chains holding Troy rattled.

It should have drawn some reaction from him—nobody with an arm broken that badly could hold back a groan at the very least. But he hung silent behind me.

My stomach roiled as I panted, shaking my head to clear the sweat dripping into my eyes.

With all my bonus power spent and Troy fading fast, I had to end this. Now.

Evangeline recovered first. She darted to attack me when I lunged to finish her grandmother. My elf-killer sparked against a blade that matched Troy's. Maybe even was his.

Okay, so I might have underestimated the brat's combat training and toughness.

A rattle of breath behind me made my heart twist.

Troy was still alive. I broke away, conflicted.

"What're you gonna do now?" Evangeline's arms were coated in blood nearly to her elbows. She'd been an active participant in whatever had happened here. "Kill us? Or save that traitor? Tick tock, bitch. He's almost dead."

"He's your *brother*." I wanted to vomit at what she'd done.

"I have no brother. Not anymore."

I couldn't tell whether she thought she had the upper hand or was just that hateful, but I didn't have time for this. The main house was fully in flames, lighting the interior of this room in orange, and sirens screamed in the distance. The brazier had fallen over, and smoke filled the air in the kitchen as the wood floor smoldered.

Keithia coughed and shook her head to clear it.

"Fine." I said. "Then you don't have a grandmother either."

Horror twisted Evangeline's face as I borrowed the glowing embers from the brazier and used them to send a wave of pure flame at Keithia.

Those who believed revenge was best served cold didn't have control over Fire.

"No!" Evangeline howled, dropping the blade and whirling to try putting out the flames.

Keithia just screamed, raw howls of agony that nobody outside the building could miss.

I was out of time.

On the chance that the longknife Evangeline had been wielding was Troy's, I snatched it. It was too dangerous to leave with her. Combined Air and Earth let me split the crack in the ceiling wider and tear the chains free. I gathered Troy's dead weight to me, doing my best to ignore the sticky warmth of his blood and praying I didn't tear any more skin from him than his family already had.

Evangeline reeled away from the heat of the fire that was Keithia and lunged toward us.

I threw up a wall of Air and grabbed at Duke's callstone. "Time to get the hell out! Go!"

The elf princess snarled, her deadly secondary teeth bared. "Where do you think you're going to go, elemental bitch?"

It was a good question. We didn't have time for Duke to walk Troy and me through the Crossroads. Not if I was going to get Troy back alive.

"Elegba!" I shouted.

Troy's pulse was thready and slowing. I prayed he was close enough to death to qualify as a corpse, rather than a person.

"Eshu-Elegba, I call in my favor!"

Time slowed as a portal opened. Evangeline's face shifted to shock in slow-motion, and her move to shield her eyes looked like she was trapped in molasses.

The orisha himself sauntered through the portal in the corner of my eye, grinning as he tossed popcorn into his mouth. "Well then. What a fine mess this is. Well done, my dear."

"I beg passage through the Crossroads for myself and my—my cargo," I said.

Elegba leaned closer, tilting his head and squinting. "Looks like a man to me, though maybe not for much longer. The favor was for you alone."

I scrambled to find something that would appeal to him. "He's nearly dead. An elf. You know carrying a being of shadow through the Crossroads will kill most of them in the best of health. If he dies, the trick will be on me. If he lives, it will mean discord for those who didn't honor your Crossroads behind the Veil and chaos for his House. For his whole people."

Dark eyes flickered with mischief and flame as a piece of popcorn was flicked into the air to fall between his teeth. "Indeed. Do you promise?"

"Chaos?"

"Yes. Balance."

Was chaos balance? I didn't know. I was out of time. "I will see to it myself that the local Houses will fall. If he lives, the Wild Hunt will falter."

"Quite the promise." Elegba studied me. "So much chaos in you, little trueborn." His eyes shifted to Troy, whose breath rattled as he labored harder to breathe with the smoke from Keithia's corpse filling the room.

"Please!" I begged. Time was slowed, not stopped, and it was running out fast.

Elegba laughed. "An elemental humbling herself to save an elf. *This* elf. And I suppose you did leave me an offering." Popcorn crunched as he considered. "Very well, girl. Think of where you wish to go, and I'll part the Veil for you."

"Thank you," I breathed. "Thank you."

I pictured my bedroom at home, my most private space, the one place that was all mine. Focused on its every detail, the smell of the room with Zanna's fixes, the way the air moved, the way the light and shadow fell.

With a feeling like I was being torn in half, the world shifted. I clutched Troy's suddenly lifeless body and screamed until I had no breath left.

Landed hard. Opened my eyes. Wished I hadn't as wracking pain squeezed me in a vice.

My body spasmed. Met resistance from the wood floor beneath me. My hands felt bruised from where they had slammed to the ground around the knives I still clutched.

Troy lay at my side. Not breathing. Mind empty.

"No, no no no, please no." I fought disorientation and pain to push myself up.

I laid Troy flat and did a round of CPR. Battled the hangover of traveling the Crossroads twice in a day, bent Chaos to my will, and poured it into him.

Troy gasped. Flopped. Went still.

Another round of CPR, my hands sliding across the blood on his sternum. He coughed another breath. Blood dripped from my nose to his forehead as I clasped his temples and dove in, looking for the fragments of who he was as I had when Artemis had pushed us into Callista's basement.

Something else was wrong. I still couldn't get a sense of him.

There. Blood-smeared silver glinted under the shackle on Troy's right wrist. I gagged as I realized the band was so tight around the joint that his hand was swollen and black. Between that and the compound break in the same arm, he'd be lucky to hold a blade again.

Air didn't want to cooperate, but it had been my first element. I'd make it work.

I forced molecule-thin tendrils between the braided strands of metal. Heated them with as much Fire as I dared until I could flex the band free and throw it into the corner.

Another gasp, accompanied by a spasm this time.

I hammered on his chest and leaned on Chaos as hard as I could. Pried his mouth open and pushed Air into his lungs. "Damn you, *keep breathing!*"

Troy coughed, a deep, wracking hack that seemed like it would never stop until it did. Slow, painful breaths continued.

When I leaned over to listen to his chest, his heart beat with a slow, reluctant thud.

"Oh thank fuck." Shifting to his head, I tried again to find the fragments of his mind and soul. They were there, hovering, quivering, equally ready to rejoin his body or flee and leave him a husk. Casting a wide net of Chaos, I wrestled with magic and the fragments, urging them back to Troy. "I'm not finished with you yet. You don't get to just die. *You owe me!*"

With my shout, the fragments shuddered, glittering like needle-sharp glass shards in my mind's eye...and shot back to him.

Troy arched up with a tearing gasp that turned into watery breaths. His secondary teeth slid from his gums as he snarled in pain. Every muscle in his body seemed to tighten enough to break the bones that weren't already broken.

His mind relearned mine in a series of heartbeats, the Aetheric tag searing through us both.

I flinched, tears making hot tracks down my cheeks and gut roiling from Troy's unfiltered pain and fear and heartbreak swamping me. He groaned, long and low, until he finally slumped, drenched in sweat smelling of rotted herbs.

Reeling, I staggered to the kitchen and the burner phone I hadn't dared to take, dialing the one number in the address book.

"I have Troy," I said, too fast, hardly breathing, when someone picked up. "Get here. My house. Now. With your Sequoyah. Before he dies again." It was the only chance he had to see the morning, let alone regain the use of his sword arm.

"Arden?" Allegra said. "How—"

I hung up and grabbed the first aid kit on my way back to the bedroom. They'd get here, or they wouldn't. I had to keep Troy breathing until then.

He'd died for me today. I had to make sure he'd live for tomorrow.

Not daring to move him, I did what I could for the worst wounds, cleaning and bandaging, taping what I didn't have the tools to stitch or staple. I kept having to stop and choke down bile. Aside from the wrist and broken arm, they'd beaten the hell outta him, leaving him black and blue from head to toe. They'd seared the House tattoo off his chest, cut or burned him in half a dozen non-fatal places, carved a word in elvish across his belly, and practiced flaying him.

The scent of lemon peel cut through the stench of blood and burnt skin.

"Goddess," Duke muttered, crouching at Troy's bare feet. "You see now why I have no qualms about hunting elves? They do this to all their worst enemies. Including any djinn they can trap in corporeal form. They would have done it to your parents if they could have captured them alive, and they will do it to you if you're caught again."

I didn't stop my work, even as my eyes blurred with more tears. Keithia had deserved to die. I had no regrets for making it painful.

Had I made a mistake in leaving Evangeline? She'd been part of this, child or not.

Regardless, I couldn't allow elven power to stand in the Triangle. This was not how Othersiders would conduct themselves in *my* territory. Not now, not ever, and especially not with the Wild Hunt coming. If they—and everyone else—had to learn the hard way, so be it. Maybe if I crushed all three Houses, people would get the fucking message.

When I was at a loss for what else to do, I had Duke fetch a washcloth and a bowl of water, cleaning what unbandaged skin there was as best I could and smoothing arnica cream over the bruises. To my surprise the djinni helped, as quiet and solemn as I'd ever seen him. Then I stretched out next to Troy on the floor, my head pillowed on my arms, exhausted. I didn't dare move him but Allegra had said being close to me would let him heal faster. I prayed she was right.

Stay alive, asshole. Stay alive.

Chapter 32

I hadn't realized I'd fallen asleep. I woke to the fluttering of a hand at my throat, finding consciousness in slow, groggy degrees until the fingers tightened.

Fear shocked me fully awake in a heartbeat.

"Arden?" Troy's roughened voice, broken and disbelieving, jerked me upright.

I winced at the stiffness that had come from falling asleep on the floor then flinched at his hiss of pain, not having realized I'd migrated closer to him in my sleep and jostled him when I sat up. It had been his hand around my neck, and I frowned.

"Hey," I said, doing my best to wrench my mind into some semblance of function. The first hints of morning crept through the windows, showing the mess they'd made of his face already healing to a painful-looking green. "How are you feeling?"

"This is— Fuck you, Keithia. I know she's dead. I know you—"

Cold shock washed over me. "What? Troy, it's me. It's Arden. You're—"

My words cut off as, with the strength of the damned and the lost, Troy surged up and pinned me, his hands around my throat. "Let go of me, Keithia, or I'll kill this one, I swear to the Goddess. I'll kill her myself. I won't tell you anything."

Tears streamed down his face as his fingers, weakened but still strong enough, closed around my throat.

"Troy, no!" I raised my voice as much as I could with him choking off my air. "Duke! Allegra!" I didn't even know if the elfess was here, but I didn't know what the hell else to do. I didn't want to hurt him.

The bedroom door slammed open. Allegra burst in, Iago on her heels.

Duke appeared behind them.

"Troy! Troy, no, it's her. It's for real Arden. Stop!" She skidded to kneel beside him and slipped a hand over his forehead as I gasped for breath and drew on the elements. "Troy, chill! Arden, don't hurt him!"

I wrestled down the crackle of lightning building in me as the scent of burnt marshmallow filled the room.

He fought Allegra's command with everything he had left. The tatters of the bond made me live every painful second of it until he finally succumbed, slumping to the floor and sobbing at whatever evil lived behind his eyelids.

Iago blocked me from rolling away, heartache painted on his face. "Stay where you are until Allegra anchors him. Please, Arden, or we'll lose him."

My blood pounded in my veins as Allegra leaned close to Troy's ear and whispered something in elvish as the scent of Aether grew even stronger. Bile sloshed up to my throat, and my skin was too tight.

"What the hell happened to him?" I asked when Troy slumped into an uneasy half-sleep and Allegra straightened.

She looked at me with the expressionlessness of someone who had nothing left to feel. "Keithia found a human woman who resembled you. Beheaded her. Mazed Troy and threw the head at his feet. For no reason other than to hurt him."

Horror gripped me with sharp, cold talons, and I had to hold my breath to stop from heaving.

"She found the one thing that would break his spirit, and she used it. They had him strapped with silver and lead. No bond, and delirious with pain and the effort to resist it. He thinks you're dead. That's when I left the house. There were too many for me to defeat and get him out alone. I came here looking for you. Your car was here, but you weren't and you weren't answering the burner. I thought she'd gotten you too."

The fast-shallow breaths of trying not to throw up were all I could focus on.

Who the fuck did something like that? At all, let alone to their own blood? And after peeling skin from him in strips and breaking bones?

"Then I'm glad the bitch died in fire," I said bitterly.

Allegra gasped, and Iago's jaw dropped. Duke just smirked, dravite eyes sparkling in ugly amusement.

"Keithia's dead?" Allegra asked, wavering. "That's why I passed out? The House oath is broken?"

Given my knowledge of elven House oaths was a thimble above jack shit, I shrugged.

"Evie?"

I shook my head. "She's a kid, Allegra. I—I couldn't do it."

"A mistake," Duke murmured. "Considering she likely did a good amount of *that* to your princeling."

Furious but unable to deny it, I took a breath to snap at him.

"Can we get Troy up on the bed?" Iago interrupted gently. "We couldn't rouse either of you so we left you and hoped it was just a deep healing sleep. Fi Sequoyah was here and accelerated what you'd already done with treating him. He might regain the use of his arm if the double bond is everything we hope it is."

I nodded, mind racing. Strange elves had been in my bedroom? And I'd been too lost to the world to even notice? I shuddered, only then realizing how cold and drained I felt, as though some of my vitality had gone. Maybe into Troy.

"I was here, Arden. Don't worry," Duke said in response to my obvious thought as Iago and Allegra hefted Troy up and onto my bed.

"I—I need a shower. Can you—"

"I'll sit with him. Make it quick," Allegra said flatly.

Even with the hot spray, I felt cold. I couldn't stop shaking. I hadn't eaten in too long and now that I wasn't running on adrenaline, a power hangover pounded to the fore. Less than it should have been given how much I'd used, probably because of all the power I'd stolen from the elves. Or from finally growing into my own power. I finished as quickly as I could, pulled on an oversized T-shirt and boxer shorts, and stumbled out. Exhaustion had me tripping over my own feet as I used the wall to get back to the bed and climb into it on the far side.

Wordlessly, Duke extended a bottle of wine. Regardless of the hour, I took it and drank straight from the bottle. A packet of jerky was on the side table, and I ate some of that before drinking more of the wine. When the power hangover had eased somewhat, I slid down and closer to Troy and closed my eyes.

The next time I opened them, Duke, Allegra, and Iago were gone. It was just me and Troy. His labored breathing sent daggers into my chest. I sent tendrils of Chaos back, hoping they'd break whatever enchantment Keithia had set on him and not make everything worse.

This was my fault. I'd make sure he healed—physically, at least. I curled my arms around Troy's head. "I'm alive. You didn't fight in vain. Come back to us. Come back to me."

***

I didn't mean to fall asleep again, but I did. Troy's sharp gasp woke me.

"Easy. Easy, Troy, it's me. I'm not dead." I cradled his head, surreptitiously checking his pupil reflex then his pulse. Good. He was getting back to his usual, even if he burned with a low fever. His right arm, wrist, and hand looked much better as well, although I suspected the scar from the silver-and-lead cuff would be permanent, as would that from the burn under his collarbone where his House tattoo had been.

The usual flecks of gold in his gaze were dulled as he fixed on me blurrily. "She showed me your head."

"Not me. It wasn't me." I choked up at the woman who'd died for me, to hurt him, and opened the bond as completely as I could.

Panting, he focused on me again. His shaky hand found my cheek. "Arden. It's really you?"

I leaned into it then lifted a hand and made lightning dance over my fingertips. "Alive and well."

"How…" He swallowed.

I reached past him for the water someone had left on the nightstand then helped him drink. "Steady," I murmured. "Or you're gonna throw it up, and I've already cleaned you up once today."

He grunted, and I set the glass back on the nightstand.

"How did I get here?" he asked.

I cleared my throat and flushed. "I, ah…blew up Keithia's house and called in a favor with the orisha of the Crossroads."

After a long, disbelieving blink, he rasped, "You what?"

"There was a lightning strike that, um, must have hit a gas main or something. And maybe an earthquake. The house was in pieces. And on fire."

His breathing picked up to just shy of hyperventilating. "Keithia?"

"Dead," I whispered.

Troy's gaze shot to mine. "You?"

I nodded. "Immolated. Allegra passed out when the House oath broke, so we're pretty sure she's dead dead."

Relief slapped me in the bond before being replaced by fear again. "Evangeline?"

"I—Troy she's a kid, I couldn't."

He closed his eyes and started shaking. "She won't let this go."

"Duke said as much. I'm sorry. We'll figure something out. Just rest for now, okay? If you're feeling stable, I need to go see what's going on."

"Okay," he whispered. Unease curled through the bond, making a counterpoint to the throb of pain.

Whatever this Fi Sequoyah had done had only been enough to save his life, not to heal him completely. I shuddered for what that might mean in terms of how close to death he'd been and, for the first time, wondered if the tangle of the Aetheric bond between us would pull me down with him, whether into insanity or death.

Pushing that cheerful thought aside, I rose, only to lean on the bed again as a wave of dizziness struck me. Troy grimaced, and I muted the bond a little, resolving to ask Allegra exactly what the impacts of a double bond were.

I frowned when a low hum of voices reached me as I got closer to the door and stiffened at the sight that greeted me when I opened it.

My house was full of elves.

"Arden?" Anxiety laced Troy's voice.

Allegra and Duke straightened from where they'd been leaning over my dining table. I made myself relax—mentally, at least. I couldn't make my limbs loosen.

"It's fine. We have company is all," I said to him.

"Guard present!" Allegra barked as I slipped out and shut the door behind me.

I blinked as every elf in the room stomped a foot as they saluted.

"Hail the queen!"

"Uh…hi y'all." Flushing, I made myself keep walking, completely at a loss.

Duke smirked, a merry twinkle lighting his eyes. "You said you needed the Ebon Guard. Here they are."

Not knowing what else to do, I fell back on formality. "Be welcome in my home. My table is yours, my hearth is yours, and my roof is yours, while you are here."

The assembled elves answered in unison, but using a response I'd never heard before. "Our queen honors us. Your home is ours to defend. Our strength is yours to direct."

Allegra was grinning now as well.

I ignored her. "Um. Thanks. As you were."

They all bowed then returned to their quiet busyness. I leaned to peek around the corner of the wall that made the bathroom and found them filling the living room, speaking in near whispers and gesturing at the maps and charts pinned to the walls. There had to be over a dozen elves packed into my little house, which appeared to have been turned into some kind of HQ in the—I checked the window, finding it dark out—twenty-four hours I'd been occupied with keeping Troy alive.

What in the ever-loving nine circles of hell is this?

"A word? Outside?" I said when I reached Duke and Allegra.

They followed me out the front door, and Duke busted out laughing when I lifted my brows and waved in the general direction of the interior.

Still grinning, Allegra said, "We couldn't risk a retaliatory attack on you and Troy. I conferred with my colleague"—she glanced at Duke—"and he agreed that bringing the Guard here would be best. We secured the appropriate permissions from Terrence and Ximena first, of course."

Having councilors and captains was going to take some getting used to. I scrubbed my fingers through my curls, grimacing when I found them tangled from having gone to bed with unwrapped wet hair, and swayed on my feet as another wave of dizziness hit.

"Sit before you fall," Duke said.

I glared at him and locked my knees. He just rolled his eyes.

"Report," I said brusquely, completely thrown by having my house full of elves and too fucking tired to find tact.

"Keithia is confirmed dead," Allegra said flatly, straightening into the parade rest stance Troy usually took. "Evangeline is on the run with a cabal of Monteague loyalists. Humans are investigating the family home in Chapel Hill. No deaths are being reported, so they either mazed the first responders or took the bodies along. Probably both. The media circus is fueling the riots, but the mundanes have no idea what kind of magic could call down a lightning bolt so they're baffled. For now."

I grimaced, hoping I hadn't endangered Val, Laurel, and Sofia. Maybe I should call them here. "Fine. Otherside? What's going on with the other Houses? The wolves?"

Allegra pursed her lips. "Sequoyah and Luna are in civil war. My fa—the Captain is keeping the Darkwatch out of it. We're getting reports of assassinations and sabotage as the Houses and their vassals split on vengeance against you or allegiance to you. The Guard are feeding into it with misinformation. We'll take direct action if necessary, but for now only the Monteagues and low-bloods are free from House oaths.

"Last report from Asheville is that Roman and Sergei have their hands full with the Farkas pack. Ana arrived safely in Durham, but she and Vikki took refuge with the cat prides rather than stay here, as did a small retinue of progressive wolves that escorted Ana across the state."

"Any news from the fae?"

Duke shook his head. "I imagine they'll have heard what happened and have renewed debates in the Chamber of Lords over whatever they might have decided up to now."

"Okay." I frowned into the darkness. A flash of pain broke through from Troy, and I winced as I rubbed my chest where his burn was. "I need to get Troy some painkillers or something. First though—Allegra, is there anything I should know about the double bond? Troy told me a little about the political reasons it's forbidden for elven men to bond, but do I need to worry about like, dying if he does?"

"Not from the second bond, no. That's purely hormonal on his part. As he said, no impact to you other than some cultural obligations nobody expects you to fulfill given you're not a full-blooded elf." She squinted at me the way she did when she was reading the spells affecting my aura, a rare talent particular to her. "The Aetheric bond though...hm. That twists more the stronger you get." She studied me a few heartbeats longer. "It might allow energetic exchange soon, if it doesn't already. Maybe even more of a connection than location and general emotion."

Duke scoffed. "Are you saying they'll be telepathic? Like vampires?"

"Something like that, maybe." Allegra shook her head. "Impossible to know until and unless it happens. We don't dare break it though."

I sighed and scrubbed a hand over my face. "Yeah. Troy mentioned side effects."

"If you call the potential for memory loss, insanity, or death by stripped aura a side effect, sure. You're twined too closely together now to separate you safely. Like symbionts, feeding off each other for mutual support."

Duke grunted in surprise and I stared at her, stomach clenching at the enormity of the situation. "Is that all?"

She shrugged, her face a stiff mask. "We have other theories. As with everything else with you two, it's impossible to know until it happens, given none of this should have been possible in the first place. We don't even know how much is related to you being an elemental and how much is pure Chaos, given the lack of credible information about trueborn elementals."

Fuck. I almost did sit down then as my mind raced to come to terms with the new info. There were bigger issues though. Decisions to make. It didn't change what I'd already been thinking about. I set it aside. "Fine. If there's nothing to do about it, I need to focus on Luna and Sequoyah. I don't want to wait for the remaining elves to decide what to do. I keep waiting for them to be decent, and they keep fucking me over. We need to be ready to push as soon as Troy is on his feet."

They both frowned at me, and Allegra crossed her arms. "Why wait for Troy?"

I wasn't quite ready to admit the decision that was solidifying in the back of my mind, so all I said was, "The double bond with him gives me a tie to elven Aether. The blood tie to Duke gives me djinn Aether. Chaos is easier to manage with one or the other of them around, and I needed it to stop Keithia's Aetheric attacks. Having both Duke and Troy would probably be better if I'm going to face two queens and their entourages at once."

Duke smiled slyly as he studied his nails. "Not to mention you could use the blended power to sever elves from Aether."

Allegra and I both gaped at him.

"That's possible?" I said when I found my voice again.

He shrugged. "Hypothetically. There are oblique references in a few scrolls. A fate worse than death, some might say."

From the sick look on Allegra's face, she agreed.

Me? I thought it was just deserts. "You have until Troy recovers to teach me."

Chapter 33

Between regular Sequoyah workings and the bond with me, Troy healed faster than anyone had a right to. Even so, all of Otherside went into hiding and held its collective breath for the three days it took while the human riots spread beyond the Triangle.

I still wasn't used to the elves camping in my fenced back yard and passing in and out of the house. I had to resist flinching every time I nearly ran into one or they called me "queen" without a hint of irony or derision. My world was upside-down in every way possible, the mirror image to what Callista had raised me to believe.

I mean, yeah, there were plenty of elves plotting to kill me right now. But I'd never imagined that any at all would be willing to help, let alone be in my house planning a rebellion when they weren't doing my chores and grocery shopping. It inspired me. Troy, Allegra, and Iago had already sworn to me. I had the beginnings of my own House Guard. And how better to protect myself and those I cared about than to claim every resource available to me?

I could do this. More importantly, I *wanted* to do this. I wanted a say in how my corner of the world worked. I wanted a chance to do better for me and everyone else. It seemed dissatisfaction had been brewing in the Houses for a generation—ever since Keithia had taken over. The Redcaps had been one extreme manifestation. My Ebon Rebellion was another.

Allegra ran it all with crisp efficiency, and Duke chipped in with esoteric knowledge and reports gleaned via spying from the Crossroads. I was conferring with them both on final plans for the parlay I'd insisted on having with Sequoyah and Luna when I felt Troy make a decision in the bond. I cut off mid-sentence and spun to the closed bedroom door, shaking my head.

"Don't you even," I grumbled under my breath.

"Arden?" The note of concern in Allegra's voice made her a worried sister rather than a captain speaking to her queen. The chatter in the room quieted.

I waved over my shoulder as I headed for the bedroom. "He's fine. Just—give me a minute."

Troy was on his feet, wearing only his briefs, steadying himself with a hand on the wall when I burst in. His beard had grown in while he'd been down, and he looked like a wild man.

"What are you doing?" I shut the door behind me a little harder than necessary. The sense I was getting through the bond was peaky and pained still, and it was all I could do not to grimace at the scars now covering him.

He'd been lead poisoned and hurt too badly to heal without a mark, like usual. The small divot under his right collarbone from a high-caliber bullet echoed the arrow scar and Lichtenberg lines I had under mine. The burn-scarred tattoo, now looking shiny and older than it really was, mirrored it on the other side of his chest. The word carved into his belly had faded, but a braided scar matching the cuff that'd bitten into his wrist stood out.

"I'm done being in bed," he grumbled, scowling at my evaluating look. "And I'm more than done with Alli spelling me to sleep."

Fists on my hips, I scowled at him, not convinced that he was ready to be up.

He glared right back, but it quickly melted into an expression I couldn't read even with the bond.

Uncertainty? Doubt?

When he knelt, I darted forward, afraid that he was collapsing. I stopped, hands hovering, as he pressed his right fist to his heart and bowed his head.

"My queen, I would return to your service, though I don't deserve it."

I flushed. "Are you—what are you even talking about? Stop that. Get up."

He didn't move.

"I mean it, Troy."

"I failed you." His voice cracked, and the words were wracked with emotional pain that echoed the physical.

Seeing as he wasn't going to get up, I dropped to the floor and caught his chin to tilt his head up. "What the hell are you talking about?"

He dropped his eyes. "You shouldn't have had to come for me. Not at all, but especially not to the heart of Keithia's power. Risking yourself like that…I'm not—"

"If you finish that fucking sentence with 'not worth it,' I swear to the Goddess I will—" I bit my tongue and snarled in frustration. I wouldn't threaten him with violence, not with what he'd just been through. Taking a breath, I sought calm. "Troy, look at me. *Look at me.*"

When his eyes lifted to mine, I stopped muting the bond. He rocked back with a gasp as I let him into the emotional depths of what I'd been mulling over the last few days.

Waking up next to him at random times in the night, afraid that he'd stopped breathing again. Watching him sleep, worried about how badly his family had broken him and whether he'd be able to recover his full strength. Staying as close to him as I dared, given his occasional thrashing from the nightmares that tortured him, trying to make sure whatever healing magic was going on would be as strong as possible.

It wasn't just concern for an ally. It was…more. Something deeper and scarier than I'd ever felt, even with Roman. What I'd learned about the double bond should have made me stay away. I didn't want to. I wanted him. Us. A House with him at my side. The first bond had been a fucked-up accident. The second had been his choice. Now it was time for me to choose.

I gathered my thoughts. "It is *not* your fault you were taken. Shit, they tricked me into going to Chapel Hill—when you specifically told me not to go—and took me from the damn police department."

"But—"

"Shut up. I claimed you. You're *mine*. My shield. My Hunter. And…shit." It was my turn to glance away, and I dropped my hand as I worked up the courage to give voice to what'd been growing in my heart. "I happen to have decided to rebuild the elven power structure in the Triangle, starting with my father's House. I…could use some help."

Troy went completely still. "Help?"

"Fuck, Troy. I'm choosing you, okay? You chose me, over and over again. You—" I stopped before I could say he'd temporarily died. I started again in a softer voice. "You could have saved yourself the trouble and given me over to Keithia. Or left town. Something. Anything less than what you went through." I shrugged, completely uncomfortable. "Look, do you wanna be Prince Consort of House Solari or not?"

With a soft thud, Troy sat all the way on the floor. "What?"

"You're gonna make me say it again? You said sex was off the table until I could wake up without panicking when I smelled Aether or elves. What the hell do you think I've been doing for the last four days? Okay, so I was panicking, but it was because I was afraid I was going to wake up and find you dead." He stared at me, and I rushed on. "It's not just that. It's that even when it cost you literally everything, you chose me and you didn't ask for anything in return. I don't—I've never had anyone do that. Ever. It's...I can't find words today."

I was still looking wildly around the room. One that now smelled like both of us in a way that made it feel good.

This time he took my chin and made me look at him. I shivered at the blend of heat and anger in his eyes as he said, "Don't you dare offer this if it's out of pity or some twisted reward for—"

Frustrated as hell with the both of us, I leaned in and kissed him.

He pulled away, falling back onto his elbows. "I mean it, Arden," he said breathlessly. A wild blend of want and fear, hope and disbelief rampaged through the bond. "I won't—"

I straddled him and shut him up with another kiss.

"You chose me. Let me choose you," I said hoarsely when we broke for air.

A tremor ran through him.

Both of us jumped at a banging on the bedroom door.

"Are you two done yet?" Allegra called. "Goddess save me but the *tension*—"

"Go away!" I shouted back, sending a burst of Air to thump the door and hoping it thumped her eavesdropping ear as well.

She cackled. "Yes, my queen. Don't break him. We've only just put him back together again."

Embarrassment heated me at the thought of a roomful of elves hearing that. Then I decided I didn't care. I raised an eyebrow at Troy. "So?"

He cupped my jaw in both hands, studying my face with something like wonder, then pulled me down to kiss me just as thoroughly as I'd kissed him. For a guy who'd momentarily died a few days ago, he was damn lively now.

My blood ran hotter as it pounded in my veins.

"I don't think I'm quite up to consummating anything right now," he said the next time we parted. "But as soon as I am…"

"We'll get there. We have a power structure to rebalance first, *Prince Consort*."

He shivered under me, and it was all I could do to force myself to get off of him and offer a hand up. We stared at each other, getting a feel for our new situation, until he cupped the back of my head to pull me to him and press his forehead against mine.

"I'm still not quite sure I believe this is happening," he said, "but I will always serve you."

I swallowed past the lump in my throat. Part of it was fear at the idea of a forever, but part of it was anticipation for the future. "One day at a time."

He pulled away and offered a small smile. "Hopefully starting with clothes."

I barked a laugh. "What, you don't want to go out and face the Ebon Guard in your briefs?"

"If you ordered it…" He shrugged, looking completely unconcerned.

I blinked. "Ah. No." My wandering gaze made its way down his body and landed on the way he was obviously happy with our new arrangement. My face heated all over again as I pointed to the pile of black on top of the dresser. "Clothes. Definitely clothes if you're going to insist on getting out of bed."

Watching him put them on made me want to order them off of him again, and the way he smirked at me when he was dressed told me he knew it.

"Ready?" he asked once he'd finger-combed his beard and hair into a semblance of order.

"Yeah. Let's go kick some ass."

The elves in the main room of the house fell silent as we emerged.

I froze, Troy at my side, at the expectant looks on the faces turned our way. Duke looked skyward and leaned back against the half-wall behind him, sighing.

Allegra was clearly fighting not to beam, her honey-colored eyes bright. "My queen?"

I flushed. "And your prince consort. House Solari is reborn."

The cheer that rang out at that declaration forced me to shield hard at the assault of the agitated air molecules. Troy touched the small of my back briefly, reassurance and pride coming through the bond.

Allegra approached and knelt. "As Captain of the Ebon Guard, I live to serve and protect House Solari and those elementals sheltered by it."

My head spun. I hadn't considered that the other elementals could join the House. But fuck it, it was my House, and the Ebon Guard had been founded to protect the elementals of old. Why the hell not?

"We're lucky to have you," I said.

The rest of the elves lined up and swore to the two of us.

Duke was last in the line. "Djinn don't swear fealty," he said seriously. "But we have our deal."

"So we do, cousin." I acknowledged him as family despite the shit we'd been through over the years. "The provisional terms were fulfilled. I'll hold to the full bargain."

Duke's gaze darted from me to Troy and back, the faintest hint of jealousy sparking them carnelian before they resettled as dravite. "I'm pleased to hear it. Shall we get on with this parlay?"

"Yes. What's left to do?"

We nailed down the final details around my dining table. I squeezed Troy's shoulder at the relief that echoed at being able to sit down but kept my attention on the discussion. My Ebon Guard—my head still spun to think of them as mine—had worked the Sequoyahs and the Lunas into a frenzy. There'd been a few deaths. All it'd take was a nudge to topple them like dominos.

"Well done," I said when the details had been laid out. "Where?"

"Undecided," Allegra said. "Did you have a preference?"

I thought fast. There weren't many places in the Triangle we could do something like this, but one came to mind. I watched Troy as I said, "We go back to where this all began."

He stiffened, and alarm echoed through the bond. "The boathouse."

"The boathouse." I had to face the ghosts of the recent past if I was going to claim my future.

Allegra frowned as she glanced between us. "Where's this boathouse then?"

"Jordan Lake." I pulled up the pin I still had saved in my phone and showed her.

"Remote. What's the terrain like?"

Troy leaned back in his chair and crossed his arms, his gaze going distant. "Heavily wooded. Aetheric wards and security systems already in place. The main building is an abandoned boat storage and repair facility that was acquired by Leith Sequoyah, expanded to include living space and abandoned again this past winter. Two sheds on the property, one holding supplies, one converted for prisoners. One road in, one dock with water deep enough for a motorboat. Cell phone dead zone."

"How convenient." Allegra's eyes narrowed. "Do I want to know what happened there?"

"No," I said when Troy's eyes cut to me. That was nobody's business but ours now. "But it'd be wise to do a sweep first."

She studied us a moment more. "Fine. When?"

I lifted my brows at Troy in question, and he grimaced. "Tomorrow. Sunset."

When Allegra looked to me for confirmation, I nodded. If Troy thought he'd been ready by tomorrow evening, I'd trust him on it.

"Leave it with me," she said.

While the Ebon Guard made final preparations—some heading out to Jordan Lake for a sweep, others prepping weapons and wrapping up infowar campaigns—I checked in on my factions and updated them on the elven situation. Maria was stressed but holding her nest. The Miami and New York contingents were still in hibernation. The local weres, including Vikki and Ana, were lying low and staying indoors, as were the witches, the fae, Doc Mike, and our various newcomers. After wrestling with the decision, I called Roman, only for it to go to voicemail. I left a message for him to call me back, wondering what the hell was going on out west and hoping that Evangeline hadn't gone out that way to meet him.

The elementals, I saved for last. With all the hardship it had taken to get here, it felt damn good to give them the news that I was making progress on the one thing they'd ever asked me for: the possibility that they might live as openly as elementals as I was. Those calls had me in happy almost-tears that made Troy reach across the table and squeeze my hand. He didn't say anything, but the blend of pride and support in the bond was all I really needed.

A ray of sun hitting me in the eyes made me frown, wondering how it was already sunset. In an echo of the other night, I glanced at Troy. "So...you sleeping over?"

The spark in his eyes made the gold in them flash, even as he kept his expression neutral. "If I did and we made it a thing, we could shift the Guard's headquarters to my safehouse temporarily."

I bit back my enthusiasm at the idea of getting my home back. "You'd give up a safehouse?"

His expression flickered between amused and smoldering. "If it got you to relax a little and us some privacy…"

Desire raced through me. "Do it."

Troy's laugh at my quick answer made me warm even as something in me eased. Nightmares lingered in the back of his mind, waiting for him to sleep, but if he could laugh, we might both settle into what had happened.

We just had to end the other two Houses first.

Chapter 34

The boathouse was, for better or worse, exactly as I remembered it when we pulled up. It loomed next to the lake as waves lapped the shore and a breeze whispered through the trees before making a loose hinge on one of the sheds creak. The day's warmth lingered in stark contrast to my last visit, and the trees ringing the lake were varied shades of green, not bare and snow-covered. I clung to the changes in the landscape as though they would cement the change in myself.

But I still shivered, swallowing hard as I remembered being dragged out in handcuffs.

Troy was tense in the passenger seat, though whether it was the past or the present tightening his shoulders, I couldn't tell. Maybe both. It sure as hell was for me. Dark circles smudged the skin under his eyes, both from the late night of planning and the nightmares that had woken him. I didn't think he was a hundred percent yet, but he burned with a desire to drag some good out of what had happened to him. That, I definitely understood.

He leaned in to brush a tentative kiss on my cheek then flowed out of the car as soon as I parked in the large, open space fronting the boathouse. With a job to do, the bond was nothing but focus. Allegra emerged from her car when she parked beside mine, and they put their heads together, Troy filling her in some more now that they were present.

We were early. The two former Monteagues wanted half the Ebon Guard to sweep and secure the area a second time, not trusting the Lunas, Sequoyahs, or any Monteagues who may have caught wind of the parlay to arrive honestly. The other half, led by Iago, would stay in reserve, scattered across Durham and Chapel Hill, in case anything happened.

Duke materialized next to me in a burst of lemon zest when I got out. "So this is where it all happened."

"Yeah," I said hoarsely. "It was colder. Snowing. Helps that it's summer now but…"

"Never easy to face the past."

I glanced at him, surprised by the unexpected empathy. "You were more of an asshole when I was growing up."

He grinned to show pointed teeth that looked terrifying in a human face. "I still am. But Callista is gone, and I finally have a chance at getting Iaret back."

I snorted. Should have guessed there were ulterior motives.

My jaw clenched hard enough to give me a headache as I took my courage in hand and strode toward the shed where I'd been held. Duke followed soundlessly, having agreed to play bodyguard while Troy busied himself with using his knowledge of the location to secure it. Everything looked exactly as it had in the winter, down to the dried bloodstain on the floor. I wondered whose it was and whether the elves had recovered all the bodies from the lake.

That wasn't what I was here for though. I had a parlay to lead. A position to secure.

I whirled to leave then jumped and barely bit back a shriek when I found Troy standing directly behind me, looking miserable. I'd been so wrapped up in facing my memories that I hadn't sensed him coming closer, and I rarely heard him even when I was paying attention.

Duke sighed and drifted away as Troy backed up immediately, hands fisting as though he was stopping himself from touching me.

"I'm sorry," he said softly. "Not that anything I say is enough for what I put you through here or how badly I managed that mission. But for what it's worth..."

My heart hammered as my mind's eye showed him standing there, unbruised and with snow in his hair. His face had been as cold as the weather, his voice expressionless, neither giving me the depth of emotion I picked up now, even without leaning on the bond. I closed my eyes and bowed my head, seeking calm in breathing exercises. When I had myself under control, I lifted it again and reached for his chest, brushing my fingers lightly over the burn scar peeking from the collar of his shirt. "You've paid for it. I won't keep making you pay if I can help it."

The muscle in his cheek jumped as he squeezed my hand then held it when I didn't pull away. "You don't have to make me do anything. I'll do it anyway. Every damn day."

I let my fingers twine with his as we approached the boathouse together. I refused to go inside again, not seeing any reason to disturb myself more than I already had and preferring to watch the sun set over the lake.

Troy sat beside me with a careful space between us. Surprise and relief echoed through the bond when I closed it and leaned against him. This was why I'd chosen this place, and why we hadn't had sex the night before. One more test of my choice. I think we both needed it—me, for a chance to find any sparks of vengeance toward him hiding in my heart; him, to see if he could live with the guilt.

When I didn't straighten back up, Troy curled an arm over my shoulders and pulled me closer before resting his head on mine. We'd be fucked if we were ambushed, but I decided to trust the Ebon Guard. And us.

As the last sliver of the sun sank below the horizon, a shout from the front brought us to our feet.

The compactly built former Darkwatch agent who approached us at a run—Thana, I think her name was—bowed as she skidded to a halt in front of us. "My queen, Prince Consort, they're here."

"Late," Troy murmured as we followed her back. "Probably an intentional slight."

"To say what?" I asked.

"That you're not legitimate. But they wouldn't blow it off completely, given what you did at Keithia's." His voice tightened a bit on his grandmother's name, and a spike of fear, quickly suppressed, flashed through the bond. "Let me do the introductions. It'll balance things out a little by suggesting they're not fit for you to treat with directly."

I nodded, happier than ever I'd killed Keithia, and gave him a last sideways hug before we rounded the building. He paced slightly ahead of me, given that that was where the known danger was, and I let him do his job, even if it bugged me a little.

"Catrionne Sequoyah and Mireia Luna." Troy stopped us beside Allegra where she waited with her back to the boathouse. He stepped aside enough for me to see two queens.

One had long, golden-blond hair and startlingly ice blue eyes, much as Leith had. The other had shoulder-length dark hair and eyes dark enough to be black. Both their faces were lined, and their hair threaded with enough silver that they had to be over a hundred. Both had a small cluster of elves behind them. All of them were dressed in black.

I wondered what it said that I only had Troy and Allegra, with the rest of my retinue scattered in the trees and Duke waiting in the Crossroads.

"Did you take the time to look for Evangeline this evening?" Savage mockery cut in Troy's tone. "You shouldn't have troubled yourselves. My queen did a thorough job running her out of town after taking justice from Keithia."

"Queen? I only see an elemental bitch, one of the Houseless, and a traitor to the Darkwatch." The blond elf I took to be Catrionne sneered as her eyes lit on the three of us in turn, all attitude. "I told you this was beneath us, Mireia."

At a nudge in the bond from Troy, I lifted my chin and my pendant. "I think you'll find that House Solari has a queen, a prince consort, and a captain, though I suppose I shouldn't be surprised that petty bitches like yourself couldn't find enough courtesy to greet your hosts as such. Or read a map well enough to arrive on time, for that matter."

Mireia rolled her eyes at my pendant. "Please. Those are easily replicated."

"If I may, my queen?" Troy murmured.

I had no idea what he wanted to do, but I nodded and managed not to jump when he cupped my father's pendant in one hand. Aether prickled over me as he whispered a few words of elvish. The pendant glowed with a sigil I didn't recognize.

"She is the rightful heir of House Solari, lost and found, and you *will* treat her as such," Troy said in steely tones, glaring at them something fierce. "I am honored to stand as her prince consort. And I will not tolerate your disrespect."

I hadn't known the pendant could do that, and only long practice as a private investigator allowed me to keep my reaction locked down.

Our opponents did not have such control.

"Impossible," Catrionne snarled, stopped from lurching forward by her lieutenant. Her secondary teeth dropped, sharp in open threat.

"Rumor in House Luna says you tried to drown her," Mireia said slyly. "In this very lake."

Allegra grunted at my side, and I had a feeling Troy was in for a tongue-lashing later.

Smoothly, he said, "And yet here we are. Fearmongering won't work, Mireia. You can't use the vengeful elemental trope or conjure up fears of a second Atlantis when she has met threats with diplomacy."

"Diplomacy like destroying House Monteague's family stronghold and killing its queen with elemental power? No. We can't let her—"

I interrupted them with a laugh, unable to help myself. "Seriously? Keithia murdered my parents, destroyed my House, usurped the Solaris's place, threatened to kill me on more than one occasion, arranged to have me kidnapped and held for torture—a kidnapping where I was shot in full view of the mundane public, by the way—and then captured and tortured nearly to death a prince I had rightfully claimed as blood payment for the death of my father. And you bitches *seriously* want to have something to say about me carrying out justice that all of Otherside would agree is right and fair?"

They had nothing to say to that, which was fine because I wasn't done.

"Given my damn good nature, I'm offering a one-off deal. Dissolve your censured Houses, free your people from all oaths and obligations, and re-swear to Solari. Or get the fuck outta the state. I don't know whose idea it was to be involved with Callista, the Volkovs, or the human riots, but I know all of you either outright approved or sat by and let the situation here go to hell in the hopes of maintaining elven supremacy." I gave them my most unfriendly expression and spoke over them as they opened their mouths. "Those are your only options. Swear. Or leave.

Wait, there's a third: I kill you both and burn your Houses to the ground. Just like I did with Keithia."

They stared at me in hatred.

I tilted my head. "It really didn't have to be this way. I tried to include the elves in the alliance, on equal footing with the rest of Otherside, despite my deeply personal reasons not to. I tried being better. Y'all wouldn't have it and you pushed the Triangle into unrest and riots. So, as Troy said, here we are."

The two queens exchanged glances.

Behind them, their people started to spread out, hard-eyed and angry. This wasn't going to end well, and we were all armed. We hadn't even bothered making entourage size one of the conditions, knowing they'd break it anyway.

"How many people do you have in the woods?" Mireia asked. "You wouldn't be alive still if you were so cocky or stupid to show up with a pair of half-trained Darkwatch agents playing at leadership."

"Enough to cover us." I curled my lips in a mocking smile. I saw no reason not to admit it. They probably had more people as well. Fine by me. It was time for a demonstration. "But they're mostly here to keep the fire under control."

They recoiled as I opened myself to Air and Fire. Superiority fled, leaving stark fear in its place as my eyes glowed—the only hint they had that something was about to happen.

"We're here for parlay!" Catrionne said, her voice harsh.

"And yet you bring nothing but insults." I pushed my voice into a low growl. "So. A demonstration to help you make your choice."

Without letting them get another word in, I clenched my fists and called three lightning strikes out of a clear night.

The visiting queens shied as the bolts struck the ground between us. Troy and Allegra each rested a hand on my shoulders, relying on me to be a living lightning rod, but the other queens and their retinues screamed and swore as phones exploded in their pockets and metal jewelry burned.

I couldn't help a grin of pride. That had been my most controlled strike yet. I was getting better.

"We could kill you for breaking parlay and be well within our rights," Mireia snarled when they had themselves under control again. Or almost under control—some shook with fear or outrage, and the clearing stank of rotted herbs and marshmallows burnt to ash.

"Could you?" I tilted my head. "I suppose you could try. But then again, given that it was two Sequoyahs and a Monteague in the party that shot me, I'd certainly be within my rights to seek vengeance. Gotta be honest, Mireia, I'm surprised to see the Lunas here. I'd heard some of you had come to your senses about the betrayal of Solari."

That struck a nerve. Mireia started to answer then grimaced and glanced aside as her people shifted their feet and muttered.

The automatic lights on the boathouse roof came on, painting the clearing in a dull, orange glow. The scene looked more than ever like it had the night I'd been caught here, and I wrestled away a spike of remembered fear.

"What'll it be, ladies and gentlefolk?" I said in a harder tone.

I was tired of this damn place and the nasty memories, tired of dealing with elves who refused to see me as a person, let alone a queen, and tired of having to do this same shit over and over. And over. Fighting for what I deserved, what I was owed, by every law in Otherside. Fighting even harder so that the other elementals could have a choice in how they lived.

Catrionne's decision showed in the ugly twist of her expression just before she spat at us and drew a bronze knife the size of my elf-killer. "Rot in hell, elemental filth."

Something broke in me. I'd called the bluff. Now I had to follow through.

Troy and Allegra eased away from me, drawing their black blades and cloaking themselves in shadows. Duke shimmered in at my side from the ethereal plane, drawing disgusted shouts from the elves. We'd known it might come to this, but the usual naive part of me had still hoped it wouldn't. That this time would finally be different.

Catrionne didn't do more than raise the blade before I swatted her away from her people with a burst of Air that connected with the snap of bones, following it with a crackle of lightning. She arched up, screaming until the lightning dissipated. Troy burst from the shadows and cut her throat with a silent snarl before fading back into the night.

The Sequoyahs dropped as their House oaths were abruptly broken. Mireia's followers stared in wide-eyed horror.

We stood, motionless, waiting for the fallen elves to regain their senses and find their feet.

"Who's next?" I asked in a harsh whisper.

All of Catrionne's people drew weapons with shaky hands. Aether rose so strongly that the warm night felt like winter's chill on my skin.

And I just smiled.

Chapter 35

Half of the Lunas drew weapons. The other half wavered as the Sequoyah contingent threw themselves at me. Mireia stared in shock—she clearly hadn't actually thought I'd follow through, despite having already killed Keithia.

I raised my hands and pushed, sending a wall of Air forward to knock them all off their feet. Earth obliged me by opening a pit beneath them in the waterlogged ground before they could rise. I sauntered to the edge of it. At the small of my back, the godblade Troy had argued against me bringing itched to be used. I leaned into my magic and resisted, not wanting a repeat of what had happened during my kidnapping. I didn't need it yet. My enemies were trapped.

I set a wall of Air on the top of the pit before leaning over—and a good thing I did, because one of the fools tried shooting me. I didn't flinch as the bullet ricocheted and struck someone in the pit. They fell with a muddy splash and a cry of pain.

Crouching, I waited for Duke, Troy, and Allegra to rejoin me. When the elves released their shadows and Duke swirled over the pit like a malevolent dust storm, I asked, "What do you think? Lava? Pull the lake in? Fill the pit? Or just let them smother?"

If my people were surprised by my unwonted cruelty, they didn't show it.

"Whatever pleases my queen." Troy's neutral tone suggested he didn't care. Maybe he truly didn't. The only emotion I caught from the bond was fury. He'd dispatched those who'd attacked me before without a hint of regret. Even if he was willing to do it again, I didn't want him to have to.

I squeezed his arm and got an answering burst of something softer in the bond. "What would please me," I said in a louder voice, "would be not having to do this fucking shit every time I try to get something done on behalf of Otherside when the gods are going to call the Wild fucking Hunt any damn day now."

Down in the pit, Mireia gaped. "I thought that was one of Callista's ploys."

"Believe it," Troy said. "Lady Artemis dragged my queen and me through the Crossroads so we could end Callista."

"Bullshit." She sounded muffled through my barrier of Air. "We can't travel the Crossroads."

"He can." I twisted my lips in a snarl. "I've carried him through twice."

We didn't need to mention the shattered mind and shredded aura part of it.

Over the disbelieving mutters of the elves below, I said, "I'll ask y'all one more time because I'm tired and I want to go to bed. What's your choice? Swear to me, get the fuck outta town, or die? Keeping in mind that because y'all saw fit to be unreasonable, I'm gonna need assurances if you pick options A or B. Talk amongst yourselves. I'll give you five minutes."

Rising, I moved away and hugged myself as I looked out over the lake. The moon hung amidst sparkling stars, a thin crescent that reminded me of a sickle. No matter how tightly I squeezed, I couldn't stop the shakes. I didn't want to do any of what would have to come next, regardless of what they chose.

Troy scuffed a foot in warning as he came up behind me, and his warm hands rubbed my arms. When I leaned back, he embraced me from behind, gathering me in against his chest with a sigh.

"You did everything possible to do this the bloodless way," he said in a voice barely louder than a whisper. "More than I would have."

"For all the good it did," I said bitterly, giving in to the shakes.

His arms tightened. "Their reaction was never yours to own. If they choose death, it'll be quicker than the one they would have given you or the one that was waiting for me." He shuddered. "If they choose life, being cut off from their magic is the least you need to do to keep yourself and the rest of us safe. This was never going to be an easy path to walk. But I'm with you for every step of it."

"I know." I twisted just enough to kiss his jaw and was rewarded with a small flash of pleasure breaking through all the grimness in the bond. "It's just...it was easy to kill Leith and Keithia. This? Not so much."

"That was personal. They'd harmed you directly, and you knew it. These queens sent their people after you. But everyone here would have gotten the same infowar messages from the Guard about choosing a side. We made it very clear, both the choice and the consequences. All of those here made their choice. They would have celebrated your death." He shuddered again and held me tighter before freeing me. "Come on. Don't let them think you're losing your nerve, or they'll keep trying to bargain."

I pulled myself together and steeled my heart and soul.

When I leaned over the pit again, uncertainty and hatred painted most of the faces.

I sighed, wishing that this could have had a better ending. "Well?"

Mireia shook her head. "I will not swear to an elemental, and I will not run. But I will accept justice on behalf of my House for the wrong committed against Solari and the results it has had."

"Death, then," I said, just to be clear.

She nodded with a sharp jerk of her head then knelt. "I only ask that those of my people who choose life be allowed to leave in peace."

I had to give her credit for courage and bloody-mindedness. "So be it. The rest of you?"

All but two of the Sequoyahs said, "Death," and knelt beside the queen. The Lunas were split, a handful kneeling but most backing away to opt for exile.

The two Sequoyahs and five Lunas fisted their hands over their hearts, and one of the women said, "We will swear."

I glanced at Troy.

He squinted as he read their auras for falsehood. One of his personal tricks, one I hadn't taken advantage of before. "They're telling the truth."

Being careful not to expose myself to any weapons, I lifted those out first with Air, one by one. Their eyes bugged to be touched with elemental magic they couldn't see, but they all knelt as soon as they were on the ground. I put up a wall of Air around them. "Stay put."

Those who chose exile I lifted out next. They wavered, looking at me suspiciously as they refused to kneel. The magic that would sever them from Aether was complex, and I didn't bother wasting words as I held out a hand to both Duke and Troy. It took a knife of Chaos and primordial power to sever Aether, and it would hurt all of us like a bitch.

I fumbled the first attempt. The elves in front of me cried out in pain.

"What are you doing to them?" Mireia shouted from the pit.

"Taking assurances," I snarled, trying again. I got it on the third attempt. It might have been easier with a Luna to help me, but Allegra could read Aetheric residue and Troy could read auras. We got it done.

With another shout of shock and disbelief, the elves dropped to the ground as I severed them from Aether in quick succession. My stomach twisted, and I swallowed bile. They would live, but they would never use magic again. I'd be merciful enough to let them leave, but I was done being foolish enough to have them at my back at their full strength.

"Get up and go," I said when it was done. "You have two hours to get at least fifty miles out of the Triangle. My Ebon Guard will be watching, so don't try me."

They stared at me, haunted and reeling.

"Well? Go!" I shouted, wanting them out of my sight.

They staggered to their feet and made their way to their cars. Allegra made a quick phone call then nodded to me. Iago would see them gone.

Now the shittiest part.

Embracing Earth again, I refilled the pit from below, just to make the point to the elves who'd chosen to swear to me that I could. Those who'd opted for death rose out of the ground, all but Mireia with wild, frightened expressions.

When the mud settled, Troy stepped forward, longknife at the ready.

"Wait." I stopped Troy with a hand on his arm. He paused, expression impassive but the bond roiling as he bit back a challenge.

The elves here didn't believe the gods were coming. There needed to be an object lesson.

I'd tucked Artemis's ring in my pocket as a last-minute failsafe just in case shit really hit the fan. Kneeling, I slipped it on. "My lady Artemis."

Blood drained from Troy's face, and he dropped to kneel beside me, keeping his eyes on the prisoners.

"Shit." Allegra's eyes darted around the edge of the clearing as she knelt, as though she was placing the members of the Guard we had in the trees.

Even Duke morphed into his favorite corporeal form, grimacing as he took a knee on my other side.

Trusting my people to keep watch for betrayal, I closed my eyes, bowed my head, and reached for Chaos, Duke and Troy both within touching distance. It danced into me like with the oscillation of a sound wave, not steady, but more predictable with balance. Holding it like I would a bird, I touched the ring and called to the gods who'd been visiting me since January.

"I beg your attention, lady Artemis. I have an offering of blood and bone. My lady Neith, I offer tribute. My lord Mixcoatl, come take your due."

Cries rang out in the clearing as a sudden, unbearable pressure—physical, mental, and auratic—toppled everyone but me, Troy, and Duke.

The gods had arrived.

Neith, in her strip-leather armor and red kilt, eyes heavy with kohl, took in the clearing with her *was* staff tucked under her arm and her ankh spinning on its leather thong. Mixcoatl, striped in red paint, with the galaxy shining in place of his eyes behind a fanged mask, deer-hoof spooled earrings hanging heavy, his damned bow and lightning arrows making the scar on my shoulder ache. Artemis, her stag-red hair in braids, dressed in a white tunic and brown, conifer-patterned belt, the blood moon in her eyes brighter than ever. And though I hadn't called them, Odin's child-sized ravens quorked and spread their wings.

"What have you been up to, little primordial?" Neith's voice was like the wind howling through a desert wadi. Everyone but me covered their ears and groaned in pain. "What is this?"

"An offering of blood and bone," I repeated, the words thick in my throat. "I—I invite you to hunt."

Laughter like a braying stag rang out as Artemis circled the elves. "You invite us to do your dirty work for you."

"With respect, lady, I can do my own work." I gestured to where Catrionne's still smoking corpse lay.

Mixcoatl phased over and crouched to examine it. "You did this with lightning?"

"Yes, my lord. And I destroyed another enemy with lightning and fire just days ago. Her house is ashes, her people scattered. Her prince and knight are now mine."

Smiling as though she already knew the answer, Artemis asked, "What did this enemy do to deserve this fate?"

"She murdered my family and usurped my birthright. Then she stole my Hunter and tortured him nearly to death." I hadn't expected the rage that suffused every ounce of my body and seeped into my voice.

At my side, Troy quivered, equal parts remembered fear and current fury.

The stag's braying broke out again. "So fierce. This pleases me. You will need it to join our Wild Hunt."

"I will accept the offering." Something in Neith's tone set me on edge as she looked over the elves who'd refused to be cut off from their magic. "All of it. But only if you take the heart of their leader with my gift."

Mixcoatl straightened. The ravens hopped closer, pinning me with a beady-eyed gaze.

I didn't need Troy's panic in the bond or Duke's hissing intake of breath to know it was a bad idea. But I'd called the gods here. I'd wanted to make a point. Now, as with everything in Otherside, I had to follow through.

Mireia didn't bother to beg as I approached. She just looked up at me with hatred.

My hand shook as I drew the godblade from the sheathe at my back. I'd watched Troy kill a Sequoyah boy a few months ago, a neat stab to the heart, blood payment for Javier Luna's death here at this same damn lake.

"Mireia Luna," I said, voice rough as I fought emotion to keep it steady and pitch it loud enough for everyone to hear. "For the crime of usurping the place of House Solari and for leading and agitating the humans into riots that resulted in physical and reputational harm to members of the alliance, and all of Otherside, I hereby—"

"Oh just get on with it," she snarled. "Stop pretending that you—"

She gasped when I plunged the blade into her heart, exactly as I'd watched Troy do it before. The Lunas who'd opted to swear collapsed, groaning, as their House oaths were broken.

This time when the red film washed over my vision, I was prepared. I stood rigid, fighting it, panting as though I'd run fifty miles. When a *push* came through the bond, I used it to build a wall. The tangy, lemony warmth of djinn Aether seeped into me from the callstone at my throat—Duke couldn't affect other *people* with Aether, but he could manipulate enchanted objects.

I drew on them both, wrapping myself in a shroud of Chaos until my mind cleared and I found myself standing rigid in the clearing. Troy embraced me from behind, whispering fervently in elvish. Duke's hand was splayed wide on the callstone, over my heart.

The red ebbed away, and I took a deep, relieved breath.

"That is very interesting indeed," Neith said in a dangerously soft tone.

As Troy and Duke slowly eased away, I grimaced. Being more interesting to the gods was something I'd been trying to avoid.

"Quite the show," a new, masculine voice agreed. "Though it seems I was right about her needing to be bonded to one of equal power."

I spun to find Ogun. The tall, bald, Black orisha was sharpening his machete.

Neith shook her head. "No. She's become a primordial all on her own. With a little help from me, perhaps. That gift was always in her, even if she had to be pushed to find it. This Hunter, the trick with the djinni…this is something new. Tools we did not have in the last cycle."

I didn't like the anticipatory smiles all the gods wore at that statement, and in the back of my mind, Troy went wary and still.

"Honored Ones, does the sacrifice please you?" The words were tacky in my dry mouth.

They exchanged glances before answering in unison. "It does."

I freed those who'd chosen death from their bonds of Air. "Run."

None needed a second prompting. With a ululating cry, Neith raised her bow.

Chapter 36

It was getting on toward midnight by the time Troy and I made our way back to my house. Allegra and the Ebon Guard were heading to Troy's safehouse with the handful of elves who'd sworn to me and House Solari at the lake. Duke had returned Veilside to report to the Djinn Council. Troy had made all the necessary calls to Maria, Vikki, Terrence and Ximena, Doc Mike, Val, Laurel, and Janae, giving me space to stew in my thoughts.

And by thoughts, I meant my self-recrimination and the flashes of bloody memories that followed me home.

He was leaving me to it, although the sense I got from the bond was of a predator biding his time. I'd walled him out, wanting space to process what I'd done. I hadn't lied when I'd told Troy I didn't have any bloodlust, and yet in the space of a week, I'd drenched myself and those close to me in blood. Troy didn't seem bothered in the slightest by anything I'd done. He wasn't disgusted. He wasn't accusatory. He wasn't angry or disappointed or upset.

No, those were feelings I saved for myself. Because sometime between the bath where I decided I needed to heal and tonight, I'd made choices that couldn't be undone in the name of finding that healing. In a way, it was just how shit got done in Otherside. We weren't human, not even me, no matter how much time I'd spent hiding amongst the mundanes. With my power signature stronger than ever, my magic growing, and the gods on the verge of calling the Wild Hunt? I could never go back to even pretending. Hawkeye Investigations was finished, as much from outgrowing it as from my neglect.

I didn't know what to do with that.

"I'll check the grounds," Troy murmured when we pulled up to my house.

Leaning forward, I rested my forehead on the steering wheel and didn't answer, trying to unsee the carnage the gods had joyfully wrought at the lake. I jumped when the driver's side door opened a little while later.

"All clear," he said. "Come on, Arden."

"How can you even look at me after what I just did?" I asked in a ragged whisper.

"What you just did? Is that what all this is about?"

I shrugged, not lifting my head.

He sighed. "You secured your place in Otherside. Defended the alliance against a much bigger, far better-resourced faction. Had the courage to claim the justice you were owed when nobody would extend it to you, after trying the peaceful way for months in the face of death threats and kidnapping. You came for me and showed that forgiveness is possible."

Something in his voice made me look at him, despite the tears I was fighting.

"Arden…I'm proud of you."

That did it. Tears made hot trails down my cheeks.

Troy knelt in the car's open door. He reached up with both hands, cupping my jaw and sweeping the tears away with his thumbs. "You want to tell me what's really bothering you?"

I froze. "How did you——?"

Tilting his head, he offered a look that said *Really?* more clearly than words could have. "I don't need the bond to tell me when the woman I was assigned to watch for the last six months is running from her feelings again."

My lips pressed into a firm line, not wanting to shape the words. But I couldn't hide with him looking up at me.

"I don't feel guilty," I whispered. "I was *owed*. I did those fucked up things and killed all those people. And *I don't feel guilty*. What kind of monster does that make me? Who the fuck am I now?"

"Not a monster. A survivor. And a queen. Just like you always have been."

I recoiled. "I—"

"Always had that in you," Troy insisted firmly. "You were just content to live in Callista's little box, or Keithia's smaller box, until you had no other choice."

Blinking, I sat and stared at him.

"You going to walk in, or do I need to carry you?"

He backed up when I shifted, got out, shut the door, and locked the car. Didn't touch me when I hugged myself as I stomped up the stairs of my porch, a noisy contrast to his perpetually silent movements. I shifted the block of Air...and, for the first time since I'd lived here, didn't reset it. I had strong wards. I had stronger powers. And I had Troy.

The house still smelled of elves, but after tonight, I didn't think I'd ever fear it again.

"Go on and take a shower," Troy said. "I'll make dinner." When I just stared at him, he added, "Or you can be miserable with a power hangover instead of..."

The flash of his brows left no question.

"Oh," I whispered. Heat raced over me at the realization that he was feeling much better today than he had yesterday. And that meant we could...

"Uh. Right." I fled for the shower. Made it a quick one, just enough to get clean, and used my fancy lotion. Pulled on the cute but comfy boxer shorts that made my legs look long and a thin camisole, before going back to the kitchen.

Troy glanced back from where he was broiling lamb chops, from the smell, then looked again. His eyes widened as they traveled over me from head to toe then back up again. He muttered something in elvish as he reddened and pulled the chops out of the oven, plating them with enough salad to satisfy me.

I felt saucy and emboldened by his reaction. "What was that?"

He cleared his throat and set the plates on the table, waiting for me to seat myself before taking a chair. "Um. I was wondering if I hadn't actually died. Because this is not anything I expected to have the luck for in this lifetime."

Ohmigod is he actually sweet? Not just dutiful?

I had no idea how to respond to that, so I settled for a smile and thanked him for the meal. We ate in silence, our eyes as much on each other as our food. Tension grew to almost unbearable levels until it crackled between us.

"I'll wash up while you shower," I said.

Troy looked like he was going to argue then thought better of it when I took his hand and bit one of his fingers. Then it was a rush to the bathroom.

I was waiting for him in the bedroom with candles lit when he finished, inspired by his earlier reaction to change into a black silk nightie I'd worn maybe once and make this more romantic.

He paused in the doorway to the bathroom, hair slicked back and a towel around his hips. His breathing quickened, and the towel bulged as I approached him.

"You feel up to helping me forget the end of the world for a little while?" I asked.

His low hum of pleasure sent chills over me, followed by a flash of heat. "If that's an invitation to play hotshot again, then yes." He leaned in to whisper. "Only this time…"

I looked up at him, heart pounding, as I realized this was it. Make or break, do or don't. Our futures danced together on the point of a pin as he waited for me to be sure.

And for once, I was. "This time, I want it all."

Troy cupped my jaw in a big, warm hand.

I shuddered at the emotion that rushed over me and leaned into it, wanting him, wanting to be with him, even if I was still a little afraid of what it would mean, given what he'd said after our first night together.

He ran his thumb over my bottom lip and that, combined with the heat in his gaze, sparked into flame the embers burning in me whenever I was near him.

"You're sure?" He leaned closer, too close for me to see him but just far enough that our lips didn't touch, giving me permission without taking the choice.

My body ignored my racing mind and made the slight lean needed to press against him, my arms slipping around him. His other hand slid around my waist and stopped there, waiting for me to decide.

Closing my eyes, I tilted my head back and tried to just breathe. The caress of his thumb made it difficult. I needed to think, to be sure. He'd said that being with me was a path to kingship for him. He might be using me…but I didn't care. I had what I wanted.

His thumb stopped, and he started to step away as he sensed my hesitation.

"No." I pulled him back. "Come here." What we'd had these last few days had been too real, his need too raw for it to be a power play.

I was tired of second-guessing him.

Troy grunted as he took our weight hitting the wall behind him. Then his hands were back to cradling my face as his lips fell on mine. His abdomen was firm with muscle and ridged with new scars as I pressed against him, savoring the rosemary taste of his mouth and the taut skin under my fingers as I skimmed my hands over his body.

"Is that a yes?" he mumbled into our kiss.

I searched deep in my heart for the grudge I'd carried, my last chance to push him away and run. I couldn't find it and was tired of carrying its weight.

"Yes," I breathed back, tugging his towel free.

He nudged my head to the side to nibble a trail down my neck as he slid the nightie from my shoulders. His hands caressed my curves on their way back up, a little bit of nails, the hint of a thumb over my nipples. Tingles raced over me, partly from the physical touch, partly from the Aether that ebbed from him even when he wasn't trying.

We were really doing this. My control over my shields slipped and was gone in a buffet of wind. I winced when he pulled away to look at me. "Sorry."

"I just want to be sure you weren't afraid. If you're not, I'm going to make you do that again."

My breath caught.

Troy took advantage of my distraction to back me to the bed and pin me to it when I toppled backward. "Still good?"

"Yes. Drawer. Condom. Now."

With a satisfied half-smile, Troy obeyed. He'd been playing every move so carefully and subdued up to now, but my desire seemed to give him confidence. When he was finished with the condom he returned to my body with gusto, everything he'd teased me with the other night and more.

Faster. A little rougher. Still an act of worship but one that was tinged with demand. Taking cues from my reactions, adjusting before I had to say a word.

Until I did, gasping every word.

"Troy—I need—"

As though that was a signal he'd been waiting for, he joined with me in a single smooth push. Between his body and the open bond, all that existed in the world was carnal pleasure.

Distantly, I heard a crash as a burst of Air sent a lamp toppling. Smelled smoke as the candles went out. It didn't matter. Nothing mattered but his body moving against mine. His fingers tangled in my hair. The salt-sage taste of his sweat. His lips and a brush of teeth over my throat. The prickle of restrained Aether on my skin.

He leaned away, eyes on me in the dark, and held me down with a hand splayed over my collarbone as I tried to buck, tried to keep my heart pressed against his.

"Troy!"

"Arden."

The growled utterance of my name combined with a smooth movement of his hips sent me over the edge. He didn't stop moving as he pressed his lips to mine, drinking in the sound of my completion.

"May I?" he asked when I was spent.

All I could do was nod—and then hold onto him as he moved harder, faster, driving toward his own climax. A second one shook me as he finished. The windows rattled as a storm beat against them from within the house.

The scent of meringue and herbs filled my nose as Troy growled, tensed, and relaxed, propped over me with his face tucked against my neck as we both panted.

If this was what it meant to have Troy Monteague—no, Troy *Solari* now, since mine was the only House he claimed—as prince consort...yeah. I could live with this.

***

The scent of herbs tickled my nose the next morning and weight around my waist pinned me to the bed. For once, it didn't scare me half to death. I smiled and squeezed Troy's arm, knowing if anything had come for me in the night, he would have known about it—and stopped the threat.

Behind me, he exhaled heavily. Relief rippled through the bond when I snuggled closer rather than panicking.

I twisted to kiss him.

"My queen," he said in a gravelly, sleep-thickened voice when we separated.

"Prince Consort." I squirmed a little to acknowledge him as such, but that was the deal. I was okay with it. More than okay. I just hadn't ever imagined being here or being with him.

The flash of pure joy in the bond combined with another kiss then eased into desire to make it a damn good morning.

When we'd finished with round two, sweaty and sated, Troy pulled me to him. "We have a lot of work to do."

I grinned. "We do."

He shifted as though he was trying to read my face. "A lot. Quelling the human riots. Getting the elves back into order under House Solari and finding Evangeline before she can do more damage. Handling the Blood Moon succession out west and Vikki's coup here. I'm assuming you sent Zanna to the fae lords and ladies. Then there's the East Coast coteries. All before dealing with the gods and the Wild Hunt, assuming—"

With a growl, I pushed up and straddled him, kissing him to shut him up. "I deserve one. Good. Morning. To think of myself and not the rest of the world. I hereby declare today Arden's Day."

Troy tried for seriousness, but his face twitched until a smile won out. "As my queen commands."

"That's more like it." I leaned down to steal another kiss.

For all I'd sacrificed, all I'd lost, every betrayed dream and naive hope dashed to dust, I'd still triumphed. Troy was part of it, but he wasn't all of it. Nobody was, except for me. My strength. My growth. My power. I'd never needed anyone to choose me. It felt good, but in the end, I'd had to choose myself first.

Yeah, I still had to face the humans and Roman and the gods. I still had to fix everything. Take up the mantle of Queen, Arbiter, and Mistress of the Hunt. Lead Otherside into a strange new world where we lived openly alongside the mundanes with equal rights. Avert the Wild Hunt. Hell, Callista wasn't confirmed dead yet.

But fuck it.

Nobody was standing in the way of what was mine ever again. I'd make sure of it.

Acknowledgments

I continue to be wowed by the support for the Shadows of Otherside series and me as an author. It's easy to get lost in anxiety while writing, wondering if the vision in your head is one anyone else will want to share in. Thank you to all those readers who are still joining me in this world!

As ever, big thanks go to my family, friends, and colleagues cheering me on in this journey. I've been rearranging my life these last few months and have only been met with "How can I help?" To have that level of support is both humbling and encouraging. Thank you.

Huge thank you to my editor Jeni Chappelle, not only for doing yet another great job with pointing out where things are off but also for making me genuinely enjoy the editing process. I cackle at edit notes, y'all. It's fun times.

Thanks again to Stephanie, my beta reader, as well. Her early read lets me know whether the tone I've set and the targets I'm aiming for have landed and based on the reader reviews for previous books she's been spot-on with feedback.

I want to make sure to give a shout-out to book bloggers this time as well. Their work is so often unappreciated, but they're a huge part of getting the word out about a book and introducing it to new readers. Working with Bri's Bookish, The Gem Chronicles, Indie Spines, tata.lifepages, Sistah Girls Book Club, and Bookish Valhalla on reviews and promotions has been an absolute pleasure. I'm grateful for their work and that of many others who have featured my books on social media and blogs.

Last but certainly not least, thank you to those readers who have been so enthusiastic in reviewing the series online, sharing updates, and supporting me on Patreon.

Also by Whitney Hill

The Shadows of Otherside series

Elemental
Eldritch Sparks
Ethereal Secrets
Ebon Rebellion
Eternal Huntress (coming late 2021)

The Flesh and Blood series (as Remy Harmon)

Bluebloods

Praise for *Elemental*

"Arden is a winning protagonist, pushing against PI stereotypes in small but telling ways, and the denizens of Otherside— particularly the vampires and djinn—have well-developed personalities. Hill also has a fine ear for dialogue and a good sense of timing, and the story builds steadily and believably, resulting in a genuine page-turner." —*Kirkus Reviews*

Praise for *Eldritch Sparks*

"…although Hill's worldbuilding will draw the reader in, it's the strong-willed, hard-boiled protagonist who will keep them engaged, as Arden's narration ties the speculative elements together and brings a sense of simmering urgency to the proceedings…A compelling book of Otherside that goes from strength to strength." —*Kirkus Reviews (starred review)*

About the Author

Whitney Hill is the author of the Shadows of Otherside contemporary fantasy series. The bestselling first book in the series, *Elemental*, was the grand prize winner of the 8th Annual Writer's Digest Self-Published E-Book Awards.

When she's not writing, Whitney enjoys hiking in North Carolina's beautiful state parks and playing video games.

Learn more or get in touch: whitneyhillwrites.com
More books by Whitney: whitneyhillwrites.com/original-fiction
Sign up to receive email updates: whwrites.com/newsletter

Join her on social media:
- Twitter: twitter.com/write_wherever
- Instagram: instagram.com/write_wherever
- Facebook: facebook.com/WhitneyHillWrites

Get bonus content on Patreon: patreon.com/writewherever

Learn more about the publisher, Benu Media, at benumedia.com, or sign up to receive newsletters with the latest releases at go.benumedia.com/newsletter

One Last Thing...

If you enjoyed this book, please consider posting a short review, recommending it on Goodreads or BookBub, or telling a friend who might also enjoy this story. As always, thank you for reading, and for your support!

CPSIA information can be obtained
at www.ICGtesting.com
Printed in the USA
LVHW092334150921
697901LV00002B/186

9 781734 422788